Cafe Berlin

Cafe Berlin

HAROLD NEBENZAL

AVON BOOKS NEW YORK

AVON BOOKS
A division of
The Hearst Corporation
1350 Avenue of the Americas
New York, New York 10019

Copyright © 1992 by Harold Nebenzal
Published by arrangement with The Overlook Press
Library of Congress Catalog Card Number: 92-9079
ISBN: 0-380-72169-4

First Avon Books Trade Printing: January 1994

AVON TRADEMARK REG. U.S. PAT. OFF. AND IN OTHER COUNTRIES, MARCA REGISTRADA, HECHO EN U.S.A.

Printed in the U.S.A.

OPM 10 9 8 7 6 5 4 3 2 1

The political and military events described herein are historically sound and in no way fictitious.

I SPEAK the Arabic of my native Damascus; Hebrew, the language of our faith; French, as taught by the Alliance Israélite; Ladino, the ancient Spanish of the Sephardim; sufficient Italian; the Russian I have learned from my kitchen help; German, the language of my seemingly last way station; and English, the language of those, other than my parents, whom I have served faithfully and well.

Other than invoices, bills of lading, and an occasional postcard, I have never written much in any of them. I shall use the language of those in whom lies the hope and salvation of the world. As we say, "Con el pie derecho y el nombre del Dio" — "With the right foot forward and with the name of God" — I commence: in English.

DANIEL SAPORTA, SON OF EZRA
Berlin, November 14, 1943

November 14, 1943

I HAVE BEEN IN HIDING *since the sixteenth of December, 1941—
one month short of two years. Why I waited this long before starting
to write, I cannot say. I suppose it took this long for the realization
to sink in that my enforced residence would not be terminated by
some fortuitous event. I am older, sadder, wiser, and have learned to
eat the bitter bread of patience. Thus these memoirs, whose uncomfortable
beginnings you witness here.*

*Lohmann comes almost every day but he hasn't been here since
the tenth, which means I haven't eaten in three days and I feel quite
light-headed. What could have kept him? I miss him and I miss
what I call the feeding ritual. It has become important to me, as
have my recently resurrected morning and evening prayers: anything
to give some meaning to the monotony of my days. I have also tried
push-ups, an exercise in vanity, to keep the body in shape. The
rewards were headaches, accompanied, strangely, by a toothache I
am not anxious to reawaken.*

*Lohmann's entrance never varies. First, I hear footsteps on the
wooden attic floorboards and the shifting of an armoire, followed by
his entrance into my refuge. There is a truncated lifting of his hat, a
dry, brisk handshake with a stiff bow, and the appearance of a
package from the depths of his overcoat pocket. He places the package
on my little table. It is of wrinkled brown paper, firmly secured by a
length of twine.*

*Lohmann then carefully unties the string, wraps it around his index
and middle finger, and places the loop on the table. Next comes the
unfolding of the butcher paper—it has been the same for weeks—
which he smooths free of folds and wrinkles. Folded into a tidy
square, it joins the twine on the tabletop. He repeats the process with
the sheet of waxed paper that enfolds the reason for this exercise: a
piece of gray rye bread with a white coating of pork fat, or, perhaps
a Schrippe, the crusty bread roll of the Berliners, with a piece of*

Harzer cheese or a thick slice of onion in its middle. At the beginning there were cutlets and pieces of stew meat, but food is getting scarce and I am grateful for every potato, for every winter apple, that Lohmann brings.

He does something else for me: he removes my wastes. Unquestioningly, he carries the galvanized bucket to the communal toilet on the fourth-floor landing and, after emptying it, returns it to me. He is cautious and has so far not been observed. It is not a problem now, during the icy winter months; I keep the bucket outside, well concealed by the dormer window. Whether I shall still need the bucket when the weather turns warm depends on Lohmann. Actually, my very life depends on him. Should he be killed or injured during the air raids, should he be taken ill, should he be denounced to the authorities, it would signal an end to the twists and turns, the small glories and the greater shames of an existence that began in Damascus thirty-two years ago.

November 15, 1943

DURING THE NIGHT, my recurrent dream of Damascus. We are sitting on the balcony of my father's house: my father, my mother, my brother, Victor, my sisters Fortuna and Sultana. The air is heavy with the scent of jasmine and mimosa. The maid, Fawzia, has been sent to a neighborhood restaurant; she has returned with a platter piled high with grilled pigeons. They are pungent with lemon juice and flat leaf parsley. My father, fez on his head, says the blessing: "Blessed art thou, Lord, King of the universe, through whose Word all things are called into being." We devour the pigeons, a mountain of them. The gramophone plays in the living room: "Zourouni kol sana marra"—Call on Me Once a Year—by the Egyptian composer Sayyid Darwish. This song of love and pain is my father's favorite. The ululations, the beat of the derbakke, are physical; the repetition narcotic. The soars, the gasps, the plunges of Arabic song are beyond those of the West. They touch our soul, our genitals, with rose-scented fingers. We are glassy-eyed with sated torpor. My father sips his Turkish coffee. His tiny cup releases the sweet bitterness of the grounds, laced with the essence of orange blossoms; the perfume blends with the heady blooms weighing down our balcony. The thought remains unspoken: that this may last for all eternity, Inch'allah.

November 18, 1943

TODAY LOHMANN'S OVERCOAT *pocket turned out to be a veritable cornucopia of delicacies: slices of meat loaf—mostly bread, of course, with precious little meat, held together with fat but delicious nevertheless. There was a jar of cabbage and turnip soup and half a loaf of bread, a length of hard sausage, and some rather stiff fried doughnuts.*

Lohmann explained that while crossing the Nollendorf Platz he had run into a friend, a waiter by profession, who had been in Lohmann's sapper company during the First World War. They had served together in the trenches of the Marne in 1916. He now had a permanent billet with the Winterhilfswerk, a welfare organization set up by the Nazi Party to assist the needy and, principally, those bombed out of their homes by Allied bombing raids. The Winterhilfswerk distributes blankets and warm clothing and doles out warm meals from mobile kitchens known as "goulash cannons." The ex soldier-cum-waiter works in the commissary branch, which allots comestibles to the vast network of the Winterhilfswerk. This regimental mate had invited Lohmann to grab while the grabbing was good. Lohmann also brought a supply of old newspapers. Not only are they my lifeline to the world but, more importantly, they keep me warm in my Spartan attic. Newspapers, when wrapped around the arms and legs and about the torso, beneath shirt and trousers, preserve body heat to a remarkable degree. I also sleep between layers of newspapers: a bottom layer over the icy cushions of the horsehide couch, a top layer secured by my overcoat and ragged quilt. I owe my very breath to Lohmann, and in my mind, at least, I have never done anything for him commensurate with the kindness he lavishes on me at great personal risk.

I met Lohmann in 1929, shortly after Herr Landau had thrown me out of his house. Landau had accused me of seducing the children's nursemaid, who was showing signs of morning sickness. It was a black-hearted lie. It was I who had been seduced, not by the nursemaid but by Frau Landau. The old saw holds true: the husband is always the last to know.

Thus, at age eighteen, I found myself in the streets of Berlin and unwilling to return to Damascus, where my father's fortunes had begun to sour. The French had dethroned King Faisal and occupied Syria, thus awakening nationalist fervor in the Arab and Druze masses. This in turn created a sense of insecurity among the Jews, Armenians, and Maronite Christians, who now cast a nervous eye toward potentially more hospitable lands.

I had no great incentive to return to the limiting life of the Levantine middle class, but in the fall of 1929, things did not look promising in Germany either. On the twenty-ninth of October the stock market of New York crashed. It plunged the United States into depression and sent such shock waves throughout the world that here in Germany the painful recovery from the inflation, which had raged between 1922 and 1925, ground to a halt. During the inflation, the little nest eggs of widows, war veterans, and retired civil servants had evaporated; their pitiful mark notes stuffed into mattresses or into sugar bowls on kitchen shelves had become as the old newspapers that scudded in the frozen gutters. The inflation did not spare the substantial savings of the middle class either, but it took the great crash of 1929, with its ensuing depression, to devastate the well-to-do, the businessmen and entrepreneurs: the very class of people to whom the others looked for jobs and security. Unemployment, and with it membership in the Nazi Party, soared. But in the midst of this gray fear, which enveloped the country like a deadly fog, I, Daniel Saporta, was rich! Rich because of my mother, may her name be blessed until all eternity, amen. Rich because she had sewn into the waistband of my best suit a row of Turkish hundred-piaster gold coins. They were of the Monnaie de Luxe variety, struck by a special mint for their beauty. They were distributed, in the Ottoman days, by the titled and wealthy to important guests and retainers as a sign of favor. In my family they were given on the occasion of a bar mitzvah, the birth of a son, and the New Year. They were to serve me well.

Before being cashiered from their household, I had often accompanied the Landaus on their evening outings, to the theater and to restaurants. I was aware that although the German masses suffered cruelly, plenty of people were doing well during this period. There were the businessmen who had some sophistication in their dealings, those who had foreign accounts, those who had saved foreign currency, those who bought when others sold, and vice versa. There was also a class of profiteers: Germans who had holdings abroad; foreigners from every continent who had come, during the inflation, to pick up the pieces. And there were the purveyors of cocaine, heroin, cannabis; also the pimps, active in both import and export. They fetched country girls from the impoverished farms of Pomerania and Silesia with offers of work as waitresses and salesgirls. Once in Berlin, the young women were drugged, debased, and debauched until they were tractable and started to turn a profit on the sidewalks or in the many brothels that dotted the city. True blondes who showed promise in their newly acquired trade were shipped off to Cairo and Buenos Aires, to Port Said and Caracas, where an appreciative clientele awaited them.

To accommodate and anticipate the wishes of this free-spending class, the city offered an incredible variety of restaurants: provincial German, Austro-Hungarian, Polish, Czech, Russian, Chinese, and strictly kasher. All this was available in infinite gradations, from the luxury of the Adlon, the Bristol, and Horcher's to comfortable lunchrooms and beer-and-sausage emporiums. There were bars for draymen and coal and potato dealers, for homosexuals, lesbians, and every other persuasion. There were nightclubs with telephones on each table, from which one could request a fox-trot or proposition guests at other tables. There were clubs with female impersonators, clubs featuring political satire, and clubs where people fornicated on the stage, in which pastime the public was asked to join. And did.

I must stop. My hand hurts. I have difficulty extending my fingers. Is it arthritis, or is it the damnable cold?

November 19, 1943

I LEARNED ABOUT nightclubs from my cousin Eli. Eli is four years older than I and worked in my father's warehouse. Although he was a dutiful son and supported his widowed mother, he spent most of his money in seedy nightclubs and on the prostitutes behind the Hejaz railroad station.

My mother would say, "Eli est un voyou" —Eli is a scoundrel.

My father defended him. "Eli is a good boy. He has a feel for the business. He can look at peppers and tell you where they were grown within a hundred dunams. He's only seventeen, and right now he's letting his little head rule his big head."

"Ezra, I must ask you not to be vulgar in front of the children—or in front of me, for that matter. You know I cannot abide it." My mother said this grandly, in the manner of the French convent school she had attended.

My mother's protests notwithstanding, I was attracted to Eli and his evil ways. Eli was already a man of the world. He slathered and combed his hair with Bakerfix until his coal-black mane shone like a raven's wing. Bakerfix was a French hair cream Eli bought in the souk. It was named after the American Negress Josephine Baker, who was the toast of Paris. My sisters knew her hit song, "J'ai deux amours, mon pays et Paris," by heart. La Baker's picture was on the tube of hairdressing, emphasizing the mannish, patent-leather look of her coiffure. Eli also affected gray suede shoes trimmed with patent leather. He assured me the look he cultivated was totally Parisian.

What I admired most in Eli was that he already commanded the attention, if not the respect, of grown-ups. The coffee vendors balancing their brass trays, the shoeshine men banging their brushes against their boxes, never failed to greet him in the street. "Marhaba yah Eli!" they would shout. Eli would give them a hand salute, in the fashion of Arab politicians, or share his cigarettes with them, or the purple Violettes de Parme, the crystallized candy blossoms, which he carried in his vest pocket. I was also impressed by how the doorman of the Semiramis nightclub greeted Eli. The doorman was a pockmarked Kurd, whose fierce countenance was embellished by a huge mustache and a blind milk-blue eyeball. The good eye, merciless in its glare, became merry when he recognized Eli. The doorman proffered the traditional "Ahlan we sahlan"—You are welcome—upon seeing us and, after a whispered conference with Eli, ushered us into the club itself. The Semiramis was a second-class establishment at best: dark, yet gaudy, illuminated by multicolored light bulbs—the sort used in the West for Christmas decoration. Hard chairs and small tables crowded a barely elevated stage from which the management presented its nightly entertainment. This never varied and consisted of the house orchestra: oud, kanoon, derbakke, and violin. They backed the belly dancers, who were spelled by singers of either sex. These artistes all reappeared after several months' interval, completing the circuit that took them to Homs, Aleppo, Latakia, and Basra or, as the result of a fortunate booking, on an occasional foray into Beirut or even Baghdad.

This particular evening was a turning point in my life. There is no question in my mind that it was this evening, at the Semiramis, which led me to buy the Kaukasus Klub, in Berlin, twenty-four hours after having left the Landau household.

We were seated in a darkened loge where, I suppose because of our tender years, we could watch the entertainment unobserved by the customers.

The Kurd brought us a narghile, a water pipe, which contained hashish mixed with leaf tobacco. We puffed, I for the first time, and soon I felt a rush of heat to my extremities, followed by the sense of detached amusement Eli had so often described to me. By the time the first belly dancer had taken to the floor, the Semiramis had filled up quite respectably. Most of the customers were small businessmen. I recognized Abou Issa, one of our customers, a spice dealer in the Attarine market. There were lesser government functionaries, two Armenian goldsmiths with a customer, some pomaded procurers, and a tableful of Bedouins from the Hejaz, judging by their dark complexions and the manner in which they wore the kaffiyehs. They alone among the clientele abstained from drinking the rotgut arak. This, along with pistachios and olives, was the champagne and caviar of a Levantine boite.

According to cousin Eli the first dancer was Jamila, twenty-six years old, from Egypt. She had been the mistress of a banker in Beirut. Eli shared this knowledge with me as a European would speak of a well-known soccer player. I was already under Jamila's sway. How could a boy of fourteen react otherwise to a graphic presentation of his sexual fantasies?

Interminably, Jamila twirled, lifting and lowering the aquamarine veil with which she covered her breasts and abdomen. Suddenly the drum beat picked up and became an unabashedly coital rhythm, which the cognoscenti greeted with a ripple of applause. Jamila dropped her veil, revealing full breasts encased in an embroidered brassiere. Her smooth, white, slightly protruding belly was barely held in check by a coin-decorated belt, which snaked down to cover her pubis, her lokoum or "Turkish delight," as Eli preferred to call it. Jamila undulated, shook her breasts, stood still, made them quiver, resumed her dance, and then slowly started to thrust and withdraw her pelvis, as if it were impaled on the zoub of some invisible lover. By this time I was totally tumescent. Eli, who could read me like a book, nudged me with his elbow, grabbed his crotch, and rolled his eyes wildly. He had seen me as I saw myself—a dog in heat, the red organ out of its sheath—and I hated him for it. But Jamila was not through. She now stood on the corner of the stage facing our loge, and her odor of sweat and patchouli came to us. She stood quite still. Only the muscles in her belly started an imperceptible ripple, which she maintained to the beat of the drum. I could see drops of sweat snake down between her breasts, joining the rivulet that coursed to her navel and then ran down into the waistband of her belt. The ripples became waves. She undulated her belly as if it had a life of its own. She kept this up as the beat increased. Then, with a cry, she dropped to the floor, arched her back, spread her thighs, and rolled over, head hidden in the crook of her arm, as if in a gesture of shame and humiliation. It was a touch the audience appreciated. The applause was tumultuous. I was brought out of my reverie by Eli. "Yah, habibi!" he said. "That Jamila has some muscles in her kous! She could slice bananas with it."

The next performer was a singer: a soft, pudgy young Greek, probably from Alexandria, judging by his Egyptian accent. He too had admirers. I later saw one of the Bedouins slip his gold watch into the Greek's pocket.

November 20, 1943

I LEARNED A GREAT DEAL that first night. I saw men who seemed not to have rent for their market stalls slip their last piasters into the brassieres and waistbands of dancers. I saw waiters, following the exchange of monies, bring the dancers to the tables of the patrons. I saw men, already glassy-eyed, being served more arak. I saw a policeman getting his baksheesh from the manager. And I understood from all this that a nightclub, even one as tawdry as the Semiramis, was a place where customers could leave their cares at the entrance. Business failures, betrayals by partners, mothers dying of cancer, fat or indifferent wives, sluttish daughters, stupid sons, usurious debts to moneylenders in the bazaar, the hopelessness of uncertain futures: all that which renders little people helpless in the face of an uncaring fate was left at the door. I saw that celebrants—of birthdays, of business deals satisfactorily consummated—were small in number. Most were lonely, worn down by a hard life, making the flesh, presented on stage, their own.

As we slipped into the dark and windy street, Eli suggested that we visit the sharmutas behind the railroad station. I was afraid of the late hour and of discovery by my father. I was also afraid of the whores themselves, certain that they would not measure up to the charms of a Jamila.

On the subject of whores, Eli's favorite subject, he offered to share with me, his favorite cousin, his personal approach to a satisfying sexual union.

"I masturbate before I go to the whorehouse," he said.

"Why would you do that?" I asked, in utter innocence.

"Because the second time it takes longer to come, you donkey. And that way you get your money's worth."

Eli had always had an exceptional head for business. He proved it in 1925, when the Druze uprising against the French began. He married Yvette Alkalay, the docile but unattractive daughter of a well-to-do cotton merchant. Using her dowry, he took wife and unborn child and, in the dead of night, left Damascus and headed for São Paulo, Brazil. Within five years he was truly rich, the owner of a knitwear factory with outlets in Recife, Salvador, Rio, and Belo Horizonte. Yvette gave him five wonderful children and in 1932 they took a trip around the world. I met them in Paris. Eli had not lost his good looks, but he'd become fleshy and vulpine. Yvette was no longer a shy mouse; she was a self-assured, well-satisfied matron. They spoke Portuguese to one another, which was no great linguistic feat. Portuguese is related to our Ladino, as one of the lesser Iberian languages.

"Daniel, habibi, get out of this Germany of shit," Eli said. "The thing with this Hitler will go badly. There are Polish and German Jews in my business, and they are getting their families out."

"It's a passing phase," I said. "The Germans who matter are much too sophisticated to buy this nonsense."

"Daniel, you are still a donkey, living in the clouds. Come to Brazil, open a nightclub, come into my business—anything. Everyone makes money there except the Brazilians. Please."

Of course I did not listen. In the lavatory, Cousin Eli showed me photographs of his mistresses. He specialized in mulattas with gray eyes. They were uniformly beautiful, with mountains of glossy hair, great breasts with dark nipples, and wonderful haunches. Eli kept the photographs in the back of his Brazilian passport. Whether he shared them with the customs officers at border crossings, I do not know.

Lohmann, where are you? What stale, crumbly, greasy delights do your pockets hold for me this time?

November 21, 1943

LOHMANN CAME LAST NIGHT. *His pockets were bulging with some good-sized potatoes, and he unwrapped a fatty piece of smoked pork loin, which appeared to have come off someone's plate. "I'm sorry," he said, as if reading my thoughts. I often wanted to put my arms around him in a show of thanks, but I realized this would have been painfully embarrassing to him. I really think he would have preferred an upbraiding, even a reprimand: "Lohmann, what is this garbage you are bringing me? See if you can't do better in the future." He would have straightened his back and barked an affirmative "Jawohl, Herr Saporta."*

As I said, I met Lohmann the night of my exodus from the Landau family. He had taken refuge from a flurry of December snow in the underground station at Kurfürstendamm and the Uhlandstrasse. I was about to take the underground train to Halensee, to a pension that had been recommended to me. Lohmann had taken off his sandwich board and set it up in the tiled underground entrance. His frayed overcoat and visored blue workingman's cap were at odds with its seductive promise:

KLUB KAUKASUS
Sascha and his Gypsy Orchestra
Don Cossack Dancers
Shashlik
Chicken Kiev
Entertainment
Meinekestrasse 142 (in the courtyard)

Lohmann sized me up correctly: a well-turned-out young foreigner with no place to go. Deferentially, he touched the tip of his visor with a forefinger that showed through a hole in his woolen glove. He studied me for a moment and pointed to the sandwich board. ''All that is a lot of tripe, but the cook is excellent and we have a few good bottles left.'' He picked up his board, slipped it over his head, and started up the stairs toward the street. I followed.

Hours later, I still sat in the stained, purple ugliness of the club. In front of me were the remains of an outstanding borscht. I was sopping up the juices of a Pojarski cutlet with a piece of bread, and we were well into the second bottle of wine. ''We'' refers to the owner, a White Russian entrepreneur, and myself. Lohmann hovered in the shadows, fetching bread, lighting his master's cigars when so ordered. The only waiter had already decamped. The owner told me of the injustice that had befallen him. Unscrupulous and dishonorable people were conspiring against him with accusations of complicity in drug deals and even white slavery; imagine! he who had fought for the Czar! The Little Father had personally decorated him. And now he was ordered to present himself to the police at eight o'clock in the morning. As a foreigner I would understand the mentality of the Prussian bureaucracy, the tendency of the Berlin police to see everything in black and white, their lack of tolerance for the human factor. That he, an innocent man who had fled the cruelties of the Bolshevik revolution, who had added his intellectual gifts and creative talents to the leaven of this city, was now faced with the prospect of spending the winter in Moabit Prison...

I no longer heard his litany. All I could see was Jamila, dancing on the stage of a redecorated Kaukasus. I saw imported belly dancers from Turkey, from Egypt, sloe-eyed Armenians, Circassians, Sudanese, Egyptians: quivering, jiggling, driving the German clientele wild. For this was a period in which the Germans were besotted by exotica; Negro saxophone players from America, uniformed doormen from Senegal, mulatto chorus girls from Havana were all the rage. My mind was made up. I excused myself, slipped a fork into my pocket, and headed for the WC, where I closeted myself. I removed my trousers. With the tines of the fork I opened the waistband and slipped out some of the coins.

The bill of sale was made out on top of the upright piano. The White Russian made off for Paris, where his sister maintained a similarly notorious establishment, and I, Daniel Saporta, eighteen years of age, recently of Damascus, became the owner of a business in Berlin! With a stroke of the pen, spice merchant had become nightclub impresario.

The Arabs say that when the camel was asked its occupation, it said it was a spinner of silk. Had I remembered this bit of folk wisdom, I might not be sitting here today.

The cook, Frau Tatyana Novikov, Lohmann, and I celebrated my succession until five o'clock in the morning. We ate scrambled eggs with chives, caviar in the Russian manner, soup spoons of it heaped on thickly buttered bread, and smoked salmon with capers and olive oil. A passable German Sekt served us nicely. Frau Novikov also drank vodka until she became tearful, sobbing that she had not been paid in several months. I looked to Lohmann for confirmation. He nodded. It was the cook's turn to tell me that Lohmann had received no salary at all, just meals and the tips he made opening doors and chasing taxis. I put them both on proper salaries. We drank a final toast to the success of our enterprise and declared it was time to go home. Frau Novikov lived near a Russian Orthodox church, where she and fellow émigrés lit candles, breathed incense, and prayed for the speedy restoration of the House of Romanov. It was her employer and Lohmann who were homeless. I told Lohmann he could sleep on the banquettes, provided he did not get brilliantine or boot blacking on them. As for myself, I moved my scanty belongings into the club's office, where I slept a few fitful hours.

When I awoke, I already regretted the decision I had so brashly taken. Other than furtive visits to the Semiramis under the tutelage of my cousin Eli, what did I know of nightclubs? I was vaguely aware of licensing regulations, of leases to be signed with a landlord, of contracting for towel and linen services and other practical considerations. Who was to advise me in these matters? I would have to rely on Lohmann, he of the sandwich board, whose cabaret expertise was limited to fetching taxis and opening doors.

More than anything else, I needed someone to whom I could unburden myself. In view of my expulsion I was too ashamed to call on some of the Landau regulars who had befriended me. I suppose I could have turned to Lotsi, Herr Landau's brother-in-law, but in view of his cavalier view of regulations and ordinances I felt he was not the one to give me counsel. Who then remained in this suddenly unfriendly city? I reached into my black kid-skin wallet, a going-away present from my sister Sultana. Between a photograph of my mother and one of my entire family standing in front of the ruins at Baalbek, I retrieved a calling card: Prof. Dr. Steinbruch of the Pergamon Museum. I lost no time in contacting my former traveling companion from the Orient Express.

Dr. Steinbruch received me in his bachelor quarters within the hour. His pleasure at seeing me was obvious. He made me welcome, dismissing the incredible disorder of his rooms with a deprecating gesture. There were books by the hundreds; they covered the tables, the buffet, the chairs, even the windowsills. Clippings, foolscap, magazines, reams of newspapers filled all the remaining nooks. In spite of the mess, a not unpleasant odor, a mixture of the aroma of good cigars and eau de cologne, impregnated the place. It reminded me of the compartment we had shared on the wagons-lits.

I unburdened myself to Dr. Steinbruch. Had I committed a dreadful error? Should I take my loss and try my fortunes in the spice business somewhere else? I could not return to Damascus. The disgrace of my premature return, even if the cause of it were unknown, would be obvious to everyone. I could not expose my parents to such shame.

I had given Dr. Steinbruch an opportunity to indulge in his favorite pastime: the delivery of a pedantic monologue, buttressed by historical underpinnings. "My boy, now that you've been pushed out of the nest, so to speak, the decision as how to pursue your life must be yours. All I can do is help evaluate the possibilities open to you. I suppose I should advise you to return to the warmth of the Mediterranean, where you could pursue any career of your choosing among kindred spirits. Your many languages and the educational discipline to which you were subjected by the Alliance Israelite would stand you in good stead."

He paused, looking at me over his steel-rimmed spectacles.

"I suspect that this is not what you have in mind, so let me examine the alternative you seem to have chosen. I find your concept of opening an oriental cabaret a sound one. Germans are tired of the gray depression, tired of the gray weather, tired of their circumscribed lives. Suggestive oriental music and exotic dancers with full breasts and shapely bottoms are bound to bring you not only all of Berlin's low life but the repressed bourgeoisie also. If you handle your affairs in a businesslike fashion, you will have success on your hands. In that sense I approve. It seems an enterprise to which you are eminently suited."

He chose a cigar, cut off its tip with his boar's-tusk cutter, lit it with a wooden match, and savored the aroma momentarily.

"But I would be remiss if I did not speak to you of my apprehensions for the future of this country. They arose in Munich in 1923 when I gave a lecture at the Ethnographic Museum. There I became witness to the Nazi putsch, which was spawned in the beer cellars of Munich. I saw a collection of misfits, criminals, degenerates, and drug addicts, the scum of German society, challenge constituted authority. In six short years these murderers have gathered such a following that today, in 1929, they speak of the day when they will come to power."

Steinbruch glowered at me, turned to the bookcase in back of him, and took a newspaper off the shelf.

"You've been in Germany a year, Daniel. Have you heard nothing? Have you seen nothing? Do you not know of Hitler and his National Socialists? Do you not know what they have in store for your people?"

"Of course I know," I replied. "It is a constant topic of conversation among the Landaus and their friends. But they also say that there had been periods of anti-Semitism in Germany before; that it always blows over. That the contribution of the Jews to German culture makes their future secure."

"Let me tell you how secure their future is." He reached for the newspaper on his lap. "This is what Julius Streicher, a former lower-school teacher and now Hitler's expert on the Jews, says in his weekly paper, *Der Stürmer.*"

The content of that article was so incredible I have retained the highlights. Streicher's theory, accepted by the Party faithful, was that a woman's womb absorbs the sperm of her sexual partner into her bloodstream. Therefore a single sexual encounter with a Jew would poison the woman for all time. Worse, with this alien semen she would also absorb the soul of the Jew. Even if this woman were subsequently impregnated by an Aryan, she would be incapable of giving birth to anything but bastards. That is why, Streicher reasoned, the Jew uses every means of seduction to sully German girls of tender years; it is why Jewish physicians anesthetize and rape their Aryan patients. It is also why Jewish women permit their men to have intercourse with German women, so that they, contaminated by Jewish semen, would no longer be able to bear racially pure German children.

Dr. Steinbruch put the article away. "That's the official position of the Nazis who are waiting to take control of the government."

"Surely most Germans don't believe such nonsense," I interjected.

"That is unimportant," said Dr. Steinbruch. "The industrialists see the Nazis as a way of dealing with the unions and the Left. The General Staff looks down on the brown-shirted rabble but is quite pleased to have them pave the way for remilitarization. The opposition is hopelessly divided. The Social Democrats write anti-Nazi articles, mostly for their own consumption; the Communists brawl in the streets with the Brown Shirts, but Social Democrats and Communists cannot overcome their class differences to unite against the Nazis. And in answer to your question: yes, there are millions of Germans who believe Streicher's claptrap."

"Should I be the first to run, Dr. Steinbruch? Run before the German Jews do? Even with the protection my French passport affords me?"

"Daniel," he replied, "I do not wish to alarm you unnecessarily. I do not wish to stand in the way of your potentially successful career as a cabaret impresario. I cannot tell you exactly when they will come to power; it's just my conviction that they will. All I ask is that you take a page out of the book of the Marranos."

"The Marranos? The Conversos, you mean? Converts to Christianity, betrayers of the Convenant?"

"You miss the point, my boy. The Marranos practiced their Judaism secretly, to avoid the long arm of the Inquisition. Once in the safety of Moslem lands, they emerged as devoted to Jehovah as ever before. And if the father could not come back to the Torah, the son or even the grandson would. Make them your example, Daniel Saporta, for you are of the same lineage as those who clung to their faith in spite of torture and exile."

He saw the shock, the disbelief on my face.

"What I counsel you to do is to distance yourself completely from your former contacts. I suggest that before you open your cabaret you assume a new name and in the process create a new persona for yourself. The best of luck to you and to your cabaret."

He shook my hand. I turned to go, but he restrained me.

"One more thing, Daniel."

"Yes?"

"You might start by removing that absurd symbol of Arab manhood—your mustache."

November 22, 1943

THE ATTIC *in which I am confined is identical to all the others that top the great middle-class apartment houses built in nineteenth-century Berlin. Many of these buildings are double-winged structures surrounding courtyards; thus the attics tend to be enormous affairs, covering the entire floor space beneath the rooftops. They are generally maintained for the convenience of the tenants, each family having an allotted space for the storage of trunks, suitcases, and excess furniture. These storage areas were built of rough lumber extending from floor to ceiling, with spaces between the slats, in the manner of fences. The attics were subdivided into long rows of corridors, which, crossing at right angles, create a veritable maze. Some of the tenants finish the interiors of their cubicles with sheets of wood, thus making their contents less visible to nosy janitors or housemaids. There is also sufficient space in these attics for clotheslines on which to dry sheets and laundry in the case of rain or snow. Fortunately this custom has fallen into disuse.*

It is the generous layout of this attic that saves me from total claustrophobia and atrophy. At night I can leave my cubicle and roam up and down the corridors in stockinged feet, to pause at the dormer windows, which afford me a view of the nighttime city. The cold-water tap in the laundry area serves me in good stead, and usually my only companions are stray rats scampering about.

It was Lohmann, of course, who secured this haven for me. To which tenant the cubicle belongs, I do not know. Probably to someone in the vast network of friends he has from "the old days." Mostly these are waiters, commissionaires, prostitutes, taxi drivers, petty criminals: in short, people who live by their wits, all survivors of one sort or another who refuse to be politicized. Lohmann and I try not to compromise each other's relative safety, in case of apprehension by the authorities, by sharing information that might prove incriminating. Thus I do not know the identity of the benefactor whose hospitality I am enjoying here. I only know that I am in the Charlottenstrasse, halfway between the Anhalter Bahnhof and the Spittelmarkt, which would place me somewhere near the center of the city.

November 25, 1943

I'VE HAD LITTLE SLEEP *these last few nights. The air raids, which should be a cause for jubilation on my part, were intense and left me frightened in my isolation. I heard the drone of the approaching aircraft and the howling of the sirens and could see the ghostly beams of the antiaircraft searchlights trying to penetrate a foggy night sky. The bombs were not long in coming. They seemed like thunderous footsteps marching across the central part of the city. The explosions were muffled at first, then louder and more defined as they passed nearby, gradually tapering off as the bombers left the city behind them. I could see the reddish glow of the clouds, reflecting raging fires below, through my dormer window.*

Last night, or rather around four in the morning, the all clear sounded. I had just wrapped myself into my rat's nest of rags and newspapers when a heavy delayed explosion went off down the street. It sent a shower of dirt and dust down upon me. It filled my eyes and lungs and started an interminable attack of coughing that left me drained and exhausted. Worse, I was overcome by waves of self-pity, which led me to curse the chain of events that brought me to this damnable place.

By and large, the Damascene Jews lived in the Haret el Yahoud, the ancient Jewish quarter, which lay just south of the Street Called Straight. One reached it by descending a cascade of levels and ended up in a rabbit warren of ancient buildings, where workshops, stalls, living quarters, and synagogues existed cheek by jowl. The inhabitants of the quarter were mostly artisans: tin, silver, and copper smiths, tailors, drapers, petty jewelers, and bakers of traditional breads.

As in all Jewish communities, extending from the shores of southern Arabia to the shtetls of Russo-Poland, there was also a class of professional optimists: men who had no trade or calling but who managed to feed their wives and children from the meager droppings of deals in which they were able to bring together those who had merchandise with those who had the money to buy it. My mother's distant cousin Abou Moussa, for example. Having neither trade nor schooling, he depended on the Almighty to provide for his wife and six children, but he was also no fool. He knew that sometimes even God needs help.

Thus Cousin Abou Moussa went to Beirut once or twice a month on the railroad. By moving from coach to coach without ever claiming a seat, he avoided the ticket collector. When cornered, he would bribe the collector with a few paras, which the collector would pocket avidly, since he was easily as poor as our cousin. Abou Moussa was not a mean or dishonorable man, far from it, but he needed his money for matters more pressing than the corrupt railroad administration: bread, for one. In Beirut, Abou Moussa would haunt the waterfront and sleep on the hard benches of local synagogues. He would always find a compassionate gabbai to unlock the doors for him and give him a glass of tea in the morning. On these business trips, he had virtually no expenses. He ate the local flatbread with parsley or scallions, nothing else. He knew all the ships that came into the harbor, as well as their ports of call. What interested him was the cargo and the condition of the goods. He spoke to the navvies who unloaded the ships. He buttonholed customs brokers. He offered himself as a guide to foreign sailors. He would follow ships' captains into the harbormaster's office to read the bulletins announcing ship arrivals and departures. Often he was booted out, but no matter. The fact that he only spoke Arabic was no impediment. He had picked up enough English and French to make himself understood. He jumbled them together, his hands and eyes adding emphasis in case of a breakdown in communications.

After a few days Abou Moussa's dossier was complete. Before the merchants in Beirut or Damascus had an inkling, he knew what merchandise was damaged, what had been seized by customs, what had been refused by the consignee. With this information he would hurry back to Damascus, to the souks and the wholesalers, to factors and jobbers. A hundred bolts of water-stained cotton from India. Tinned goods without labels from Germany. French wines with seeping corks. Nuts and bolts with inch specifications, shipped by an American manufacturer to a factory with metric needs. Austrian Christmas cards mistakenly sent to Moslem stationers. No matter. In the Levant, one can always find someone to buy if the price is right.

This information was Abou Moussa's stock in trade. He needed no offices, no filing cabinets, no telephones, no messenger boys. He carried his entire business in his head, above his frayed collar. His reward depended on the generosity or niggardliness of those who availed themselves of his intelligence. But modest as it was, it was sufficient for Abou Moussa to play out his role as husband and father in relative dignity.

November 26, 1943

LIFE BECAME HARD for the Jews of Damascus in 1870. The opening of the Suez Canal killed off the remunerative trade with Persia, which had always moved by camel caravan across the Syrian desert. The Jews had benefited from this as middlemen, as dragomans or commercial interpreters, as bankers and expediters. By the turn of the century, steady emigration to Beirut and to the Americas had left the community in the condition I describe.

Of course we did not all live in the Haret el Yahoud. Families who were well off, such as mine, lived in villas on tree-lined streets overlooking the Barada River. We lived in amity with our Moslem neighbors and in conditions best described as civil, measured, and courteous.

Which brings me to my bar mitzvah. For months I had gone to the Jewish quarter after school. A strict and mean-spirited haham—rabbi in western parlance—had drilled into me the portion of the Torah I was to read in front of congregation and guests on the day of my acceptance into the covenant. At thirteen, we became men, entitled to wear the tallith, to be measured among the ten men required to constitute a minyan, the quorum required for communal worship.

Not content with following the service with the usual party given for friends and relatives at home, my father had, months before, reserved a private dining room at the Orient Palace Hotel. He was resolved to celebrate his son's bar mitzvah in the European manner, in lavish surroundings. He would invite not only family but business friends and local notables with whom he had dealings. Six months before this exalted event, my mother had written invitations in French, in the beautiful calligraphy taught her by the nuns, to relatives and friends in Alexandria, in Aleppo, in Salonika, in Jerusalem, even in Germany. Also invited were some of my father's Moslem friends, most prominent among them the chief of the customs house and a high-ranking police official. The Haham Bashi, or Chief Rabbi of

Damascus, and bankers from the Zilkha and Safra banks headed the list of Jewish notables. My father's principal customer in Europe, Herr Jakob Landau of Berlin, answered by telegraph:

MY WIFE AND I ACCEPT WITH PROFOUND HONOR YOUR INVITATION TO JOIN YOU IN DAMASCUS ON THE OCCASION OF THE BAR MITZVAH OF YOUR SON DANIEL. MAY A BOUNTIFUL GOD SHED BLESSINGS UPON THE HOUSE OF SAPORTA. YOUR DEVOTED FRIEND, JAKOB LANDAU.

The acceptance of the Landaus created a sense of excitement among us. Although Ashkenazim—German or Eastern European Jews—were an object of ridicule or even derision among us, we secretly admired and envied them. They were physicians, philosophers, scientists, and great merchants, while we Sephardim were mostly small traders and peddlers in the backwaters of the Ottoman Empire. There were exceptions, of course: the Sassoons, Hardoons, and Kadoories of Bombay and Shanghai, the legendary Montefiores of London. Though they were not, historically, exiles from Spain but originally from Baghdad and Italy, we saw them as Sephardic grandees and happily accepted their schools, hospitals, and charitable institutions. Thus, in a reversal of roles, we saw the coming of the Landaus as an exotic illumination to our drab surroundings.

Had they only remained in the frozen wastes of their native Prussia!

November 27, 1943

"AND YE SHALL have no power to stand before your enemies. And ye shall perish among the nations, and the land of your enemies shall eat you up. And they that are left of you shall pine away in their iniquity in your enemies' lands...and they shall confess their iniquity and the iniquity of their fathers, in their treachery which they have committed against me...and they be paid the punishment of their iniquity.... Then will I remember my covenant with Jacob, with Isaac, with Abraham, and I will remember the land. For the land will lie desolate without them, they shall be paid the punishment of their iniquities because they rejected mine ordinances, and their soul abhorred my statutes. Yet when they are in the land of their enemies, I will not reject them, neither will I abhor them.... But I will for their sakes remember the covenant of their ancestors, whom I brought forth from the land of Egypt in the sight of the nations, that I might be their God: I am the Lord. These are the statutes and ordinances and laws, which the Lord made between him and the children of Israel in Mount Sinai by the hand of Moses."

I had chanted without making a single mistake. I laid down the pointer with which I had followed the handwritten letters on the parchment scroll. I spoke the final blessing:

"Blessed art thou, Lord our God, King of the universe, who gave us a Torah of truth and planted within us eternal life. Blessed art thou, Lord, who gives the Torah."

I slipped the prayer shawl off my head, folded it around my shoulders, and turned to face the congregation. Thus it must have been in the Holy of Holies, a vision of purity: the lamps, the silver, the velvet embroidered with gold, the men covered in their white prayer shawls, their faces and western suits hidden from view. The spell was broken as my father hurried toward me with open arms. At the same time, the women broke out of their gallery, trilling their tongues in the wild ululation peculiar to Arabs. When they were within reach, they showered me with a rainfall of gaudily wrapped sweets. I was bar mitzvah.

At the Orient Palace Hotel, I sat at the table of honor with my parents, my maternal grandparents, my brother and sisters, and, at my insistence, Cousin Eli. The guests of honor, the Landaus', were also at our table. Herr Landau was a large man in his forties, already going bald but compensating for it with a heavy black mustache. He wore a pince nez and, with his sallow complexion, did not look out of place in these oriental surroundings. Frau Landau, some ten years junior to her husband, was something else altogether. She was a true pale blonde. Not a reddish blonde, as were the Jewesses of Aleppo, but fair pale, like an Englishwoman. At least, that was our point of reference. Her husband explained that his family came from Frankfurt, the town in which the House of Rothschild had originated, but that his wife was Hungarian or Romanian: anyway, from Budapest or Bucharest; we couldn't tell which. They both spoke French, not well and heavily accented. Obviously these Ashkenazim, as my grandmother later commented, knew nothing of modesty either. This woman was dressed in a pale gray satin dress, without sleeves, and a décolletage that revealed the full orbs of finely powdered breasts. When she laughed or moved, her nipples showed through the silk. Cousin Eli was already in love with her. He demonstrated this exalted feeling to me secretly by rapidly plunging his stiffened index finger into an orifice created by his clenched fist.

After the departure of the guests we remained at our table drinking champagne. Herr Landau asked me to sit between him and his wife. He handed me a package, which I was asked to open. A velvet case emerged. In it was a wristwatch, fabriqué Suisse. My joy was complete. This was a period when most men still carried stem-winders in their waistcoat pockets. I rose to shake Herr Landau's hand in gratitude and turned to offer my thanks to his wife. She ignored my outstretched hand and instead pulled me to her bosom, to kiss the top of my head. I smelled the sweet odor of her rice powder. I felt the silkiness of her breast against my face. I knew that I was scarlet to the tip of my ears.

Although I had become, in religious terms, a man, I was in reality still a child. The day following the festivities found me back in my appointed seat in the school run by the Alliance Israélite Universelle.

Instruction was in French, covering all the disciplines required to take us into the twentieth century. We studied mathematics and geometry, history and geography, physics and science, and French interminably; also composition, logic, grammar, poetry, recital. There were music and piano lessons for our sisters; there was shop for the boys. The school was not exclusive in nature. On the contrary, the Alliance had been set up primarily to educate the children of the Jewish masses.

This gave us an advantage in life that would eventually earn us the envy and distrust of the Arabs. Moslem boys attended the madrasa, usually nothing more than a one-room school in which a mullah would pound the suras of the Koran into them; these the children would repeat in unison at the top of their lungs. Beyond the native gift that eastern people have for business, assimilated more from bazaars than from teachers, the average Moslem was ill prepared for the modern world. By the time the French were installed in Syria-Lebanon and the British in neighboring Iraq, it was the Jews who filled the infra-structures these colonialists needed. Jews worked in banks as tellers, in counting houses as accountants. They were the clerks in the courts and then lawyers before the bar. They were official interpreters and guides. Through no doing of their own they came to be perceived, by the Arabs, as the handmaidens of the accursed faranjah, the occupying foreigners.

Before the Landaus left Damascus for Berlin, I was summoned into my father's office. It was located on a mezzanine landing, from which he could observe the activity in the warehouse below. The building itself lay in a ramshackle neighborhood between the Bab el Faraj, the Gate of Deliverance, which led out of the ancient walled city, and the Moslem cemetery of Dahda.

I loved going to the warehouse, with its intoxicating odor of spices and the comradeship extended to me by the elderly Arabs, who had worked for the Saporta family for years. They let me share their bread and sour milk. On payday they might buy me a sfihah, a little meat pie that was hawked in the streets.

To earn pocket money I had worked in the warehouse, after school and during vacations, since I was ten. I knew the contents of every bin, the origin of every burlap sack. I knew how to grade cardamon, cumin, turmeric, and saffron, each according to their quality. I had sacked and weighed coriander, mastic, sumac, cinnamon, and ginger. We had every shade of paprika, varieties of aniseed, caraway, fennel, and cayenne. We had nuts of every kind, as well as seeds and dried fruit and dried peppers. Our inventory came from India, Yemen, Zanzibar, Turkey, and Persia. We shipped our wares all over the East, and we had special customers in Europe, of whom Herr Landau in Berlin was the foremost.

Herr Landau was sitting in my father's office when I came in. I kissed my father's hand, and, taking the hint from the lift of his head, I reached out for Herr Landau's hand to pay him the same respect, but it embarrassed him. It was Herr Landau who addressed me. He said my father and he had discussed the political situation in the Levant and it was their mutual opinion that the position of our people could not but deteriorate in the years to come. The British and the French, by slicing up the Ottoman Empire, had infected the Arabs with a sense of nationalism they had never known before, and there were already isolated attacks on our people in Palestine. None of this was over the head of a thirteen-year-old boy. Politics were a matter of life and death for us. A new king, a new prime minister, a pact made or broken, spelled the difference between prosperity and misery, between home and exile. It was the major topic of conversation in the family, in the office, in the coffeehouse, and in the bazaar, and the children were raised on it.

Herr Landau continued, saying that the future lay in the West and that he had offered to take me into his business, in Berlin, as an apprentice, whenever my father decided the time was ripe. I would live with the Landaus. I would be with them as in my own house. My father said that if I pursued my studies at the Alliance diligently, I could go on my seventeenth birthday. The men shook hands and I was dismissed.

The minute I was on the warehouse floor, I sought out Eli to tell him of the career that had been planned for me.

"Hamdul'illah!" he said. "You will get to see more than her tits, I wager."

I had never thought of Cousin Eli as a prophet.

November 28, 1943

LAST NIGHT *Lohmann brought a bottle of bordeaux, a ring of French garlic sausage, two tins of sardines, and a jar of cherry jam. This was an extraordinary windfall, considering the turn the war was taking for the Germans. Lohmann explained its acquisition. He had visited an elderly aunt in Zehlendorf, a working-class district of the city. An air raid had delayed him on the way home and, after the all clear, he had continued through the darkened streets. Passing some small shops, he heard a crunching, tinkling sound behind him. When he turned, he saw that the window of a modest jeweler's had suddenly disintegrated: a delayed effect of the bombing raid. Without thinking of the consequences—certain execution for looting—he had grabbed a few watches and rings. He made it back to his aunt's, where he'd spent the night. In the morning he had gone to the Schlesischer Bahnhof, one of the main railroad stations, where soldiers on furlough arrive from France. Many of them were stationed in the countryside and brought back veritable treasure troves of French produce and merchandise. Lohmann, veteran nightclub doorman of many years' service, was able to evaluate a man's standing or intellect with uncanny accuracy. Looking for a likely customer, he had isolated a young artilleryman, a Friesian giant of limited mental resources, and had traded off a silver-plated watch and a couple of rings for the delicacies.*

Lohmann also left me a copy of the Völkischer Beobachter, *the Nazi Party organ. Its news dispatches are larded with vainglory, threats of secret weapons, noble deeds, and appeals for more sacrifice. Catastrophic defeats are described as strategic withdrawals, but everyone knows that the Russian front is starting to collapse. The Russians have retaken Kursk, Kharkov, Smolensk, and, finally, Kiev. The Japanese are being forced back in the Pacific; the Americans have recaptured the Solomon and the Gilbert Islands. The Germans have surrendered in North Africa but are holding firm in most of Italy. The end is not yet in sight.*

November 29, 1943

THE FOUR YEARS following my bar mitzvah passed uneventfully. I continued my studies at the Alliance and spent more and more time in my father's warehouse. I was already bringing in some business of my own and accompanied my father on buying trips into the provinces. I wore a business suit with a vest, a shirt with starched cuffs and high collar, and the inevitable red fez, the traditional local head covering worn by Moslem, Jew, and Christian since the days of the Ottomans. Prompted by Cousin Eli, I too had become a devotee of Bakerfix and sported a sparse and silky mustache. While European boys my age were in college, enjoying membership in rowing and tennis clubs and going to dances with young ladies of their social circle, we in the East were already businessmen. Besides commerce, there remained only marriage to fill out our lives.

Shortly before my departure for Germany, my sister Fortuna was married. By this time, marriages were no longer arranged, but parents still saw to it that the young people were of the same background so their children could maintain the same station in life—or, better yet, augment the family fortune, through dowry and position within the family business. My sister had been courted by a young man who had graduated from the Alliance several years ahead of my class. He was Daoud Saleh, a thoroughly nice young man whose family owned an important textile business in the Grand Bazaar. My father liked him and gave his approval.

My mother raised petulant, unconvincing objections: Daoud's family were not Sephardim; they did not experience the expulsion from Spain in 1492, as did the Saporta family and her own clan, the Toledanos. The Salehs were Musta'rabs, Jews whose presence in Syria predated the arrival of the Sephardim. They were looked down upon by the refugees from Spain for being Arabized and without our literary and historical pretensions. When my father turned a deaf ear to my mother's elitist talk, she brought out what she perceived to be the heavy artillery of logic. "Ezra, my dear. You told me yourself that the Saportas were nobles in Catalonia, and the Toledanos were sharaf bashis, communal treasurers, appointed by the sultans in Alexandria." When my father asked her if she didn't really mean the provincial town of Alexandretta rather than the Egyptian metropolis, she became confused. She flounced out of the room with a "Faites comme vous voulez"—Do as you wish—only to reappear minutes later with tea and sweets, signaling her surrender.

I was to hear similar elitist discussions in the dining room of the Landau household when they entertained their intimate friends: the Rosenfelds, the Kohnheirns, the Wertheimers—mostly attorneys and businessmen. The conversation invariably turned to the Polish Jews: ill mannered and unhygenic, bearded and sidelocked, wandering the streets of Berlin in broad-brimmed hats and black caftans, giving the Germans a distorted view of Jews. It was by holding up these Ostjuden, or Eastern Jews, as examples that Hitler was able to influence public opinion against the Jews of Germany. Or so the Landaus and their friends chose to believe.

In any event, I had graduated from the Alliance Israélite Universelle school shortly after my seventeenth birthday and the fateful moment had arrived. The Saporta and Toledano families had assembled in the Ottoman splendor of the Hejaz railroad station to see me off to Constantinople (Istamboul since 1930) and points west. I kissed them all, some twenty-five in number. Everyone's tears flowed, including my own. I inclined my head before my father, who recited the traditional blessing: "The Lord bless you and keep you; the Lord make his face to shine upon you and be gracious unto you; the Lord lift up his countenance upon you and give you peace." Then I boarded the train. The whistle shrieked, my mother wailed, and, leaning out the carriage window, I saw my family diminish in size until they were out of sight.

My father, alav ha shalom, died in 1931. I was not there to say kaddish at his grave. In 1932, my brother-in-law, Daoud, moved my sister and their two children, my mother, and my unmarried sister, Sultana, to Beirut. My brother, Victor, never much of a businessman, moved to Palestine and settled in a socialist kibbutz in the Galilee. Over the years the other Jews disappeared into the alleys of the Haret el Yahoud or sought self-imposed exile, leaving their flourishing businesses and comfortable homes behind. What was left of the Saporta business was run by a distant cousin of my father. The warehouse was destroyed by the anti-Jewish riots of 1935. Street mobs set a torch to it, after hearing a radio broadcast by Hajj Amin el Husseini, the Grand Mufti, saying that the Jews had burned down the mosque on the Dome of the Rock in Jerusalem. Although the authorities knew this to be a lie, they did little to stop the violence. Unnoticed by the world, it spelled the end of a community that had been in existence since biblical days.

November 30, 1943

Lohmann came in around midday, an unusual time for him. I detected a rosy hue to his cheeks and nose. He soon confirmed its origin by producing a bottle of slivovitz, which had arrived in the musette bag of a soldier only this morning. There was also a tin of stuffed peppers, a length of bread, and a piece of hard Balkan cheese. Lohmann sipped from the bottle and insisted I drink with him. Good for the digestion, he said. He had news for me. Frau Novikov, our cook, had been bombed out, and Lohmann had moved her in with his aunt in Zehlendorf. They had taken an immediate liking to each other. This, in spite of Frau Novikov's poor German and the fact that his aunt, who came from East Prussia, viewed Russians and Poles, "the whole filthy pack," with misgivings. We spent an hour chatting about the early days of the Kaukasus.

Lohmann, Frau Novikov, and I had almost single-handedly redecorated the club. We did have the help of Lilo, a homosexual streetwalker who knew how to wallpaper and paint. Lilo was a protégé of Lohmann's; his professional beat was our neighborhood. When Lohmann brought him into my office I was taken aback by his appearance: long black hair, a face powdered ghostly white, Rimmel on his eyelashes, and, I thought, a touch of red on his lips. He held his hand out to me as if he expected it to be kissed. Fortunately Frau Novikov came in to hug her beloved Lilo since he was, obviously, a favorite of the establishment. I became aware that Lohmann, too, disapproved of my negative reaction.

My year with the Landaus had been relatively sheltered, and I still carried with me the middle eastern baggage of prejudice. Homosexuals were objects of contempt in Moslem literature, as they were in Jewish Law, and their vile and loathsome sexual activities were the cloth of dirty jokes told in the market stalls. We were raised with a whole grab bag of prohibitions. They included blood, both menstrual and animal, the spilling of seed in the manner of Onan, the loss of virginity, and, among the Moslems, female pubic hair and the clitoris.

I made a quick and reasoned judgment. If Lilo was good enough to be treated affectionately by Lohmann and Frau Novikov, I could do the same. Eventually Lilo was murdered, not by a homosexual pervert, as the press trumpeted, but, according to Lohmann, by Nazi bullyboys.

Within a week after having bought the Kaukasus, the four of us scoured it as it had never been cleansed before. We stripped the vile purple off the walls. We sanded and lacquered the dance floor. Lilo covered the walls with heavy silver wallpaper, procured from a friend in the theater. The woodwork was lacquered in black; the banquettes and chairs were reupholstered. The final touch was due, inadvertently, to Frau Novikov, who mentioned that while she was cleaning her church with the other ladies of her congregation, they had come across a number of Russian icons stored in the basement.

Her church was bitterly poor. The members were mostly, like herself, elderly refugees from the Bolshevist terror: once respectable matrons, mothers and wives, now widows working as charwomen or attendants in public rest rooms. The few men, once generals and colonels in famous Cossack regiments, were now driving taxis or working as uniformed doormen. This remnant sustained its church through faith, hardly through contributions. Thus I persuaded Frau Novikov, over her vehement objections, for she knew of my imminent recruitment of belly dancers, to let me have ten of the largest icons for the Kaukasus Klub. I paid generously, and the icons, banked with ivory candles, transformed the club from an elegant boite into a Caucasian fairyland. It was a deal from which everyone profited. The Orthodox priest and his church enjoyed a windfall, Frau Novikov was raised to a position of preeminence among the congregants, and the clients of the Kaukasus would enjoy the protection of Madonnas and obscure Slavic saints while they ate, danced, groped each other under the table, or cheated one another in business deals.

In spite of my misgivings, I had discovered early on that Lohmann was much more than a commissionaire. He had learned the management of a cabaret from his previous employer, the unsavory White Russian, with great skill but had never been given a chance to exercise his expertise. With his new employer, Lohmann was out to prove himself. Thus it was he who interviewed the waiters, the bartender, the ladies and gents' toilet attendants; it was he who made the deals with the furnishers of wine, beer, liquor; with the butcher, the baker, and, yes, the candlestick maker.

I perceived Lohmann to be an honorable man, but he undeniably still maintained his links to the Berlin underworld. Al hamdul'illah! Late one night as we shared a bottle of wine in the kitchen, I broached the subject raised by Dr. Steinbruch. I told Lohmann that mine was an old-fashioned family, and I wanted to save it from the embarrassment of having a son in the cabaret business, especially one specializing in belly dancers. And now I came to the point: I wanted to run the business under a name other than my own. Did he, Lohmann, know how to go about this? I am sure I did not fool him for a minute, but he praised me for the show of filial concern. A rare quality nowadays, he added.

An hour later we were in a smoky bar within hailing distance of the Alexanderplatz, ironically the headquarters of the Berlin police. Lohmann and I sat across the table from a surprisingly cultured and artistic young man who was subjecting my French passport to careful analysis. The change from Saporta to "Salazar" was not apparently insurmountable. He needed time, also a new photograph without mustache, for I had already removed my proud Arab shawarib and would require my hand to become accustomed to the new signature. Lohmann handled the financial details. It had been as simple as that. Ten days later it was as Daniel Salazar that I registered my acquisition of the Kaukasus Klub with the governmental Chamber of Commerce.

This has been one of the longest visits that Lohmann has paid me, and I feel buoyed by it.

Perhaps it is the slivovitz that makes him talkative, but I am aware of something else also. Whereas, by all accounts, the average citizen is being ground down by the deprivations, dangers, and seeming hopelessness of this war, Lohmann is flourishing. As the fortunes of war are slipping for Germany, Lohmann is gaining daily in self-assurance and even in weight. It becomes him; I think I detect new shoes and a couple of Sumatra cigars in his jacket pocket. I wonder if his experience with the shattered jewelry store window has opened new vistas for him.

December 1, 1943

IN MY ENTRY of November twenty-ninth, I wrote of my departure from Damascus and the tearful family left behind. Wishing to appear a man of the world, I had wiped away my own tears, blown my nose, and lit a cigarette. Thus fortified, I looked out the window of my railroad carriage. The city was soon left behind, but suddenly the train banked into a long curve and I saw it all once more—a sand-colored jumble, its minarets reaching for heaven. A cloud bank parted, and the city exploded in a reddish glow. This is how the Greeks, the Romans, the Byzantines, the many desert tribes, the Mamluks, the Mongols, and, finally, the Turks must have seen Damascus as they advanced upon her and, once more, when the city expelled them.

Damascus is not an ordinary place. It is the oldest inhabited city in the world. Here the great sultans had ruled: Nur ad Din and Salah ad Din, who had ridden forth to put an end to the ambitions of the Crusaders. Here John the Baptist had trodden the Street Called Straight. Damascus of the incredible mosques: the Umayyad, Sihan Pasha, Darwish Pasha, Al Aqsab, the Al Qual'ah. Damascus of the Citadel, of the Azm Palace, of the great gates. Damascus of the bazaars: the Souk el Khayyatin, el Miskiyya, the Souk el Kabir. Yes, even Damascus of the Haret el Yahoud. Suddenly, the track straightened and the city was gone.

The Syrian plain was monotonous, dun-colored, and interrupted only occasionally by villages of stone and mud brick, clustered around a solitary mosque. Peasants in the fields with their beasts straightened their pain-wracked backs, stared at the train with empty eyes, and went back to work. Miles of nothing. Then a farmyard, a blindfolded camel plodding its endless round, grinding wheat. Children, bright-eyed, playing in a muddy ditch. A train of camels and donkeys, burdened with the crops of the fields. Then, shepherds with their staffs, their abbayes pulled about them against the wind, and their flocks by the thousands. It was biblical. I remembered a passage from the synagogue: "And there was a man in Ma'on whose business was in Carmel; and the man was very great, and he had three thousand sheep, and a thousand goats...."

I tired of the landscape. I opened my suitcase and removed the Berlitz German Language Course, a gift from my grandfather. I immersed myself in the jumble of hostile Gothic letters. To my consternation, Mr. Berlitz brought home to me that a German sentence could ramble on interminably, reserving the qualifying verb until its very end. And until that revelation, one never knew if the subject had been admired, adored, loathed or loved; killed, hung or eaten. How would I ever master the grammar, the hostile Gothic letters?

In Constantinople, I was taken in tow by a distant relative who deposited me at a modest khan for the night. In the morning he treated me to a postman's holiday: a visit to the spice market, where he introduced me to small stall keepers as "Saporta's son." From there, he took me directly to the station where the Orient Express was getting up steam. Of the vast city, throne of empires, cleft between Europe and Asia, I had seen nothing. I was resolved to remedy this in the future.

December 2, 1943

I WAS INFECTED for all time by the glamour of the Orient Express, by its glistening gold and blue carriages, the shouts of the hamals shifting their burden of luggage, the whistles of the stationmasters, the steady hiss of steam, the sudden bark of the impatient locomotive, the many languages of the travelers, and the wonderful odors escaping from the kitchen compartment of the dining car. Getting on a train meant leaving the humdrum, the familiar, to head for new, unknown places where God only knew what temptations, triumphs, or disappointments lay in wait.

The train itself was a wonderland of discovery for me. I marveled at the intelligent way my compartment had been fashioned, particularly the comfortable seat with its backrest, which the wagon-lit attendant converted into an upper and a lower berth at night. I admired the wall panels of rosewood, with their insets of floral motifs. Everything had been considered: reading light above each berth, elastic netting to hold one's slippers and dressing gown, even blue running lights to make the passenger feel secure in the dark. Everything was perfection: the woolen blankets emblazoned with the Wagons-Lits' coat of arms, the crisp linen sheets, changed every day; the little ladder, on which to climb to the upper berth. I examined the washbasin with its hot and cold water faucets and its mirrored cupboard, containing heavy cut-glass tumblers and carafe with fresh water. The only thing I had missed was the little trap door beneath the washstand. It contained the "vase de nuit": a white porcelain vessel, looking rather like a large sauce boat, into which I saw my travel companion relieve himself during the night. I wondered what he would do with the contents of the vessel into which he had so copiously gurgled. What he did was to slip the vase back into its compartment and close the door on it. Monsieur Georges Nagelmackers, the Belgian who had founded the Compagnie Internationale des Wagons-Lits et des Grands Express Européens, had thought of everything. The vase de nuit emptied itself onto the tracks below.

I had barely finished my examination of the compartment when my fellow traveler was shown in by the sleeping car attendant. His luggage followed. To my surprise, this European thanked the hamal in Turkish and, having counted his pieces of luggage, turned to me with a smile.

"Steinbruch," he said, holding out his hand.

"Enchanté, Monsieur," I replied.

He laughed. "No, your name, young man."

"Saporta of Damascus," I said.

"Bravo," he said in accented French.

He sat down and started to pat his pockets in search of something. By the time he came up with a card case, I had studied him carefully: probably German, of some forty years, quite bald, wearing steel-rimmed spectacles, with comfortable belly, smelling of a not-unpleasant mixture of cigars and the eau de cologne which, I was to learn, the Germans who had invented it called Koelnisch Wasser. He handed me his calling card:

PROF. DR. THEODOR STEINBRUCH

PERGAMON MUSEUM, BERLIN

I handed him mine:

DANIEL SAPORTA

ÉTABLISSEMENT SAPORTA, EPICES EN GROS

RUE MANAKH, DAMAS.

I didn't come off too well in comparison, I felt. A spice merchant exchanging cards with a university professor, as though these pieces of stiff paper conferred equal merit on their owners? But the German thought otherwise.

"Daniel Saporta," he said. "I like the sound of that name. Very aristocratic. Rich with historical implications."

By saying "Rich with historical implications" he was actually telling me "I know you to be a Jew." I must have involuntarily drawn back, but I had misjudged him.

"Young man." He smiled. "I am a professor of history, a curator of Near and Middle Eastern Art. I envy your background. Few of us are privileged to have so illustrious a history."

Whereupon he reached for a well-worn briefcase and pulled out a bottle of raki, the Turkish arak. He placed it on the folding table beneath the window and set the glasses and carafe beside it. He poured water into the glasses first, then slowly added the arak, enjoying, as did I, the spectacle of two colorless liquids turning cloudy white upon being joined.

I smiled in approval. "You are an expert. My father says that serious arak drinkers always pour the water first."

Dr. Steinbruch raised his glass. "Sahtak," he said in Arabic.

As he put the glass to his mouth I became aware of the pink rosebud shape of his lips. I quickly squelched a mounting feeling of revulsion, replying "Sahtak"—To your health.

Next, he brought a leather cigar case from his vest pocket and took out two stubby gray cigars. He gave me one and then produced a cigar cutter mounted on a yellowed boar's tusk from the end of his watch chain. He clipped off the end of his cigar and did the same to mine. "A proper brit milah," he added.

A clumsy Germanic joke, I thought, but certainly not wide of its mark. I was astounded that he knew the correct Hebrew term for the ritual of circumcision. I shook off my irritation. He was a gracious, generous host, and as we sat sipping our arak and savoring our cigars, he was addressing me, a boy of seventeen, as his equal.

December 3, 1943

LOHMANN CAME, *in a good mood, and he enjoyed my childish pleasure at the goods he produced from his coat pockets: a tube of Chlorodont toothpaste, a new toothbrush, a whole box of Eberhard Faber pencils, stale but good dinner rolls, and, out of the inevitable brown paper parcel, a large slab of roast beef. When I started to compliment him for what must have been difficult to come by, he waved me off, saying that it was really horsemeat but cooked to perfection by Frau Novikov. Without much prodding he told me of his new enterprise.*

As I suspected, it has something to do with his experience at the jewelers. He is taking advantage of the ever-more-frequent bombing raids and takes to the streets long before the all clear sounds, smashing small shop windows with a brick, which he carries in his briefcase. He is selective in his acquisitions, preferring watches, rings, fine wallets, ladies' wear easily folded and concealed, tobacco, cigarette lighters, cigar cases, and watch chains. He has made himself familiar with the railroad stations. He knows which units are returning home from the front lines or from occupation duty, and to which station. Soldiers still come from France, Belgium, Scandinavia, or from Italy and Yugoslavia, with sausages, slabs of bacon, smoked hams, tinned fruit, vegetables, and bottles of wine or local schnapps. Lohmann does not fear the Kettenhunde, or "Chained Dogs"—the military police, so-called for the breastplate and chain around their necks. They loiter in the railroad stations with orders to arrest black marketeers. Lohmann, an old soldier himself, knows their modus operandi and their mentality. There is nothing furtive about Lohmann. In black overcoat, bowler hat, and gloves, with Party emblem in his lapel and Völkischer Beobachter folded under his arm, he is the embodiment of the solid German burgher.

He accosts the soldiers in the public lavatories or in the dank tiled passageways that lead out of the stations. The soldiers, still ignorant of the true conditions on the home front, trade off their foodstuffs for Lohmann's stock-in-trade: gifts he assured them will delight a dear mother and enchant the wonderful Fräulein awaiting her brave soldier with open arms.

In the Kantstrasse, a few blocks from the Kaukasus, he has found an apartment that belonged to a long-departed Jewish family—Lohmann made a gesture of regret—and which, through some bureaucratic muddle, remains unoccupied. The janitor of this building, whose loge and living quarters are below street level, is a friend of his. The janitor and Lohmann have come to an understanding, and the apartment has been turned into an exclusive dining club.

The patrons were solicited by Lohmann from among our former customers. Some are high-ranking Party functionaries, others staff officers from the War Ministry. They come with their secretaries, not their wives. In turn, these dignitaries bring in other fat cats from the fringes of society. Frau Novikov performs miracles with the goods that Lohmann acquires at the railway stations. These usually end up as zakuska: appetizers of whatever sort, presented in the Russian manner. Since cabbage and potatoes are plentiful, there is always a borscht. The meat for the main course is procured from our former suppliers, and sometimes from Lohmann's comrade of the goulash cannons.

To accompany these dinners, which are served in the dining room and salon, there is dinner music, played on the big Bechstein that stands in the salon. The pianist is an amputee who left his right leg on the Russian front. This presents some problems with the pedals, but, as Lohmann explained, not enough to matter to the diners. This pianist regales these new bon vivants with American jazz. That, at least, is what Lohmann thinks it is. And, after dinner, when the mood is introspective and mellow, there are the proscribed lieder of Richard Tauber.

Lohmann functions as majordomo and sommelier, Frau Novikov is in the kitchen, and his aunt serves. They have even found a black dress for her, complete with lace-edged white cap and apron, which the former owners, on their flight to God knows where, thoughtfully left behind. They also left Meissen and Rosenthal china, crystal glassware, and English silver. It is all put to good use by this new class of Feinschmeckers, who eat off the Bruges lace tablecloths. It annoys me to think that the family who amassed this finery over the years, was, in all probability, friendly with the Landaus. I might even have met them. It would be wrong of me, however, to extend this criticism to Lohmann. True, he is enjoying the fruits of their deprivation, but he cannot be held responsible. He has merely taken advantage of a situation and has kept me alive in the bargain.

December 4, 1943

AS THE ORIENT EXPRESS SPED through Turkey, Bulgaria, Yugoslavia, and Austria, Dr. Steinbruch and I became inseparable companions. After our toilette, we breakfasted in the dining car. He would not hear of coffee taken in our compartment. "Only for women of easy virtue," he said. We would return to our compartment, now restored to sitting-room status by the attendant. He would drill me in the intricacies of the German verb and help me with conversational German. We would occasionally peer out to view the marvels of Pithion, Dragoman, Dimitrovgrad, Crveni Krst, and Jesenice, which rattled past our window. We were killing time until the gong called us to the premier service in the dining car, where Dr. Steinbruch's appetite was something to behold. It came, he assured me, from an iron constitution, free-flowing gastric juices, and the discipline required to reject the ordinary: to eat only what was first-rate.

"I will only eat marmalade made in Scotland. I will eat French baguettes but no other white bread. I will eat Viennese Tafelspitz but no other boiled beef."

I was deeply impressed by so rigorous a regimen. However, for reasons best known to himself, he never applied it to the meals eaten in the dining car. I watched him ingest:

Hors d'Oeuvres Varies
Consomme Double
Omelette Fines Herbes
Daurade au beurre noir
Rosbif, Yorkshire Pudding
Salade
Fromages, Corbeille de Fruits
Glace Wagons-Lits, Petits Fours

Between meals, he prepared me for my stay in Berlin. He spoke of the energy of the Prussians, who had unified Germany; of the causes and results of the Great War; of the injustices visited on Germany by a vengeful Versailles treaty; and of Germany going through hard, though fascinating, times. He thought it would be difficult for democratic institutions, such as were known in France, Great Britain, and the United States, to take hold in Germany. He feared that the Germans would prefer stronger leadership. He was sure that if I stayed in Germany any length of time I would see history in the making. He gave me advice.

"Read the newspapers, all of them, not just those that make you comfortable. Read the Marxist Left and get it through your head that there are millions of people who want to put an end to your privileged life. Read the papers of the German Right. They see traitors under every bed. They want honor restored to the German soldier. They blame the Versailles treaty, the Jews, and the Communists for every misfortune.

"Daniel"—and that was the first time he addressed me by my first name—"keep your eyes open and your wits about you. Don't let German Gemütlichkeit ensnare you. You are from the East. You have that special Fingerspitzengefühl, that feeling at the tips of your fingers, that keeps you on the alert. It comes from living among all sorts of people, from speaking languages. The world is huge. Our lifetime is short. Try and see it all." He paused, fixing me with a look over his spectacles. "If that makes you a Wandering Jew, make the most of it."

It was a lot for a boy of seventeen to digest. I've certainly thought of his advice, so generously given me, in the years since.

Dr. Steinbruch showed great interest in my family. I spoke of my father and my mother, of our many relatives, and of some of the Moslem notables my father knew.

"So your uncle, who was with the Banque Ottomane, is now with the Japhet Bank in Jaffa? Is that your Uncle Nessim Saporta?"

"No," I replied, "that is Uncle Saadia Nessim, on my mother's side."

"How well does your father know the imam of the Sunni mosque, the one you said is now at Al Azhar University in Cairo?"

"They met in Dr. Azoulay's waiting room. They both had pro-state problems, and their visits fell on the same days. He came to our house once in a while. He said there was nothing like my mother's kasher cooking."

"Try to remember the name of the Kurdi sheikh, your grandfather's friend. You thought he moved his family to Mosul."

When my interest strayed:

"Young man. I am fascinated by your cousin Abou Moussa, telling you of camel caravans that still cross over to Persia. Do you recall the itinerary? The oases?"

What possessed him? I thought. Enough. And so it went until the dinner gong.

The train traversed Carinthia and we passed the legendary resorts, Badgastein and Salzburg. In the early evening, we steamed into the Hauptbahnhof, Munich. Dr. Steinbruch saw to it that our luggage was transferred to the Berlin night express. We had a full hour before the departure of our train. Dr. Steinbruch made the suggestion that I purchase flowers to present to Frau Landau upon our arrival in Berlin. In the station's flower shop, I chose a bouquet of roses. He returned them to the florist's vase, instead picking out a modest three or four flowers, with ferns. He anticipated my objection.

"You cannot give blood-red roses to a married woman. They speak of passion. We have a flower code in Germany. Be sure to learn it."

Before boarding our train, he rushed me over to a refreshment stand.

"You cannot leave Munich without tasting the Weisswurst. They deserve a greater reputation than the local beer."

Two pallid sausages with speckled mustard were placed before me. I cut into them and tasted them without enthusiasm. Dr. Steinbruch intervened.

"No, no. You cannot cut Weisswurst like that. They must be sliced once lengthwise and then once across, without severing the skin. Then you peel back the four equal pieces."

What a country, I thought. First a flower code, now a sausage code?

On the Munich-Berlin sleeper, we finished the arak. Dr. Steinbruch spoke of his museum, the Pergamon. It was Berlin's answer to the Louvre. His department, of which he was curator, specialized in the antiquities of the Near and Middle East. Next to the British

Museum, and perhaps the Louvre, they had the most extensive collection of statues and artifacts in the world. He invited me to visit him and was mildly surprised that, being from that part of the world, I knew so little of its treasures.

He told me of the excavations in which he had participated as a younger man. In 1912, he was at Samarra on the Tigris with Herzfeld and Sarre, lengendary historians and countrymen of his. He had helped sort the shards, the pots and vases, the vials and wall decorations. These came from the early capital of the Abbasid caliphs.

He had been at Cordova with Velásquez Bosco in 1909, when they unearthed the Medina es Zahra, the tenth-century seat of the Omayyad caliphs. He had been to Turkey, to Persia, and had just now come from Palestine. With a glint in his eye, he took a small suitcase out of the overhead rack. Humming to himself, and after much fumbling with a key ring, he opened it. He removed a jumble of balled-up newspapers, socks, and woolen underwear and, from its midst, an object swaddled in cotton wool and strips of cardboard. He placed it on the table between us.

"I bought her in the walled city of Jerusalem, right inside the Damascus Gate. She is authentic, beyond a doubt." He pulled off the protective covering. "Here she is: Astarte, Ashtoreth, Ashtoroth!"

There stood a figure, some fifteen centimeters high, her female attributes clearly outlined, her eyes squinting a sexual challenge.

"A goddess of love, worshiped by your ancestors," Steinbruch whispered hoarsely.

Also by Cousin Eli, I thought.

Steinbruch raised his glass to Astarte and to me.

"L'chayim," he said.

December 5, 1943

LOHMANN CAME LAST NIGHT. *He recounted a little comedy of errors that had taken place in the stairwell. On the second-floor landing he had run into a boy in Hitler Youth uniform. Lohmann was afraid the boy might be a self-appointed block Spitzel, or spy, who reported to his superiors all unusual activity, conversations critical of the war's conduct, and other disloyal behavior, even on the part of his parents.*

The boy had immediately addressed him with a snarling: "What is it you want here?"

Lohmann started to mumble, "I'm looking for..."

When the boy saw his oversize swastika button, identifying him as a veteran Party member, he changed his tune. "Fräulein Inge and Fräulein Jutta are on the fourth floor left, sir." And, as an afterthought: "Heil Hitler."

Lohmann laughed. The presence of two tarts in the building would prove to be a blessing in disguise. To be on the safe side, he had actually visited the girls before coming up into my attic. They were no great credit to their craft, he said. The two were actually salesgirls, who preferred to augment their income in this time-honored way rather than assemble mortar fuses in an armament factory. There had been another client on the premises. He was a portly over-age major in the supply corps. They had run into each other in the living room on their way out. Far from being embarrassed at an encounter in a house of assignation, they had recognized each other for what they were—two men of the world having a bit of sport before returning to home and hearth. The girls had produced a bottle of brandy from the dining room sideboard, and the major had eagerly accepted one of Lohmann's cigars. After introductions, they sipped their brandy and flirted with the girls, and Lohmann had seen to it that an easy friendship was cemented between kindred souls. Before leaving, Lohmann had invited the major to his new dining establishment. He made certain the major understood that his patrons consisted of high-

ranking staff officers, with whom the major probably "had a great deal in common." The major could hardly wait to rub elbows with his betters and promised to bring some army flour and sugar in the bargain. It was a successful evening. Not only would the major's connections with the supply corps prove to be most helpful to Lohmann's new establishment but the two whores were to serve us well, legitimizing, as they did, Lohmann's frequent visits to the building.

Lohmann gave me three bars of Sarotti chocolate and a box of the little brandy-filled chocolate bottles so dear to the Germans. He apologized, saying he would bring more substantial fare soon. I did not have the heart to tell him that chocolate gives me excruciating toothaches.

I am sipping the brandy out of the chocolate bottles first, deluding myself into believing that in this way my teeth will be less sensitive to the chocolate. I try eating the bottles on the left side of my jaw, but as soon as my saliva liquefies the chocolate, an insidious stream seeps around the afflicted molar on the right, making the pain unbearable. But I have the solution: I will swallow the bottles whole. They will dissolve in my stomach, to give me the nourishment I need and at the same time avoid contact with my teeth. At last I am putting to use the finely honed logic so studiously acquired at the Alliance Israélite.

I hear the whistle of a departing train at the Anhalter Bahnhof, a short walk from here under normal circumstances. Dr. Steinbruch and I disembarked there fifteen years ago.

The Landaus had been waiting on the platform. I pointed them out to my new friend. Herr Landau wore a light gray homburg with a malacca cane hooked across his arm. Frau Landau was in gray again: a Persian lamb coat draped over her shoulders and a cloche hat, which pushed her fair hair forward. Steinbruch turned to me.

"My God, you were right. You should have bought red roses after all!"

I practiced my German as I introduced them. "Herr Landau, Frau Landau, darf ich Doktor Steinbruch vorstellen."

The men now executed a little dance, which I found remarkable. They faced each other, lifted their hats in unison, replaced them, shook hands, bent stiffly at the waist, and brought their heels together with an audible little click. Dr. Steinbruch then bent over, as if to kiss Frau Landau's extended hand, but his lips stopped in midair just above it. Another code to add to that of flowers and sausages. My turn to give Herr Landau a manly handshake, to present the flowers to Frau Landau. She smiled and I became aware of a silvery thread of saliva in the corner of her mouth. I took command of myself. Cousin Eli, I said silently, unhand me. Do not stoke the fires of my lust. Let me enter the house of my father's friend in honor and gratitude.

We took our leave of Dr. Steinbruch, and from our taxi I caught my first glimpse of this metropolis of three million souls: so large its boulevards, so massive its buildings, that it took my breath away.

December 7, 1943

*COULD NOT WRITE YESTERDAY. A powerful air raid during the night
kept me fearful and trembling. During the day I was beset by toothache
and stomach cramps, punished for having attempted to thwart the
natural order of the body by swallowing twelve miniature chocolate bottles.*

The Landaus' apartment in the Kellerstrasse was in one of the
massive blocks built for the middle class in the eighteen sixties. Large
chestnut trees fronted the enormous wooden doors. These led into
a courtyard, which in early days housed horses and carriages in their
stalls. Now, dustbins and bicycles were stored there. The high vaulted
entryway, which connected the street with the courtyard, had two
smaller doorways as well, each leading to two identical wings of the
building. Each wing contained a lift within its stairwell. Its iron cage
traveled up and down on a hydraulic stem. The staircase, which encir-
cled the lift, was fashioned of polished dark wood. It smelled heavily
of wax. No wonder every apartment house in Berlin had a warning
sign on the ground floor: VORSICHT! FRISCH GEBOHNERT—ATTENTION!
FRESHLY POLISHED.

These signs, in ominous Gothic letters, were only one example
of the multitude of prohibitions the Prussians of Berlin posted in every
public place. In the parks: THE STEPPING ON THE GRASS IS RIGOROUSLY
PROHIBITED BY THE POLICE. In hallways: BEGGING AND PANHANDLING IS
FORBIDDEN. In the railroad stations: ACCESS TO THE PLATFORMS IS STRICTLY
LIMITED TO THOSE WITH VALID TICKETS. DOGS: NO ENTRY! Many years later,
park benches would say, NO JEWS! ARYANS ONLY! These signs were
meant to impress on a citizenry imbued with great energy and a rich
and cynical sense of humor that there were limits to their freedoms.

The Landaus lived on the second floor, in a large apartment
crammed with heavy oak and mahogany furniture, of a type I can
only describe as oppressive. Highly ornamented decor, mirrored,
columned, and fluted, with dark oil paintings, heavy damask drapes

over lace curtains: all this added to the darkness of the antechamber, the salon, and the dining room. There was even a small library with leaded windows, depicting Nordic knights in armor and maidens with flaxen hair. The family bedrooms, the nursemaid's room, and finally my own all led off a long corridor culminating in the pantries and kitchen.

I was introduced to the staff who served the Landau household: Frieda, the maid; Frau Polnow, the cook; and Hilde, the nursemaid. I gave my full attention to Hilde. She was a striking young woman in her twenties, with apple cheeks and a firm handshake. She was dressed in slate blue, with heavily starched collar and cuffs and a starched cap, with a slate-blue train down her back, covering her hair. A small enameled pin, identifying a nurses' order, and a little watch pinned to her breast like a medal completed the costume. I learned there was a certain snob appeal to having your children prammed through the Tiergarten by one of these young women. Only English nannies were considered more chic, a word much used locally and pronounced "schick." The Landau children, Ernst, age three, and Trude, a more recent addition, both adored Hilde.

My room was the guest room, to which the Landaus had thoughtfully added a small bookshelf stocked with German, French, and English dictionaries. A small writing table held a full inkwell, a penholder, and a little box of new pen nibs. There were flowers in the room, chocolates on my nightstand, and a flat box from Tietz, one of the better department stores, with six white linen handkerchiefs initialed "S". A card was enclosed.

> Dear Daniel. We welcome you, the son of our dear friend Ezra Saporta, into our house. If you will let us, we want to think of you as our own. In the same spirit, we welcome you into the firm of Landau & Cie., where you will start tomorrow. With heartfelt wishes, Jakob and Elizabeth Landau.

How fortunate I was. Seventeen years old, halfway around the world from my beloved family, to be welcomed by people to whom, but for my father, I was a relative stranger. I resolved to repay their faith in me by exemplary behavior and by hard work in the office. I would make the Landaus and my parents proud of me. Imbued with this admirable resolve, I sat down and wrote my parents a long letter. I spoke of my trip, describing my traveling companion, Dr. Steinbruch, and of my warmhearted reception here.

In the morning I accompanied Herr Landau to his office. It was on Unter den Linden, one of Berlin's most elegant thoroughfares, named after its many lime trees. Its splendid buildings contained famous shops, restaurants, hotels, commercial enterprises, and offices. As we walked up the broad marble staircase, passing varnished doors with polished brass signs, I wondered how a spice merchant could stock his aromatic inventory in what appeared to me palatial surroundings. Of course, this was not a warehouse such as ours in Damascus. Herr Landau's office was strictly commercial in nature. With the exception of the salesmen, no one could tell turmeric from saffron. Most transactions were conducted via correspondence and telephone. Herr Landau ran this very efficient and highly successful business with an iron hand from the confines of his elegant office. I discovered that he had created a near monopoly of the spice trade. His firm dealt with the major German bakeries, with hotels, with chains of restaurants, with the railroad administration, with coffeehouses, and with manufacturers of lemonade and orangeade. I had no idea that people in the West, whose diet was so different from ours and whose food tasted so bland to us, used such a variety of spices.

Yet Herr Landau sold tons of poppy and sesame seed to bakers and confectioners all over Germany. He sold them vanilla, in bean and extract form. He sold them cinnamon bark and powder, ginger and food dyes and coffee and tea; paprika and saffron and rosemary and cloves, thyme and nutmeg. He sold everything. So much for my quaint notion that most Europeans used nothing but salt and pepper, and precious little of that.

To my surprise, most of the employees I was to meet were not Jews. At home, the only Arabs in my father's business and others like it were the workers in the warehouse, or in the knitting mills, or loading docks. The people who ran the business, even on the second or third level, were our own people. Conversely, in Moslem enterprises they also employed their own. But here it was different. The chief accountant, Herr Klein, was Jewish and turned out to be Frau Landau's brother. He had only recently arrived from Györ, in Hungary, and spoke with an accent that endeared him to the other office workers. Dr. Grunauer (Doctor of Economics) was head of the Commercial Section. Herr Schapiro handled Advertising and Customer Relations. This comprised the entire House of Israel in our establishment. There was one more: Warschauer; he was not afforded the dignity of a "Herr" to precede his name. Warschauer was old, shabby, spoke German with a Yiddish lilt, and had that unfortunate appearance resulting from generations of Ghetto in-breeding. He was sent off to stand in line for theater tickets, to go to the bookmaker's, to the apothecary's for aspirin or belladonna; he chased across town to buy something at wholesale; he took Frau Landau's shoes to be heeled; his was every mean or petty task. In rain or snow he hopped the tramway, the buses, or the underground.

I am sure he received only a pittance in return for his services, but he had his own chair in the reception area, where he read the scandal sheets. Herr Landau had asked him not to bring his Yiddish newspaper to the office. In spite of his demeaning existence and the charitable nature of his employment, I never saw him despairing or ill-natured. Far from it; he was always in good spirits, ever helpful, fetching coffee or running little errands even for the secretaries, who were not really entitled to his services.

In spite of his lowly status, Warschauer was a regular at the Landau table each Sabbath and on Jewish holidays. This was not an act of charity on the part of the Landaus. It was their observance of an ancient custom—the opening of one's home to the less fortunate on days of merit—which transcended their assimilated German ways. Even when important people, bankers or journalists, were invited, Warschauer would be there, slurping his soup, dipping his challah into the gefüllte fish. He was spiritually related to my mother's cousin, Abou Moussa, and I liked him at once.

To my distress, I learned that the Landaus did not keep a kasher house. They ate pork with impunity, as if there were no injunctions against it. I decided to refuse that which offended me without making an issue of it. At least they observed the Sabbath. I gave thanks for small favors.

December 8, 1943

HERR LANDAU SUGGESTED that I acquaint myself with the operation of Jakob Landau & Cie. by observing the various departments at work and by getting to know the personnel. He ran his extremely efficient business in the German manner. He was the Chief. Instructions were autocratically issued by him, or possibly by the department heads; these, in turn, were punctiliously executed by the lower echelon without comment or grousing. I had become a witness to that much-vaunted German efficiency carried out with almost military precision. It was a far cry from the Levantine ways of my father's warehouse. Here, there were no leisurely cups of tea and coffee consumed with clients or with friends coming by to pass the time of day. Here, there were no friendly games of shesh-besh after lunch, no lengthy siestas on the couch my father had covered with carpets from Bokhara. Here, people came with files under their arms, not with amber worry beads with which to click the time away in gossip or politics. Here, accounts were settled on time or credit was suspended; no one could say as they did to my father, "Yah, abou Daniel"—Oh, father of Daniel,— "things are slow this month; I need time until Kippur, until Ramadan."

Although barely eighteen I understood that one system was not superior to the other, but that each functioned in its own sphere. In these first few weeks everyone was extremely helpful to the exotic stranger. Imagine, the young man, all the way from Damascus! I also understood that with the exception of Dr. Grunauer, Herr Schapiro, Herr Klein, and Warschauer no one really understood me to be Jewish. With my Spanish family name and my exotic provenance, it was a cultural somersault the average German could not make.

I spent my lunch hours with Herr Klein, Frau Landau's brother from Hungary. He had insisted that I address him as "Lotsi," the diminutive of his first name, Lazslo. Although he too was a recent arrival to Berlin, he already knew all the little restaurants, cafés, and bars in the neighborhood of our office. He also knew the waitresses by their first names, and I judged by the looks that passed between them that their acquaintance transcended the Wiener schnitzels we were having for lunch. When he offered to fix me up with one of the girls, I declined. Not that I was disinterested, far from it, but I wanted to learn German properly; I wanted to immerse myself into the spice business. The last thing I wanted was another Cousin Eli in my life, another resident voluptuary urging me to share his carnal pleasures.

One evening Lotsi and I walked from our office to the Adlon Hotel, which gave on the Brandenburg Gate and the French Embassy. It was heady stuff for two young men to sit in the bar, order drinks, and discuss world affairs. My German was still rough at the time, and we conversed in French, which Lotsi handled masterfully. His German was excellent too, but, as I was to learn, that was part of his cultural baggage. In the days of the monarchy, the Jews of Hungary had made it their business to speak the language of the Austrian crown, the dominant power in the Austro-Hungarian Empire. In the same manner the Jews of Syria and Lebanon spoke French in order to converse in the language of their rulers.

Lotsi turned to me. "Daniel, I'm not much older than you are, but I want to give you some eitzes."

"Eitzes?" I played with the word for a moment. Then the penny dropped. The Ashkenazi Jews, in their atrocious pronunciation of Hebrew, had created a jargon of words that I was learning to interpret. "You mean 'etzah—advice—don't you?"

"Eitzes, 'etzah: Daniel, you need a lot of it. I heard that Landau wants you to register with the Einwohnermeldeamt. Don't do it."

"What is it, and why not?" I replied.

"It's a government office where everyone, citizen or foreigner, must register. Every time you leave town or move, you have to deregister and then reregister in the next place of residence. It's their way of keeping permanent track of you."

"What do I care? It's the law, isn't it?"

"Daniel, you've only been here two weeks, and you're already thinking like a Yecke."

There was no end to my ignorance. "What is a Yecke?"

"A Yecke is a German Jew, like my brother-in-law. Just because the Germans condescended to let them join the army and gave them a few medals, they've become more German than the Germans. They are most happy when they are decorating their Christmas trees and singing *Deutschland über Alles*. Millions of Germans hate them, but the Yeckes pretend not to notice."

Much of this was new to me, and I let him continue.

"Why do you think I work as a bookkeeper? Don't you think I had the brains to attend university? In Hungary you have to be baptized to study medicine or law. That's why I'm sensitive to all this registration, to all these police procedures. If something goes wrong, I want to grab my toothbrush and run. Why am I telling you all this? It's because this part of the world is not as the Yeckes imagine it to be. When they start cracking skulls here, I don't want some policeman to come looking for you with a copy of your residence card in his hand. Verstehst? You could be my little brother. Do as I tell you."

I did, and I had ample opportunity to be grateful for Lotsi's "eitzes."

December 9, 1943

I WAS GIVEN A DESK, with telephone, in the shipping department. The other desk was occupied by Herr Stemmler, who was in charge of shipping, transport, and the interminable paper war with the customs office. He had been picked for the job, so Frau Becker, Herr Landau's secretary told me, because he had been an officer in the war and knew how to deal with bureaucrats of every stripe. He was the first German I met who had dueling scars. It was a way of advertising that one had attended university and had the honor of having been admitted into a fraternity, which encouraged having one's face slashed with a saber. The resulting scars—engorged by heavy intake of alcohol—would, in the course of one's lifetime, serve notice on ordinary mortals as to whom they were dealing with.

In a way, the dueling scars I was to encounter in Germany, the proud flesh that proclaimed "Heidelberg" or "Göttingen," reminded me of something similar in the Middle East.

Similar, but different. Frequently, we would encounter someone with a shiny scar the size of a coin on his cheek. We called it "the rose of Baghdad." It was seen mostly on people from Iraq who had been bitten by a certain fly, whose bite and the subsequent infection scarred its victim for life. But the rose was an act of nature; the Schmiss, like a tattoo, was self-induced mutilation and according to our laws an offense in the eyes of God.

Perhaps Herr Landau had intended that Herr Stemmler take me under his wing. He corrected my German from the first day on, he made me read the newspapers in their Gothic alphabet, and he insisted that I learn to write in Germanic rather than Latin script. He was a hard taskmaster, probably a carryover from his years in the army. He wore his dark gray suit like a uniform. He changed his shirt twice a week, and his collar and cuffs three times. He wore his hair short on top, the sides and the back clipped to the scalp. That look signaled a conservative point of view and was cultivated by a large number of Germans.

One day Herr Stemmler braced me. "Permit me to speak openly with you, Herr Saporta. You are spending your lunch hours with Herr Klein."

Sensing the criticism implied, I started to reply, but Herr Stemmler cut me off.

"He may be the Chief's brother-in-law, but he is a notorious skirt chaser and not the best of company for you. He has brought his Hungarian ways with him, and I would not want you to make them your own."

He anticipated my protests.

"I have nothing against Hungarians. I am speaking of an attitude you will find also among the Viennese. They see work as something that interferes with idle hours in the coffeehouse, with chasing secretaries, with gossip, with horse races and long lunches, preferably with another man's wife. Look, young man, I am not a prude. When I was in the army, stationed in France, I too enjoyed long lunches and my liter of wine, but in Berlin I bring my sandwich to the office. It's economical, and I give Herr Landau a full day's work. I am inviting you to spend your lunch hour with me. I'll drill you in German, and above all we'll push the work along."

From that day on, Frau Polnow, the cook, prepared two sandwiches for me, which, wrapped in waxed and brown paper, I took to the office. Herr Stemmler and I would sit at the worktable across from each other, open a bottle of mineral water, and ritualistically unwrap our sandwiches. He unfolded his packages as painstakingly as Lohmann would, fifteen years later. The sandwiches, or Stullen, were always cut in two. Herr Stemmler told me that, as a schoolboy, he and his mates had exchanged the second halves with one another. It was fun to eat what the other boys' mothers had provided. I offered to share that simple pleasure with him. Thus I ate half the sandwiches Frau Stemmler prepared, and he got to eat Frau Polnow's rather richer fare.

I learned a lot about German sandwiches. They were made of rye bread, of pumpernickel, at times of hard rolls. Often, they combined two sorts of bread in one sandwich. A Swiss cheese Stulle, hard roll on the bottom, black bread on top, was a gourmet's treat.

Frau Stemmler made sandwiches with a spread of white cheese, sliced radishes, and chives. Wonderful. At first, I politely refused the roast pork, with its spread of white pork schmalz. But after two to three months, I realized that everything I touched was terefah—unclean—anyway, and I made peace with local custom.

December 10, 1943

Sometime later, Lotsi took me aside at one of the Landaus' Sabbath dinners. He asked me into the library and closed the door.

"Daniel, you live your life and I live mine. I have no wish to intrude on you. But must you spend every moment with Stemmler? He's a Nazi. The whole office knows it."

I objected. "I cannot believe this. Herr Stemmler has befriended me. My German is improving because of him. Why would Herr Landau tolerate him, if this were true?"

"In the first place, it's true. Frau Becker saw him in a café on a Sunday afternoon reading the *Völkischer Beobachter*. He was so absorbed in it he failed to see her. In the second place, I am sure the Chief knows he's a Nazi but Stemmler is needed in that job. He's our front-office goy.

To me "goy" was a word from the Bible. Goyim meant the other nations, as opposed to the Hebrews. "What is a front-office goy?" I asked.

"Daniel, you really are a schmuck. You may be a Jew from Damascus but you don't have a yiddishe Kopf. Can't you smell the atmosphere here? There's not a Jewish-owned company in Berlin that doesn't have a front-office goy: a good-looking gentile, preferably a former army officer or someone with an aristocratic title, who goes out and deals with the authorities or the public."

I must have looked at him uncomprehendingly, like the boy I was.

"Daniel, when Stemmler deals with the Chief of Customs, he's probably talking to a fellow officer. They see each other as equals and settle matters between them in a correct manner. But if you went, there would be a subtle change: the customs official would know you're a Jew, and you'd know that he knows you're a Jew. Now the man may not be an anti-Semite, but you would be handicapped in representing the company as forcefully as you should, because you'd be afraid he'd think you a cheeky Jew. So we're better off sending Stemmler." ·

"How do you expect me to handle this? We share the office, we even share our lunches. I cannot cut Stemmler out of my life."

"Daniel, I don't suggest that you give up your lunch hours with Stemmler. He knows his business; learn from him. But I had to tell you the facts."

I nodded and rose to join the others in the living room. Lotsi motioned for patience.

"To confuse you a bit further, you should also know that there are a lot of right-wing people in Germany who consider themselves "national": true to German culture, traditions. They are mostly jingoists. But that doesn't necessarily make then anti-Semites. So, Daniel, you've got to learn to pick and choose. Verstehst?" He opened the door for me and we joined the others.

Lotsi had poisoned my hours with Stemmler. I was hoping to prove him wrong but I did not know how, or perhaps did not dare, to involve Herr Stemmler in a discussion of the Nazis or anti-Semitism. But day by day as we sat across the table, munching our sandwiches, I wondered if Herr Stemmler really hated the Jews, and, if he did, why he had chosen to work for Herr Landau. Actually, I was able to answer that question myself. Jobs were scarce; at Landau's he enjoyed a position of some importance, which earned him the respect of his fellow workers and of those he met outside the firm. Also, the work was nonpolitical in nature, quite different from publishing, theater, films, fashions, or art, and his employer, Herr Landau, was German born and German educated. I don't know how Stemmler perceived me in those early days. I believe he saw me as some sort of Levantine, hailing from an ill-defined area settled by a mixture of lesser people—Greeks, Arabs, Spaniards—anyway, people who ate garlic and idled their time away in sun-baked marketplaces. That I could be Jewish, that there were a million and a half Sephardim in the Orient, was surely outside his sphere of knowledge. That he was to know better at a later date hinged on political developments yet to come.

It was Herr Stemmler's own fault that I was able to confirm the Nazi sentiments alluded to by Lotsi. Stemmler had gone to the customs authorities and had carelessly left his briefcase beneath his desk. By this time I had become aware that most Germans carried briefcases. It was a way of stating subtly that one was an educated person: an academic, a student, a businessman, a bookkeeper, a lawyer. It separated the briefcase carriers from those who did manual labor. In fact those briefcases usually contained nothing more important than a liverwurst sandwich and a newspaper. I had noticed that businessmen of note, real entrepreneurs such as Herr Landau, never carried them. If there were papers or documents to be carried, it was done by chauffeurs or secretaries.

The battle with my conscience over the propriety of looking through someone else's briefcase was quickly won. I unfastened the two neatly buckled straps and snapped open the nickel-plated lock. The odor released by the ghosts of thousands of cheese and sausage sandwiches rose from the case as I pulled out the neatly folded wrappers of brown and wax paper. They were followed by the pièce de résistance, a copy of Julius Streicher's *Der Stürmer*. Unhappily, the mere presence of the hate sheet in Herr Stemmler's case was enough to confirm Lotsi's worst suspicions.

The front page of *Der Stürmer* carried a large cartoon depicting two evil-looking caricature Jews, bloodstained knives in their hands, gathering in a bowl the life blood which poured from the severed throats of angelic-looking blond children. The accompanying article, which covered the entire page, was headed JEWISH MURDER PLANS AGAINST NON-JEWISH HUMANITY REVEALED. It informed the reader that since time immemorial, the Jews had sacrificed Christian children after subjecting them to unspeakable torture. They needed their blood for the baking of matzah, an unleavened bread required for the sinister and secret ritual of Passover. Unhappily, this satanic story was not new to me. The same infamous charge had been leveled against the Jews of Damascus by the Capuchin monks in my grandfather's day.

I had read enough. I slipped newspaper and sandwich wrappers back into the briefcase.

From that day, I saw Stemmler in a different light. But I was learning to play the game, and until my apprenticeship ended abruptly and unexpectedly, Stemmler and I exchanged salami and mortadella, Land and Jägerwurst, Harzer cheese and Tilsit, while we polished my German and pushed Herr Landau's enterprise.

December 11, 1943

In yesterday's entry I spoke of Stemmler, my immediate superior in the Landau office, and of my discovery of the *Stürmer* in his briefcase. That was not the end of my involvement with him. More was to come.

Sometime late in 1934, the year after the Nazis had come to power, I sat in my office at the Kaukasus and reminisced over my early days in Berlin. Driven by concern, curiosity, or perhaps perversity, I dialed Flora 2119, the telephone number of the Landau office. Instead of replying with the customary "Landau and Company," an unfamiliar voice said, "Deutsche Gewürz Gesellschaft." German Spice Corporation? "May I speak with Herr Landau, please." There was a short pause at the other end. "Herr Landau is not with this company any longer." In the anonymity of my office I decided to carry the game further. "Would you connect me with the office of the managing director, please." There was a pause as the call was being transferred. A secretary came on the line. "Herr Stemmler's office. May I help you?" She repeated herself and, in response to my silence, disconnected.

Although the information came as a shock to me, I was not really surprised. Shortly after the Nazis came to power, a "legal" process of Aryanizing businesses perceived to be in Jewish ownership had been instituted. The process was simple. The governmental Chamber of Commerce appointed new managing directors, usually from among the Party faithful. If possible they were appointed from within the business itself, thus assuring a commercial continuum. In this manner countless employees whose Jewish employers had put bread on their tables for years moved out of their Spartan offices and established themselves behind the polished mahogany desks of their former bosses. Stemmler was one of them. I could see him sitting behind Herr Landau's desk, strangely out of place in the elegant office. But his patience and envy had been rewarded. The prosperous business so carefully nurtured by Jakob Landau for so many years was now his to run.

Lohmann has just left. He also has his share of problems: the Anhalter Bahnhof took direct hits during the last week of November. The bombs demolished much of the area behind the imposing station entrance, and trains were being rerouted while the clean-up operation was in progress. He had just come from the station and said with some pride that the tracks had already been relaid. Most of the rubble had been carted away, and the Reichs Railroad Administration had posted signs saying that the station would be in service shortly. Lohmann had gone to the Görlitzer Bahnhof and the Schlesischer Bahnhof, both major stations, in search of provisions, but according to him the poor devils returning from the Russian front were lucky to bring back their limbs, let alone food. Even the usually resourceful sailors arriving at the Lehrter Bahnhof from Hamburg and Wilhelmshaven came empty-handed.

His new friend, the supply corps major, was worth his weight in gold. He was diverting respectable amounts of staples to Lohmann's dining club from his stores. This was not a difficult task because, when it came to food, everyone was corruptible, clerks and lorry drivers above all. The major had become a regular at the nightly dinners, basking in the company of staff officers and luminaries of the demimonde, blissfully unaware that they held him in contempt for what he represented. Doubly so, because they surmised him to be the source of the food on which they were gorging.

Lohmann also recounted two events of personal interest to me. Frau Novikov had been arrested, interrogated by the Gestapo, and subsequently released. During a recent air raid, she had sought the safety of a neighborhood air raid shelter. The ensuing raid had been particularly intense, sending a torrent of plaster and dirt on the huddled pack of misery congregated in the shelter. A woman, near hysteria and clutching a small child, had overheard Frau Novikov speaking to a neighbor. Upon hearing her heavy Russian accent, the woman had sent up a hue and cry that a Russian spy was in their midst. After the all clear, some zealous citizens turned Frau Novikov over to the police. Those stalwarts had more immediate problems and sent her over to the Gestapo. Her papers were in order, of course; she had been in Germany legitimately since the October Revolution of 1917. Even so, she was asked to give a quick rundown of her employment during those years. When she mentioned the Kaukasus Klub, they gave her a cup of ersatz coffee and were soon joined by a more senior official with a file folder in hand. He asked her repeatedly if she had any news or information about the "Spaniard" Salazar or, rather, Saporta. Frau Novikov, who in her lifetime had already dealt with Czarist and Bolshevik authorities, was not greatly intimidated by the Gestapo. Her Spaniard was called Salazar, and she had seen him for the last time in November or December of 1941, in any event shortly before the authorities padlocked the Kaukasus. Her present occupation was that of caretaker of her church; no word of Lohmann's dining club. She added her fervent hope that the victorious German army would soon free her beloved Russia from the godless Bolsheviks.

Looking at her simple peasant features, the Gestapo could not tell if she was jesting, since everyone knew that the German armies were in full retreat from her Motherland. They decided she wasn't. They apologized for detaining her and had her driven home.

Lohmann also told me he had been to a neighborhood cinema last night. He had missed "Der Grosse König"—The Great King—starring Otto Gebühr, Kristina Söderbaum and Gustav Fröhlich. Like most Germans, Lohmann had a passionate interest in Frederick the Great and never missed the films about him, which the Germans, regardless of regime, turned out with regularity. This time, the Nazis were using his memory for propaganda purposes, to further the war effort. Perhaps, subconsciously, the people were yearning for this ruler, who was not only powerful but wise and cultured, who counted Voltaire among his most intimate friends, who spoke French at his court, and who had built the magnificent palaces at Potsdam, which the Prussians considered their spiritual home. In short, a far cry from the house painter who was now leading them to certain defeat.

Be that as it may, Lohmann and his friend from the goulash cannons had run into Hilde, the Landaus' former nursemaid, in the lobby of the cinema. Hilde was with a friend, also a nursemaid, and the four of them had gone to a beer parlor nearby. According to Lohmann, Hilde, now perhaps thirty-five, had filled out a bit. She was still, he thought, Herr Saporta's cup of tea.

Lohmann, of course, knew Hilde from the Kaukasus days when she and I had had a torrid love affair of several months' duration. I had last seen her in the summer of 1930, at which time she was still looking after the Landau children. Hilde told Lohmann she had stayed with the Landaus until Christmas of 1935, when she had returned to her family in Silesia. In September of that year, several laws pertaining to racial purity had been issued. One of these was entitled "Law for the Protection of German Blood and Honor." Under Paragraph Three thereof, Jews were not permitted to employ German females under forty-five years of age. The law became effective January 1, 1936. The separation from the Landau children had been traumatic for Hilde as well as for them.

Late in 1936 she returned to Berlin and went into service with a number of well-to-do families, but she never wore her blue uniforms again. She told Lohmann that sometime in December of 1938, shortly after the infamous Reichskristallnacht, the Crystal Night in which synagogues and Jewish shops were put to the torch, she happened to find herself in the Kellerstrasse. She went up to the second floor. The brass plate LANDAU was no longer there; another was in its place. In the stairwell, she ran into the janitor. He told Hilde that the Landaus had emigrated in 1937. They had gone to Johannesburg, in South Africa, where Herr Landau had relatives in the candy business.

I ran into Hilde one late-summer afternoon, in the Tauentzienstrasse, in front of the KaDeWe, the big department store. It was several months after my departure from the Landaus, and the Kaukasus was already in full swing. I had just returned from Constantinople with my initial shipment of belly dancers. Hilde, in a trim two-piece suit, looked the picture of good health and propriety. Her little nurse's pin held the collar of her white blouse together.

"Herr Saporta!" she said. "I am so truly glad to see you! Without your mustache I almost did not recognize you. You look even younger than before!"

We went to a café and ordered glasses of Mampe's rich orange-flavored cordial. Hilde wanted to thank me again for having come into her room that fateful morning when she had been so ill. She wanted to tell me how sorry she was that her condition had led to my expulsion, when I, the young Herr Saporta, was innocent of any involvement. But Herr Landau would not listen, would not believe, and the Landaus never spoke my name again. As far as Hilde was concerned, the earth had opened and swallowed me. Yes, she had been pregnant, and Frau Landau had taken her to a reputable doctor who had terminated the pregnancy. It was either that or go home in disgrace—or, worse, submit to the ministrations of a midwife in a filthy tenement.

I had to know if it was Herr Landau who had gotten her into that predicament. Hilde looked me in the eye and said no, it was a man from her hometown whose business frequently brought him to Berlin.

So the mystery was finally solved. Herr Landau had found out I was his wife's lover, and he had used the opportunity, presented by Hilde's morning sickness, to put an end to our affair.

I walked Hilde over to the Kaukasus. Frau Novikov served one of her better dinners: ikra, the eggplant appetizer, which reminded me of my mother's baba ghanoush; pelmeny, the miniature Siberian dumplings in broth; a pink lamb shashlik; and, for dessert, kisel, the opaque fruit jell, which was my favorite. We drank champagne, Hilde for the first time. We went to my office and I locked the door. We kissed. She bit my lip. She unfastened her nurse's pin and saw the time on the watch pinned to her bosom. "I've got to get back. I promised to be in by eight. Next week, I promise."

Before she left, I explained to her that to avoid the disgrace that had befallen me I now called myself Salazar, and if she valued my friendship she would tell no one she had seen me.

"I will do anything you tell me, Herr Saporta." She smiled. "Herr Salazar." And she was gone.

December 12, 1943

I REMEMBER the first Friday night in the Landau household. Herr Landau had invited his parents. Landau's father still dressed in the old fashion, wing collar and frock coat, much like Dr. Azoulay in Damascus. He and his wife, who was stone deaf, nodded constant approval of everything around them. No wonder. Their son had done more than well: a prospering business, a wonderful wife, beautiful children. Their old eyes lit up when Hilde brought Ernst and Trude to be kissed and taken off to bed.

Lotsi was there, in his capacity of brother-in-law, and of course Warschauer, who sat quietly shaking his head from side to side, as if listening to some inner melody. There were two other couples: the Friedländers and the Breslauers. Friedländer was an attorney, Breslauer in ready-to-wear. They resembled the Landaus: the men well turned out, their wives in silk, lace, and pearls. Herr Landau made a little speech, again bidding me welcome to my new surroundings. He asked me to preside over the table and offer the traditional Sabbath blessing in the beautiful Hebrew they had been privileged to hear in Damascus.

I excused myself, went to my room, and returned with the colorful embroidered kipah, or scull cap, my father had bought for me in the Bokharan quarter of Jerusalem. I went to the head of the table and, in the Sephardic fashion, poured the wine into the silver kiddush cup, so that instead of stopping at the lip it overflowed copiously into a saucer I had placed beneath the cup. I raised the cup and chanted that portion which told of God having completed his work of creation, the heavens and the earth and all the hosts thereof.

"Blessed art thou, O Eternal, our God, King of the Universe, who created the fruit of the vine."

I drank from the silver cup and offered Herr Landau the next sip. Then, observing the Sephardic tradition, I offered the cup to Frau Landau, all the men present, and finally the women. I then chanted our thanks for the gift of the Sabbath, the day that ranks first among the holy convocations, in remembrance of our departure from Egypt. I removed the starched white napkin, that covered the loaf of braided white bread in front of me.

"Blessed art thou, O Eternal, our God, King of the Universe, who bringest forth bread from the earth."

Ignoring the large silver knife next to the loaf, I tore the bread with my hands, dipped bite-size pieces into salt, and, to the astonishment of hosts and guests, tossed the pieces to each one at the table.

They wanted to know why I had not cut the bread and passed it from hand to hand, as was their wont. "It is God's bread. How can *I* give it?" So much wisdom in such a young man! The women beamed at me and the men smiled at one another. But I realized that I was the only man whose head was covered. Only Warschauer made common cause with me: he had knotted the four corners of his not overly clean handkerchief and put it on his head.

The dinner started. First, the gefüllte fish: cutlets of poached carp, their centers filled with a forcemeat of carp, pike, onions, almonds, and meal of matzah. It was served cold in its own jelly with fiery horseradish. It is a dish beloved of all Ashkenazim, whether from Russia, Hungary, Romania, Poland, or Germany; rich or poor, Orthodox or assimilated, Communist or freethinker, they all love gefüllte fish. In my ten years among the Ashkenazim, I never learned to like it. From this first night onward, I disliked the peculiar flavor: at once bland, sweet, and salty. I have given this much thought. It is gefüllte fish that separates the Ashkenazim from the Sephardim. It is not the arrangement of benches in the synagogue, not the manner in which they mispronounce Hebrew, not the ritual melodies, not the minute diversions in tradition: it is the gefüllte fish. I have never met a Sephardi who could countenance it. Give it up, and the house of Israel will cohabit forevermore!

The rest of the dinner was always wonderful: the chicken soup, rich and deep golden with its ravioli-like dumplings, sometimes served with flat, yellow, homemade noodles; the main course, usually chicken or incredibly tender boiled beef with its side dishes of cucumbers and sweet-and-sour wax beans, cooked with pears; cakes fragrant with vanilla, almonds, and raisins, accompanied by mixed fruit compotes.

On this first Sabbath at the Landaus, the dinner was more

elaborate. After the sacramental wine had been removed, French red wine was uncorked to accompany the crisp duck, served with kasha, a grain from eastern Europe similar to the burghul we use in the Levant. It was a cheerful evening. Much wine was consumed and my presence was toasted. Everyone made little clumsy speeches. Dr. Friedländer stood and declaimed couplets, which, I was told, were Heinrich Heine's. Herr Landau explained that he was a great German-Jewish poet, but I had never heard of him, and I doubted that he measured up to the splendors of Ibn Ezra or Judah ha-Levi, the great poets of our golden age in Spain.

There was more wine. I had difficulty following the rapid patter of the conversation. The men were now addressing one another. The ladies, in turn, were speaking of fashions or servants or children or whatever it is that women discuss together. Only Warschauer and I were still enjoying the poppyseed strudel. It was then that I felt a hand slip beneath the napkin in my lap. Warm, nimble fingers sought me out, under the layer of navy-blue serge. The fingers found what they were seeking, and my zoub leaped into the hand as a trout heading upstream.

The hand, I discovered, belonged to Frau Landau, who, leaning forward, was speaking intently to Frau Breslauer. It was as if her hand were no part of her but, rather, a disembodied limb acting out of its own volition. It lingered, withdrew, and the dinner came to an end. Everyone got up. I sat for a moment, my heart pounding, waiting for the excitement to subside. Then I joined the gentlemen in the salon.

I lay in bed later, but sleep would not come. I recalled Cousin Eli's prophecy: "You'll get to see more than her tits, I wager." But I did not want to live out Eli's prophecy. I wanted to be decent, honorable; I wanted to preserve our ways. I became indignant. I recited a charge sheet of their transgressions: they did not keep the dietary laws, the men sat uncovered at the table, they even smoked on the Sabbath, and Frau Landau, that sharmuta, had given me an erection at the Sabbath table. Oh, shame, shame! I resolved to stay out of her way, to prove my loyalty, my devotion to Herr Landau.

My resolve was of short duration, as I heard her high, clear laugh in the corridor. It was followed by Herr Landau's deep rumble as he closed the bedroom door on them. How I hated Landau for possessing

December 13, 1943

LOHMANN HAS LEFT ME *a package that includes two pairs of army issue stockings and some perfumed soap. I can put both to good use. The package was wrapped in yesterday's issue of the* Völkischer Beobachter *and, as I glanced at the second page, with its clumsily concealed reports of more military disasters suffered by the German forces, I was brought up short by a boxed article, with heading in heavy print. I translate it here with deep pain and sorrow.*

TRAITOR EXECUTED
Berlin, December 13, 1943

On the 11th of December, the 64-year-old museum curator Dr. Theodor Steinbruch was executed by firing squad in front of the War Museum. The People's Court had condemned him to death for suspicion of espionage on behalf of a foreign power. Adding weight to the verdict was his cowardly conduct in seeking refuge in his academic post when his knowledge of languages should have been placed at the disposal of the various security organs. The site of the War Museum was chosen because of its proximity to the Pergamon Museum, where Steinbruch had been employed since 1924. It will serve as a reminder to those defeatist elements in the academic community that the German people, through its institutions, will protect the nation against treason and defeatism.

This sorry news brings me back to March 31, 1933. The Kaukasus was completely sold out. It could have been New Year's Eve. The guzzling, red-faced clientele was celebrating the assumption of power by Adolf Hitler, who had combined the offices of President and Chancellor and had modestly designated himself Reichsführer. A sober figure among the celebrants tugged at my sleeve. It was Dr. Steinbruch. I had not seen him since that day in 1929 when he had given my purchase of the Kaukasus his blessings. We retired to my office, and he reminded me that his worst predictions had come true. He wanted to assure himself that I was safe, that I had taken his counsel seriously. He appeared to be satisfied with my new name, even with my forged passport. But his jolly humor, his bonhomie, was gone. He sighed deeply. "Daniel, difficult, cruel times are ahead of us. Remember that you have a friend in me. Call on me if you should need me. In the meantime I shall keep an eye on you."

In spite of Dr. Steinbruch's forebodings, nothing had really changed in my life. Although I was aware of the brutal anti-Semitic tenor of the Nazi Party, it had simply never touched me. The nature of my nightclub, the people with whom I associated, did not bring me to the attention of the Party or of the authorities. As our Jewish clientele gradually disappeared, more and more Nazi functionaries, in uniform and out, gave us patronage. Again, as Salazar, a Spaniard, supposedly a subject of General Franco's fascist state, I was seen as the citizen of a country sympathetic to Nazi Germany. Life went on and I prospered. But on that fateful date, I burned my tallith and my kipah. I would say my morning prayers without them—a minor transgression that I was certain would be overlooked by the Merciful One.

It was also the last time I wrote my family, begging them to understand that I did not wish to call attention to myself with the receipt of mail from abroad.

Dr. Steinbruch reappeared in the Kaukasus on the eleventh of November 1938, exactly forty-eight hours after the infamous Reichskristallnacht. The rampage undertaken by the Nazi hoodlums had been particularly fierce in the area of the Kurfürstendamm. The normally grand and colorful thoroughfare was littered with the shards of countless shopwindows smashed by the Brown Shirts. It was the broken glass on the sidewalks that gave the Crystal Night its name.

I had mixed with the nighttime street mob to witness the collapse of the burning synagogue in the Fasanenstrasse, where I had attended services with the Landaus. A holiday atmosphere prevailed as smoke and flame poured out of the windows and doorways of the venerable gray stone building. It appeared that the spectacle was to be interrupted by the arrival of the fire brigade. But it had come, not to extinguish the flames but to protect adjoining Aryan property against the furor of the fire. To the cheers of the crowd, the roof of the synagogue caved in, sending a comet's tail of burning embers into the sky. But in a show of defiance, the twin lions perched atop their stone columns, guardians of the temple's gate, refused to come down. Even after the collapsing edifice had detached itself from the gate, the lions remained in place, snarling their fury at the tormentors of the people whose Torah they had guarded over the centuries.

I sought to escape the mob and had worked my way toward the brick arches which supported the S Bahn, the elevated train farther down the street. I passed a crowd gathered in front of an apartment house.

There was a curious atmosphere in the air as the press of bystanders grew, augmented by drunken idlers from the many neighborhood bars. All were eager to watch the brutal spectacle that was unfolding in their midst. I heard shouts of "Get them!," "No mercy!," "May Judah perish!," and caught a glimpse of two men, perhaps a father and son, on their knees, blood streaming down their faces. Men in brown uniforms were raining blows upon them with rubber truncheons, kicking them brutally with their jackboots. The crowd enjoyed the sport and people were laughing. Two policemen stood by, enthusiastic spectators.

Suddenly there was a cry. "Sali! Josef!" The mob looked up. A woman had clambered up on the decorative stone balcony of her third-story flat. A gust of wind parted her bathrobe, revealing stout thighs encased in a pink corset. The crowd roared its amusement. The woman screamed "Murderers!" and jumped. She seemed almost graceful, the bathrobe flapping in her wake as she plunged. The laughter stopped as the crowd scattered. The last thing I saw were the three bodies lying close to one another.

It was after two o'clock in the morning when I returned to the Kaukasus. Lohmann was waiting for me. His relief was so great that he shouted at me, an extraordinary occurrence. "Goddammit, you stay off the streets, do you hear?" I think we were equally surprised by the outburst.

The following morning, on the tenth of November, the newspapers appeared on the streets with well-orchestrated explanations for the furor of the Kristallnacht: the German people had risen as one, to show their fury and disdain of the Jews. Why? Because a member of that accursed race, a seventeen-year-old boy, Herschel

Grynszpan, had assassinated the third secretary of the German Embassy in Paris, one Ernst vom Rath.

Dr. Steinbruch had aged in the past five years. He had put on weight, and what hair remained had turned gray. While we sat in my office he kept his overcoat on, with his hat and gloves in his lap. He was here to remind me that his scenario for the future of Germany was unfortunately correct.

Dr. Steinbruch felt that after dealing with domestic dissidents such as Jews, intellectuals, uncooperative clergy, and Communists, Hitler would turn his attention to the countries he said were threatening Germany. War, Dr. Steinbruch thought, was only a matter of time. He told me of the true extent of the destruction that had taken place during the Kristallnacht. Hundreds of synagogues were destroyed, most of the major department stores were set on fire, countless private homes were vandalized. Almost a hundred Jews, mostly shopowners, were killed in the street. Thousands of businesses were smashed and some twenty thousand Jews were arrested. So much for the spontaneous uprising.

He drew his chair close to my desk and leaned over towards me. We were almost eye to eye.

"Daniel, I am going to speak openly to you and, in the process, put myself into potential danger. I hope you will do as I say, but if you decide not to I only ask that you treat this conversation as if it had never taken place. I also promise that you will never see me again."

I nodded for him to proceed.

"My wish is that you leave this country and join your family—in Beirut, in Palestine, in Brazil, wherever they are. That would make the most sense. But in my heart I hope you'll stay here and help me in my fight against the 'Brown Shame,' against Hitler and his murderers." I must have looked at him as if he were a madman. "Daniel, I am not alone in this matter."

"Dr. Steinbruch," I said, "I'd like to know who is with you."

There was a long pause before he spoke again. "We have allies, and powerful ones at that."

"Who are they?" I insisted.

Steinbruch took a deep breath. "This is very difficult for me," he said. "You know me to be a proper and orderly German, and I know that you are amused by my pedantic ways. But it is precisely because I am an orderly German that I abhor the brutality, the swinishness, with which the Nazis rule. They not only degrade Germany but one need not be a Cassandra to see they have a similar fate in store for the rest of Europe." He paused to assure himself of my attention. "Now comes the difficult part," he said. "I may have told you that I read history at Cambridge. I made many lifetime friends there, fellow academics. After much soul searching I have decided to acquiesce to their request. I have decided to assist them. It is the most direct way to work against Hitler."

"You're going to be a spy for the English?" I said with naive admiration.

"I am going to gather information. If you are the man I suspect you are, you will join me. In days to come, your family and your people will thank you." He extended his hand to me. Innocent that I was, I shook it solemnly.

December 15, 1943

I NEXT HEARD from Dr. Steinbruch in June of 1939. The shameful Munich accord had already sacrificed Czechoslovakia to Hitler's ambitions, and the Germans were mounting provocations against Poland. The story was the same. The Poles were accused of heinous persecutions of their sizable German minority. Dr. Steinbruch was being prophetic. If Germany invaded Poland, France and Great Britain would have to honor their commitments to go to war. He felt that this could happen at any moment. He was sure that Hitler would treat the various conventions regarding the treatment of enemy aliens and prisoners of war like scrap paper. Dr. Steinbruch was concerned for me. He felt that with my spurious French passport, even though it had been legitimately renewed by the unsuspecting Vice Consul of France in Milan, I might find myself in jeopardy. He suggested that I proceed to London and secure a new passport at the consulate of Spain.

On the following day, I took the night express to Paris. I continued on to London on the sleeper, which was shunted onto the Channel ferry. I arrived in London refreshed and, following Dr. Steinbruch's instructions, presented myself at the consulate of Spain, requesting to be received by the Vice Consul. He turned out to be a Señor Irigoyen, a polished Basque, in a Prince of Wales suit. I told him I considered myself a political refugee and, since I was "de lingua Hispana" — "of the Spanish tongue" — I was respectfully requesting the citizenship so graciously offered by General Franco to those who could demonstrate their links to Spain. I explained all of this in the fluent but archaic fifteenth-century Spanish known as Ladino. I tried to filter out the Hebrew, Arabic, and Turkish words with which our language is studded. When Señor Irigoyen smiled, I knew I had lapsed. Either I had used a Spanish word no longer in usage or, through sheer lack of practice in modern Spanish, the Turkish bastardization of a word. Señor Irigoyen said little. He smiled from time to time, his perfect white teeth accentuated a carefully dyed black mustache. I could not tell if his smile was one of sympathy or, if in his mind's eye, he was already condemning me to the fires of the Inquisition. Luckily it was the former, because Señor Irigoyen showed me to an outer office, where I completed a sheaf of printed forms and then waited, by the hour, for the passport that was being prepared for me.

A stern Generalissimo Franco, threatening even on canvas and oil, and a black crucifix on the wall looked down upon me, ensuring that I did not desecrate the Host or commit other acts of apostasy. I studied the Generalissimo in his olive uniform, his breast crossed by a silken blue sash, his hand grasping a marshal's baton. I looked at the Semitic face under the uniform cap, the dark calculating eyes. The name "Franco" alone established kinship. To us, Franco is the most Sephardic of names. It is inconceivable that a Franco is not from the seed of Abraham. Our poetic and rabbinic literature abounds with the name. The mind boggles at the twists and turns of history. In 1492 General Franco's forebears could submit to expulsion and go into exile or accept conversion and remain in Spain, that is if they were not first burnt at the stake as backsliders by an ever watchful Inquisition. Somehow the general's ancestors overcame the opprobrium "marrano" — "swine" — the name given to these new Christians by their fellow Catholics, and eventually joined the Spanish mainstream. And in 1936 General Franco came across the straits from Spanish Morocco at the head of Moslem troops to recapture a now Republican Spain with the fervent prayers of the very church that had martyred and expelled both Jew and Moslem. This, with the active support of the Hitler regime! Franco, habibi, I thought, you owe me this passport.

I returned to Berlin a full-fledged Spaniard. When I let myself into my office at the Kaukasus, I had a package under my arm. Lohmann came in just as I was hanging the crucifix on the wall. He looked at me, rolled his eyes heavenward, and withdrew.

In spite of the fact that Dr. Steinbruch had initiated my change of citizenship, he did not contact me again for several years. But he had left the unmistakable impression that his plans for me would surface at a later date.

But now he is gone. I know the contrived article in the hateful newspaper can only be half the story. They must have taken him to one of their blood-splattered cells in the Prinz-Albrechtstrasse. God knows what they did to him to break his body and spirit. I wonder if "Saporta" crossed his lips. But I dismiss the thought as unworthy. I suppose it is because of my poor condition, but I feel tears of grief, tears of loss starting to flow. It is true; he drew me into his net, and it is because of him that I am incarcerated here. But I was recruited of my own free will, and it was Professor Doktor Steinbruch who brought me to the first act of selflessness and courage in my life.

December 16, 1943

THE LAST TWO DAYS have not gone well. Terrible toothaches have come and gone like waves of nausea, coupled with a deep sense of depression at the loss of Dr. Steinbruch and the realization that my options are few: to be incinerated in a bombing raid; worse, to be finally found out by those who unearthed Dr. Steinbruch; or, if something were to happen to Lohmann, to die of starvation. I discussed all this with him when he came yesterday afternoon. His loyalty and his good nature cheered me somewhat. He sat with me until I had fallen asleep. In regard to my toothache, we agreed that the tooth had to come out lest a more serious infection set in. He would procure a pair of jeweler's pliers and a bottle of schnapps. He would extract the tooth, a relatively small matter. He had performed real surgery in a shell crater in the no-man's-land of the Marne, when his sapper section was cut off from medical help.

I notice that I avoid coming to grips with my affair with Frau Landau. "Affair," indeed! Affair implies a sexual liaison between a man and a woman, entered into as equals. No boy of seventeen can be considered the partner of a woman in her thirties. It was not an affair. I was a love slave, the toy of this lubricious woman. I return to those days in 1929.

My work at the offices of Landau & Cie. had become routine. I was at my desk each morning at eight-thirty and tackled the correspondence Herr Stemmler assigned to me. Soon I was dealing with freight forwarders, insurance agencies, and customs house brokers on my own. Stemmler was proud of me. Herr Landau and Dr. Grunauer had decided that I would reply to our foreign correspondents in their own languages. We had customers and suppliers in Morocco, in Spain, and in Italy. My relative fluency in those languages was a vast improvement over the atrocious English or French both parties used as a lingua franca. Herr Landau praised me. The flow of mail was greatly accelerated, and above all he detected an amiability on the part of our correspondents, a greater show of goodwill because of my endeavors. Herr Landau proposed that the firm pay tuition for me to attend the Berlitz school at night, to bring my English up to the level of my French. I accepted readily. English came easily to me, and the classes gave me an opportunity to meet socially with Germans of a class and background quite different from the ones I encountered at work. I again learned that the Germans would not readily understand my origins. It was too exotic, too arcane. After all, the new student's name was Saporta, he spoke Spanish, he had black hair; obviously he was a Spaniard. Thereafter I was called "Der Spanier" behind my back.

I had been with the Landau ménage about six weeks when it happened. Not that I wasn't prepared for it. Riding in taxis or at dinner in restaurants, Frau Landau always managed to press her leg against mine. That and the memory of the incident at the Sabbath table kept me in a state of constant excitement. When I heard at the office that the Chief was taking the train to Frankfurt and that Warschauer had been dispatched to the Kellerstrasse to pick up Herr Landau's suitcase, I knew that mischief was unavoidable. To my credit, I did not rush home. I wanted to postpone this encounter as long as possible. I knew that things would never be the same: I would be cuckolding my father's friend, I would be abusing the hospitality so generously given, I would be spitting in the face of the man who had stretched out his hand to me.

I put off the much-awaited moment by going to the cinema after the office. It was an American film, *The Jazz Singer*, which had been playing to full houses for weeks, the story of a cantor's son who breaks his father's heart because he does not want to follow the family tradition, and it moved me deeply. Al Jolson, the actor, and his cantorial renditions moved me to tears, and their effect on me was cleansing, healing. I would not shame Herr Landau. I would honor my father. My mind was made up.

When I let myself into the apartment, I saw to my great relief that everyone had retired. Silently, I walked down the corridor and entered my room. I switched on the reading lamp by my bed. The orange hue of the silk lampshade cast a golden glow on Frau Landau. She lay on my bed, beautifully and bountifully naked, as I had always seen her in my fantasies. She was a woman of few words. She demolished me in minutes. It was during the second and third time that I started to assert myself, taking satisfaction in the effect my movements were having upon her. Her hands and thighs were guiding me to a rhythm of her own needs when suddenly she arched her back, went rigid. Her breath exploded in ever-increasing huffs. I pushed a pillow over her mouth, terrified that Hilde, in the adjoining room, might hear her. I marveled. So that was the orgasm of which Cousin Eli had spoken! And now I had caused it, with my strength, with my cunning, in this blonde goddess beneath me. She turned tender, kissing me, telling me she had already known this would happen when she first saw me in Damascus as a bar mitzvah. I caressed her body: the incredibly white skin, the pink nipples, the soft tendrils under her arms, the pale blonde hair, abundant, frothing up between her legs like the foam of freshly poured champagne. What she did next, Eli had also described to me, but since the sharmutas in Damascus would not do it I could not imagine that a woman of good family would. In this manner, she reminded me of my duties. Again, I pushed her over the brink. This time she bit the pillow. We were getting used to each other.

She left me at five in the morning. I was too tired to gather my thoughts. Herr Landau did not return until forty-eight hours later, and by that time she had possessed me as if a jinni from the *Thousand and One Nights* had enslaved me. Who was going to exorcise that jinni? No one, I hoped. That's how besotted I was. Worse, I had no feelings of guilt or shame. It was I who met Herr Landau at the station and escorted him home, one might say to the very bed in which I had enjoyed his wife only hours before.

It is not my intention to describe here what passed between Frau Landau and myself. There are limits to the ways in which man and woman can couple. Suffice it to say that she omitted none of the possibilities. Years later, when business took me to Paris, I learned the term to best describe Frau Landau: "vicieuse." The English word "vice-ridden" does not translate the true meaning. It is, of course, a pejorative, but used by Frenchmen with a degree of admiration for a woman who is the compleat mistress of sexual activity. No voluptuous act, no depraved refinement is beyond her. That she should also be a loving wife and an exemplary mother was difficult for a

December 17, 1943

THE YEAR CAME TO AN END; 1930 was upon us. I had turned eighteen and my "affair" with Frau Landau continued unabated: trysts in seedy hotels, assignations in the luxurious apartments of her girlfriends, stolen moments at home, a madness in Hilde's room while Hilde was at the zoo with the children. We were never detected. One morning, Herr Stemmler brought me up short.

"Herr Saporta, permit me to say something of a personal nature to you. Of course you may tell me to go to the devil. That is your right. But I think in view of our friendship I deserve to be heard."

I swallowed hard and listened.

"You were never a heavyweight, but you are wasting away in front of my very eyes. You are overly thin, you have black circles under your eyes, and, what is more, you are no longer punctual and I have observed you dozing at your desk more than once."

What could I say?

"I suggest you put yourself into the hands of a physician, or..."—here he paused ominously and meaningfully—"you must totally give up the sort of life you are leading."

The "sort of life" I was leading came to an unexpected and sudden end. It was about seven o'clock in the morning. I was at the washstand in my room, just starting to lather my face, when I heard the sound of retching coming from Hilde's room. Clad only in pajama trousers, I rushed next door. Hilde was on her hands and knees, vomiting into the ceramic bucket which, in those days, stood next to the washstand. Upon seeing me she stood and, feeling faint, started to slip to her knees. I caught her and put my arms around her, trying to comfort her as one would a child. At first, my display of tenderness brought tears, then hysterical sobs on her part.

"Herr Saporta, ich bin schwanger," she said over and over again. She was still repeating her litany, "I am pregnant," when the door was flung open. Herr Landau burst into the room, followed by his wife.

In all fairness to the Landaus we must have presented a less than reassuring sight. I was in my pajama bottoms. By holding Hilde upright, I had inadvertently pulled her nightshift up around her waist. She had her arms around my neck, repeating her self-accusation of pregnancy. However, I was not prepared for the ferocity of Herr Landau's reaction. What followed was like a scene out of a silent film: the melodrama of the exaggerated. Herr Landau tore Hilde out of my arms and manhandled me out of the room, into the corridor, and into my quarters.

"You little shit. Is that how you repay our hospitality, by compromising our nursemaid? Have you no decency? No shame?"

Frau Landau had clamped herself to his right arm, in an attempt to calm him. That, and my trying to respond, made him all the more apoplectic. He tore himself free from his wife.

"You filthy swine! You dirty dog! Get out, do you hear? Out, by the time I get home! Out! I want no trace of you left behind! Ingrate! You,—you,—Arab!" There was spittle on his mustache.

In retrospect and seen with the maturity of years, Herr Landau's self-induced rage was not only good catharsis but an intelligent bit of theater. In one fell swoop he had purged himself of his anger and rid himself of his wife's lover. He had saved their marriage. It had become unnecessary for the Landaus to admit to each other that he was a cuckold, and she the wanton who had put the horns on him.

The Landaus' apartment was unnaturally quiet while I packed my belongings. Herr Landau had left for the office; the maid had been sent out; Frau Landau and Hilde had taken the children. There came a soft knock on my door. It was Frau Polnow, the cook. She had been my special friend, spoiling me with little delicacies left on my bedside table. She had been crying and wiped her nose with her apron. Although her late husband had been a sergeant in von Lettow-Vorbeck's army in the war against the British in East Africa, her sense of geography was limited.

"I've heard the terrible news," she said. "Is the young Herr Saporta going back to...there?" she asked.

"No," I said. "I think I'll stay in Berlin, but I don't really know where."

She went to the kitchen and, moments later, returned with an address written in pencil. It was that of a pension owned by the Gräfin

Schwerin, a general's widow who rented rooms to refined people such as the young Herr Saporta. Frau Polnow insisted on helping me into the street with my luggage and to hail a taxi. It was midafternoon, but typical of Berlin it was already getting dark and snow had started to fall. I took the luggage to the Zoo Railroad Station and left it with the baggage master. I would treat myself to a Chinese dinner, perhaps go to the Eden bar and think my situation through. Later that evening I would go to the pension and look it over.

Several hours later I ran into Lohmann in the underground station at the Uhlandstrasse.

December 18, 1943

LOHMANN LEFT ME, *I do not know when. I woke up late, with
a headache and the taste of blood in my mouth. He had brought a
large piece of kulibiak, a sort of Russian cabbage strudel, and a liter
bottle of Steinhäger, the clear spirit that the Germans chase with
beer. We drank more quickly than I care to, and I remember saying,
"You're trying to get me drunk."*

*"Indeed I am." And with that he reached into his pocket and
withdrew a small gleaming pincers. "Today your tooth comes out."*

*When I protested that it was not hurting anymore, he became
avuncular. "Yes, yes, just drink up, and Dr. Lohmann will pull that
nasty tooth."*

*I drank the full tumbler and pointed the offending tooth out to
him. Without waiting a moment, he had my jaw in a bear's grasp.
The pliers seized my tooth, and with a powerful rocking movement he
had pulled it out. Blood and pus gushed. He had me rinse with salt
water and then with the Steinhäger. He scraped the tooth with his
penknife and declared himself satisfied that the root had come out.
He gave me aspirins, and then sat at my side and waited for my
sleep to come.*

*Lohmann was not only an accomplished dental surgeon, he was
also an intuitive psychologist. His years as a cabaret doorman had
given him a special insight into the foibles, weaknesses, and needs of
his fellowman. As if reading bedtime stories to a child, he began to
reminisce about our early days at the Kaukasus, those early creative
days, which he knew I had enjoyed so much. He reminded me how
the three of us, he, Lilo, and I, and sanded and painted around the
clock, interrupted only by Frau Novikov's wonderful meals; how
early one morning, the four of us stood on the little raised dance floor
and looked about at the jewel we had created. The silver walls
glistened, the icons were in place, the candles blazed, and the huge
antique mirrors reflected and refracted the beauty of our handiwork. I*

had said, "All we need is the entertainment and the customers."

"You get the dancers, and I'll take care of the customers,"
Lohmann had replied.

The next day he had seen me off to Constantinople.

December 19, 1943

UPON MY ARRIVAL in Constantinople, I sought out the luxury of the Pera Palas. The hotel was an imposing mélange of Ottoman and Victorian splendor, highlighted with Russian, Byzantine, and Persian artifacts. I reveled at being back in the Orient. Sitting in my enormous marble bathtub, I could hear the cries of the tea and sherbet vendors in the street below.

I called upon Ehmet Bey. He was an important spice dealer in the Attarine market who had been dealing with my father for many years. With the openhearted hospitality of the Easterner, he immediately suspended his business activities so he could be of "some meager assistance to the son of his great and highly respected friend, Ezra Bey." He decided that the best place to give me his full attention was at one of the seafood restaurants on the banks of the Bosporus.

We sat on the terrace, sheltered by a trellis, through which grape leaves and their tendrils cast sun-flecked patterns across our table. We ate our way through the endless varieties of mezze; eggplant salad and stuffed zucchini, ewe cheese with oregano and oil, lady fingers of ground lamb, dried roe, and mutton chops the size of gold piasters. This was accompanied by glasses of fiery Turkish raki, probably the best in the East, with the possible exception of that made in Zahle, in the foothills of Lebanon. Between the annihilation of the mezze and the arrival of the plat de résistance, charcoal-broiled cubes of sturgeon en brochette fresh from the depths of the Caspian Sea, Ehmet Bey heard me out.

"You devil." He laughed. "I thought you were here to buy our spices, but it's the other sort of spice you want. When it comes to oriental dancers, my son Toufik is an expert. He can afford them. He has his own business in the Covered Bazaar. You two will get along famously. He will collect you at your hotel this evening and show you what this town has to offer."

Ehmet Bey was anxious to hear of my life in Berlin and my

opinion of the political and social unrest in Germany. He had been a Youz Bashi, a captain in the supply corps of the Turkish army, and had seen combat in the Hejaz against Arab levies raised by the British. The Turks, as allies of the Germans, were schooled in the Prussian manner and maintained an emotional attachment to the Germans. Ehmet Bey wondered if this Hitler was not a sort of German Kemal Pasha, who would some day lead his country into a bright tomorrow.

I said that Kemal Pasha, who wanted to ban the fez and the yashmak, or veil, and replace the Arabic alphabet with Latin script, would lead Turkey into the future, whereas Hitler, with his rantings of a pure Aryan race and his xenophobia, would lead the Germans back into the darkness of the Teutonic forests. When I saw he was not entirely convinced, I said I was not speaking as a Yahoudi but simply as a foreigner in Germany, molded by the logic of a French education.

Ehmet Bey told me he had the highest regard for my "community"; not only through his business dealings but from his days in the Army in Palestine, where he had met a number of young Zionists, mostly of Russian origin, who were draining the swamps of the Huleh. He held them in high esteem for their education and energy, which they maintained in otherwise slothful surroundings. He probably meant what he said, as he was less generous about the Arabs. As an officer he found Arabs poor material, bandits rather than soldiers, and he doubted that the victors, the British and the French, could drag them into the twentieth century. That he would speak to a Jew about fellow Moslems in this fashion was not in itself remarkable. Eastern people see their part of the world as inhabitated by Sunni and Shia, by Maronite and Melkhite, by Copt and Chaldean, by Druze and Kurd, by Armenian and Jew. These endless religions and sects eat the same foods, enjoy similar music, pray to their deities, and live in relative harmony. The concept of nationhood, created with pen and ruler by the European colonialists, had only recently been foisted on them.

Later that evening, Ehmet Bey's son Toufik presented himself in the lobby of the Pera Palas. He had the reddish hair and blue eyes that always surprise the foreigner on a first visit to Turkey. Of course these people were not Semites but the very Aryans so dear to Adolf Hitler's heart. Toufik was boisterous and outgoing, but why not? At age twenty-three he was already a partner in a carpet business. He had another young man in tow: a sad-eyed Armenian, a former classmate at the university. The young man presented his calling card:

Karnig Minassian
Theatrical Impresario
Hemediye Cadasi 27

We wasted no time in descending on the fleshpots of the city. Toufik and Karnig were known everywhere. The nightclub owners kissed the hand of Toufik but not that of Karnig. We watched dancers of every nationality, of every talent. With Karnig at our table, they smelled business and directed their gyrations toward us. Karnig asked me to take notes. He would study them and scribble the going price into the margin with a huge orange Parker fountain pen. Before returning me to the Pera Palas, the young men took me to an all-night hamam, a Turkish bath, built by God knows what sultan, hundreds of years ago. There we steamed in the hot waters and had the raki massaged out of us. Then we sat drinking Turkish coffee and sorted out the night's merchandise. We had jotted down some fifteen names in all, and Karnig asked me to indicate my preference. He dismissed my choices as a racetrack tout would a lame horse.

"She dances more on her back than upon her feet"; "Has difficult menses, you will lose ten days out of the month"; "She will not leave her mother"; "Cannot travel, she has a six-month-old daughter"; "A troublemaker with the evil eye."

Ultimately, Karnig the expert settled the matter for me. I needed three girls. Three girls who were pretty but not exceptional dancers, because the Germans wouldn't know the North African from the Persian style of dancing. Three girls who were eminently affordable. I would also need some musicians; I had forgotten that. We settled on an oud player and a drummer. I could flesh out the rest of the orchestra with musicians in Berlin: Greeks or Russians, who have an ear for the beat of oriental music.

We agreed to meet the following day at Karnig's office, where I would meet the artists personally, draw contracts, and prepare salaries and commissions. Karnig would take care of passports and travel documents.

The impresario's offices, on Hemediye Cadasi, were above a

cinema and behind its projection room. The whirring of the projectors and the clanging of the reels supplied constant background music to our negotiations. The three girls were in costume, and I could only agree that Karnig's choices had been good ones. Lailah, aptly named because she was dark as the night, was a Sudanese beauty whose black skin was highlighted with a reddish-cinnamon blush; Latifa, an ample ivory-colored Egyptian with pitch-black but finely kinky hair; and, finally, Shukran, a wiry Turk with a hardly perceptible dark down on her upper lip, the best dancer by far.

Then there was Selim, the oud player, who turned out to be a drug addict of major proportions, and Mehmet, the drummer, a vicious catamite who was to brutalize Lilo. Lohmann would beat Mehmet within an inch of his life with a Polizeiknüppel, a leather-covered length of steel spring, which he kept in the cloakroom. Eventually, I would replace the pair of them with unemployed students from the Berlin Academy of Music who had picked up the melodies, which were, to their ears, an exercise in repetition and monotony. But I am getting ahead of myself.

December 20, 1943

KARNIG HAD MADE all the travel arrangements. The men were sent ahead, third class. The dancers needed more time to augment their wardrobe. This cost me a pretty penny, addicted as they were to sequins, jingling coins, fine gauze and satins. Later I would learn to order costumes for a tenth of this price from a theatrical outfitter in Berlin.

I stood on the platform in front of the Orient Express while I waited for my charges. I was assailed by the movement and color that swirled unceasingly through this terminus connecting Europe with Asia. Its glassed roof, its vaulted arches, are both mosque and cathedral, a totally logical blending of East and West. The station had been the point of arrival and departure for the Ottoman Empire. It was from here that one left for Macedonia and Bulgaria, for Syria and Palestine; it was also here that one returned from Egypt and Bosnia. Masses of Turkish peasants, Anatolians, Kurds, and Druze, many still in their native clothing, carrying carpets and bundles, cheap suitcases and wicker baskets, sometimes on their heads, created a kaleidoscope which, in another decade, would largely disappear.

Suddenly Karnig stood before me, my dancers in tow. I could not believe the spectacle, for that's what it was. The three women were tarted up in what they believed to be western chic. I realized that I had seen them only in their dancing costumes, but there they stood, heavily rouged, with blood-red lips and coal-black eyelashes, swathed in layers of brocade, a-sparkle with fake jewelry and ratty fur pieces. I cursed myself for being condemned to travel with this circus. I could already see the knowing smirks of fellow passengers as they boarded the train. But this was only the beginning of a journey which I shall not soon forget.

The wagons-lits conductor shouted "En voiture!" and we boarded the train. We installed ourselves in our compartments, and I ordered a table for four in the dining car. As the train sped through the darkening Turkish countryside, I heard the gong being struck in the corridor with the cry "Premier service!" Feeling much like a despised gawad, or pimp, I led my gaudy troupe into the dining car single file. They had left their coats in their compartments to expose more brocade and an expanse of décolleté bosoms, against which strands of pearls and rhinestones jiggled. As we moved through seemingly endless sleeping cars on the way to the diner, we attracted much attention, both supercilious and amused. When we entered the dining car, all heads turned, and forks and knives were suspended in midair.

The maître d'hôtel seated us and handed the menus to my charges, knowing full well they couldn't read their own names. *I* ordered. The food came and my embarrassment grew. My ladies were accustomed to the Arabic way of eating: bread was used to pick up meat and salad; rice was eaten with a spoon. They were blissfully unaware of my embarrassment. Smarter than I and certainly wiser, they were enjoying the wonderful fare, smacking their lips, belching delicately, and taking second servings.

I became aware that a man whom I judged to be Italian by his good looks and well-cut clothes, seated across the passageway, was winking at our table. Surely not at me, I thought, and, shifting my gaze, saw that Latifa the Egyptian, seated to my left, was reciprocating with a wink of her own. Under my breath I told her that in her spare time she could do as she pleased, but not while traveling with me. I was certain that this would be the end of it, as she shifted her attention back to the profiteroles on her plate. On leaving the dining car, however, the Italian made a little bow in Latifa's direction and, without dignifying me with a glance, went on his way.

I paid the bill, having to endure once more the smirk of the maître d'hôtel, and our colorful caravan made its way back to the sleeping car. I had a compartment to myself. The adjoining one was occupied by Shukran and Lailah. Latifa was in the next compartment by herself, as the train was not fully occupied.

I was already in pajamas and bathrobe, ready to retire, when I decided to look in on my charges to ask them if they had ordered breakfast, which was available from the car attendant. I let myself into the passageway and knocked on the adjoining door. It was quickly opened, and I stepped into a compartment heavy with perfume. Any anger or impatience I might have had with Shukran and Lailah evaporated when I saw them. Dressed in flame- and orchid-colored nightgowns, they were jolly as schoolgirls on an outing. They had opened a box of Rahat Lokoum and were gorging themselves on the sticky confection. Their fingers, noses, and lips were covered with the fine dust of confectioner's sugar. They insisted that I sit on the lower bunk and have some with them. They were irrepressibly happy and started the Arabic "almendras de miel," the "honeyed almonds" or soft soap on me.

"Oh, beloved. We are so happy, so proud to travel with you. You, sweetheart, you are the best-looking man on the train. All eyes are on you in the dining car."

And on you also, I thought. The mention of the dining car set off an alarm of misgiving. I quickly wished them pleasant dreams and stepped back into the passageway. I stopped in front of Latifa's compartment and knocked on the door. Complete silence: only the rhythmic clacking of the bogies on the track. Suspicious by nature, I glued my ear to the polished rosewood door and was rewarded by that certain silence which is more than a silence—the silence generated by someone holding his breath.

To my embarrassment, I was surprised in that demeaning position by an elderly Englishwoman on her way to the WC. As she brushed past she hissed at me through her dentures. "Disgraceful. You people stop at nothing."

The "people" she referred to were obviously those of us not fortunate enough to be British. "The dagos start at Calais," as her countrymen say. I sought out the sleeping-car attendant in his little cabin at the end of the carriage.

"La dame du seize se trouve mal. Ouvrez-moi le compartiment, s'il vous plaît."

He opened the door for me, and I was greeted with a classic spectacle. The handsome Italian stood, in more ways than one, in a position of laughable disadvantage. Dressed only in his singlet, which came to his milk-white hips, and still wearing his shoes, the socks held in place by garters, he was facing the lower berth in which Latifa was preparing to receive him. I decided that, if ever I was to control the tawdry business in which I was embarking, this was the moment to assert myself. I reached into the lower berth and pulled a nude

Latifa out by the crown of her hair. As she slipped to the compartment floor, I rained blows on her body and slaps on her face and tugged at the roots of her hair.

"Sharmuta! Whore!" I bellowed, an empty and laughable curse, it occurred to me. "Daughter of a whore, sister of a whore!"

The Italian, whose manhood had abated, was pulling his trousers on. He now felt equipped to address me.

"Leave this lady alone, you infamous pimp," he shouted.

I uncorked my elegant Italian. "Agli mortacci tua." A curse on yours. "Va fa in culo, figlio de la mignotta," I added for good measure; take it up the arse, son of a whore.

I gave the cowering Latifa one last kick in the rump and threw the half-dressed Italian into the passageway, hurling his shirt and jacket after him. Leaving a sobbing Latifa, I returned to my compartment. The Italian was nowhere to be seen.

After I had climbed into my berth, I turned off the reading light and lay in the darkness waiting for the motion of the Orient Express to rock me to sleep. But sleep would not come. Instead, I pondered what I had done with my life. Only a year ago I had lived at home, beloved of mother and father, protective of my sisters and my rather inept brother. I was a decent young man with good prospects in business, a regular in my synagogue, a candidate for the hand of the most virtuous daughters in Damascus. What had I done? I had betrayed the trust placed in me by my father's good and loyal friend, a man who had taken me into his home and treated me like a son. I had become his wife's lover—her plaything, really—whom she had sucked dry like a prune, while I had slept the mornings away in her husband's office. And now, what was I now? A pimp, a whoremaster, traveling with his sharmutas. Ah, bitter, bitter, I was thinking when long fingernails played a tattoo on my compartment door.

December 21, 1943

THE TATTOO was insistent. I turned on the reading light and unlatched the door. It was Latifa, backlighted by the night-lights in the passageway, who stepped in and closed the door behind her. She too wore a peignoir in spumoni colors. She sank down on her knees, placed her head on my breast, and, accompanied by tears of contrition, commenced her own almendras de miel:

"Oh, you sweetheart, you are so strong. You are so masterful, my beloved. You were right to beat me. Your blows made my breasts ache with desire. What a fool I was. Please forgive me. I thought you were just a stripling, but I can tell you are a man made of iron."

With the lack of character peculiar to youth, I had permitted her to slip under my bedclothes. With only minimal cooperation on my part, she was now straddling me and slowly commencing the pelvic movements peculiar to her profession.

As Latifa sat with her hands on her hips, commencing to rock while intently studying the expression on my face, the voice of Mohammed el Masri came to me. He was an elderly worker in my father's warehouse, an inspired storyteller in the classical tradition. He would hold Cousin Eli and me enthralled, as he imitated the style of Alf Lailah wa Lailah, the *Thousand and One Nights*.

"Now the king said to his wazirs, 'He who bringeth me a maiden who shall give pleasure such as I have never known; him I shall appoint tax collector for all his years and he shall have my daughter and my handmaidens to abate his pleasure.' Then he rose and gave to the wazirs gold and silver purses, that they could go forth in their quest. And while the Wazirs clucked like pigeons pecking grain, not knowing where to commence, one of their number, a Cairene named Hassan, hurried to the Great Gate. There he mounted a she mule and rode for a full moon until he came to Al Yamam. This Hassan hied himself to the dwelling of the wise women who schooled handmaidens so that they should minister to the pleasure of the sheikhs of that land.

"Now Hassan took a portion of the gold and silver in purses and gave it to the women, so that he could observe the school which attached such merit to their pupils. And they hid him behind a lattice in the hamam, where he saw young girls of excessive beauty, with white bodies and pomegranate breasts. Presently the wise women came in with baskets. From them they gave squash to one and all, and the women said, 'Use them as we taught thee and make that which is most precious to men snap shut like a fist catching flies.' And the maidens did as they were bidden until they were told to rest. But one damsel, Dalila, went before the women and quoth, 'Behold, I am ready.' And she fitted the squash into the perfumed gate and contracted her belly, and the squash fell at her feet in a shower of coins...."

As the Orient Express rocketed through the night, I was in the grasp of a modern-day Dalila, who seemed to have learned her artistry in the hamam of the wise women of Al Yamam. Between Vzunkopru and Svilengrad she brought me to climax five times without releasing me. When I tired, she would remind me of my duties with "a fist catching flies." When she finally let me go, it was daylight and the train had stopped to take on coal.

Up to this point, my experience had been limited to sharmutas and Frau Landau. Cousin Eli had finally prevailed on me to join him in the brothels behind the Hejaz railroad station. These affairs, bolstered by hashish, usually took place in the dark cubicles of those tattooed women, and I was never sure if I ejaculated in their vaginas or in their nimble hands. It was a trick of which Eli had warned me. Of course I had also attended the rigorous school, in session for over a year, between Frau Landau's white thighs. In the course of those demanding exercises, I had learned certain key phrases which appeared de rigueur in the lovemaking of occidental couples.

It seems that western man is not allowed to enjoy his orgasm without reservations. No. Immediately thereafter he is expected to feel pangs of guilt and remorse and ask of his mate, "Did you enjoy it? Was it as wonderful for you as it was for me?" Or, with less refinement, "Did you come?"

If the answer is in the negative, it is assumed to be his fault and he is expected immediately to make good his blunder. Instead, good reason dictates that he take a deserved nap. Non-European men are not burdened with such guilt feelings. Far from it. They ejaculate, withdraw, and immediately enjoy the sleep of the just. If, upon awakening, desire seizes them again, they mount their women and have their way with them. The result of this selfish behavior is that the men of the East are potent at age ninety-five. Western man, at forty-five, has problems of neurasthenia, premature ejaculation, or "nervous weaknesses."

Of course I knew none of this at the time and, being well schooled by Frau Landau, I turned to Latifa, who was now lying in the crook of my arm.

"Oh, you sweetheart, did you feel wonderful?"

No answer.

"Did you come?"

Instead of answering, she brought my right index finger to the spot where I had just idled the hours away.

I touched a rough area, too small to define.

"You know the tiny zoub that women have? The seat of pleasure?"

Indeed I knew.

"They took it from me when I was ten."

I had heard of this Moslem custom, but it was difficult for a boy to understand. Yes, Jewish boys were circumcised on the eighth day after birth, to keep the covenant God made with Abraham. Moslem boys were circumcised before the tenth year, because that was when Mohammed's foreskin was taken. But to circumcise a girl? Latifa continued.

"I was raised in a village not far from Asyut. I had just turned ten and I was in the hamam with my mother, aunts, and married sisters. We enjoyed going to the bathhouse. It brought relief from the hard work and from the confinement of our daily lives. In the bathhouse we laughed, we played: young and old. We steamed in the hot water, we soaped each other, we washed our hair. I was sprouting little breasts, like the tips of lemons, and a feather's wisp showed between my legs. My mother and my aunts were looking at me and then at each other, looks heavy with meaning. I knew what these looks meant. My friends and sisters had been similarly inspected. From that day on I dared not go to sleep, for fear that the village midwife would come with the knife. But for how many nights can a child fight sleep?"

Latifa paused, lit a cigarette, and inhaled deeply. Fortified, she continued.

"They came in the middle of the night. My mother held my arms. My aunts pulled my legs apart and held them in claws of iron. The midwife pushed my night shift up to my belly. She fumbled in a little bag and brought out a knife, a razor, I do not know. With the other hand she parted my secret lips. 'See the button, how large it is. Thank Allah I can relieve her of a life of shame and protect your family from dishonor.' She grasped the button between thumb and blade and sliced it off. The blood spurted and I screamed. I fainted. My little kous became infected. I could not join my legs for weeks." Latifa barked the dry laugh of the addicted smoker. "But I was pure. Satan would not make me a wanton. I would not disgrace my father and brothers by becoming a sharmuta."

Latifa fell silent. She had relived the event, and there were tears in her eyes.

I kissed them away and held her close. "Does that mean you cannot come? Ever?"

"When a woman is in love she can come. When she feels the love, the tenderness of her man, she can come—without the button. I was in love only once. I was so young. He was a student from Tripoli. He studied law. He had red hair and wore glasses!" She chuckled in recollection. "How we loved each other! When Omar kissed my breasts, I came. When he entered me I fainted. But his father put an end to our love. He said I stood in the way of Omar's career."

"And since then?" With the conceit of youth, I was still waiting for Latifa to compliment my performance.

"It is difficult, my darling. But if I have enough hashish, and the man has enough to give him the strength of a lion, then I can come—sometimes."

I became incensed. "Is it a commandment in the Koran?" I asked.

"The Koran does not call for it. But all the mullahs in the mosques of Egypt do. And the people are afraid and do as they are bidden," Latifa replied.

"But you sleep with men even if you have no pleasure."

She shrugged. "A woman finds pleasure in being wanted, and

men have wanted me since I was fourteen. I excite them, and their generosity grows with their excitement."

Sharmuta, I thought in my disappointment.

She must have read my mind. "You foolish boy, do you know how large my family is? I support them all: my mother who held me for the midwife, my father who didn't know I was alive, my brothers for whom I was a servant. I keep them out of jail; I keep them in hashish. I buy the meat for the holidays; I pay the taxes."

"What about Lailah and Shukran?" I wanted to know.

"All the girls support large families."

"No, I mean, have they also been cut?"

"Shukran, no. The Turks are hard but they have never done this to their women."

"And Lailah?"

"In the Sudan it's even worse. They cut off the button, and they sew up the lips. The threads are not removed until the girls are given in marriage."

Merciful God! So much cruelty, so much hardship in their lives. And yet they were still capable of girlish laughter, of warmth and generosity. From then on I would see them in a different light.

December 22, 1943

LOHMANN JUST LEFT. *He left me several days' supply of food, as well as packets of German army rations, no doubt courtesy of the major. "For a rainy day," Lohmann said. He also brought me three French novels, two by Pierre Loti,* Le Roman d'un Spahi *and* Mon Frére Yves, *and* Chairs Ardentes—Ardent Flesh—*by someone preferring the anonymity of Flora to her full name. No matter. The contents are incendiary and of absolutely no use to someone in a condition of enforced celibacy. The books had come off the shelf of the study in the Kantstrasse, where Lohmann managed his dining club. Dear, thoughtful Lohmann. He had brought only the worthless French paperbound books, the sort in which the reader separates the pages with a pen knife, rather than make off with the linen and leather-covered tomes which stood a dusty vigil, awaiting the unlikely return of their owner.*

He also told me he had been seeing Hilde's friend, the one he had met at the cinema. "A nice bit of fluff," as he put it. He had invited her and Hilde to the dining club, where two lieutenant colonels of the General Staff had made a big fuss over them. Hilde had expressed the hope to him that Herr "Salazar" had left Germany in time to avoid all the ugliness that had descended on them.

Lohmann also told me that a disaster of monumental proportions was in the making on the Eastern Front, which could shorten the war by many months. Lohmann did not gloat at this turn of events. He was no Nazi but he was a German, and a veteran of the First World War at that. But he wanted to give me some hope, the feeling that, with total collapse imminent, I might walk out of here alive. I sensed there was something else he wanted to say, but he only sighed and took his leave.

The opening of the Kaukasus Klub in the winter of 1930 was spectacular, even by the blasé standard of Berlin nightlife. I give most of the credit to Lohmann. I knew no one outside the narrow circle of Landau household intimates. Lohmann knew the big spenders of the underworld and the substantial citizens who take pleasure in rubbing elbows with them in nightclubs, at the races, and at boxing matches. Lohmann knew the prostitutes, not just the streetwalkers but the high-class girls, who had one or more benefactors on their string, usually men in marginal businesses who entertained their friends and hangers-on in a grand manner. Lohmann had also made the rounds of the luxury hotels—the Adlon, the Bristol, and the Eden—and promised commissions to the doormen for sending well-heeled foreigners to us.

Frau Novikov's church turned out to be an unexpected source of personnel for the Kaukasus. On opening night, we had a Circassian general and two Cossack colonels in full uniform, opening the doors of the Daimlers, Mercedeses, Maibachs, and Horchs, bottling up the Meinekestrasse. Three elderly Russian ladies, identical in appearance to our cook, were helping out in the kitchen, creating truly memorable Russian dinners. By ten o'clock we were sold out.

I asked Lohmann to secure the front door with the red velvet cord and told the Circassian general to prohibit all further entry. I looked at the guest book: Max Schmeling, Vicki Baum, Jan Kipura, Baron Gottfried von Cramm, Fritz Lang, Joseph Goebbels (!), Brigitte Helm, Emil Jannings, S. Z. Sakall, and Siegfried Arno were names I recognized. Everyone was in dinner jacket or evening dress: society and riffraff, wives, mistresses, whores, transvestites, gamblers, six-day bicycle racers, pimps, and the police president himself. This august body ate mountains of sturgeon and caviar, mushrooms in sour cream, piroshki, roast goose, and chicken Kiev. Vodka and champagne gushed. Baklava disappeared by the tray.

Throughout the dinner service my musicians, the two Turks augmented by a Greek, a Bosnian, and two Russians, played softly on kanoon, oud, and violins. At a signal from me Lohmann dimmed the house lights, permitting the candles in front of the icons to cast wild and unruly shadows. I gave the musicians the nod and they commenced the classical *Tam-tam, tam-tam, tam*, the pelvic rhythm of Arabic music.

The spotlight flooded the dance floor. There stood Lailah, the Sudanese, the reddish blackness of her skin highlighted by her emerald-green ensemble. She raised her arms, and her finger cymbals picked up the rhythm of the orchestra. She permitted herself a sexual shudder. The audience clapped its approval. Lailah threw back her head and laughed. She already had them in the palm of her henna-stained hand. She had never had such an audience, and she pulled out all the stops. After the preliminaries, she dispensed with her veil, went into the expected variations, and then retrieved the veil from the floor. She tied a heavy knot in one end and tied it around her waist so that the weighted end hung between her legs. Then she arched her back and caused the knotted length of the veil to rise and fall between her legs to the rhythm of the drum: a symbolic display of coitus I had never seen in Damascus. By the time she started the finale, the contraction and rippling of the abdominal muscles, the crowd was on its feet.

Then, in an interval long enough to take orders for more wine but short enough to maintain the tension, Latifa, my Egyptian protégé, took the stage. Where Lailah had been orgasmic in her movements, Latifa, fuller and softer, was languorous, tantalizing. She held back, teasing the audience with slow soft pelvic movements, only to become demure: dancing up to the tables with little steps. At that point two well-dressed men, Egyptians judging by their black hair and well-trimmed mustaches, joined Latifa on the dance floor and, in Arab fashion, without embarrassment, started to dance opposite her, inserting handfuls of mark notes into her brassiere and into the waistband above her buttocks and her pelvis. The crowd understood quickly. Perspiring burghers got onto the floor and attempted to add their bills to those already bulging out of Latifa's costume. Of course the Germans lacked the grace of the Arabs, which lent humor to the proceedings. A stunning lesbian in dinner jacket and trousers lovingly slipped money into Latifa's brassiere, to the roar of the crowd. In a show of defiance, she took the red carnation out of her lapel and put it between Latifa's breasts.

More champagne, more vodka, and it was Shukran's turn. Where the others had been seductive, feminine, Shukran was muscular and intense. She moved with great precision, a superb dancer, escalating the preordained evolutions until she stood still, only her pelvis thrusting and withdrawing, in hard little movements that had the men in the audience sucking in their breaths. The good Berliners shouted their approval.

December 23, 1943

IT WAS SEVEN O'CLOCK by the time the last glass had been washed, the last ashtray emptied, the last bit of refuse taken out. I had just counted the night's receipts: an incredible 2,900 Reichsmarks. And no wonder. We were charging 21 Marks for a bottle of G. H. Mumm, 1921 Cordon Rouge, 20 percent more than at the Kempinski around the corner. Our prix fixe dinner was 7.50 Marks, high by prevailing standards. Zakuska, a selection of appetizers and the favorite for the second show, was 10 Marks for two. It included pâté de foie gras, smoked salmon, crayfish cocktail, cold lobster, Roquefort with celery, butter, and toast. Our bar and the table service of champagne, wine, vodka, and cognac had generated almost half our receipts. To all of this we had added a 10 percent service charge. Including those seated or standing in the bar, some twenty in number, we had served in excess of a hundred customers per performance.

As I left my office I heard the sound of music coming from the kitchen. All the other help had left; only the Russians had stayed behind, seated around the chopping block, drinking vodka and eating black bread and cabbage soup with great dollops of sour cream. The two Russian musicians had brought their balalaikas with them. They accompanied themselves as they sang: songs heavy with nostalgia, probably pining for the good old days, when they as serfs had felt the landowner's knout on their backs. With their Czarist manners, they rose to a man when I entered the kitchen. The military saluted me; the old ladies each kissed me three times in their fashion; they all congratulated me on the success of the Kaukasus and made room for me to join them.

I thanked them, but I was in desperate need of fresh air and a clear head. I asked Lohmann to come with me. We bundled up in our overcoats. Together we walked up the Meinekestrasse, turned into the Kurfürstendamm, and breathed deeply of the brisk Berlin morning air. We walked silently, and I had time to digest the night's success.

Although I was a neophyte in the nightclub business, I had been involved in my father's enterprise since childhood. I had my year at Landau's. In the final analysis business was business and through a number of circumstances I had hit on the right combination. Unless the unforeseen such as war, civil disturbance, or an act of God intervened, I should make a good living from the Kaukasus, Inch'allah.

We turned into a café just opening for the morning's business, and I felt that special feeling of well being—the coming in from the cold, the good odors of coffee and fresh rolls, the greeting of the owner to his first customers, the smile of a good waiter taking the order, the panorama of newspapers hanging from their racks, the gleam of the multihued bottles, the polished copper, the brass and wood of the bar, the gloss of the leather seats, the gleaming black and white tiles on the floor: each element adding to the total pleasure of the senses. Sometimes one feels this more intensely than ordinarily, and this was such a day for me. I recalled that our people have a blessing for every wondrous thing. It is said a hundred can be recited each day: on seeing a rainbow, on perfumed herbs or flowers, on fragrant trees and bark, on the wonders of hearing, sight, and smell, on hearing thunder, on candles and their special uses, on the immersion of a convert, on spices, on something new, on bodily functions, on circumcision, on good tidings, even on learning of a death.

I was thinking, irreverently, Why not a blessing on entering a coffeehouse in the morning? But as I mentally ticked them off my fingers, I saw that the rabbis had already covered all eventualities.

I turned to Lohmann and told him that as far as I was concerned he would never have to wear the navy blue doorman's overcoat with gilt buttons we had bought for him. If we needed a doorman, we would hire one of the Russians. I promoted Lohmann on the spot to manager without portfolio, his duties ill-defined, but my second in command. I told him to get himself fitted for a dinner jacket, since his girth precluded buying one off the rack.

Lohmann nodded, excused himself, and went to the WC. His eyes were red-rimmed when he returned. He had been crying. I realized that Lohmann was a member of that proletarian substratum which, in postwar Germany, had no right to aspirations and the hope of a better life. I had seen them in the ink drawings of Käthe Kollwitz, of Zille: drab men in their visored workingmen's caps doing menial and odd jobs, living in the gray tenements so aptly called "rental barracks" in German. Lohmann told me later that his first regular job after being demobilized in 1918 was with the infamous Russian, the first owner of the Kaukasus. Between 1918 and 1925 he had sold newspapers, both Nationalist and Communist, had pimped for some slatterns off the Friedrichstrasse, and even occasionally delivered coal and potatoes from the cellars that sold them throughout the city. And now a foreigner had come who not only treated him like a mensch but had actually given him a leg up in life. It was hard for Lohmann to assimilate all this so quickly.

It was no great act of virtue on my part in bettering Lohmann's lot. He was intelligent, loyal, and had the street smarts that are invaluable in the cabaret business. Also, in the Orient we are not so class conscious. In the mosques and in the synagogues, the men sit row upon row regardless of station in life. Women are not part of this, so the finery of the well-to-do is not demonstrated. All it took was some success in the souk—a favorable deal in cotton or copper, in silk or silver—and a man could join the merchant class. This mobility was simply not known in Europe.

Lohmann and I shook hands, downed a brandy with our coffee, and went back to the club. There was a lot of work to be done in preparing the Kaukasus for the night's business.

With God's blessing, the business prospered and continued unabated. The work became routine. All I had to do was change the dancers every three or four months and the club—its formula holding, al hamdul'illah!—almost ran itself.

December 26, 1943

I BOOKED THE BIGGEST SUCCESS the Kaukasus ever enjoyed under peculiar auspices. I was having coffee and a piece of Streuselkuchen on the terrace of the Romanisches Café. I was reading when a shadow fell over the newspaper. I looked up. There was Chayim Spiegel, a little Polish Jew, an insignificant spice merchant, whom I had met several times in the Landau offices.

"Shulem aleichem, Saporta," he said in his lamentable Yiddish-accented Hebrew.

"Ve alechem shalom"—And to you, peace—I replied with Sephardic condescension. "And by the way, Saporta has left Berlin; it's Salazar now."

"Saporta, Salazar, it's all the same to me. It's not a name for a Jew in either case, if you ask me."

But having lived under unfriendly regimes all his life, he had an unquestioned understanding for my change of name, whatever the reason.

He gave me a moist handshake and, without being asked, installed himself at my table. He made no reference to my having left Landau's, nor to my new vocation. He broke off a piece of my cake and savored it.

"You are just the man I need, but I didn't have the good sense to realize it until I saw you sitting here."

I ordered coffee for him and he started to unburden himself. His brother-in-law had just arrived from Romania; he had been a cook, working on the passenger ships that plied their course between Constanza and Salonika. He, Spiegel, had rented the premises of a defunct cafe on the Friedrichstrasse. It was his intention to open an Italian restaurant there. The Friedrichstrasse was fast becoming the headquarters for the film companies, and these film fellows were enterprising and had money to spend. Why an Italian restaurant? Because the ingredients were not overly expensive, and his brother-in-law, being a Romanian, poor fellow, could cook this hazerei of tomatoes, garlic, and lokschen—noodles—with his left hand.

"How do I fit into this grandiose scheme?" I wanted to know.

"Look, young man," said Spiegel. "My brother-in-law Shloime and I are stateless. Our passports are not kosher. Chances are that if we leave Germany, they'll arrest us upon our return and the authorities, the cholera on them, will deport us." He submerged the rest of my cake in his coffee. "Your papers are in order. You speak languages. Take a trip for me. Everything first class—train, hotel. Go to Italy, set up a connection so that my place has a steady supply of oil, hard cheese, tinned tomatoes, olives, wine. My brother-in-law will prepare a list and the monthly amounts required. You must have connections with wholesalers. The better the deal you make, the larger your commission. I don't know you very well, but I know I can trust you."

I was calculating as he spoke. The Kaukasus was running itself, I could use a week in the sun, and I would use the occasion to buy some antiques for the club in Rome. A week later I was on the Express bound for Italy via Austria. In Milano, I changed trains and headed for Genoa and the offices of the Sorelle Bartoli, wholesalers in produce, wine, and manufactured comestibles. The sorelle were ancient spinsters who had inherited the business from their father, Cesare. They were both huge, mustached, and incredibly kind to me.

"Do not preoccupy yourself, figlio; this matter is already settled. We understand the sort of restaurant it is. Food of second order."

As for the wine, they suggested I visit the vineyards on the slopes above the Mediterranean within easy driving distance of Genoa.

"Make your own deal with the locals. The wine is respectable, and at prices we cannot beat."

I hired a car and driver and proceeded to spend several pleasant days in villages whose names I have long forgotten, sampling simple country wines. Sitting in rough taverns, drinking coffee, haggling, never very seriously, over the price of the wines, filled me with nostalgia. Eating figs, olives, white cheese, and bread reminded me of Syria. Sitting in the sunshine of a café terrace, I indulged in the luxury of introspection. How wonderful this simple life was! I saw myself returning to Damascus, being embraced by family and friends, welcomed by the ancients in the family warehouse. I would help my father run the business, look about for a likely wife, enjoy our children. I would be decent, upright, and wise; people would kiss my hand on the Sabbath. But it was a dishonest game I was playing with myself. I wanted to return to Berlin and its sinful excitement just as surely as our ancestors lusted for the fleshpots of Egypt.

A hubbub of voices broke into my reverie. Across the road from my café, a small open-air market had been set up from which the peasants sold rabbits and chickens, eggs, fruit, and vegetables. The little market was crowded with women, mostly dressed in black, and in the midst of this crowd an ugly spectacle developed. A woman in her forties, dressed in widow's weeds, broke out of the market, dropping her modest purchases. She was pursued not only by children, who threw dung and stones at her, but also by ancient crones, who cursed and spat upon her. The unfortunate woman slipped, fell, and was quickly surrounded by a mob that hurled invectives and worse. She was saved by the arrival of a lone carabiniere on his bicycle, who forcefully dispersed the crowd, helped the woman to her feet, and ensured her safe departure.

I turned to several men in the café, asking for an explanation. I was treated to a typically Italian spectacle. The men pulled down the corners of their mouths, shrugged their shoulders, and lifted their palms outward, as if in surrender.

December 27, 1943

SHORTLY BEFORE OUR INTENDED DEPARTURE for Genoa later that day, a rainstorm started. It was of such intensity that the chauffeur of the hired Fiat suggested we spend the night at the local inn, and after dinner I found myself alone with the innkeeper.

He invited me into the kitchen, warm and cozy with an ebbing wood fire in the stove. Over coffee and brandy we established the easy intimacy that often occurs between strangers. He spoke of his concern that the fascists, under Benito Mussolini, would gradually take away the freedoms the Italian people had historically enjoyed. Mussolini had begun by first abolishing the right of women to vote and then instituting a voter's tax, which reduced the number of people voting from ten million to three million. And now, in 1930, he had prohibited abortion. I spoke of the growing power of the National Socialists in Germany, of their storm troopers, who already roamed the streets with inpunity, and the political murders they were committing. Our conclusion was that the millions who had died in the Great War had died—for what?

We sighed, filled our glasses, and went on to lighter subjects. I regaled the proprietor with tales of the Kaukasus and my trip on the Orient Express with the three belly dancers. I may even have been indiscreet and alluded to my affair with Frau Landau. My host was now in a jolly mood, and I felt that this was the time, without giving offense, to request an explanation of the peculiar event at the market that afternoon. In reply, he told me that within driving range of a modern city such as Genoa and in rural areas such as this, a tradition of superstition was kept alive, especially by the older women, who, being for the most part widows, filled their empty hours with gossip. This, was naturally often malicious and caused many domestic troubles. Thus stories came to husbands that they had been cuckolded, to wives that they had been betrayed. Add to this tales of werewolves and of shameless women who fornicated with the devil—the penchant for mischief was great.

The crones in the village had started a rumor that the unfortunate woman, victim of the attack in the marketplace, was a strega, a witch, who had given herself to Satan on Christmas Eve some sixteen or seventeen years before. Normally she was just shunned by the villagers, but today something had occurred to set off the old hags. What? Perhaps she had retorted too sharply to the price of a cluster of garlic, certainly nothing more important than that. He added that the village priest was seventy-five years old and it was patently beyond him to attend to his parochial duties—baptisms, funerals, masses, the keeping of parochial records—and still address himself to the supression of superstition. The practice of it, unfortunately, gave pleasure to all except its victims. Thus it was left to the carabiniere occasionally to come to the rescue of the unfortunate woman and her daughter.

I could tell by the expression on his face that he had said more than he intended. Then he shrugged, took a couple of waterproof capes off their hooks on the kitchen wall, and handed one to me. He took two large loaves of bread and a butt of smoked ham out of the larder and opened the kitchen door into the courtyard and the driving rain.

Silently, ignorant of our errand, I followed the innkeeper through the night until the streets, actually streams of mud, gave way to a stony goat track, which ascended between stone hovels where the poor dwelt, on the periphery of the little town. We stopped at the stout wooden door of such a dwelling. The innkeeper pounded on the door.

"Donna Clara. Please do not be concerned. It is I, Federico."

Soon, dim light seeped through the cracks of the wooden shutters and the door opened. It was the woman from the marketplace, holding a kerosene lamp. We entered the fetid dwelling, nothing more than a large room, with a brick oven at the far end, a wooden bench, and a couple of pallets, one of which she had just vacated. She pushed aside a heavy-uddered goat and shooed some chickens off the bench so we might sit. Federico walked over toward the oven, where he deposited his gift of bread and meat. The woman kissed his hand. The simple gesture brought a pang to my heart. How long had it been since I kissed my father's hand on the Sabbath?

Federico brought me out of my reverie. "In return for what I've asked her to show you, she wants a gift. It's not for herself, she wants you to know." I looked into her infinitely sad eyes, her prematurely lined face, and agreed.

The woman walked over to the far corner where I had discerned the second pallet. The kerosene lamp now illuminated a sleeping figure, covered with blankets of hide and burlap. A crucifix and lithographs of saints gave some protection to the sleeper. The woman knelt down.

"Svegliati, cara, svegliati."

The figure came awake. The mother placed the lantern on the shelf and we saw the figure of a girl, or young woman, disengaging herself from her jumbled bedclothes as if from a cocoon, clad only in a mended cotton shift. Then she stood up and faced us. Seeing a stranger she cast her eyes downward. The mother suddenly became brisk and businesslike, as if wanting to be done wth some distasteful task. She took the girl's chin in her hand and forced her head up, presenting to us a face of angelic beauty: alabaster skin, deep dark eyes, a face ringed with a mass of matted dark-brown hair. The mother now stepped behind her daughter and stripped the cotton shift off her shoulders. We stood silent, marveling at the beauty of the breasts, small but pointed and seemingly marble firm. Then the mother lifted the breasts in each hand, as if in offering to us. There was bitter triumph in her gesture. Finally, with a brusque movement, she pushed the girl's shift down over her hips until it fell about her ankles. The girl's pudenda lay in the shadows. The mother knelt at her daughter's side and, reaching between her legs, brought a penis and scrotum into the light; an uncircumcised penis, pointed as a horseshoe nail, and testicles smooth as robin's eggs lay in her open hand.

"You want to see the devil's work?" she said. "Here it is."

We drove back to Genoa at daybreak. I sat next to the chauffeur and pondered the events of the night before. The strange and beautiful girl was in the car behind me.

December 29, 1943

I LEARNED from the poor androgynous creature that although she felt herself to be feminine, she was believed to be a normal boy at birth. With the advent of puberty she began to grow breasts, her face never taking on the masculine characteristics of mustache, beard, and sideburns, which make their appearance relatively early in southern climes. She described her childhood as a "calvario"—the sufferings of the Stations of the Cross. When her father realized what he had sired, he abandoned the family, which included, besides the mother and herself, three older brothers and sisters. They, too, left the village as soon as they were able. She was sent to school, nominally as a boy, but when her female traits became obvious she no longer knew which latrine to use. One day she was waylaid by boys from the village and dragged into a barn, where they stripped her and, with the innate cruelty of children, took sexual liberties with her. From that day on she had not returned to school, had not even left her house, except at night to take fresh air. She was illiterate and ignorant but, in spite of her tragic childhood, an intelligent and graceful creature.

"Creature" is exactly what Lohmann called her when he first saw her. "What does Herr Salazar intend to do with this poor creature of God?" was how he put it. I was not about to be put on the defensive by Lohmann or anyone else. I described how I had taken her out of a hovel—a cave, really—where she lived like an animal without ever seeing the light of day, a dark humid place where she was sure to die of consumption before her twentieth year. I described vividly how she and her mother were scorned by the village, how they lived in danger of life and limb and depended on the generosity of the innkeeper to stay alive.

Lohmann weighed his words very carefully. "Now that Herr Salazar has brought her to Berlin, does he intend taking her to Professor Sauerbruch at the Franziskaner Hospital, where something surgical might be done for her? Or does Herr Salazar intend to place her in some vocational school, where she could learn a craft that might sustain her throughout her life?"

His disapproval, evidenced by his use of the third person, enraged me. "Neither hospital nor school, Lohmann," I said. "If Anita Berber can dance in the buff, so can this one. And keep you in tarts and pocket money in the process."

I slammed the door to my office. My heart was racing. What was happening to me? I wondered. What had happened to the boy who would hold up a red pepper and discourse for five minutes on its hue and burnish? To the boy who made his father smile by comparing Spanish saffron to Moroccan in poetic Arabic? What had happened? He had become a procurer, who shuttled his tarts from Istanbul to Berlin. A gawad, become expert in the flesh of women, who evaluated breasts and buttocks as do the Bedouins the teeth and fetlocks in the camel market. And now I was going to exhibit "this poor creature of God" to this sated audience of mine, hoping she would get a rise out of their uncircumcised prickles or spark a spasm between the thighs of their fine ladies! If my fortunes failed, I could always own a string of sharmutas behind the Hejaz railroad station.

My instincts proved to be correct. Her appearance on our stage was an enormous success. The preparations took a month and were relatively simple. She boarded with Frau Novikov, who treated her with maternal affection. "My golobchik, my little pigeon," she called her. I took the little pigeon to the hairdressers and had her hairline plucked to make her appear less primitive; had her manicured, pedicured, massaged; and took her to a doctor for inoculations. I bought her a wardrobe and had costumes designed to show off her breasts and slim waist—to increase the shock when she let the skirt slip to the floor. To earn a few lire her mother had shown her off to strangers occasionally, so it proved less difficult than I had imagined to talk her into the act we were creating for her. A friend of Lilo's, an out-of-work choreographer—everyone was out of work in those days—taught her the rudimentary steps of the strip tease. The orchestra would play Rimsky-Korsakov's *Coq d'Or*, thus maintaining our eastern motif. The spotlight would follow her, and at the moment of the great revelation a purple gelatine would be slipped before the projector. All in the very best of taste.

We mounted a publicity campaign, the central thrust of which was: "Maria or Mario? You be the judge." Sandwich men with this provocative riddle on their boards covered the entertainment areas of the city. We even had posters on the Litfassäulen, the cylindrical advertising pylons that stood on the street corners. In the meantime, the columnists in the scandal sheets had a heyday with salacious innuendos.

The opening night and all ensuing performances were sold out. As an afterthought, I had Maria-Mario photographed by a fashion photographer and had her sit at a flower-laden table in the vestibule. There she autographed, in an unformed hand, the film fan postcards of her likeness. She became enormously popular. For a couple of seasons, she became the darling of the young monied set. She was taken sailing on the Wannsee and became the celebrated hermaphrodite deity of the orgies that took place in the candlelit villas of Dahlem. There was even talk of a love affair with the heir to a large armaments fortune, a handsome but weak-chinned young man of uncertain sexuality.

For two years the Kaukasus benefited from her presence. Then, suddenly, the audience tired of her. It was just as well; she had become difficult. Without telling me, she had made a short film for an independent producer from the Friedrichstrasse. It was not truly pornographic, it was merely exploitative—and lacked the element of restraint that surrounded her act at the club. Equally annoying was the fact that she had withheld her considerable payment from me; monies that under the terms of our contract were rightfully mine. I let her go. As she took her leave—quite graciously under the circumstances, I thought—I marveled at her. Two years ago she had been a wild, furtive animal nesting in a heap of goatskins and rags. Now she was a well-groomed beauty in a smart dress and fur coat. This transformation—that's what the film should have been about, not an idiotic prancing by the lake shore. I should have made the film myself, and I berated myself for my lack of foresight. I accompanied her into the street where her "friend" was waiting. It was the film producer at the wheel of his Opel. He wore a pinstripe suit with black shirt and white satin tie. He didn't get out of the automobile to open the door for her.

Lohmann shook his bearlike head with foreboding. "I fear for her, Herr Salazar," he said. "I see suicide or worse."

"You want to replace her act?" I replied. "Lohmann and his crystal ball?" I was really getting tired of his moralizing.

December 30, 1943

BETWEEN 1939 AND 1941 I had intermittent contact with Dr. Steinbruch. These meetings usually took place in the Tiergarten, a large expanse of greensward and shade trees, which abutted the zoo and the so-called diplomatic quarter. Walking among the strollers or sitting on a park bench was an unobtrusive way of keeping in touch. During these meetings Dr. Steinbruch would give his own views on the progress of the war. As the months went by, he had ever more information about the Jews in the territories occupied by the Germans. He spoke of massacres in Poland and Romania, of mass deportations in Holland and Belgium. I believed him because I had had a fore-shadowing of things to come during the Kristallnacht, but I wondered if he was exaggerating to weld me more firmly to his cause.

Sometime in 1940, we met in the reptile house of the Berlin Zoo. It is a large, steamy structure, lushly planted with palm trees and tropical foliage. From a bamboo bridge, one could observe crocodiles, alligators, and caymans dozing in the brackish waters below. It was a place avoided by mothers and nursemaids. The beasts frightened them more than it did their charges. It was there Dr. Steinbruch first told me of his suspicions that a Nazi-Moslem rapprochement was in the making. The attacks on the Jews of Palestine were growing in direct ratio to the successes achieved by the Nazi juggernaut. Behind these attacks—murders, really—the gray eminence of Hajj Amin el Husseini seemed to be hovering. The name Hajj Amin was familiar to me. He had sparked anti-Jewish riots in Palestine beginning in 1920, and he was behind the Arab general strike against the British in 1936. Although Hajj Amin had no religious education, he was nevertheless appointed mufti, or interpreter of Koranic law, by the British. By naming him to the most important Moslem post in Jerusalem they had hoped to ensure, or rather to buy, civil behavior on his part. Of course they were to be disappointed. This much I knew about him.

Dr. Steinbruch knew a great deal more. Hajj Amin was born in

1893 to an old Jerusalem family. He attended Turkish schools, including a military academy, and joined the Turkish army during the First World War, serving as an artillery officer until his capture by the British. Once a prisoner of war he conveniently changed sides to fight in the Hejaz with Bedouin tribesmen who were recruited by the British to fight the Turks. The British rewarded him with a position in the Palestine customs administration. It was Sir Herbert Samuel, a Jew and High Commissioner for Palestine, who then appointed him Grand Mufti of Jerusalem. True to his colors, he now again turned against the British and was sentenced by them, in absentia, for instigating large-scale riots against the Jews. Now, in 1940, he was a fugitive from British justice and, according to Dr. Steinbruch, hiding out in Iraq. It was inevitable, thought Dr. Steinbruch, that the Nazis and the Arab fanatics, both committed to the eradication of the Jews, should eventually come together. It was to be our task to prepare for that day.

January 1, 1944

IT HAS BEEN *a disastrous year for the Axis powers. Yet victory for the Anglo-Americans seems a long way off, especially as seen from my attic. The Americans are gradually retaking the Pacific from the Japanese; the British and the Americans have swept the Germans and the Italians out of North Africa; Mussolini has resigned. Shortly after the fall of Sicily the Italians sued for peace. The Allies are in southern Italy, but the Germans are resisting fiercely. After the surrender of General Paulus at the battle for Stalingrad, the Germans are fighting a holding action, with the Russians on the attack everywhere. Eventually, the Allies have to liberate France and the rest of Western Europe, but my hopes rest with the Russians, who, for revenge's sake alone, will burst into Berlin.*

This is not an ideological hope because, as a deist and a capitalist devoted to the good life, I have little sympathy for Communists. It is, rather, my hope that biblical justice be done. Let the aggressor die by the sword. Let them pay for the millions of dead, for the thousands of villages burned, for the martyred widows and orphans.

I had often wondered if the staunchly anti-Soviet Russians in my employ felt the same way. On one particular occasion, the two Cossack colonels had come to help out. I opened a bottle of vodka in the kitchen and asked them about their feelings of the bloodletting that was taking place in the East. The Cossacks were cultured and educated men who at one time had served at the court of the Czar. They were still loyal to him, as they were to their church. The colonels hardly qualified as Communist sympathizers, but Russia was holy to them and, without anger at the German people whose hospitality they had enjoyed for decades, they prophesied a coming Armageddon. The Russian armies would come out of the East, they said, led by their shock troops: the Cossacks, the Uzbekis, the Kalmucks, the Tadzhikis, the Kazakhis, and the Mongolians. They would put Germany to the torch. They would rape and plunder and kill until it was brought home to the Germans that to the Russians the soil of Mother Russia was holy, no matter who ruled: hetman, Czar, or commissar.

Thus I look for the day when the Red Army, in its greatcoats and long bayonets, will come down Unter den Linden and hang the Nazis from the lampposts. May I be preserved until that day!

Today is the first day of the New Year, hardly an event to warrant celebration by someone in my condition. But it is a day that lends itself to introspection, to reviewing the transgressions and achievements of the past. All the more because of the knowledge that these memoirs— or my life, for that matter—could be cut short without warning.

Thus if it is God's wish that someone read these ramblings, I wish the reader to know the burdens of shame that embitter my existence. They are how I dealt with Chayim Spiegel, with Samira Mansour, and with the unfortunate Maria-Mario. I sent Chayim Spiegel to a certain death. I might as well have killed Samira, destroying her as I did and robbing her of her only chance at a decent life. And, in a way, I even consider myself responsible for the death of the poor hermaphrodite. Nonetheless, I can say with perfect justification: I had no choice. Greater issues were at stake. I struck a powerful blow against the German war effort, which alone should serve as balm for my conscience, but it will not wash. During the night I can see Samira's eyes, dark, tear-filled with hurt and indescribable pain, and those of Chayim Spiegel, light blue, suffused with the blood of hatred and contempt.

So much for taking stock. I am cold; my right hand throbs. I hope Lohmann will come and spend some time with me.

January 2, 1944

LOHMANN CAME YESTERDAY *afternoon. He had not gone home after his New Year's celebration and was, in fact, still drunk—if from the previous night or from the hair of the dog that bit him, I don't know. He brought a lot of food, which I devoured while he watched me silently. He produced a bottle of Korn, a strong, clear spirit, which he insisted I share with him. As during a prior visit, there was something on his mind, something that weighed down upon him, and I was prepared to wait for him to regurgitate it.*

Suddenly it came.

"Herr Saporta, I have kept something from you because I was ashamed, and I had hoped it was exaggerated and not true." He paused and cracked the knuckles of his fists. "But if we ever get out of this, I will hate myself for not having told you. And you will hate me even more for the same reason. That is something I do not wish to face." He looked away and studied the caps on the toes of his shoes.

My intuition told me what was coming: the fate of the Jews. It was a subject I had buried in my subconscious. Although Dr. Steinbruch had spoken to me of massacres in the Ukraine, I chose to lump this together with the execution of partisans, of Communist commissars, not unexpected during the conduct of total warfare. I had swept the earlier brutality of the thirties under the rug, dismissing them as an internal German matter. After all, the Jews were allowed to emigrate until 1938. In Yugoslavia, in 1941, I was told of large-scale massacres of Serbs by the Croats, and that it had been the misfortune of the Jews and Gypsies to suffer the same fate.

But other than the Kristallnacht in Berlin and the gutted synagogue in Sarajevo, I had never come face to face with the violence directed at Europe's Jews. I had used that cultural separatism of the Sephardim to keep the problem at arm's length. I suppose it was a way of dealing with my guilty conscience, and if I was to function in

Dr. Steinbruch's network, I could not let my already overly active imagination paralyze me with fear.

But now it seemed the long-delayed moment of facing the truth had come. Lohmann started by speaking of the New Year's festivities at the dining club. Fortunately, in view of what ensued, there had been no Party members present. The New Year's dinner had been reserved by a group of army officers, mostly majors and above in rank, men of maturity, some veterans of the First World War. Hilde and her friend were present, in the company of their admirers.

At first things had gone very well. The tables were beautifully set. Frau Novikov had brought votive candles from her church. She had prepared a colorful zakuska, quite copious under the circumstances. There was boiled carp with parsleyed potatoes, and the supply corps major had outdone himself with egg substitute, sugar, and powdered milk, which had enabled Frau Novikov to bake respectable pastries. The officers themselves had brought wine, champagne, and cognac from their respective messes, or from caches hauled back from occupied territories.

Lohmann fortified himself with a deep draft of Korn and continued his recitation. The dinner had gone well. Yes, some of the officers were getting drunk. Some of their ladies laughed too shrilly. He, Lohmann, had to caution those present that there were police patrols in the streets, and that one wanted to protect the premises against the uninvited attention of the civil authorities. There had been restrained shouts of "Hear, hear" in approval of his admonition. Shortly before midnight, Lohmann's aunt had brought in a cake ablaze with brandy. At this, the rotund supply corps major, heavily in his cups, had risen to his feet. According to Lohmann, he raised his glass and proposed a lengthy toast to the Führer, who was leading Germany into greatness, who was hardening the steel of the nation in a crucible of fire, who had gotten rid of the Jews.

Most of the officers had looked at their plates with some embarrassment, but an infantry lieutenant colonel with the Pour le Merite pinned to his field-gray tunic had jumped to his feet and dashed his glass of wine into the major's face. He then grabbed the major by the throat, shouting that he was a bloated swine, sitting in Berlin on his fat arse while half a million young German dead were lying on the frozen steppes of Russia; that while the army was fighting, the SS was gassing millions of Jews in the death camps of Poland. The *officer was clearly hysterical or drunk or both, and his fellow officers tried to disengage him from the major, who had turned purple. They tried not to do him violence but managed to overpower him only with great difficulty. Fortunately, a medical officer was among the guests. He fetched his kit from the vestibule and gave the officer an injection right through the uniform sleeve, putting him out of commission. To compound matters, the supply major was showing all the signs of a cardiac crisis.*

It spelled the end of the New Year's celebration, and the officers filed out silently, leaving their two fellow officers in Lohmann's care. Hilde, who had a diploma as a nurse's aide, chose to stay with Lohmann. Her friend, who said she didn't want to be involved in any of this, talked their admirers into going on to an officers' club.

Lohmann said that he and Hilde made the lieutenant colonel comfortable in one of the back bedrooms and installed the supply corps major on a living room sofa. Both men had been sedated. Several hours later, when the infantry officer came to, Hilde brought him something warm to drink and Lohmann entered the room with her. The man was now totally calm and collected. He said he was returning to the Russian front within forty-eight hours with minimal hopes of returning to his family in Westfalia. He told them that what he had said, possibly under the influence of drink, was the gospel truth. And in Lohmann and Hilde's presence he spoke of Hitler's master plan, called the Final Solution, for the liquidation of the Jews of Europe. The officer said that this task was well on its way to completion; camps were in existence—Lohmann remembered only Maidanek, Treblinka, Auschwitz, but the officer had named many more—where millions of people were being systematically gassed and then incinerated. Whole communities, the Jews of villages, of major towns, of whole countries, were going up in smoke. And the cattle cars with their grisly freight were rolling toward the camps every day. As a Christian and as an officer with an aristocratic background, he had wanted to unburden himself, whatever the cost. He apologized for having spoiled the celebration and went on his way.

When Lohmann and Hilde went into the living room, the supply corps major was gone. His greatcoat still hung on the coat rack in the hallway. Still drunk, he had wandered into the street, where he suffered a fatal heart attack. He was found in a doorway, appropriately frozen stiff, covered with a coat of newly fallen snow.

Lohmann had said things to me that were painful to him as a German and as a friend. He sat silently and waited for me to say something. What could I say? What could he say? He fumbled for my hands, blew his nose, and left me.

To be honest, the scope of the catastrophe was too large to assimilate all at once. Had I been told of the massacre of some small Jewish community, I would have seen, in my mind's eye, the bloodied corpses wrapped in their prayer shawls laid out in the synagogue courtyard. I would have heard the wailing of the widows and orphans, and tears would have come to me. But this was beyond imagining. For my sanity, I decided to say kaddish, the prayer for the dead. I took a blanket off my couch and covered my head and shoulders, so that I was enfolded within the wool as if in a tallith. I stepped up to the little dormer window and looked over the rooftops of the darkening night. I started the gentle rocking on the balls of my feet, and soon the Aramaic majesty of the prayer came forth:

"Yitgadal v'yitkadash shemei rabbah.... Magnified and sanctified be His great name in the world which He created according to His will.

"And may He establish His kingdom, and make His salvation spring forth, and bring nigh the Messiah."

And as I was starting the next phrase, I heard a humming, as of angered bees from afar, and then the first bombs dropped across the city and the flames leaped up and turned the black of night red.

January 4, 1944

HERR LANDAU had induced my father to send me to Germany, because "Daniel should have the benefit of exposure to western culture." Was this not among the most cultured of European nations? I've had no schooling in the arts or literature, but did this country not give the world an extraordinary number of writers, poets, musicians, philosophers, and scientists? Were the Germans not the most literate, the most educated? Was there another country with as many schools, universities, symphony orchestras, opera houses, libraries, and theaters? I had been here long enough to know that in Germany even the poorest went to school, read the papers, took part in the political process. If this savagery is true, how many Germans does it take to murder millions of people? How many does it take to drag the victims out of their homes, put them into railroad cars, and consign them to camps where they are killed and burned? It is not a task for a hundred SS fanatics. By my reckoning it takes thousands and thousands of soldiers, policemen, railroad employees, jailers, and finally executioners. And the Nazis are not alone. According to Lohmann's informant, the Slavic and Baltic peoples have a hand in this. Even the French gendarmes were rounding up Jews for the Germans. Western culture?

All this cruelty from a Christian world that held the Moslem East in contempt as barbarous and uneducated? Since the beginnings of Islam in the seventh century we had never experienced this sort of savagery. And even before Mohammed brought his faith to the desert tribes, we had lived among the same people and continued our communal existence. Not that there were not occasional excesses, but the bloodlettings of the Crusades, of the Inquisition, and now of the Nazis were visited on us by the Christian West.

Even the Damascus blood libels, an infamous accusation against the Jews of Damascus, were fabricated by the Maronites, not by the Moslems. We all knew the story of the Capuchin Friar Thomas, an

Italian who, in 1840, was murdered along with his Moslem servant. The friar had a reputation as an unscrupulous businessman and was probably done in by some of his clients. The Capuchin Order of Damascus, however, accused the Jews of ritual murder, of using the friar's blood in the making of matzah for the Passover. Since the Capuchins were French, under the laws then obtaining the French consul, Ratti-Menton, should have investigated the affair. But he did nothing, and the Governor General carried out an investigation of great brutality, with torture and false arrests, while the Capuchins, using bones found in the Jewish quarter as evidence, built a shrine to Friar Thomas. It was not until the intervention of Great Britain, the United States, and Austria, and the dispatch of Sir Moses Montefiore and Adolphe Cremieux to the sultan Mohammed Ali in Cairo, that the Jews were absolved. This did not prevent the Catholics of Damascus from making an attraction of the tomb of their so-called saint "who had been martyred by the Jews." Incidentally, this affair led to the founding of the Alliance Israélite Universelle, an organization founded to protect the Jews against this sort of libel. The Alliance then organized the school system I had attended.

Lohmann came shortly after dark. He brought two string bags full of food, some wine bottles full of soup, and a bottle of schnapps. He placed most of the food outside the dormer window and covered it with snow, thus assuring concealment as well as preservation. He tells me that with the death of the supply corps major, the principal source of comestibles for the dining club has dried up and that, in view of the many witnesses to the tirade delivered by the infantry officer, he has decided to lie low for a while. This accounts for all the food—a liquidation of assets, so to speak. So far there have been no repercussions over the death of the major. The alcoholic content of his blood must have been high enough for the police to ascribe his death to accidental causes. Lohmann took care to burn the major's greatcoat in the tiled Biedermeier stove in the living room, having first removed buttons and epaulets, which he threw down a storm drain.

Lohmann also told me that Hilde and her girlfriend had a falling out over the events at the New Year's celebration. According to Hilde, her friend had berated her for her sympathetic attitude toward

January 6, 1944

STRANGE, I THOUGHT, *the role that Lohmann had chosen for himself. With the veteran Party emblem on his lapel, he could have walked away from the Kaukasus and his tainted employer and easily have survived the war in some provincial town. Instead, he had appointed himself torchbearer to the memory of the Kaukasus, becoming responsible for the survival of employer and cook. And now he had drawn Hilde into that inner circle, which had its origins in the club. Although he was the only one who knew of my existence, he kept the link intact by speaking of them to me and quite certainly keeping my memory alive with them. Knowing that within spitting distance, so to say, there were people who thought about me and cared for me has been a great source of inner strength during these last months.*

Hilde, dear Hilde. I was eighteen and she must have been twenty the night we met in front of the KaDeWe, the night I took her to the club and she ran away, saying she had promised Frau Landau to return by eight. She said she would return the following week, and she kept her word. She had shown up in time for the early show, breathless, happy. Frau Landau had given her the night off to spend with a girlfriend from her home town. And now we sat at my table, drinking champagne as the show started.

Women can always tell when there's romance in the air, and my dancers conspired to raise the erotic temperature of the club so that the little Almaniah should positively fight her way into their employer's bed. Shukran came out first, and after the mandatory gyrations demanded by the rigidly traditional routine of the belly dance, concentrated on her finale for Hilde's benefit. She shook, she quivered, her abdomen rolled, and all the while she looked directly into Hilde's eyes, the perspiration building little beads on Shukran's fine, downy upper lip. Hilde was scarlet, with champagne and with excitement, yet she remained self-assured, seemingly not embarrassed, without maidenly shyness.

Lailah, of course, had to outdo Shukran in her provocations. She snared an unsuspecting Hilde with her scarf, pulled her out on the dance floor, and, with the scarf firmly around Hilde's waist, guided her into the slow pelvic motions of her dance. The musicians, dirty dogs all, were accentuating the coital rhythms with heavy drumbeats, which underlined the violent shaking of Lailah's hips. Lailah, in the Arabic manner, kissed Hilde on both cheeks and brought her back to the table. Hilde was as if mesmerized, her eyes bright, her breath coming in little gasps. I poured more champagne.

When Latifa came out, I could see by the set of her mouth that she was angry—angry because, since our affair on the Orient Express, she considered me her property, boasting to the others that the boss was hers. And now I was publicly disputing her claim. Yet as an artist she was not going to let the others eclipse her in lubricity. She danced in her usual languorous way and, when the beat picked up, performed the remaining number at our table, directly at Hilde's feet. Since Latifa wore pantaloons, she had freedom of movement. Without warning, she sat on Hilde's lap, straddling her so that her breasts were right under Hilde's face, and by spreading her arms like wings she made her orbs quiver and bounce in Hilde's face. But under her breath she was addressing me in Arabic.

"Dog. Enjoy the blonde bitch. May she give you such a burning pox that your little zoub drops off. May you fall into that orifice of hers and fall out through her tiz. Pimp! Don't ever touch me again!"

In that manner, Latifa defined the end of our relationship. But I already had Hilde by the hand and was leading her toward my office.

We locked the door and did what young people who think they are in love generally do. To my great surprise I did not encounter a shy maiden but an energetic, accomplished woman.

While I was smoking a Simon Artz, my favorite Regie Turque cigarette, Hilde turned to me and laughingly said that the dancers had made her "geil." It was not exactly an elegant word, corresponding as it does to the English randy, or sexually excited. I failed to understand why a girl would be stimulated by dancers who were here for the pleasure of a male audience. Girls were supposed to like Tino Rossi, Rudolf Forster, or Clark Gable.

Hilde said she had a secret to tell me. She whispered that she had on several occasions listened to my lovemaking with Frau Landau.

She had been so excited that she had helped nature along. I was amazed; she said this without any shame, to me an unthinkable admission from a woman. She said she had been jealous, but now that we had made love all that had vanished. I was flattered that she should have been jealous of Frau Landau and told her so. I was in for another surprise.

"I wasn't jealous of Frau Landau." She laughed. "I was jealous of you."

I must have looked stupid, uncomprehending.

"Silly. Because she was making love to you instead of to me."

Hilde now told me that Fran Landau had seduced her during a summer holiday. They had taken the children to Heringsdorf, a resort on the shores of the Baltic Sea; Herr Landau had remained in Berlin.

One evening, after the children had been put to bed, a summer thunderstorm had started to rage. Frau Landau had used this as a pretext to come into Hilde's bed. Hilde found it strange that she should be nude, but who was she to question her employer's foibles? Anyway, Frau Landau was so wonderfully perfumed, so gentle, so knowledgeable that she made Hilde a willing accomplice to her antics. That relationship had continued for over a year and had terminated just before my arrival from Damascus. At first Hilde had blamed me for her deprivation, but she had overheard a shouting match in the Landaus' bedroom. Herr Landau had bellowed that his wife was to "treat the nursemaid like the servant she is and save her caresses for her children."

It was principally to accommodate this burgeoning affair with Hilde that I took up bachelor's quarters in the adjoining Uhlandstrasse. The club was highly profitable, and I could afford it. The day I moved out of my office, Lohmann also moved into a neighboring pension. We were becoming respectable. I had Lilo furnish my apartment, and the result was a bit more flamboyant than my personality warranted, but its theatrical effects seemed irresistible, especially to my female guests. The Jugendstil or Art Nouveau, with its swirls, flowers, and dreamy idealized figures, had run its course. It was being replaced by the so-called Art Decoratif, the application of geometric patterns in the use of glass, wood, and chrome. Lilo wedded this style to overlapping layers of Bokhara and Tabriz carpets. He created a sleeping alcove within a paisley tent, its bed—a low couch, really—covered with a tiger's pelt. There were standing gooseneck lamps of chrome—Lilo had borrowed from the theater by ingeniously putting colored filters into the lamps, so that they cast islands of orange, yellow, and rose. There was a large oil painting, in the style of Persian miniatures, depicting Omar, sharing his inevitable jug of wine with a bare-breasted houri. There were wall sconces made of tortoiseshell, Bauhaus chairs of black leather and chrome, and the pièce de résistance: a life-sized alabaster nude into whose encircling arms one could place a gladiolus or a long sprig of lilac, the bottom of the statue being a slender Grecian vase. Lilo had illuminated this statue with a spotlight, thus creating not only a center of visual attraction but a central theme for my overheated love nest.

I come from a background where interior decoration consists of placing as many armchairs as possible against the walls of the living room. The backs of the chairs actually touch the walls, giving the overall impression of a physician's waiting room. Family and guests sit in this arrangement and talk, shout, or gesticulate across the room, depending upon where the conversational partner is seated.

My flat was on the gaudy side, I know, but I infinitely preferred it to the somber arrangement of the Landau apartment and the heavy furniture that passed for good taste in those days. Gaudy or not, I was rather proud of Lilo's creation of this, my own first home.

January 7, 1944

IT WAS TO MY APARTMENT that Hilde came on her infrequent days off. Those were the times when domestics were given Thursday or Sunday afternoons off; rarely did the masters give them leave to stay out overnight. The infrequency of her visits heightened our passion. There were occasions when the flame burned too bright, too hot, and she would forego her morning outing with the Landau children in the Tiergarten, instead bringing them over to the Kaukasus in their double pram. On these occasions I would ask Lohmann or Frau Novikov to wheel the children back and forth under the chestnut trees, while Hilde and I did our best to quench the flames.

Of course I also had affairs with my dancers. This always entailed a great deal of nostalgia. We would lie in my tented bed in the darkened room smoking cigarettes, and whether it was Noura, Amina, Bulent, or Mouna I would be treated to an oriental litany of the wrongs they had suffered at the hands of their families or unscrupulous men. These men were either young, terribly handsome, with eyes black as kohl and skin like snow, or old, rich, but hard-hearted and cruel. Their virtue had always been taken by a cousin; in one rendition, a grandfather had deflowered the girl. This was inevitably followed by flight to the city, marriage in the village no longer possible because of their ruptured maidenhead. In the city they were exploited and only their great talent for dance, their grace, their deep feeling for music saved them from a life of shame.

The stories were identical, whether they had their origin in the Nile valley of Egypt, the Bekaa of Lebanon, the slums of Baghdad or Teheran, in a village of Anatolia or on the plains of Thessalonia. Often I had to suffer tears for children, all beautiful and intelligent, left in the care of a grandmother or older sister. Sometimes there was a decent young man, a clerk or a policeman, who was saving his piasters, drachmas, or dinars for her return. And their favorite dishes! Oh, you sweetheart! What I would give for a slice of konafa! I can taste the syrup on my tongue! Oh you darling, the figs in our village! The lebeniyah is white as the moon! Oh my love, the sayyadiah, the ful, the torshi, I would give my soul for it. They brought all their favorite dishes into my bed. And once the German winter set in, they pined for the sun of their homelands. Their fly-specked, wind-blown villages suddenly became glistening white, lush with blossoms and greenery, forever basking in the balmy days of a benevolent sun. One would have thought they were describing the resorts of the French Riviera.

Much of what they said was probably true, but the monotony of it reduced their lives to the banality of an Egyptian film. The studios of Cairo turned these out at a rate of some three hundred a year, each one telling precisely the story I received firsthand in my bed.

My afternoons with Hilde were never that dull. The fact that we had both been schooled in Frau Landau's bed created an erotic bond between us. We exchanged confidences at her expense that served to inflame us further. I told Hilde that, while making love with Frau Landau in the bedroom of one of her friends, she had reached for the bedside telephone and, while motioning for me to continue doing what I was doing, had called the girlfriend whose apartment we were using. She had then proceeded to describe to her friend every detail of what was transpiring in her bed, finally delivering herself of an orgasmic scream into the mouthpiece.

I told this vignette with such skill that it made Hilde instantly amorous again. She also told me of several outlandish experiences with Frau Landau, but I considered them so outrageous that they were designed by Hilde to stimulate me further. To be honest Hilde was insatiable, but that was only one side of her. She was a pleasure to be with, devoid of pettiness or jealousy and grateful for every little kindness and attention.

Once I surprised her with a modest gift, a little gold chain with her sign of the zodiac. She put her arms around my neck.

"You are so kind, so thoughtful. You always say beautiful things to me, even when we make love."

"But Hilde," I replied, "what could be more natural? We love each other, you are adorable, you have the softest skin, the prettiest eyes, a funny little nose, and a mouth in which I could drown. Why wouldn't I say beautiful things when we make love?"

In reply she started to tell me of her affair with the man from her hometown who had been the first in her life. He was a married man, an employee of a large textile mill, who periodically came to Berlin to call on the manufacturer of their looms. He was an acquaintance of her brother, who also worked in the mill. This man had called her, saying that he had a little present from her brother, and he had then taken her out for a stroll and a beer on her Thursday afternoon off. Hilde described him as being in his early forties, just this side of handsome, strong-willed and domineering. On his second visit he took her to his room in the pension where he was staying. After a few cursory kisses, he pushed her onto the bed and with his weight and strength soon penetrated her. It was not rape, Hilde said; she was willing and excited by the prospect, but he had not let her exercise any choice in the matter. And now Hilde got to the point of the tale: while this man was mounting her, instead of addressing her with words of passion or tenderness, he started a monologue in which he likened her to a sow. Hilde repeated it for my benefit.

"You swine. This is how I fuck a sow like you. Move your hams, porker. Now, you pig! Let me feel it, you sow!"

When he was through with her he sat back in bed, lit a cigar, and told her to wash his travel-soiled underwear, socks, and celluloid collar in the sink, a fixture of German pension rooms. When she started to step into her slip, he told her to leave it off; he enjoyed watching her do a woman's chores in the nude. It was like this that she had to polish his boots. They had maintained this relationship, and her position of subservience had become routine. I expected her to condemn it, but she was only making a comparison between him and me, her new lover.

I was to learn later that this verbal debasement of the woman, this use of porcine terms, is not unusual among a certain class of Germans. Their language and customs are larded with it. They use the word "schwein" the way we use "mazal" to signify luck. "You've got swine" means "You are lucky." Yet "sau" and "schwein" are also pejoratives, used at every turn. I submit a pertinent example.

When the Nazis first took over, a photograph was printed on the front pages of the Berlin papers. It was of a healthy-looking young woman, prettily attired in summer dress and pert straw hat. She was surrounded by grinning, leering, uniformed Brown Shirts. They had put a cardboard sign around her neck:

> Ich bin im Ort das grösste Schwein,
> ich lass mich bloss mit Juden ein.

> I am the biggest swine in town,
> doing Jews is my renown.

The German obsession with pigs also erupts during certain holidays when the windows of the confectioners are full of marzipan boars, pink marzipan mother pigs surrounded by little piglets, or trays of marzipan cold cuts, with piles of marzipan sausages looking like little turds. It is something I should have discussed with Dr. Steinbruch: how, at the same time, an object can be one of loathing and of affection.

After four or five months my affair with Hilde came to an end. I had waited for her as usual on Thursday at the apartment. When she failed to show by late afternoon I left, frustrated and angry. I walked the streets, and on a whim entered a café where I would treat myself to a Steinhäger, a glass of Pilsner beer, and that Berlin favorite, tartar steak. I seated myself at the front of the café, facing the street, and immersed myself in a newspaper. When the waiter brought my order, I knocked the schnapps back quickly, followed by the Pilsner. I then addressed myself to the raw beefsteak, an egg yolk nestled in its center. There was salt, pepper, Worcestershire sauce, and chopped onion to complement it. It reminded me of the kebbeh nayeh of the Lebanese, also a raw pounded-meat dish but of lamb, mixed with burghul and olive oil and eaten with white onions. Of course it was a Christian specialty, not kasher, because of the blood within the raw meat. Its consumption was a frequent transgression on my part, usually on the way home from school. I had rationalized: at least it was not khanzir—pork.

I was just starting to mix the ingredients when I was brought up short by a peal of laughter. I was sure I recognized it as Hilde's. I carefully looked up into the mirror and saw her reflection. She was sitting in a booth next to Shukran. They had not seen me. They were absorbed in each other and laughed in unison. Probably at my expense, I thought. Sharmutas! I put money on the table, pulled up my coat collar, and went into the night like a thief. I had left the tartar untouched.

January 8, 1944

IN APRIL OF 1941 Dr. Steinbruch contacted me, asking me to meet him in one of the rear pews of the Hedwig's Kirche, a Catholic church copied from the Pantheon in Rome. Because of its size it was usually deserted at any time other than mass.

When I entered the church only a few old ladies were there, telling their beads. I found Dr. Steinbruch sitting with eyes closed, in worshipful introspection. I seated myself next to him, and sotto voce he started to tell me of a recent visit to his museum of a small group of SS officers. They had not asked for a docent to guide them but were accompanied by two men in civilian clothes who, judging by the accents and rather handsome dark features, appeared to be Arabs. They spent several hours among the Mesopotamian and Assyrian antiquities, the young officers taking copious notes. The Arabs appeared to be more than guides: instructors, rather, or perhaps military officers in mufti.

Dr. Steinbruch said that, unlike Paris, with its countless North African restaurants, Berlin had no center of attraction for the Moslems. He thought that these instructors, and perhaps even their charges, might gravitate to the Kaukasus, attracted by the dancers and the food. The food of the Middle East is heavily influenced by Turkish cooking, as is the cuisine of the Kaukasus. This richly colorful and insufficiently appreciated food was probably carried to the far reaches of the eastern world via the silk roads of Afghanistan, Turkestan, and Bokhara. The aubergine appetizers, the skewered lamb with mountains of rice, were devoured in a belt extending from Asiatic Russia, through Persia and India, to the banks of the Nile. Dr. Steinbruch thought the Arab instructors might bring their SS students to the Kaukasus, as boarding-school French teachers might take their charges to a French restaurant after final exams. His request to me was to keep my eyes and ears open and, under no circumstances, jeopardize my persona as a Spaniard by speaking Arabic with anyone.

Before long, I had cause to contact Dr. Steinbruch.

Lohmann had entered my office before the last performance. He motioned toward the vestibule with distaste.

"There's eight SS out there, and with them a couple of Arabs."

My ears picked up. "So seat them," I said.

Lohmann was exasperated. "But they insist on two tables right on the floor. We've got the retirement party for the insurance company there."

"Lohmann, please be your gracious self and ask them to move; it's the least they can do for the boys in uniform."

Lohmann grumbled and went on his way. The old front fighter in him took offense at the incredibly handsome, well-tailored young officers. The revelers made way for them. Anyone who did not move for the SS was foolhardy, to say the least.

I waited for the SS to consume their champagne. When Nailah, one of our dancers, had attracted their attention, I sidled up to their table, unctuously asking if everything was to their liking. They hardly gave me a glance, dismissing me with a "Alles in Ordnung"— Everything in order. The young officers, propaganda-poster blond, immaculate in their black uniforms and leather, could not take their eyes off Nailah, a particularly exotic and black-haired Anatolian, a superb provocative dancer. The SS was falling in love. I had noticed that these Germans—and I am only referring to those who believed, or pretended to believe, the claptrap of pure and unsullied Nordic blood—lusted after my dusky dancers, endowing them in their fantasies with incredible sexual prowess.

Those were the same people who, according to the daily papers, had accused a Jewish woman of crimes against the Aryan race, because she had "genetically poisoned" a German child whom she had given her mother's milk to suckle, her neighbor's teat having gone dry.

The Two Arabs—Iraqis, I judged, by their accent—were not beset by such problems.

"I'd like to stick my zoub up her tiz and let her shake it off!" the first one enthused.

"Oh, you dreamer!" his friend replied. "These uncircumcised dogs are probably fucking them around the clock. We're not allowed to wear our uniforms, so what chance do we have with these cunts?"

This expression of Arab-German understanding made me smile

as I observed the table from the darkness of the wings. One officer stood out, older than his companions, more character to his features, more commanding his demeanor. It was he who called me over to the table and requested that the dancers join them for a bottle of champagne after the performance. I cautioned the girls, the two Egyptians among them, not to let it slip that I spoke Arabic. I was not taking a chance. They did not trust men in uniform, identifying them with the police who had plagued them throughout their professional careers.

Their host was the pacesetter in his group. It was he who poured the champagne, taking care to serve the instructors first. It was he who ordered lemonade for the dancers. He was leaning forward, about to engage the two Egyptians in conversation. I did not intend to miss this and hurried over to the table, playing the solicitous owner. I saw him smile and lick his upper lip.

"Hal hathiil' bousta?" he said to Noura. Is this the post office? The devil was practicing his Arabic!

"No," she replied. And with the ready wit of the Egyptians: "But you can slip your letter in nevertheless."

The girls screamed with laughter. The SS lads looked at each other dumbfounded. It was the turn of the instructor.

"Nein, aber Sie können ihren Brief trotzdem reinstecken," the Iraqi translated, rolling his *r*'s like a music-hall Arab.

The SS roared, manfully slapping the knees of their well-cut breeches. As they left the Kaukasus, I heard the senior officer promise Noura that he would be back to see her.

What my Lothario did not know was that my girls were going back to Istanbul in the morning, to be replaced by three new protégés of Karnig Minassian. Had I known what was to happen I would have kept the old bunch here.

January 9, 1944

FOR SEVERAL YEARS after the Exposition Coloniale of 1931 I recruited my talent in Paris. The French, with their usual good taste, had built a fairyland along the banks of the Seine, in which the glories of colonial France were brought home to the metropolitans. They had erected Moorish palaces, Tonkinese pagodas, the temples of Angkor Wat, and whole African villages in which the Parisians, and above all their children, could marvel at the territories the French had—and I use their term—"pacified." There were Cambodian temple dancers, dervishes from Saharan marketplaces, bare-breasted Negresses from Central Africa, and military drills by the meharistes, the camel troops on their white racing camels. There were Foreign Legionnaires, Goums, Tunisian sharpshooters, Annamite infantry, all in their colorful uniforms and with their military bands. It was the last time that the French Empire was on parade before the Germans put an end to that illusion in 1939.

I had visited the exposition several times, taking a special interest in the Algerian, Tunisian, and Moroccan exhibits. There were some excellent dancers from those countries, and I made it my business to get to know them. When the exposition was dismantled, some of the girls stayed in Paris, dancing in North African restaurants or in North African working-class cafés. I had hired some of these girls, their style and dress providing a change from those of the Middle East.

With the onset of the war in 1939, I could no longer recruit in France and reverted to my friend Karnig Minassian in Istanbul, Turkey being openly sympathetic to Germany. We had been in business for ten years, and Karnig knew exactly the type of girls I needed for my German customers.

We had dispatched the last three dancers, including Noura, the Egyptian who had caught the fancy of the SS officer, back to Turkey that very morning, and now Lohmann was on his way to the railroad station to retrieve their replacements. The whole process had become routine with us. We put them up in a pension in the nearby Knesebeckstrasse, an establishment run by a retired actress who took a personal interest in our girls.

I was in the midst of a discussion about a change in the menu with Frau Novikov, a discussion which, after a ten-year association with the help in our kitchen, I was able to carry on in passable Russian, when Lohmann let himself in. He had three passports in hand, which he placed on the desk before me. I leafed through the passports. Egyptian: Amina el Hindi, 29, born in Port Said. Greek: Eleni Sigaros, 27, native of Patras. Syrian: Samira Mansour, 26, from Aleppo. Nothing remarkable. I would meet them later.

In the late afternoon they came over to the club. We introduced ourselves, formally and politely, in the Arabic fashion. We had coffee and pastries to make them feel welcome.

I had learned over the years to be a loving father and a ruthless disciplinarian to the girls. It was much more than an employer-employee relationship. I took them to the dentist and to the gynecologist; I took them for their curettements and their abortions; I took them to the department stores and to the post office. They spent the greater part of their salaries on household effects, which they sent to their families. I gave advice to the lovelorn; I wrote letters and postcards in Arabic for those who were near illiterates. I got one out of jail on a drug charge, and another for cutting up an overzealous lover with a kitchen knife, the suitor being intent on adding her to his stable of streetwalkers.

To return to the new arrivals: the Egyptian girl, Amina, was perfect, the very sort the Germans liked: mysterious, exotic, with thick black lashes and waves of shiny black hair. She also seemed to have the good nature and well-developed sense of humor that was a trademark of the Egyptians. In her western clothes she seemed to be at least ten pounds overweight. So much the better: a generous rump, breasts, and belly would make for a more spectacular dancer. I took an immediate dislike to Eleni, the Greek. There was something steely to her eyes, a hard set to her mouth, and, unlike the dark tresses of her passport picture, she sported a wild mane of platinum-blonde hair. She had worked in Lebanon and Egypt and spoke passable Arabic. I told her that we were dealing with a German audience and that blondes were as the sand on the seashore. My customers expected performers who passed for what they considered exotic. Ignoring the evidence on her passport photo, Eleni protested, saying that she was a true blonde, that she had only "high-lighted" her hair. After some years in the Levant, she added, she was out to create a new image for herself, a Grecian look, more in keeping with her ancestry.

"Tu parle français?" I queried.

"Bien sûr," she replied.

"You may have heard this ditty before, but I'll repeat it for you nevertheless:

> Je ne suis pas curieux
> Mais je voudrais bien savoir,
> Pourquoi toutes les blondes
> Ont la chatte noir.
>
> Although I'm not curious
> I still would like to know,
> why the pussies of the blondes
> are black down below."

At this Amina laughed, a rich, deep-seated rumble. Samira, with the hint of a smile, studied her scarlet fingernails. Eleni gave me a poisonous look. I continued on the offensive.

"Your real hair color is of no interest to me. We're in the make-believe business. And it's your business, and that goes for all of you—to shake your arses and tits so that these sweating Almanis will come back night after night, each time in the hopes of getting more than the time before."

This bit of nastiness was received in silence. I continued.

"As for you, Eleni, there's a beauty shop around the corner. I'll give you a choice: black, dark brown, or auburn red. If you decide against it, we'll put you back on the train tonight." I let it sink in. "Dress rehearsal at five o'clock." I walked out without giving them another glance. I wanted it known in exotic dancing circles that Salazar was a man who would not take khara from anyone.

January 11, 1944

LOHMANN CAME TODAY. *He brought some slices of rye bread, a liter bottle of cabbage soup, and a block of sweating cheese. He was apologetic but hopeful. The food situation was degenerating, but he suspected that there was plenty of food in the countryside. The farmers, those cagey dogs, were always salting away provisions for themselves. Hilde had told him it was her intention to visit her parents in Silesia, and Lohmann thought he might accompany her on the train, to browse around in the countryside and make some fruitful connections. I cautioned him against his usual optimism. It was general knowledge that there were spot inspections of passengers' luggage on the trains, and there were heavy penalties for black marketeering. Lohmann laughed, saying he remembered from the First World War that any smuggler worth his salt put his stock-in-trade in the luggage rack of one compartment while he traveled in another. His normally shiny red face is pallid. I know he misses the action of his dining club and is ready to get into something else, no matter what the risk.*

My respect for him knows no bounds. He is hiding me from the Gestapo, an act that carries a certain death sentence. I have kept him in total ignorance of my connection with Dr. Steinbruch. He believes implicitly that I went to Bosnia to hire ethnic dancers for our club.

I shall put down my pen. I am weary, weary of it all. I ache in my bones and in my soul. I shall try to sleep, to dream. If I am fortunate I will find solace on the balcony of my father's house. They will all be there, my father and mother, my brother, Victor, my sisters Sultana and Fortuna. We will eat grilled pigeons, the gramophone will play, and we shall be made drowsy by the perfume of the blossoms and the warmth of the sun. Safe.

January 12, 1944

I FEEL BETTER TODAY. Weak winter sunlight floods my chamber, and pigeons are promenading in front of my little window. In my position I invest everything with special meaning. To me the pigeons are a symbol of hope, as they were to our father Noah when he sighted one from his ark, an olive branch in its beak.

I return to the dress rehearsal of our new dancers. I remember being pleasantly surprised. Eleni had dyed her hair a pitch, even artificial, black. It contrasted with her pale skin and, with her straight Grecian nose, gave her a theatrical cast my Arab girls could not achieve. Also, with the passage of years, I found the costumes had improved. There was now more emphasis on voile, more variety in colors, and more skin was laid bare by the generally scantier costumes. Also, the three were good dancers with contrasting styles. Amina was the most traditional, fleshy and wonderfully pliable. Eleni was cold and aloof, making her strangely desirable yet unattainable. Samira, the youngest, with her huge black eyes outlined with kohl, seemed doelike, innocent with the promise of hidden fire. It augured well, or so I thought.

I took my leave of the dancers. They said goodbye. Upon hearing Samira's voice, I thought I detected the hint of an inflection which put my inner ear on the alert, and in her "Ma es salame" I thought I detected the Jewish inflection of Aleppo. This was not in itself very surprising, because Aleppo had a large successful Jewish community, infinitely larger than that of Damascus, well organized, and with a reputation for scholarship and piety. But that a Jewish girl should come to Germany in 1941 seemed a bit strange.

Opening night went very well, and by the end of the week the newcomers were fully integrated into the evolutions of the club. I was watching Eleni doing her elegant number when I became aware of the SS officer sitting at the bar beside me. This was the officer who had joked with Noura on the occasion of his visit with his SS colleagues. He was a Sturmbannführer, a rank corresponding to major in the army but carrying the added clout of the SS. I studied him in the half-light of the bar, having an almost clinical view when he was caught in the glare of the spotlight that followed Eleni across the floor. He was an uncommonly handsome man in his mid-thirties, his fine, even white teeth accentuating a sardonic smile. He wore his pale blond hair as long as regulations permitted, if not a bit longer, brushed straight back from temples and forehead. I could visualize the pair of silver-backed military hairbrushes and the jar of pomade sitting on his dresser. When the spotlight swept across him again I could see the clean Schmiss, the dueling scar of his university days, across his right cheek and again at the jawline. The scars were so fine it occurred to me that he had had the scar tissue removed surgically. As he raised the glass of champagne I saw his hands. They were manicured! On his left wrist he wore a Cartier watch, the famous Santos Dumont model, named after the Brazilian aviator. I suspected that the smart shirt beneath the well-cut uniform was made to order by Knize. It was not at some department store that collars and cuffs were fitted like that. The Sturmbannführer was something out of the ordinary.

He suffered my inspection in amused silence, then turned to me. "Good evening, Herr Salazar. Permit me to introduce myself. Ewald Rabe."

"Entirely my pleasure," I replied. "Nice to see you back with us. Enjoying the program, I hope."

"Very much indeed. But to be frank with you, I have been waiting for Fräulein Noura to appear. So far in vain."

He smiled charmingly, patiently. I was tempted to ask him if it was to resume his Arabic lessons, or if the interest was of a more personal nature, but I felt no need to provoke an SS officer with my sarcasm.

"Fräulein Noura has returned to Istanbul, where she has a contractual arrangement at the Yildizlar cabaret. But of course it would be my great pleasure to introduce you to our other dancers."

He thanked me, and during the intermission I brought the three girls to the table at which I had seated him. He ordered champagne, which only Eleni sipped, Amina and Samira preferring lemonade.

I had already warned the girls not to address me in Arabic, a request they happily granted me, and I became a spectator to his attempt to practice his schoolboy Arabic.

"Kif hal hawa?"—What is the state of the weather?—he wanted to know.

"What's the difference; in your country it is always winter," Amina replied in Arabic.

Of course this went over his head, and amid much laughter the girls tried to explain the jest in broken English and French, abetted by hand gestures. I had no more patience for this kindergarten and returned to my office.

Sturmbannführer Rabe came back almost every night, only now with pedantic German thoroughness he brought a smart leather notebook with him, making entries with a gold pencil as he practiced his little phrases. On several occasions he came with fellow SS officers, but they were less committed to their studies than Rabe, limiting themselves to "Ana bahebbak"—I love you—or, after several bottles, requesting more amatory terminology.

I called Dr. Steinbruch at home; I let the phone ring twice and hung up, as I had been instructed.

January 16, 1944

DR. STEINBRUCH CALLED ME the following morning and asked me to meet him at a side entrance to the Pergamon. I presented myself at a green metal door late in the afternoon.

The door opened and Dr. Steinbruch beckoned me inside. I was not prepared for the size of the Pergamon temple and its wings, which were housed within the museum walls. The temple and its altar mount had stood since antiquity on the Turkish littoral overlooking the Greek island of Lesbos. Dr. Steinbruch explained that, as early as 1878, the Germans had received permission from the ruling Ottoman Turks to cart off this masterpiece stone by stone, until it stood completed in its present site in the museum that bears its name. Although Greece's patrimony had been abducted, the result was an inspiring marvel that left me gawking at the friezes, depicting gods in battle with lions and serpents. A gentle cough brought me out of my reverie. Dr. Steinbruch was motioning for me to follow him.

His office was also a repository of antiquities. He sat behind his desk, on which the statue of Astarte was prominently highlighted by the beam of a chrome lamp. The walls were lined with thousands of books; the center of the room held long refectory tables, each covered with shards of clay and chunks of broken statuary awaiting identification.

I sat on a straight-back wooden chair. I felt intimidated, dwarfed by the high ceiling and the hollow echoes of this huge edifice.

I reported to Dr. Steinbruch that his expectations had materialized. The SS study group he had described to me had indeed descended on the Kaukasus, and the initial group visit had been followed up by Sturmbannführer Ewald Rabe, either alone or in the company of fellow officers. I added my personal observation that, in spite of the puerile level of the Arabic spoken, these young officers were obviously taking instruction from Iraqis—I could detect the inflection even in their simple sentences. When they were off duty, they came to the club to flirt, to drink, and to practice with the girls.

I said I had made no effort, even indirectly, to inquire where these officers were stationed or what their interest in the language was. I continued to play my part as a Spanish cabaret owner, a part with which I had become comfortable, even having applied for membership in the Falange—the official fascist organization—from their headquarters in Madrid.

Dr. Steinbruch brought me up to date on conditions in the Levant. There had been a constant influx of European Jewry into Palestine, both of a legal and clandestine nature. The Arabs were embarked on a campaign of civil disobedience, against the British colonial administration and in assaults both on kibbutzim and on Jews in the marketplaces and streets of Palestine. Some of the most vociferous protests against Jewish immigration came from Arab absentee landowners who were selling thousands of dunams of overgrazed and sand-strewn land to the Jewish agency. The British, true to form, had responded by issuing a White Paper that terminated Jewish immigration into the Homeland they themselves had created under the terms of the Balfour Declaration. The Jews of Palestine had responded by saying they would fight the White Paper as if there were no war, and the war as if there were no White Paper. They were joining the British forces by the thousands. Pointedly, the Arabs were not. On the contrary, they were hoping for, even expecting, a German victory with Rommel's Afrika Korps sweeping into Palestine, at which time they would settle with the Jews.

To prepare for that glorious day, virulent propaganda and violent attacks against the Jews were mounted by Hajj Amin el Husseini, the Grand Mufti.

Dr. Steinbruch produced brandy and cigars and developed his theory for me. It was unlikely, he thought, that our young SS officers were destined for diplomatic or intelligence duties. The German diplomatic corps and army intelligence were sufficiently staffed with specialists in Semitic languages. No. He felt these young men were headed for some sort of combat duty where an elementary knowledge of Arabic and Moslem culture would come in handy. When I interrupted, saying I thought the SS was strictly political in nature, he said the Führer had ordered that combat formations of the Waffen, or weapons, SS be greatly expanded. The SS divisions, uniformed in field gray with only SS flashes on their collars or on their helmets to identify them, were slated for assignments to which the Wehrmacht, the regular army, might not prove equal. Dr. Steinbruch surmised that my young officers would be joining this sort of unit.

He changed the subject in midstream, asking me to describe to him in some detail the background and personalities of our new dancers. I told him what I knew but subconsciously refrained from telling him my suspicions of Samira's Jewish origins.

Dr. Steinbruch then proposed the following plan of action for me. I was to instigate, encourage, or, if necessary, create a liaison between one of the girls and the Sturmbannführer. The girl was to keep her ears open and report to me any and all details elicited as a result of pillow talk or overheard conversations. The information he wanted included unit designation, names of senior officers, in what institution or barracks the training took place, the names of officer unit members, what other languages were being studied if any, and what troop movements or individual assignments were in the offing or actually taking place. Also, any and all information about their instructors, whether Arab, Persian, Russian Moslem, or German, and their names, ranks, and places of origin. The civil status of Rabe and his fellow officers, married, single, or divorced, their sexual preference or idiosyncrasies, their travel abroad, their places of birth, and the occupation of their fathers—in short, everything was of interest to Dr. Steinbruch.

I was to initiate this without delay and communicate with him upon the first sign of success—or failure, for that matter.

Henceforth we would meet in parks or on the noisy Stadtbahn, the elevated train that described a loop over the streets of Berlin. But he had wanted me to see the glories of the Pergamon at least once. Plans were underfoot to dismantle the temple and the other friezes, preparatory to giving them safe burial for the duration. Obviously the intellectual community put no faith in the Party's prognosis of a short and glorious war.

On our way out, we crossed the great exhibition hall containing the Pergamon temple. Our steps created a dramatic echo, as Dr. Steinbruch headed for a wall frieze. He rested his hand on the head of a mythical dog devouring a mythical god.

"You see, Daniel," he said, "civilizations greater than the Third

Reich have fallen, their glories carted off like so much rubble." He paused, smiling at me in the half-light. "Perhaps we'll get to see the Brandenburg Gate in the courtyard of the British Museum after all this is over."

"Inch'allah," I said.

It was late when I returned to the club from the museum and time for the last show. I headed for my office. As I hung up my coat I noticed a plate, covered by another, sitting on my desk. Intrigued, I lifted the top plate and thought I would go into shock: haroset, prepared by my mother's hand!

Haroset is a fruit and nut confection, moistened with sweet wine, symbolic of the mortar with which our ancestors supposedly built the pyramids. I could smell the aroma of raisin, walnut, orange, and apricot. I took a first bite and was transported into our dining room in Damascus. The flavor was identical. I stormed into the kitchen and showed the plate to Frau Novikov.

"Where did this come from?" I wanted to know.

Frau Novikov motioned toward the cabaret with her ample shoulder. "The malinkaya made it, and it's not bad."

"Which little one?" I wanted to know.

Frau Novikov became exasperated with me. She stuck her nose into the air. "Not the snooty Greek." She shook her bottom. "Not the fat one. The little one, Samira."

I asked one of the waiters to call her to the office after her number. So Miss Mansour had found me out before I could give vent to my own suspicions. Was my own Arabic that tainted? Was YAHOUDI written across my forehead? Had I not believed with sinful pride that we Sephardim were better looking, less easy to identify, than the Ashkenazim with their exaggerated Jewish traits? And now a little nothing of a dancer had found me out. I was still pouting when she came into my office.

"I didn't know you could cook," I said lamely.

"You also didn't know it's Passover," she replied. "And Passover is not Passover without haroset."

She was besting me at every turn, and it was absurd to continue my charade. "How do you know it's Passover? What do you know about me?"

"You little donkey. Passover always comes around the Easter of the Nusranis. And as for that"—she pointed at the crucifix on the wall behind me—"it didn't fool me for a moment." She helped herself to one of my Simon Artz cigarettes and sat on the corner of my desk. "The minute I saw you, the minute I heard your voice, I knew who you were. As for the name Salazar, you can fool the Almanis here in Berlin, but not a girl from the Bahsita quarter of Aleppo."

And over endless cigarettes and sips of brandy she spoke of her family, of her childhood in Aleppo, and of the incident that had started her career as a dancer, took her to the fleshpots of the Middle East and finally, through the good offices of Minassian, brought her to Salazar's Kaukasus in Berlin.

Of the anti-Semitic excesses taking place in Germany and the occupied territories she knew nothing. She had heard that the Germans were oppressing the Jews, that this Hitler, the rais, or head, of the Almanis, hated them. But how was this different from the mood in Syria or Iraq? At a time when civilized Europeans professed to know nothing of camps, of gassings, of cremations, how could a simple oriental girl be expected to know? Certainly it was not a matter of interest, or even of knowledge, among the Arab patrons of the clubs in which she worked, how the Germans were dealing with the Jews. She added with justification that the Jews of the Arab East, many of whom lived in poverty in their mellahs, or ghettos, were separated by centuries from the Jews of Europe. She had in fact never met one.

Thus the prospect of an assignment in anti-Semitic Germany had not put her off. Like many other dancers and singers of Jewish background she was passing herself off as a Moslem, and she knew she could carry off this minor deception with ease, especially in a country where knowledge of eastern cultures was nonexistent. Furthermore she needed the money, the relatively high wages we paid, desperately.

Her father, Moshe Zechariah, was by profession a schochet, a ritual slaughterer, in the Jewish slaughterhouse. He made a precarious living from slitting the tracheas of oxen and sheep in the time-honored way. This business of slaughtering was not an assembly-line business as it is in the West. Meat was relatively expensive, kasher meat even more so, since so much of it was rejected for reasons of ritual impurity, and the poverty of the people in her neighborhood militated against meat being an everyday staple. In short, it was a hard way for a man to feed a wife, a blind father, and eight children. It was hard, but not unusual in her community. Her mother and some of her older sisters helped out by doing piecework at home for the Mercerie Meshoullam, a manufacturer of textile notions. Her older brothers had odd jobs around the slaughterhouse or worked as porters in the bazaar. None of them had had any serious education beyond religious school. She, Samira, showing the most promise, had been permitted to attend a business course given in the evenings at the Alliance Israélite. Her parents hoped she might find a position in an office and with her contribution make some inroads into the family's grinding poverty.

Samira poured herself another brandy, lit another cigarette, and continued her life story. But now she was looking at the wall directly above my head instead of at me, giving the impression that she was speaking about a third person, not really about herself. One evening she had left the Alliance school shortly after nine and, using her usual shortcuts, had headed back for the walled Bahsita quarter and home. She crossed an area where some taxis, mostly old Renaults, and some buses and lorries were parked for the night. She remembered the watchman, a rough country type, a fellah in a keffiyeh and an old French army overcoat, had started a fire for himself in an empty petrol drum. A taxi driver was with him and they were playing shesh-besh—backgammon—on the fender of a car. When she passed, they called her over, asking for the time. She told them she had just left school and it would be shortly after nine. They asked them which school, and against her better judgment she told them it was the "Israili" college. The year was 1935, anti-Jewish agitation in Palestine was at a fever pitch, and the broadcasts of the Grand Mufti had stirred up the mostly illiterate Arab masses in the neighboring countries. She could tell that both watchman and driver had been smoking hashish; their eyes were brilliant, their pupils dilated, and an open bottle of arak stood next to the shesh-besh board. The men started to bait her, calling her a "batta," a plump Jewish duck, ready for plucking by a couple of good friends who were only too willing to show her what Arab manhood was all about. She tried to back out of this encounter, but the men grabbed her, pulled her into the back of the taxi, and stuffed a keffiyeh into her mouth. They had taken turns raping and sodomizing her and probably around midnight had thrown her out of the car. The watchman had grabbed her by the hair, put a knife to her, and said that if she gave them away they would find her and slit her throat.

Samira downed her brandy and continued in her detached fashion.

She managed to get home somehow, hugging the walls and doorways in her shame and degradation. Her father, mother, and older brothers were waiting for her when she came in. They took one look at her torn clothes, her blood-streaked stockings, and understood what had befallen their daughter and sister. She fell into her mother's arms, who set up that middle eastern howl of pain that spirals ever upward, breaks off, and starts all over again. All the while she was clutching Samira, rocking her back and forth like a mad woman with a rag doll.

Her father slapped his wife into silence and grabbed Samira, shouting, "Who? Who? Who?" In shock, and further frightened by the violence that was unfolding, she was unable to speak. Her father thereupon grabbed a belt and gave her so terrible a lashing that the pain cut through her numbness and she blurted out what had transpired.

Her father took her two brothers, Latif and Ibrahim, and started out the door. He paused once, taking a leather bag containing the tools of his trade off its shelf. Then they were gone into the night. Her mother washed and scrubbed her compulsively until she was raw and Samira cried out in pain. Her mother then burned Samira's clothes—anything to wipe out the most minute evidence of their collective shame.

The men came back just after daybreak. They addressed not one word to the women. They went into the courtyard and washed under the solitary spigot the Mansours shared with all their neighbors.

Then they dressed and went to the synagogue.

It was obvious to me that Samira's father and brothers had gone to say the Amidah, a prayer consisting of nineteen supplications, the sixth of which affords the sinner an opportunity to ask God for forgiveness. Upon the saying of the words "hatanu"—we have sinned—and "pashanu"—we have transgressed—the supplicant strikes his breast with his fist. And reason to strike their breasts they had.

January 18, 1944

SAMIRA'S FATHER NEVER SPOKE of the incident, but her brother Latif told her the story several years after she had left the paternal home.

The men had hurried over to the parking lot. The fire had gone out and the guard had fled. Perhaps he had come to his senses and now feared an appearance by the Aleppo police, an encounter best avoided by anyone, especially a poor fellah like himself. But her father and brothers, helped by the light of the moon, had spotted the taxi with the shesh-besh board and bottle still on the fender. They looked into the passenger compartment and saw the profuse tokens of daughter and sister's dishonor—blood and semen—on the back seat. Their rage was distracted by the sound of snoring coming from the front. They found the taxi driver in a deep sleep induced by alcohol and drugs. His trousers were still unbuttoned; there was blood on his fly. Before he came to, the men had trussed him hand and foot, with his belt and a length of cord. They pushed a rag deep into his mouth. Ibrahim slapped his face until he was completely alert. Her father then talked to him calmly and reasonably, making sure that the man fully understood what was happening to him.

"I am the father and these are the brothers of the little girl you dishonored. Unfortunately for you, I am by profession a slaughterer at the Jewish slaughterhouse. And I have brought the tools of my trade with me."

Her father produced his knife and flicked the man's nostril; blood spurted down his chin.

"Unfortunately for you, the little girl's father is not a lawyer or an accountant but a butcher who stands knee-deep in blood all day long." Her father paused, watching the man straining at the bonds, his eyes rolling wildly. "Unfortunately for you, the little girl's father is not a rich man, who would seek justice before the bar. He is bitterly poor, and a Jew at that, and expects as little justice from the police and the courts as would a poor devil like you." Again he gave the man a long, painful moment to reflect on his fate. "So I must do what a father must do to the dog who has ruined his child. If not, he could never again face the mother whose loins gave her life. He could never again face the brothers who were raised to protect her. He could never again face the sisters who must be protected from dogs like you. Do you understand what I am saying to you?"

Desperate, the man nodded, hoping against hope to gain mercy.

"So what shall we do? Shall we take out the eyes that have feasted on my child's body? Shall we cut off the fingers that have violated her flesh? Shall we sever the hands that have caressed her before a bridegroom could claim that right? Shall we cut out the tongue that desecrated her mouth? Can she kiss father and mother, can she say prayers with lips touched by yours?" He waited. "None of your answers satisfy me. Salli la rabbak"—Pray to your God—"your time has run out. That which has offended I shall pluck out." The brothers held the man on each side; her father ripped open the trousers, brought out the penis. He pulled back as the man emptied his bladder on the floor of the car. Then the knife was brought upward in a sweep that severed the penis at the root. The man looked down and saw his lifeblood gushing out between his legs. Ibrahim, the older brother, was not through. He picked up the penis and tied it to the gaudy mashallah—the good luck amulet of blue beads and brass hands—that hung from the rearview mirror. As the man slowly died, he had that which had ruined Samira in front of his eyes.

For western ears this is a barbarous story. But in the East it is rich with symbolism, infused with the concept of terrible, irreversible desert justice. The police, the other taxi drivers who must have found the body in the morning, would understand: not only had an injury been avenged; more importantly, a warning had been posted.

But after that, things were never the same with Samira's family. Her misfortune had become a stain that drove her from the warmth and comfort of the family nest. She felt that perhaps she shared in the guilt of her defloration; she felt that perhaps she was unclean after all. When her parents tried to marry her off to the son of a rabbi, a boy deaf since birth, it was a signal to the whole quarter that there was something wrong with the daughter of Moshe Zechariah.

She ran away to Damascus. She had a relative, an old woman

who lived in the Haret el Yahoud, who was her grandmother's sister on her mother's side. She had never met her; the children had been forbidden to visit her. But Samira's mother had kept in secret contact with the only surviving member of her family. In the time of her youth, a time of incredible hardship, this old woman had been what was charitably called a "singer," or public entertainer. This trade probably combined two disciplines, singing being one, and the Syrian rabbis had acted with vigor to wipe out this disgrace to the community. Her mother's old aunt took Samira to her heart. One of her old Moslem friends had a son who owned a cabaret in the Bab Moussalla district. The man found she had a pleasing voice, and her very white skin, beautiful eyes, and virginal appearance tipped the balance in her favor. She was given an opportunity to sing the mindless popular Arabic songs, the lyrics of which consist of repeating the word "habibi"—beloved—ad nauseam. From singer she eventually graduated to belly dancer in spite of her slim figure.

It was three-thirty in the morning when Lohmann knocked on the door of the office. "Herr Salazar, with your permission I am going home. Please lock up."

Samira and I had finished an entire bottle of brandy, countless packs of cigarettes. She had told her story well. I felt as if I knew her entire family: the father become joyless, even harder than before, the mother bemoaning the daughter's fate for whom the hopes had been so high, the brothers, rough hustlers in the bazaars, living by their wits. Although I was blessed with fortunate circumstances, I knew the life she described; most of the Jews in the mellahs of the Arab world lived in similar fashion.

I walked Samira to her pension. In the silence of the chilly night, holding on to each other, that intoxicating feeling of two souls drawing nigh came upon us. When we came to her portal, we opened our overcoats to each other, so that we might stand closer. And as the streetlights went off, giving way to the morning's first light, we breathed Arabic words of love at one another.

January 20, 1944

I HAVE TRIED NOT TO RECORD in these pages every instance of fear, desperation, or pain. Those moments are, alas, altogether too frequent, and were I to record them all I would reduce these poor impressions to the level of a medical or even a psychiatric journal. Headaches, diarrhea, toothaches, pain in the joints, are spelled by moments of terror during the bombing raids, by fits of suicidal depression when I ponder my chances of survival, and the very real fear of being found by the Gestapo. I try not to give vent to these feelings of hopelessness, and Lohmann's visits, as much as the food he brings me, make my existence bearable. But until the time of this entry, he had not come for four and one half days.

Well, he has come and gone. He is very proud of himself. He is on the threshold of a new enterprise, which will not only keep "us" in food but should make money for Lohmann in the bargain.

Taking the train with Hilde, he got off on impulse upon seeing a valley of prosperous-looking villages and farms—all of them seemingly well bundled up against the winter and as yet untouched by enemy bombs—and put up at a Gasthaus. Its owner was also a veteran of the First World War, not exactly a rarity in Germany, but they discovered they had served in the same sector at the same time. Lohmann represented himself as a salesman of jewelry and indeed had taken with him, well secreted in his pockets, the inventory remaining from his nightly forays. The innkeeper introduced Lohmann to a number of well-to-do, well-fed peasants in the intimacy of the warm smoke-filled public room. It was difficult to withstand Lohmann's bonhomie, and before long he had been invited to a large farmhouse. The man wanted his wife to see Lohmann's stock in trade.

"Herr Saporta," Lohmann said, "There's a whole world out there, untouched by the war. Of course their sons are gone, but they live like maggots in a rind of lard." And he described to me how these crafty peasants had cellarfuls of smoked sausages, hams, cold-storage

eggs, potatoes, beets, cabbages, tubs of butter and lard, and homemade Schnapps made from cherries, pears, apples, plums, and apricots. And their stables full of well-fed, sleek cattle and horses generated heat that helped keep their rooms warm above. "They have money to spend. They sell their wheat, rye, oats, and barley to the army and they are ready to buy rings, watches, chains, and even larger silver objects."

Lohmann unloaded his limited inventory among three farms. In payment he took cash and produce. Some of the bounty lay on the table before me: several kinds of sausage, a large piece of smoked pork, a jar of lard, a bottle of potato schnapps. When I asked him how he intended to restock his inventory and transport it without risk of seizure, he laughed, reminding me that a professional smuggler does not ride in the same compartment as does his booty. More difficult is the acquisition of inventory, but he intends once more to take his trusted brick from his brown leather briefcase and busy himself in the aftermath of bombing raids. The Americans and the British are obliging him in this matter, with ever-increasing frequency. According to his contacts in the bars frequented by underworld characters, there are now a number of specialists who burgle while the owners of the loot sit in the relative safety of their air raid shelters. Consequently silver salvers, trays, candlesticks, teapots, and vanity sets are now becoming available—just the sort of merchandise to gladden the heart of a profiteering farmer with hams in the cellar and money in the mattress.

"Do not worry, Herr Saporta, Lohmann will see us through."

January 21, 1944

By the end of April 1941, Samira had left the Pension Stella in the Knesebeckstrasse and moved in with me. It was the first time I had lived with a woman and the closest I have ever come to being married, and it was also the closest I've come to being in a state of unrelieved bliss. Samira and I were deeply in love. We were attuned to each other through background and temperament. She was raised in the oriental tradition, which meant that her man was paramount in her order of priorities, but in the case of our people the woman is not reduced to a position of servility. She lived to please me, and I tried to respond in kind.

In spite of her late hours at the club, she was up hours before I awoke. Invariably she would bring me a cup of fragrant Turkish coffee to sweeten the waking process. By the time I was dressed and ready to face the day, she had prepared some delicacy for me. Usually it was ful, the morning favorite of the Arabs: beans cooked to a soft consistency, mashed, and topped with parsley, spring onion, olive oil, and lemon juice. In the center of the beans she placed a hamine egg, an egg cooked gently all night in onion peel, to impart to it the gentle flavor and color of the onion. She baked khubs Arabi, the bread of Syria; she made my beloved childhood pastries—there was no end to her pleasing me.

In spite of her traumatic experience as a young girl, she had not become embittered against men. Coming from a poor background, she had not been sheltered against the sexual realities of life. Even before her rape, she knew that some men abused and exploited women, taking their pleasure brutally as if it were some tribal right. She also knew that other men were considerate and loving, and she had become content to wait until such a man came along. I was to be that man. That does not mean she lived in abstinence until providence sent her into my arms. No girl can live in the milieu of the cabarets without being chosen by a patron, a protector, or, in the case of bad fortune, a procurer. It is a subject we did not discuss, but it was obvious to me that she had been wise in her choice of lovers. They had been men who had not demeaned her, men who had introduced her to her own pleasure, men who had schooled her to every nuance.

Although Lohmann and the employees of the club knew the personal nature of our involvement, it was not something that was acknowledged in front of the customers. Knowing that a dancer is the wife or mistress of the club owner makes her less mysterious, less desirable in the eyes of the public. To be blunt: it's bad for business. Consequently Samira would sit with the customers if so requested, joking, drinking, flirting—a pastime she considered perfectly normal, having been apprenticed to it early in her career.

Mindful of the instructions given me by Dr. Steinbruch, I called Amina, the delightful and good-natured Egyptian, into my office. I told her she had an admirer, at which she laughed, saying she had many. I countered by saying a special admirer, the handsome SS officer who had become a regular at the club. I told her he had come to me, had spoken of her in glowing terms, and had wondered if I might not induce her to spend some time with him to help him with the Arabic he was so anxious to master. While she was mulling over this proposition, I added that in view of the political situation in this country, good relations with the SS were imperative for me, and if she needed added inducement, I would gladly pay her generously for her time—monies provided, incidentally, from Dr. Steinbruch's special fund. In view of the constant demands made on her by her numerous family in Port Said, Amina agreed.

Later that evening I cornered Sturmbannführer Rabe and told him that one of my girls was smitten with him and had volunteered to help him with his Arabic, and that although she knew no German they could manage in French. Rabe was delighted at the prospect and asked me to tell Amina that he wanted to invite her for lunch the following day. He left his telephone number with me.

Several days after I had paired off Amina el Hindi and Sturmbannführer Ewald Rabe, Amina came to my office.

"Yah, Daniel," she said. "Now I understand why you are paying me a bonus to be with the Almani."

So far I had not discussed with her what it was that was required of her. I was at a loss.

"Did you know this Almani in the shiny boots can't get it up?" she asked. "Did you know I have to lead him around the room with his belt around his neck, like a dog on a leash? That I have to whip his afa with his riding crop, before his zoub will stand so that he can do it?" She laughed. It was not a bitter laugh, or one of disgust. She was genuinely amused at the spectacle of a grown man who crawled naked on all fours and begged for the whip. She had a purse full of Reichsmarks and wanted to go shopping to send some of the purchases to her family. Did I have time to take her, she wondered?

I asked her to describe where she had been with Rabe and what, if anything, she might have observed. Amina thought they had gone to a "soldier place." There were soldiers at the gate, just like the Inglisi have in Egypt. They drank some whiskey in a room like a small bar; there was a billiard table, and they had posters on the walls in Arabic, with pictures of the Mufti, Hajj Amin. She continued with her random observations unaware that I was hanging on to every word as though it were gold. The two Iraqis who sometimes came to the club had joined them for a drink. Only instead of the cheap suits they normally wore, they were in the costumes of soldiers.

"What kind of uniforms are they, Amina?" I asked.

"You know the gray uniforms that the Almanis wear? Well, that's what they wore, but on their heads they wore the tarboosh, just like in Egypt."

At this she laughed, finding it amusing that these two men should be wearing the red fez with their German army uniforms. Where she had been, in what part of town, let alone what the installation was called, of that she had no idea. Still, I was grateful for what she had reported, and I was sure that Dr. Steinbruch would make more of it than I could. I took Amina shopping and to the post office.

January 23, 1944

My IDYLLIC LIFE with Samira started to unravel during the first week of May 1941. We did not realize it at first, but a series of events had conspired to change the course of our lives. This started with the German invasion of Yugoslavia on April the sixth, followed by the occupation of Belgrade on the twelfth and the Yugoslav surrender on the seventeenth. Also on April sixth the Germans rolled into Greece, crushing the Greek army, a task to which the Italians had not been equal.

The week started off badly with a visit by the police, who came with an order for the expulsion of Eleni, who with the invasion of her homeland had become an enemy national. They gave her twenty-four hours in which to leave the Third Reich. When she kissed me goodbye—we had long ago patched up our differences—she said, with some terrible female intuition, "Take good care of Samira, she loves you so much."

January 24, 1944

The next disaster that befell me occurred during my encounter with Dr. Steinbruch at the Alexanderplatz Stadtbahn station. The Stadtbahn, known in Berlin as the S Bahn, the elevated railroad that covered much of the city, was one of the earliest transportation systems in Berlin, built in 1874. The old cars rattled noisily, making hearing difficult, not only on the train but in the street below its tracks. We stood on the rear platform of the last car. I reported Amina's findings to Dr. Steinbruch, infusing the meager information with as much enthusiasm as I could muster. From his increasingly somber countenance I could tell that the Doktor was having none of it.

"I am disappointed in the paucity of the information. What led you to choose this simple Egyptian country girl, who obviously has no understanding of what we are after? You've told me that you have an intelligent Syrian girl, this Samira, who speaks good French and some English, who can read and write. What stopped you from sending her in the first place? We've lost precious weeks!"

I received this bit of news with a beating heart. My previous admiration for Dr. Steinbruch turned to instant loathing as I saw my blissful relationship with Samira threatened. I immediately saw him in a different light, suddenly repulsed by his small pink mouth, gathering spittle in the corners as he pursed his lips in disapproval. Most of all I cursed myself for falling in with his scheme so easily. Finally I drew in my breath and confronted him.

"Dr. Steinbruch," I said, "it's impossible." He looked at me as if I were mad. "Dr. Steinbruch, you don't understand. Samira is a Jewess—we cannot send her to the SS. And we are in love! We're going to be married."

Steinbruch pretended not to hear. "Daniel, I am going to say some hard things to you, but these are hard times. I am going to forgive you your idiocy because you are ignorant, or pretend to be ignorant, of the true state of the war. Don't you know that Salonika fell on

April the ninth? Salonika where you told me you have relatives?"
He was speaking of the Salonika where Toledanos and Saportas have
lived since the fifteenth century. "You speak of romance and orange
blossoms with the whole world in flames. Do you think the Jews of
Salonika will be saved because they come from that princely Sephardic
line? Instead of thanking God that you're in a position to do the Nazis
some hurt, you moon about marriage—to a belly dancer."

"You don't understand," I said. "Samira is not like that." Not
like what? I knew that I sounded lame and idiotic, and Steinbruch
lost no time in bringing it home to me.

"I am losing my patience with you. Don't you understand what
a godsend it is to have a Jewish girl here? She at least will have the
motivation to do a proper job. It's up to you to handle her properly,
to convince her." He paused for a moment. "I want you to talk to
Rabe tomorrow. Tell him he can have Samira. And I want information, hard facts."

He used the German word "Kinderstube"—nursery—to describe
my unprofessional conduct and proceeded to give me a lesson in
Realpolitik.

In October of 1939 the Grand Mufti, Hajj Amin, had given up
his exile in Damascus and moved on to Iraq, where greater oppor-
tunities awaited him. With the cooperation of local politicians he had
set up his anti-British, anti-Jewish headquarters in Baghdad staffed
by hatemongers from the Palestine Arab Party. His military adviser
was the notorious Fawzi el Kaukji, organizer of the murderous bands
that assassinated Arab and Jew alike in Palestine.

The Mufti and his gang were receiving unlimited funds from the
Italians as well as from the Germans, as both fascist states tried to
enlist his services. The Mufti had managed to destablilize the government of Premier Nuri-as-Said and was successful in establishing a
pro-German government in Iraq. The new government's attempt to
declare war on Britain was just barely foiled by elements in the army
still loyal to the Regent and the Hashemite dynasty.

But early in 1941, the fortunes of the Allies were rapidly
deteriorating. The Germans were pushing the British back in the
Western Desert of North Africa, and at the same time they were
taking the offensive in Greece, where the embattled British and
Anzacs were slowly retreating. In a matter of weeks the Germans

would control Greece, Crete, and a Syria in the hands of the traitorous Vichy regime of Marshal Pétain.

"You can tell," Dr. Steinbruch said, "even from Amina's simplistic prattle that the Nazi-Moslem pincer movement against the Jews is about to start. You don't have to be clairvoyant to see what's in the offing. Unless the Germans suffer reversals, unless a blow is struck against the Mufti, the Germans will eradicate the Jews of Europe, and Arab fanatics under the Mufti's banner will slaughter the Jews in Jerusalem, Baghdad, Damascus, Cairo, and Aden. Not to speak of Sana, Algiers, Tripoli, Tunis, and Casablanca and every town and hamlet of the Arab East."

Dr. Steinbruch gave me a few moments to assimilate his blueprint for disaster.

"Daniel," he continued, "do your duty like a man. If not, someday you'll have cause to curse yourself. What I am asking of you may seem unimportant, even petty. But believe me, it is a part of a greater plan, a plan in which I envision an important role for you."

But I could only think of poor Samira, who had suffered so grievously, Samira who was so much in love with me, who had placed her life into my hands with the certain knowledge that with me she would be forever safe and loved.

I resolved to have it out with Dr. Steinbruch—to tell him that I was completely out of my element, that I did not have the stomach for his adventure, and that we should break off our relationship. By the time I had assembled my thoughts the train had pulled into the Savigny station, and as the doors opened Dr. Steinbruch stepped onto the platform without giving me another glance. I looked for him, but he was already lost in the crowd.

Oblivious to the fine rain that had started to fall, I walked toward the Kaukasus. Slowly reason began to assert itself. Could I really turn my back on Dr. Steinbruch, loathsome as he appeared to me now? Could I, a Jew, shirk my duty while Dr. Steinbruch, a German, risked his life in opposing the Nazis? Was he not giving me a unique chance to strike back at them in whatever modest fashion? After all, what was asked of me? That I should tell Samira to spend a few hours with Rabe—and return with vitally needed information. And what if Rabe should make demands on her? There is no guaranty that he would. Samira is not a virgin—to say the least. And is her obligation to our people less than mine? Is it love or just the fear of losing her that made me balk at Steinbruch's request? Is it true that I want to marry her, that I love her the way my father loves my mother, or am I just in love with her body, a slave to our lovemaking as I had been with Frau Landau? Was it my need for Samira to breathe into my ear that I was the best, the strongest, while she raked my back with her fingernails?

As I walked through the drizzle I began to define my thoughts more rationally. Defying Steinbruch served no purpose; we were hostage to one another by the seditious knowledge we shared. I would have to explain to Samira that her cooperation in a common and worthwhile cause was essential. Initially her sacrifice might be greater than mine, but as Steinbruch had indicated I figured in his plans for the future. I would explain it to Samira. She would understand.

January 25, 1944

THE FIRST THING I did was to call for Amina and tell her that I was sending her back to Istanbul. Poor thing. She started to weep, believing I was dissatisfied with her dancing. She dried her tears when I paid her contract off in full and gave her a bonus to mollify her. But it was not only the money, it was her pride that had suffered. What would future employers think if they learned she had been prematurely terminated? I solved that also by writing her a flowery letter of recommendation in Arabic. I hadn't written the beautiful flowing script in years, and I warmed to the task. I'm afraid I over-did it both in calligraphy and content. The letter turned out to be as sickly sweet as a louqmat el kadi, a pastry of my youth. Obviously I was wrong. Amina was beaming with joy as she lip-read the paean I had written about her.

With Eleni gone and Amina soon to follow, it would be up to Samira to carry the program until Minassian's replacements arrived from Turkey. I was not displeased at this turn of events. It would give me a little time to break the news to Rabe and to prepare Samira for the role she was to play.

I invited Sturmbannführer Rabe for lunch in my office. It was a means of breaking the news to him that Amina had left for Turkey and that a solicitous Salazar, ever interested in the welfare of the SS, had found an even more suitable replacement. Rabe showed up in tweed jacket and gray flannel trousers, looking more like an English gentleman than the SS officer he was. While we were having a glass of champagne in my office he studied the decor: autographed photographs of belly dancers and prominent guests, faded spaces where photos of Jewish artists had been removed. He glanced at a colored lithograph of General Franco, and even at my crucifix, with amusement and, I thought, some distaste. I was just telling Rabe that because of the sickness of her little daughter, Amina had curtailed her engagement and was hurrying back to Egypt, when Lohmann let himself in.

"Begging the Sturmbannführer's pardon. Herr Salazar, there's a tradesman outside. We need you for a moment."

I apologized and followed Lohmann through the darkened club.

"What in hell is this all about, Lohmann? I'm sitting with the Sturmbannführer and you—"

He stopped me, whispering into my ear. "There's a man in the courtyard, a man with a little red beard. Looks like one of those Polish Jews from the Moabit district. He insists—"

I barged out the front door, into the courtyard. There stood Chayim Spiegel in the shadows of the entryway. He came at me, hands extended like claws, to clutch at my sleeve. His thinning red hair was matted and he smelled of sour sweat, the odor of fear. I shook myself free of his grasp.

"Saporta, help me, I beg you. I left my place to buy a paper. When I came back twenty minutes later, they were all gone: my wife, my little boy, my brother-in-law. A deportation commando. With my own eyes, may I be struck blind, I saw the van that took them away. I came to you, a fellow Jew. I don't know where to turn."

He made as if to approach the front door of the club, but I pushed him back. Not fully grasping my intention, he continued.

"You know the right people here. All the top Party officials come to your club. For God's sake, ask someone to stop the deportation."

His voice was rising. In my mind's eye I saw Rabe coming into the courtyard to witness this discourse beween two terror-stricken Jews.

"Spiegel," I said, "you must leave at once. The SS is in my office even as we are speaking. They'll catch you, and me in the bargain." Spiegel did not believe a word of what I said. How could he? "There is nothing I can do for you, believe me. I'm sorry. Now get out." I advanced on him to speed him on his way.

Spiegel stepped back, fixing me with his pale blue eyes, now filling with the blood of outrage and hatred.

"Meshummad." He spat. "Apostate. May God curse you and yours. May you be struck blind; may you swell up; may the cholera carry you away." He paused, sucking in his breath for a parting benediction. "If you're a Jew, I'll take my chance with the Goyim. In God's eyes, the Nazi who kills me has more merit than the likes of you. Take my child's curse to your grave."

With that, he turned on his heels and slowly walked across the courtyard and out into the street.

I was shaking with impotence, with fury, with hatred for Spiegel and mostly for myself. Lohmann, who must have overheard the exchange, pulled me into the darkness of the bar. He poured me a full tumbler of vodka.

"Herr Saporta. Drink it all," he commanded. "This is not the time to go to pieces."

I did as I was bidden and returned to my office. Rabe was studying the Falange paper I received from Madrid. He favored me with a smile.

"So, Herr Salazar, Amina has returned to Egypt, to sit at the sickbed of her daughter. Very touching, wouldn't you say?" The bastard was having sport with me. I was defenseless as he continued. "Your Greek star, Eleni, has been expelled and your stable has shrunk to the most delightful Fräulein Samira, whose services you are now going to volunteer. I accept with gratitude. I find her extraordinarily attractive, and above all she has class. I am sure she will prove to be an outstanding tutor of Arabic, that language of poets and thinkers."

Yil'an abouk—May your father be cursed, I thought, and for good measure, Kous ekhtak—Your sister's vagina. But on the surface I smiled and asked Frau Novikov to serve us one of her delectable cold lunches. We finished it off with iced vodka. When Rabe took his leave he was really quite friendly. He shook my hand, thanked me for the lunch, and was gone. His appearance had been a studied display to show a Mediterranean darkling just who called the shots around here.

He had accepted Samira. All that was left was for me to deliver her.

January 26, 1944

AFTER A FOUR-DAY ABSENCE a rosy-cheeked Lohmann let himself in. He was loaded down with some first-rate provisions: smoked country sausage; hard-boiled eggs; half of a Stollen, the German Christmas twist; and a Teewurst, a soft sausage, fatty, smoky, with a distinct tea aroma. He enjoyed watching me consume the food with which he was managing to keep me alive. Circumstances had put him into a position where on an almost daily basis he could demonstrate his friendship and, by watching me wolf down the food, witness my reciprocation and gratitude.

While I ate he regaled me with the experiences of this last trip into the countryside. He had again detrained at Glogau, midway between Berlin and Breslau; he had liked the hospitality and approachability of the peasants in that area. He had traveled with his salesman's case, encountered no difficulties on the train, and had unloaded several silver objects in the village. On a hunch, he had entered a prosperous-looking farmyard and knocked on the kitchen door. A handsome woman in her late forties had made him welcome and permitted him to display his wares on the kitchen table. She bought two silver candlesticks and a pepper-and-salt set from him. Over coffee and cake she told him she was a war widow; her husband, a veterinary officer, had been killed in Poland in the early stages of the war.

Lohmann had offered his heartfelt sympathy and offered to do some minor chores around the house. In the morning he had awakened next to the widow in her red-and-white checkered featherbed. According to his recitation, he had done his homework well, and the widow had induced him to stay for another day and night. She had fattened him up with incredible meals, her cellar being a bottomless treasure trove of culinary delights. Without undue modesty, Lohmann said that the widow had begged him to stay on. When he told her business required his attention in Berlin, she had elicited the promise *that he return the following week. Lohmann was pleased with his conquest, saying that if he played his cards right, the good veterinarian's widow would keep us in sausage and Schnapps until this nightmare was over.*

He shook my hand in his formal way and was off. He still had to visit his aunt in Zehlendorf, hopefully before the air raids started.

I burrowed into my nest of newspapers and covers and thought of this man who had reversed the roles we had originally played. He had become the provider and I the beneficiary. And now that he had found himself a plump and jolly widow, common sense dictated that he stay with her—in the checkered featherbed, so to speak—until the war was over. His aunt and Frau Novikov would survive or not, like millions of others. What brought him back to Berlin was me. It was something I couldn't discuss with him, and he would have denied it. He had made my survival his life's work.

Strange, the bond Lohmann and I developed over the years, a bond that defies analysis. We had nothing in common to attract us, one to the other: not culture, not language, not religion, not some deeply felt ideology we might share; not postage stamps, or chess, or film stars, or football clubs, or authors; in short, nothing that normally creates a link between men. Other than the running of the club, or perhaps a comment on the news of the day, we didn't have much to say to each other. But we were enormously comfortable in each other's company. Our greatest pleasure was to go into the many working-class districts of Berlin—Kreuzberg, Wedding, or Moabit— and drink Schnapps and beer in neighborhood bars that had not changed since the days of the Kaisers. We would eat Bouletten, the marvelously tasty minced meatballs, a Berlin specialty; pyramids of them sat on heavy china plates on the counters of most neighborhood cafés. They were eaten at room temperature, redolent with onions and fat and complemented by sour cucumber pickles and hard rolls. These establishments were visited by what is condescingly known as the "proletariat." If this means working-class people of enormous wit, people with a trenchant cynicism that hardened them against unceasingly hard times, the appellation may be correct. Actually, "proletarian" is what they called themselves, this mass of taxi drivers, ice and coal men with their aprons of burlap, sooty chimney sweeps in their top hats, flour-dusted baker's apprentices, streetwalkers and their pimps, janitor ladies in felt slippers, hurdy-gurdy men, the beggars and the blind, both professional and legitimate, draymen smelling of their horses, and the many idlers and unemployed.

It was Lohmann's way of introducing me into his world, a world in which he was often recognized and greeted with warmth and some admiration for his new station in life. Sometimes we enjoyed neutral ground: the six-day bicycle races, the boxing matches, and the football games. During the 1936 Olympic games we shared the pleasure of watching Jesse Owens, the American Negro, dash the hopes of Hitler and his Aryan athletes.

I reciprocated Lohmann's invitations by taking him to the better restaurants and bars, and he appreciated the fine dinners at Horcher, Aben, and Schlichter. When we went to the Adlon or Bristol hotels for lunch, he never failed to shake the hands of the uniformed doormen, his former colleagues. He never felt ill at ease, no mean accomplishment for a man of his background, and sometimes when I studied him across the table I thought that Lohmann in his dark-blue vested suit and starched white collar, his thinning hair brushed back with pomade, looked like somebody's favorite uncle on a visit from the provinces. But now he too has aged, and I worry about him, as he does about me.

If God permits me to survive this, I shall leave Germany and take up my life somewhere else. I am not afraid of the future. I've thought of the possibilities: London, Paris, Cairo, Beirut, Caracas, Buenos Aires, São Paulo, Rio de Janeiro, Mexico City, to name a few. Perhaps New York. I knew the spice business from the ground up. I know the nightclub business. It doesn't matter where the business is, in which country, what language is spoken. There is always someone with whom to connect—a distant cousin, a friend of an uncle, the brother-in-law of a schoolmate. You arrive, you get your bearings, and you go to work. It is a trait we have. I know that others are resentful of it, but thus we persevere with God's blessing in an otherwise hostile world.

But I worry about Lohmann. Will he survive the aftermath of a Second World War? There will be hunger, cold, unemployment, just as in 1918. But this time no Daniel Saporta will appear in the underground station with gold piasters sewn into his waistband.

January 29, 1944

I RESUME AFTER a three-day interval. The events that transpired here, in this very attic, have left me shaken and cowering under the covers of my couch. Relief did not come until Lohmann brought me the clipping from the daily press, which I will endeavor to translate fully.

Lohmann came to me after darkness had set in on the evening of January the twenty-fourth. He had barely put my food on the table when the cupboard was pushed aside and a sixteen- or seventeen-year-old boy in the uniform of the Hitler Youth stepped in. He held an electric torch in one hand, his ceremonial Nazi dagger in the other. Lohmann and I were speechless at this turn of events. The boy turned to Lohmann.

"We meet again, you old fart. I thought you were too old to visit those whores on the fourth floor so often. You're here to feed this Jew you're hiding, aren't you? We know how to handle traitors like you—hang you from a meat hook in a slaughterhouse, and even that's too good."

Lohmann tried to bluff. "Listen to me, you pimply faced little shit. I was fighting at the Führer's side in Munich when you weren't even born. Don't stick your nose into things you don't understand."

It didn't work. Instead the boy advanced on Lohmann menacingly, dagger extended.

"Tell that to the Gestapo, you tub of lard. And now, down the stairs, both of you: march, march!" he commanded.

When Lohmann did not respond at once, the boy flicked his dagger out at him. Lohmann raised his arm in self-defense, and we could hear the dagger cut through the fabric of the sleeve, followed by a dribble of blood snaking out of Lohmann's cuff. Without thought, purely from reflex action, I picked up the liter bottle of soup and brought it down on the boy's head. My reaction at the time was one of surprise that the bottle had not broken. The boy fell to the floor but collected himself in seconds and was getting to his hands and knees. Lohmann clutched his injured arm, stepped over, and with his heavy double-soled black boots kicked the boy powerfully in the temple. He collapsed and lay still.

Lohmann determined immediately that the boy was dead. In my feverish eastern imagination I already saw the building overrun with officers of the Kripo, the criminal police. They, with the help of the Gestapo, would ransack the building from cellar to attic and eventually find me cowering in my rat's nest.

Lohmann was completely calm, urging me to keep quiet and to drink from the bottle of Schnapps I held in reserve. The first thing he did was to remove his jacket, roll back the sleeve of his shirt, and examine the cut on his forearm. He had me dribble Schnapps on it, and then we ripped a sheet, making a firm bandage. He lined his jacket sleeve with newspaper to collect any seepage of blood. When this was over he would see a dentist friend from the "old days" who would set him aright.

In the meantime he had turned the boy on his back and was carefully emptying the contents of his pockets. There was some change, a jackknife, a dirty handkerchief, keys, and a wallet with its membership card in the Hitler Youth. In its recesses Lohmann found a photograph, creased and smudged by many hands, of a naked woman most probably taken from one of the nudist magazines so dear to the Germans. Lohmann placed all of this on the table in a neat row. He then inspected the boy's face carefully. He looked relatively serene, now turning pale, only the crusted pimples still glowing an angry red. There was no blood on the boy's head, neither where I had struck him with the bottle nor where Lohmann had booted him.

Lohmann declared himself satisfied with his findings and joined me in several shots of Schnapps. He cautioned me that we must save the dregs of the bottle.

When night had descended on the city, Lohmann repacked the boy's pockets with one notable exception—he did not replace the nude picture in the wallet. He took one of my pencils and in block letters wrote the name Inge over the picture. He then smudged the writing by rubbing the paper together, making it appear that the name had graced the photo for some time. Absorbed in his work, Lohmann had kept me out of it.

"Who is Inge, for God's sake?" I asked.

"Inge is the better looking of the two whores on the fourth floor. It is exactly the type of picture a little shit like our Hitler Youth friend would fantasize over while jerking off in the toilet." Lohmann seemed very pleased with himself as he put the folded picture into the boy's shirt pocket, taking care not to button the flap. Next he forced the boy's mouth open and gently trickled some of the Schnapps into it. Lohmann took the dagger, wiped the blade clean, and reinserted it into its sheath. The last thing he did was to remove the boy's shoes. These he stuffed into his own jacket; the torch he slipped into his hip pocket. He turned to me.

"Herr Saporta, please do not concern yourself. You are still perfectly safe. Stretch the little food you have. I cannot return until the case has been disposed of. A matter of two or three days."

He rechecked the rough bandage and, satisfied, put on his hat and coat. He picked the Hitler Youth up in a fireman's carry and stepped out of my attic.

For the ensuing three days I lived in terror, certain that every klaxon, every squealing brake, heralded a visit by the police. Nothing did transpire, and on the evening of the third day Lohmann showed up. He seemed a bit smug, smelling of cologne and cigars.

He had done the following: He had placed the boy's shoes and torch in front of the girls' door. It gave the impression that someone had been looking through the keyhole, or at least had been spying on the tenants. He had then gone to the apartment door directly opposite—that is, on the other side of the landing—and had pitched their fiber doormat down the long flight of stairs, hurling the boy with all his force after it. According to him, the thumps of the cascading body had seemed relatively muffled. Lohmann had stepped over the body at the bottom of the third-floor landing and had hurried down and out into the street.

For the benefit of the police he had set the stage to suggest that the boy had taken off his shoes to eavesdrop at the girls' front door, had been surprised by footsteps, had stepped back hurriedly onto the neighbors' doormat, and, unable to stop, had ended up tumbling down the stairs. Not a farfetched idea, considering the dangerous and glassy polish on the landings of Berlin's apartment houses.

Lohmann unfolded a newspaper, pointing out an article.

JUVENILE FOUND DEAD

Charlottenburg, January 28

The coroner's office of the District Court Charlottenburg today released findings that the death of Helmut S., 17 years of age, was accidental. Evidence found on the body indicated to police investigators that the deceased had been eavesdropping on a tenant occupying the apartment above the one he occupied with his widowed mother. The tenant in question, Inge F., and her roommate, Jutta K., indicated to the police that they had been the objects of the deceased's unwelcome attentions. The cause of death was listed as the result of a fatal fall.

January 30, 1944

Once i had resolved to break the grim news to Samira that she was to take Amina's place as Rabe's tutor, I hurried over to the apartment, smoked a hundred cigarettes, and rehearsed the speech with which I was going to enlist her in Dr. Steinbruch's operation. I had decided to be matter-of-fact about the whole thing, trusting that she would see the logic of it and agree to do her job with a minimum of theatrics.

When she came in, she was playful and in a good mood. She was not yet aware of Amina's imminent departure.

"Yah, habibi," she said. "Did you hear Amina's story about her SS man? She told me in secrecy, and you must promise not to tell anyone, but before they make love he crawls along the floor on all fours, like a dog, and Amina drags him along with a chain around his neck. Can you believe this?"

Indeed I could.

"That's not all, oh, you sweetheart! She whips him on his arse to make his zoub stand up. I don't see how she can do it. I couldn't do it in a thousand years."

She had taken her blouse off and threw her arms around my neck.

"Oh, you darling, I could never again make love with another man, not for the rest of my life. You have given me such happiness, I would give my life for you."

It was as if a shaitan, a devil, had whispered words into her ear that would render me helpless. By this time she had undressed and was expecting my caresses under our paisley tent.

"Hurry," she said, "or I shall make love to the tiger instead."

To taunt me she had wrapped her arms and legs around the tiger pelt, and while simulating coitus she whispered into the tiger's ear. "Oh, you tiger, you are so strong, you are so large. You are deep in my belly, you make me feel so weak. Please, oh, you tiger, don't stop."

The damned tiger's glass eyes seemed to sparkle. A man can

only take so much. Forgotten was Dr. Steinbruch, my speech, my resolve. The only thing that mattered was that I should take the tiger's place.

The following morning I communicated with Dr. Steinbruch. Two days later we met in the Lustgarten, a public park not far from Unter den Linden. As we sat under the big shade trees I told him of the decision I had taken. I was going to send Samira out of the country, possibly to Spain or Portugal; I was going to sell the club, even at a loss, and join Samira so that we could make a life for ourselves. I had plenty of money and could afford to sit out the war in the relative neutrality of Spain, my "homeland."

This time Dr. Steinbruch did not become abusive. He heard me out calmly and then turned to me.

"Before we discuss your impending nuptials, I want to tell you what's happened since we pulled Amina off the job and remain without information."

Dr. Steinbruch religiously monitored the BBC broadcasts, and of course he had his own sources of information, which he did not share with me.

"As you may have heard, the Iraqi government, under Rashid Ali, declared war on England on May second. To secure the Arab revolution, the Germans had promised to send troops to Baghdad from Crete. But by holding on in Crete the British foiled their plans. The Germans couldn't spare the troops, and the British struck from two flanks. They landed Indian troops at Basra, and British infantry crossed the desert from Palestine and occupied Baghdad. The Rashid Ali government collapsed, and the Mufti fled to Teheran."

At this point Dr. Steinbruch paused. He put his hand on my knee, and he spoke less pedantically, more intimately.

"These good tidings, Daniel, are soured by one event that took place in Baghdad. On June first and second, before the British entered the city, mobs attacked the Jewish quarter. They killed at least four hundred people; we need not speak of the brutality and the property damage." He was waiting for me to digest this bit of information. "A committee of inquiry has decided that the outrage was masterminded by the German Legation and by our friend the Mufti. It does not take much imagination to foretell a similar fate for the Jews of Teheran, where the Mufti is now installed, or for the Jews of Aleppo— or of Damascus, for that matter."

I sat silently, waiting for him to deliver the coup de grâce. It came quickly enough.

"I refuse to believe that a man of your resources, a man who became a success at the tender age of eighteen, not only in a foreign country but in a notoriously rough-and-tumble business, is going to sit on the sidelines while his people are wiped out. I shall be giving you a heaven-sent opportunity to seek revenge. When I told you on the Orient Express many years ago that I envied your background and that few of us are privileged to have so illustrious a history, I meant it. Daniel, the Saportas and the Toledanos did not survive the Inquisition so that their issue should be reduced to being a glorified pimp, indentured to the sphincters of his dancers. Think of the glorious past, Daniel. Go forth and spy as Moses' messengers did in the land of Canaan. Go out and smite the foe as Bar Kochba did the Syrians. Then you can sit under your fig tree with Samira, but not before. Now go and do as you must."

I knew he was right. I could not stay on in Berlin getting rich from the operation of the Kaukasus while my people, perhaps my relatives, were facing certain annihilation. I would have to do my share and so would Samira, willingly or not. Having taken a final decision, I felt a weight lifted off my shoulders, but when I thought of Samira's trusting soulful eyes and her warm mouth, its corners crinkling into a shy smile, an iron claw clutched at my heart and I railed against the fates that had brought me to this accursed land.

February 1, 1944

THE SIRENS HOWLED *throughout the night and there were air raids all over the city. The building across the street suffered a direct hit. I rather think it was a stray bomb, off its course, because nothing else fell nearby, or I would have heard it and felt the concussion. The fire brigade, incredibly well organized in spite of the continuous drain on its services, responded at once. A fire had broken out, and flames were bursting out of the window that matched my own—a mirror image, so to speak, right across the street. The fire truck put its ladder aloft, and the fireman directed a stream of water into the dormer window.*

Fascinated by so exciting a distraction, I stood rooted before my own window. Without warning, the ladder swung around, and I found myself face to face with the fireman who held the now-shut-off nozzle in his hand. I could clearly see his lacquered helmet, the brass escutcheon, the leather neck piece. The man's face was reddened by exertion, his mouth opened in surprise upon seeing me: a dark, stubbly cheeked, pallid man returning his gaze.

Terror prompted the thoughts that raced through my mind. What must the fireman have thought? All law-abiding citizens were either in their air raid shelters or milling about in the street, waiting for the police to permit them to return to their apartments. He would have known that these Berlin attics, hewn together out of rough boards, are not fit for human habitation. Who then was the solitary figure? A criminal? A spy directing enemy aircraft? Unlikely. Who then? A Jew. Obviously, a Jew who had escaped the long arm of a deportation commando. Was the fireman a Party member, as were so many policemen, or was his life's work as a fire fighter prompted by feelings of compassion for his fellowman? His long gaze, before the descending ladder carried him out of my sight, gave no hint as to his feelings. Would he report me to his superiors the minute he was on the street, or would he grant asylum, for whatever reason, to the poor devil hiding out in the attic? It was a riddle that will plague me from this day on.

Today I meant to record my confrontation with Samira but the encounter with the fireman has left me shaken. I shall seek relief in Lohmann's Schnapps and hope to quiet down.

February 2, 1944

ACTUALLY, I HAD NEVER DOUBTED that Samira would carry out my orders. I only doubted my resolve in issuing them to her. Samira came from a background in which a man's word was law. Although we had maintained our religious traditions, culturally we were not much different from our Moslem neighbors. We lived in a society in which girls obeyed their fathers and brothers; later, as wives and mothers, they obeyed their husbands and sons. This was especially true among the less privileged and less educated.

Among the Moslems a woman's word has no validity in a court of law, and even among the Jews a man can divest himself of his wife by having the rabbis issue her a bill of divorcement. The woman has little to say in the matter. Powerless in the western sense, the women of the East spend their lives sweeping, washing, cooking, fetching water, mending, baking. Their chores are interrupted only by their own weddings and childbirth.

Samira's youth had not been noticeably different; she had been servant to father and brothers. Once she started to work in nightclubs she carried out the wishes of her employer or patron. I anticipated that because of our relationship she would resist me at first, but I was quite certain that in the end she would obey—slave to a lifetime of obedience.

It was the price we were to pay for her capitulation that I never calculated.

I did not want to risk another amorous encounter in our flat, so I asked Samira into the more neutral confines of my office. It was late and Lohmann had already locked up for the night. Fortified by vodka, I started off by telling her of the precarious position of the Jews, not only in Europe but also in the Arab East. By the manner in which she exhaled the smoke from her cigarette, and by the way she had of looking over my head at the wall behind me, I could tell she was distancing herself from the subject into which I was trying to lead her. Intuitively, she resolved to make my task more difficult by showing her disinterest. It only served to heighten my sense of guilt at the betrayal to which I had acquiesced at Steinbruch's urging. Wanting to be done with this hateful task, I threw caution to the winds.

"Samira," I said, "it is essential that you take Amina's place as Rabe's tutor, at least for a little while." When she opened her mouth in protest, I plunged on. "In his presence you will see and hear things which you must report to me."

"Knowing what went on between Amina and him, you ask this of me?" she said. "Knowing of my love for you, you want to prostitute me to him? Daniel, tell me what you are saying is not true. Tell me it is a nightmare."

"Samira, you are making too much of this. We are being given a chance to strike back at the Nazis. It is a risk we must take; it is a mitzvah, a worthy deed," I replied.

"Fucking Nazis is not a mitzvah. My God, I am so ashamed of you. I wish I could die."

I decided to harden my heart. If not, I would be undone once more. "There's more to being Jewish than making haroset on Passover, Samira."

"I paid the price of being Jewish at fifteen. With my blood, on the back seat of a taxi. What did you do, you bastard?" she shouted.

"Samira, last week they killed four hundred Jews in the Jewish quarter of Baghdad. Next week it could be Aleppo! The Mufti is doing this for the Germans. We must help the people who are fighting the Nazis. We owe it to our people."

"I owe them nothing. After I was raped I became as terefah as the tail of a pig. Since then I've lived by my wits—until I met you. I thought it was all behind me, that we would make a life somewhere together. It's not too much to ask, a little happiness. You know I would do anything for you. I would walk the streets for you, but don't deliver me to this animal."

My heart was breaking, but I knew that unless I provoked her into the anger, the fury, the gutter abuse of which she was capable, she would best me again. "I'm not asking you to walk the streets. All I'm asking you to do is spend some time with Rabe and report to me everything that you hear and see."

"Spend some time with him? You mean walk him around on a

chain and flog him, so he can fuck me? Is that what you want, you piece of khara?'' Her tears were giving way to fury and abuse.

"Yes, fuck him. You've fucked your way from Aleppo to Zagazig and back again, so what's one more in your life?" She came at me like a madwoman. Her fingernails raked my cheek and drew blood.

"Dog. Pimp. I'll kill you!'' She was totally out of control, starting one of the funereal middle eastern wails. I gave her a powerful slap across the face that sent her sprawling to the floor. I knelt beside her, grabbed her hair, and forced her head back painfully, until we were eye to eye.

"Shut your mouth,'' I told her. "Listen to me. You will do as I say. You will go with Rabe tonight, and you will give him his Arabic lesson. If he asks it of you, you will lead him around by his belt, and you will whip his arse. And you will do whatever else he asks of you. Whatever.'' I shook her by the roots of the hair. All the while she was glaring at me, building a growl of anger in the back of her throat. "Tomorrow you will come to me and you will tell me where you went, whom you met, what you saw, what you heard. Every last detail. And you will continue to do this until I tell you to stop.'' I gave her hair another painful yank and released her.

With an animal howl she kicked out at me, sending me sprawling. She threw herself on me, kicking, kneeing, biting, scratching. Abuse poured out of her mouth. To protect myself I struck out at her, tried to twist her arms, pin her down. We rolled on the floor, sending a chair crashing on its side. Finally I overpowered her, my sheer body weight pinning her down, my hands holding her wrists above her head. And while we were panting face-to-face, a powerful sexual urge came over us. What unleashed it I don't know—perhaps the knowledge that this would be the last time, or something more primordial, something compounded of hatred and sweat, of adrenaline and tears. We rutted on the floor, I angrily tumescent, Samira going from climax to climax. Finally we were spent. We withdrew from each other as do boxers at the end of a round.

Samira picked her clothes off the floor and faced me from across the room. "I will do as you say. I had no right to hope for a life with you. My life was determined in the back of a taxi. I loved you with everything within me. But now it's over. Don't ever touch me again.''

Every fiber of my being screamed to take her into my arms, to say, No, it isn't so! Nothing is preordained, I love you. Oh, Samira, I want to be with you forever when this nightmare is done, please. But I would not let the words escape.

Samira had already shut me out of her life. Unconcerned, she slowly put on her clothes. It was the last time I was to see the gazelle-like body which had given me so much joy, the fragrant hollows, the small high breasts, the dark elongated nipples like fresh dates, the regally fine long legs, the silken skin with its odor of almonds.

It was over. She dressed and softly closed the door behind her.

I had not wept since hearing of the death of my father. But the tears came, tears compounded of loss, of shame, of longing, of sorrow, of anger. The loss of Samira brought home to me how much I missed my parents, my brother and sisters, and my cousin Eli. For over ten years I had lived among strangers, denying my ancestry, my family, my faith—and, making it worse, enjoying the corrupt life I had eagerly espoused.

And now I had lost Samira. I could not banish the shock, the hurt in her eyes when I proposed her liaison with Rabe. Why should she not believe I was asking her to participate in some perverse charade, unable as I was to tell her that I also was acting at someone's behest?

Finally immobilized by alcohol and feelings of self-hatred, I fell asleep behind my desk. It was Lohmann who found me in this condition in the morning. Ever tactful, he withdrew, to reappear with a pot of black coffee.

I passed Samira's findings on to Dr. Steinbruch on another journey on the S Bahn. This time we met on the platform of the Ostkreuz station. Her first report had been extensive, and Dr. Steinbruch listened silently in the rear of the nearly empty car.

Rabe had taken Samira to Dahlem, the most elegant part of town, in which industrialists and bankers maintained luxurious and imposing mansions. These enormous villas were surrounded by vast expanses of lawn and trees, complete with swimming pools, pergolas, and greenhouses. The overall effect was one of elegance, and above all one of opulent privacy. Many of these fine villas had been abandoned by their Jewish owners and were now administered by the state.

Samira had been taken to such a villa on a Z-shaped street, Auf dem Graf. When Rabe sent her home in a taxi she had been able to see the street sign fleetingly. It was a billet where Rabe and his fellow SS officers, all those who had come to the club and many more, were quartered. She suspected that more than Arabic was taught here; she had seen signs in Arabic letters but, unable to read them, thought they might be Farsi—Persian, as it is known in the West. Her description of the entrance was similar to Amina's: a manned sentry post at the gate. She mentioned the same billiard tables in the public rooms downstairs. She made it a point to remember some of the officers' names: Brockmann, Schlüter, Deschamps, von Nagy. She was studying the SS ranks and the significance of the pips on their shoulder boards and would assign each man his correct rank later. She had also met the Iraqi instructors: they were both captains, Muhammad Nawabi and Mustafa Shawa, the former a Baghdadi, the latter from Mosul. They had treated her with barely concealed contempt and disdain for an Arab girl who was sleeping with these Almanis. She also reported that each was dressed in field gray, and wore a red tarboosh. There had been other Arabs, civilians, five or six in number; she thought they were students at the various universities around Berlin. The posters on the walls, many in Arabic quoting the Grand Mufti, had obviously come from his office in Damascus or Baghdad. They consisted of the usual anti-British and anti-Jewish agitation.

The officers had their quarters upstairs, while the downstairs was used for lectures. Samira reported that the dining rooms, salons, conservatories, and solarium were all used for instruction of the young officers. She had heard popular Arabic music being played on a gramophone in one of the rooms. A leader, it must have been one of the Arabs, was teaching the Germans to clap their hands to the rhythm of the music in the peculiar Arab style. Later she had heard the Moslem doxology repeated over and over, first by an Arab voice, then by a number of Germans. "Allahu akbar, Allahu akbar... God is Great, God is great; I testify there is no God but Allah, and Mohammed is his prophet."

One did not have to be an intelligence specialist to deduce that these SS men were being trained for service with an Arab or Moslem unit. Dr. Steinbruch was impressed.

"That's an extraordinary girl you have there," he said. "All that information in less than a week. Tell her to be careful. She should not overplay her hand. Just observe and report. Excellent, Daniel."

February 4, 1933

SAMIRA HAD MOVED BACK to the Pension Stella. All that remained of her in our apartment was her perfume, maddeningly impregnating the pillows, the bedclothes, the closets. No wonder I spent more and more time at the Kaukasus, getting in Frau Novikov's way in the kitchen, going through the books with Lohmann. Loyal as dogs, they indulged me, pretending not to notice my longing for Samira.

Yet it was here in my office that our debriefing sessions took place. She always made me feel inadequate as she imparted new information to me. She would close her eyes as she spoke, not only to avoid the tobacco smoke that she exhaled in a powerful stream but also to avoid making contact with me. She let me feel she was living an exciting existence with Rabe, exposed to events of historical importance, while I was no more than a desk-bound clerk.

She heightened my anger and sense of worthlessness by never complaining of Rabe and what should have been his unwelcome demands on her. I feared she had become a willing accomplice to his aberrations, deriving pleasure from them to the degree that they had now become true lovers. Perhaps her childhood experience had conditioned her to this, or, as in the case of Hilde and her brutal lover, they had found a common sexual ground.

She lit a cigarette and started her report. As usual we spoke in Arabic, the language in which we felt most at ease. When a term of precision was lacking she resorted to French or to her now formidable vocabulary of German military and political terms. Her lover, Sturmbannführer Rabe, possibly because of his rank, enjoyed special privileges, one of them being that his commanding officer, Standartenführer Heinz Jürgen Novak, closed an understanding eye to Samira's occasionally staying in Rabe's quarters overnight.

It was during the aftermath of her most recent all-night visit that she had become witness to a new development. She had ordered a taxi for the early morning hours, and was descending in response to its horn, when she observed from the darkness of the first-floor landing a group of some thirty men in the traditional position of prayer—that is, on their knees with their foreheads touching the ground—in the act of completing the Moslem morning doxology. When they arose, to her surprise, the newcomers were not only the Arabs she had become used to but red-cheeked Europeans with brown and blond hair who conversed with one another in a non-Sharki, or non-Eastern, tongue. When I pressed her for a hint of what she had heard, she suddenly broke into one of her all too seldom smiles, a smile not meant for me, but for her sudden appraisal of a fact. The men sounded, she said, exactly like Frau Novikov speaking with her fellow Russians.

She dropped another bombshell before she left my office. Rabe had told her that a seminar was taking place the week of November ninth to sixteenth, and they would not be seeing each other until the week-long seminar, in the activities of which he was deeply involved, was over. While Rabe was taking the roll call at six-thirty in the morning, she had taken a quick look at mimeographed papers littering his desk.

Although unable to read German, she had the wit to memorize a number of names appearing under the date of the proscribed week. She ticked them off: Himmler, Eichmann, Von Ribbentrop, Dr. Frank, Alfred Rosenberg, and, as she slowly ground around her cigarette out in my saucer, "Der Gross Mufti." She said it in German with a touch of triumph.

By God, she had recited the entire pantheon of Germany's fanatics and professional Jew killers! I sat momentarily speechless, assimilating this incredible information.

"That's all I have for today," Samira said. "That is, of a political nature. As I am duty-bound to report to you my sexual activities also, I have news. My love affair with Sturmbannführer Rabe has been expanded. We are now joined by Captain Mustafa Shawa of the Iraqi army. I still have to flog the Almani, but a refinement has been added. I have to rouge his lips and cheeks while Captain Shawa does him in the fashion of dogs. My services have become secondary; only when the soldiers feel playful am I called on for my talents." She stood up to go. "Daniel, I have a suggestion to make to you. Do you remember how I fixed your breakfast, waiting for you to finish your morning prayers?"

I nodded stupidly.

"When you say the Shaharit, stop using God's name or you'll choke on your own vomit." She had the maddening habit of softly closing the door behind her.

February 5, 1944

I SAT IN THE DARKNESS of the bar of the Kaukasus, watching Samira do her last number of the evening. How she managed to smile, how she maintained the stamina to dance, was unfortunately not a mystery to me. Hashish saw her though the days and through the nights. I was finishing my second vodka, but I did not need the alcohol to tell me that the Kaukasus had become tarnished, lusterless, run-down. The audience also was pathetic; the people of Berlin already understood that the quick, heady victory which had been promised them was more elusive than ever. The good wines were running out, we were serving second-rate German sekt instead of champagne, and in spite of Frau Novikov's efforts the food had lost its zest. The Russian food had become ersatz, as had everything else. Our clientele had also suffered. Gone were the high livers, the shady operators, the chic call girls and elegant lesbians, out of fashion with a puritanical government. Instead there were company-grade officers from the provinces, their ladies possessing all the charm and elegance of maids' night out. Our guests consisted of arrogant, ill-mannered Party offi-cials in their myriad mustard-colored uniforms, and of soldiers who gave lachrymose parties before being shipped off to a hero's death on the Eastern Front.

I became aware of Lohmann, who, also with glass in hand, had seated himself on a bar stool next to me.

"I know what you're thinking, Herr Salazar," Lohmann said. "Our little jewel is turning into a clump of coal" He drained his Steinhäger. "I was thinking that perhaps we should change the program. This riff-raff doesn't appreciate our lovely girls, and they don't give a shit about their dancing. They come to see 'belly dancers,' hoping to see them naked like in Sankt Pauli." He was referring to the notorious red-light district of the Reeperbahn in Hamburg, where almost everything was permitted. "When I think of the expense of bringing these girls from Turkey, the cost of putting them up in the

Knesebeckstrasse, and the cost of their wardrobe, it makes me want to weep."

Lohmann was in the throes of Weltschmerz, a peculiar form of Teutonic melancholia that can go on for hours, and I chose not to interrupt him. Besides, from a business point of view he was making total sense. "Go on, Lohmann," I said.

"Look at our beautiful place," he said. "Those priceless Russian icons, the French wallpaper, the mirrors you bought in Rome. All pearls before these swine. You've seen the conditions of the toilets; they look like the shithouse at the railroad station. I've stopped putting out our perfumed hand soap. They steal it, as they do the towels. They write filth on the walls. All the carpets are scorched because they grind their cigarettes out on the floor. I'm glad Lilo is not here to see it." Lohmann's litany continued unabated. "I've thought of putting in a mud ring. You know, two barely dressed fat sows fighting in the mud, no holds barred, lots of tits and arse. Or, if it weren't for the expense, putting telephones on the tables, like at the Resi. Or packing the bar with whores." He paused. "I once saw a chorus line of Liliputians in Hamburg, wearing almost nothing. It was terrible. The audience screamed, they loved it. There are still a couple of Cuban transvestites in town—"

At this point I was called to the telephone. The message was short: a nine o'clock meeting on the banks of the Havel.

When I returned to the bar, Lohmann had poured himself a beer, brushed back his thinning hair, and lit himself a fresh cigar. "Just a final observation, Herr Salazar, with your indulgence. Fräulein Samira has been here far too long to be an attraction. The two Turks we've brought in are bumpkins who trip over their own feet. The musicians stink."

I felt these random remarks were merely a prologue to something more serious, and I was right. He pushed aside his glass of beer and looked me in the face until he was sure we had made eye contact.

"Herr Salazar, what I am going to say to you has been like a stone on my heart for months. Let me say it, and we will speak of it no more. I am not even asking for an answer." He pulled his snow-white handkerchief out of the breast pocket of his dark blue suit and wiped his hands. I waited. "Herr Salazar, you are a better businessman than I will ever be. I remember your speaking of your early years working for your father in Damascus. You spoke to me of a world that I did not know existed. I saw you buy this dump from that Russian crook to whom I brought you, and I saw you prosper, I saw the Kaukasus prosper, and through your Menschlichkeit I prospered with you. Today the club is dying. It no longer gives you joy, it no longer gives you pride. Even the girls disgust you. There's hardly a man in Berlin who's slept with as many beautiful women as you, Herr Salazar, and with the exception of Fräulein Latifa not a bad word with any of them.''

He smiled in recollection of more innocent days. The smile quickly vanished as he looked off at the dance floor. He pointed his beer glass in the general direction of Samira, who was listlessly concluding her number.

"Look at Fräulein Samira. She was the jewel of our establishment. Look at her now. She's pitiful, she breaks my heart.''

I had said nothing, but he felt compelled to pause before getting into deeper waters.

"You have never confided in me, and I never had the right to expect that you should. I believe you are keeping this place going for the benefit of others. I believe you are here because you want to be, because God knows with your Spanish passport you could have left years ago. You've been in Germany since 1929; this is 1941, and you still don't understand us. You ignore the fact that thousands of clerks sit in hundreds of ministries filing, refiling, sorting, and resorting millions of index cards of our citizens and especially those of the foreigners in our midst. Your Spanish passport and the crucifix in your office are great camouflage, but God help you if, through a fluke, two tiny entries in two dust-covered ledgers don't match.''

I kept quiet. I had decided many years before that my surest guarantee of Lohmann's safety was to keep him in complete ignorance of my activities.

"One more thing, Herr Salazar. Over the years I've become a comfortable citizen. I've put money aside. I've gotten commissions on every pound of meat, on every bottle, on every roll of toilet paper I've bought for the Kaukasus. You know my needs: my Böhnicke cigars, an occasional roll in the hay with a bit of fluff, and my work with you. What I have is yours. I only hope you're not in deeper trouble than my nose tells me.''

He added a certain formality to the end of the monologue by doing something peculiarly German. He took my right hand into his and bowed deeply from the waist, permitting me an unobstructed view of his balding pate. He held this pose for a second, then released my hand and walked into the foyer. He never raised the issue again.

February 6, 1944

TODAY, WELCOME RELIEF *to the monotony of my days. They are repairing the damage caused by the stray bomb during the night of February first. In spite of the cold I've kept my window open so I can hear fragments of shouted orders for a sheet of tin, a wooden beam, a bucket of paint. By perching on the backrest of my sofa deep in my cubicle, I remain in the shadows, invisible to the workers even if they should glance my way. As I hear the workers shouting in their unique Berlin accents, as I hear the clink of beer bottles at midday, I realize how completely I am shut off from the most basic human contact. When the workers leave, I shall miss their cheerful voices. It is enough to start a new wave of melancholia. As I am getting low on food, I am certain that Lohmann will come tonight. His presence alone will make me feel better.*

The room is getting ice cold, but I am afraid to close the window until the workers have departed. Fortunately in February it gets dark early in the afternoon, and the workers will leave soon. I see new tin flashing, fresh paint on the window frame, a shiny piece of rain gutter.

Who but the Germans would be repairing everything as carefully as they? More rational people would wait until the end of the war, lest tonight's raid renders today's work useless.

February 8, 1944

ON THE MORNING of November 8, 1941, Dr. Steinbruch and I met at a rural café where the Havel empties into the Pichels lake. It is a pastoral enclave, many of which still exist in the lake and marshlands which have, with the growth of the city, become incorporated into it.

We sat undisturbed on the rough bench of this café, now closed for the winter. Our only witnesses were marsh birds that stalked the frozen reeds nearby.

I enumerated the cast of characters on Rabe's mimeographed roster, which Samira had committed to memory. Dr. Steinbruch's evaluation was simplistically brutal. Himmler, the chief of the SS; Eichmann, specialist in Jewish affairs who had spent time in Palestine; Foreign Minister Von Ribbentrop; Dr. Frank, Reichsminister of Justice and Governor of Poland; Rosenberg, Reichsminister for the Occupied Territories of the east—they were the prime movers in eradication of the Jews. The Grand Mufti's presence merely confirmed his complicity in this act of mass murder, with the additional attraction that this volatile and brilliant demagogue could stir up Moslem insurrections from Indonesia to the Caucasus.

The Slavic-speaking Moslems seen by Samira in the Dahlem villa presented no enigma to Dr. Steinbruch either. They were quite obviously Bosnian Moslems, possibly officers to head battalions of Moslem volunteers to be raised in Greater Croatia.

The history of the Balkans had never been my strong point, and Dr. Steinbruch proceeded to remedy this. With the capture of Yugoslavia by the Germans, that unfortunate country had quickly been fragmented. The Serbs, Greek Orthodox by religion, had sided with the British and had set up their formidable partisan units in the mountains. Their traditional enemies, the Croats, who were Roman Catholic, had set up a Nazi puppet state under the infamous Ante Pavelic and his first minister, Andrija Artukovic. Financed and armed by the Germans, the Croats had added to their own lands the old

Ottoman province of Bosnia, whose population was mostly Moslem. Up to the thirteenth century, these Bosnians had actually belonged to the Bosnian Church, but when these good Christians felt themselves and their holdings threatened by their Hungarian neighbors, they happily threw in their lot with the Turks by converting to Islam. As converts they had become fanatical in the practice of their new faith, and now, seven centuries later, they had become the willing allies of the Croats in the savage and cruel massacre of Serbs, Jews, and Gypsies.

Dr. Steinbruch, ever the German academician, was warming to his subject. Evidently we were settling down to a lengthy session because from the pocket of his overcoat he brought forth a paper-wrapped parcel tied with its little girdle of string. He untied the knot, rolled up the string, and lovingly exposed a large Streuselkuchen. This he carefully dissected with his pocketknife and gestured for me to help myself. He was now ready to face greater issues.

"My boy, sitting here under God's blue sky is as good a time as any to review our association, one that may not have been constant, but which on my side at least was compounded equally of affection and self-interest."

I did not interrupt.

"How could I not have been taken with you on the Orient Express? You were seventeen, handsome as a Grecian statue, polite, winning, but with that Levantine cunning that comes from life in the souk. But there was more to you than that. You had respect for your family and above all for your people. And at seventeen you already spoke Arabic, French, Hebrew, Italian; you even had a smattering of English and were attacking the German clauses. And there you sat in the compartment with me, drinking raki, speaking of your uncles and your cousins, of that whole crazy quilt of Levantine culture with which this Germanic mind has been absorbed for decades. When I saw you at the railroad station with the Landaus, I knew you would be creeping into Frau Landau's knickers, in spite of your protestations that she seduced you. I watched you, Daniel, until the Nazis came to power, when I first came to you. Had I been honest, I would have frightened you into leaving Germany, as good sense should have told you. But my interests in you lay in the future—and, my boy, the moment has arrived."

We sat across the rough table from each other, crumbling the lovely cake into our mouths, he waiting for my queries, I not nearly so anxious to know what was to come.

"What do you want me to do? Assassinate the Grand Mufti? As a nightclub owner, I'm singularly qualified."

Steinbruch ignored my puerile remark.

"I want you to go to Sarajevo, and I want you to hire a troupe of Bosnian dancers for the Kaukasus. You could start by advertising the performance as an appreciation for the Croatian war effort. You should have no difficulty in getting travel documents. There are many businessmen going to the Balkans to buy tobacco, produce, and lumber. When you get there take your time; don't hire the first troupe. All of this you know much better than I. Interview many artists; singers too, if you wish. It will give you a chance to get the feel and the smell of the place."

He fed more cake into his hateful little mouth and, after fastidiously wiping away crumbs with his handkerchief, continued.

"I want you to stay at the Hotel Bosphor. I'm told it's quite a nice place, kept up in the style of the Ottomans, the sort of place where a prominent Berlin nightclub owner would stay. Good food, local wines, and frequented by the local ruling classes. By that I mean the leadership of the Ustashas, the local Nazis. One of our people will contact you there, a waiter at the hotel. He will be of help to you."

"Dr. Steinbruch, I don't need a waiter to help me cast a nightclub troupe; that is, after all, my business." I was tiring of the condescension, of the hours of sitting in the marshland, where a cold wind had started to blow.

"If you were a little less egocentric you would realize that the hiring of Bosnian dancers is secondary to our cause. In fact I don't give a damn about dancers, Bosnian or otherwise. This whole business is merely a cover to give you legitimacy in extremely dangerous surroundings."

Suddenly I felt the increased heartbeat, the dryness of the mouth, the contraction of the lower bowel that Lohmann had once described to me as the soldier's reaction to being ordered "over the top," to leave the relative safety of the trenches to face withering enemy machine-gun fire. Finally I mustered the courage to ask, "What's dangerous about hiring dancers, even in Bosnia?"

"No danger in hiring dancers," he replied. "The danger lies in penetrating the Waffen SS, in avoiding the Ustasha henchmen."

I felt another wave of nausea rising in my gorge. "Surely there are others more suited than I for this line of work?" I proffered.

"Indeed there are. There are highly competent men on the ground. But they all lack your special qualification. You are a genuine nightclub owner; you are logically qualified to look for talent; besides, you speak fluent German and have been rubbing elbows with the army and the SS since 1933. You know how to talk to them, and I suspect you will know some of the officers from the Kaukasus."

It was going from bad to worse. This vile little man who had insinuated himself into my life was not satisfied with ruining my future with Samira; not content in having prostituted her, he was now planning to deliver me to the SS in faroff Bosnia.

Dr. Steinbruch read my face and in a gesture of impatience swept the cake crumbs from the table. "Try to understand this. The Mufti has been to Bosnia. He's been recruiting young Moslems into the Waffen SS. You will need help in reporting to us the success of the recruitment drive among the local Bosnians. We still don't know where the Waffen SS have set up their main headquarters. We have reason to believe they are training their levies in the local mountains. But we don't know how many, or their condition of readiness. These, Daniel, are all things I want you to ascertain before you return to Berlin."

I felt that much was left unsaid, that I was being sucked in deeper, perhaps more deeply than Steinbruch cared to tell me. But wasn't that exactly what I had done to Samira? Now that it was my turn, the fact that Samira had been at it for weeks was cold comfort to me.

February 10, 1944

I TOOK LOHMANN WITH ME when I presented myself to the army authorities in charge of Travel Authorization for Occupied Territories. They were housed in a grim fortresslike building, an adjunct to the Reichsbahn Administration. "Lose hope, all ye who enter here" went through my mind as we crossed the glacial flagstone entrance. But Lohmann felt totally at home in these forbidding corridors, with their somber nameplates in Gothic script listing ranks, departments, and subdepartments, with Roman letters followed by slashes and further numerology.

Lohmann rapped smartly on the door and was rewarded with a barked command to enter. We were received by an old-line captain whose left hand was permanently encased in a leather glove. As the First World War ribbons on his tunic indicated, he clearly belonged to an older generation. Lohmann played him like a mellowed cello. He addressed him in the third person, requesting on behalf of his employer, the highly respected Spanish impresario Señor Salazar, that he be issued travel documents so we might mount a spectacle, with patriotic overtones, with the gifted artists of our brother in arms, Croatia. I interjected that my club, the Kaukasus, was one frequented by the highest military and political circles.

At the mention of the Kaukasus, the Hauptmann looked at me and bared his teeth in a frightening grimace, caused by the fact that his left eye was of glass and neither rotated nor closed. Actually he was well disposed toward us. In the old Prussian military manner he spoke in clipped shorthand. "Ah, Kaukasus. Splendid place. Knew it well. In the old days. Great girls, eh?"

I handed him my Spanish passport, which he gave but cursory inspection before passing it on to his secretary, a strapping blond female auxiliary in army uniform. We dutifully sat through the *clackity-clack* of her typewriter, the scratchy sound of pen entries being made in a ledger, and that most German of sounds, the thud of a rubber stamp alternately hitting paper and stamp pad. The Hauptmann signed the paperwork, and the secretary handed me the passport. She was working in shirt sleeves, and I noticed dark stains of perspiration under her armpits. She favored me with a flirtatious smile, holding the passport for an instant longer than necessary before releasing it to me. The odor of female perspiration struck me, and I felt my groin respond. The hold Samira had on me was weakening.

We thanked the Hauptmann and turned to leave. Lohmann, for the benefit of the office personnel, said "Heil Hitler," but the Hauptmann ignored it. As we were halfway out the door he called me back.

"Señor Salazar. Very good Schnapps in those parts. Vinjak. Slivovitza. Rakija. Good day!"

February 11, 1944

BEFORE LOHMANN TOOK ME TO THE STATION I had him write the following letter on our office typewriter. It is committed to memory because it was not only my singular act of disobedience to Dr. Steinbruch but also my last and desperate attempt to save Samira from the situation into which I had plunged her. Lohmann promised not only to deliver it to her personally but to do everything in his power to enforce the terms of the instrument. Since the seminar was of a week's duration, I was gambling that my plan had a measure of success. It would fail only if Samira was actually bound to Rabe by sexual chains, or if he broke security by calling or meeting with her during this week of activities of a supposedly highly secret nature.

KLUB KAUKASUS
Berlin, Charlottenburg
Meinekestrasse 142

Frau Samira Mansour
Pension Stella

Frau Mansour!   November 12, 1941

Please consider this letter your notification of immediate dismissal from the Klub Kaukasus.

You are in breach of contract because of your repeated tardiness and by your addiction to narcotics which renders you incapable of satisfactorily performing the services for which you were contracted. Should you decide to make an issue of our decision, we are prepared to prefer charges against you with the Kriminal Polizei, since your narcotic suppliers are known to us.

We have under separate cover informed your theatrical agent, Karnig Minassian of Hemediye Cadasi, Istanbul, of your breach and of our ensuing decision. We reserve the right to look to you for damages suffered by us. The return ticket to Turkey, held in trust by us under the terms of our employment agreement, will be made available to you upon your understanding of, and agreement to, the termination of your employment.

With German salutations,

Klub Kaukasus, the Management

I signed it in my acquired Gothic hand.

I had worded the letter in such a fashion that, should Lohmann actually succeed in shipping Samira out of Germany, the document causing her dismissal would stand scrutiny by a probably enraged Rabe. Lohmann promised that he would use all the persuasion at his command to put her on the train to Istanbul before the sixteenth.

February 12, 1944

LOHMANN CAME LAST NIGHT. *The meager fare he brought—some poor gray bread and a piece of sausage, mostly fat and cereal—told me something was amiss. He cautioned me to ration the food for the next few days, and after watching me wolf down a sandwich he spoke of his misfortune.*

As usual he had taken the train to join his jolly widow and her ample larder. As usual he had placed his sample case into the overhead rack of a compartment distant from his own. As the result of a fortunate haul, the case was filled to overflowing with elegant vanity sets: silver-backed hand mirrors, combs with silver spines, cosmetic jars, buttonhooks, ladies and gentlemen's hairbrushes, toothbrushes, soap containers, and clothes brushes, all in a matching silver pattern.

A military police patrol had boarded the train, not an unusual event in wartime, but this time not content with checking the travelers' identity documents, they had insisted that each passenger point out his personal luggage in their search for contraband. When the military police entered Lohmann's compartment, he noticed with consternation that one of the soldiers was carrying his sample case. For a moment he feared that someone had described his likeness to the military policemen, but Lohmann knew that the travelers were united in their war-weariness and in their aversion to the MPs, an aversion imparted to them by husbands, sons, and brothers who served in combat units. The soldiers completed their inspection and left the compartment with Lohmann's sample case in tow.

A greater disaster was to befall Lohmann that day. When he let himself into the widow's kitchen, he found her red-eyed at the table with a young man in uniform, his empty right sleeve pinned to his tunic. It was the widow's eldest son, a panzer grenadier, who had unexpectedly returned from the Russian front minus his arm. He had a half-drained bottle of Obstler, a potent fruit spirit, in front of him and he took an instant dislike to Lohmann. In his dark suit, with cigar case in his vest pocket, smelling of pomade and good tobacco, Lohmann seemed to the grenadier the embodiment of a war profiteer. He accused his mother of carrying on with a fat parasite while her husband, the veterinarian, lay buried in a Polish cabbage patch. When his mother attempted to calm him, the young man started to laugh insanely, saying that the jig was up anyway, that the Russians were breaching the German lines everywhere and they would soon be rolling into Pomerania and Silesia. He would move his mother to the West and take his chances with the British and the Americans. Perhaps a profiteer such as Lohmann would buy the farm; he could buy it for a pittance now that his father and those before him had put their backs and lifeblood into it. Needless to say, the atmosphere did not augur well for a continued relationship between Lohmann and the good widow.

Lohmann said his real regret was that he had lost the source of our food supply. But Herr Saporta was not to worry. Lohmann would come up with something. Although the times militated against it, looking into Lohmann's shiny, guileless face, I chose to believe him.

February 13, 1944

THE JOURNEY FROM BERLIN to Sarajevo, normally of forty-eight hours' duration, took just under a week. We were routed via Prague and Vienna, finally crossing over into Yugoslavia at Klagenfurt and then on to the Croatian capital of Zagreb. At that point, travel gave up all pretense of being in Europe and became a Balkan adventure, consisting of hours of standing in meadows or on railroad sidings with unpronounceable names; often as not changing trains at unforeseen junctions. The reasons for this were not hard to discern. The German army, which since its invasion of Russia had captured most major cities, taken a million prisoners, and wiped out whole Russian army corps, was running out of steam. With the Germans at the gates of Moscow, Russian armored brigades in new British tanks were suddenly rolling up, and the new Russian T-34 tank proved superior to anything the Germans had. Equally catastrophic for the Germans was that the Russians and the Japanese had accommodated each other, not choosing to fight just yet, which permitted the Russians to bring battle-hardened divisions back from Siberia. As a result of these developments the German railroad, a masterpiece of technology and superb logistics, was heavily overworked.

In spite of ever increasing and ever more successful bombing raids by the RAF on Germany's cities and industrial areas, the Germans were building more locomotives than ever. They were also integrating into their system Balkan and even Russian equipment, some going back to the First World War.

So while I, Sarajevo bound, sat on railroad sidings thoughtlessly shunted aside, troop trains carrying reinforcements rattled toward Romania and endless evacuation trains, painted ominously with the red cross, were bringing the wounded and the mutilated back to Germany.

I was woefully unprepared for the journey. Dining cars had mostly been suspended, and the peasants at the provincial stations had little more than bread and apricot brandy for sale. Some very correct German army officers offered to share some of their rations with me, finding it embarrassing that they should eat while I looked out at the countryside.

Fortunately my papers were in Prussian order, because the farther I was carried from Berlin, the more hostile and surly the endless passport controls by legions of military police, plainclothes officers, and other uniformed personnel became. I saw many obviously innocent people, guilty only of some bureaucratic sloppiness visited upon them, being dragged off the train. When the black-uniformed Ustashas boarded the train in Croatia, I too felt barely suppressed waves of paranoia.

All this was forgotten as the train steamed into Sarajevo on November eighteenth. To the right of me I could see the Miljacka River crossing the valley floor and, on the hillsides of the town, the countless mosques, their sublimely graceful minarets pointing to the heavens. And everywhere green cypress groves and wooden buildings with their latticed overhangs.

The Bosphor Hotel was indeed a monument to the days of the Ottomans. It had been built with the comfort of pashas and aghas and their retinues in mind. My room faced a town square where I observed the locals sitting at little tables drinking cups of Turkish coffee. I wasted no time in joining them. In spite of the wartime atmosphere, oriental ways introduced by the Turks centuries before had imposed their own pace and measure on the people. Mustachioed men were drinking coffee or reading the papers, if not in heated discussion with their fellows. Others sat in solitary contemplation, fingering their worry beads absentmindedly. If not for the bracing mountain air, it was not vastly different from the towns I had visited with my father in Syria and Lebanon.

I strolled along the little streets and alleyways of the souk area, passing shops engaged in the sale of reproductions of silver Turkish necklaces, amulets, mashallahs, and the tiny coin-threaded chains that graced bridal pillbox caps. On my way, I admired the little cottage industries of weavers wielding their shuttles on old-fashioned looms. Many of the rugs, crafted from thick sheep's wool, were so much to my liking that under other circumstances I would have bought them for my apartment. And from every little copper smithy or coffeehouse I heard the minor key music, compounded of strings and tambour, so dear and familiar to me. The only inconsistent element was the Slavic tongue that gave voice to these old Turkish melodies.

On my way back to the hotel, my newly found enchantment with Sarajevo came to a sudden end. I had stumbled across the charred and blackened stumps of a wall I recognized as the confines of a former synagogue. The Sephardic nature of the building became clear to me by the central location of the almemar, that enclosure from which the Torah is read. Its filigreed wrought-iron partitions still stood. Attracted and repelled, I stood before it in silent contemplation. An elderly man, walking with the aid of a cane, addressed me in accented German.

"That was the synagogue of the Spanish Jews. It was very old, rebuilt many times—the largest of its kind in the Balkans. When the Germans came they set fire to it. The local Moslems helped them." He studied my reaction for a moment. There had been neither approval nor condemnation in the information gratuitously given. The tone had been that of a tourist guide. "This could never have happened under the Turks," he volunteered.

I thanked him and turned to go. He stopped me.

"We have much beauty here; see the Begova, Careva, and Ali Pasha mosques, they are magnificent. You should also visit the Orthodox Church of St. Archangel. It is the oldest in Bosnia. It contains a fourteenth century painting of the Virgin." He smiled. "It happens to be my church. I wish you a pleasant stay." I returned to the Bosphor lost in thought.

I took coffee in the lobby of the hotel. Its marble floors were still overlaid with fine Turkish carpets, passable oils adorned the walls, and the overstuffed furniture was still holding its own: a pleasant-enough setting to enjoy a thimbleful of Turkish coffee. Instead of an international crowd of well-turned-out travelers with their ladies and their children, the lobby was crowded with German officers of the Wehrmacht and SS varieties and, swaggering in jackboots and German-type uniforms, their lackeys the Ustashas. I listened and observed, occasionally taking refuge behind the *Donauzeitung*. In this particular issue there appeared an article headed by the likeness of Hajj Amin el Husseini, stating that this foremost leader of Islam had contributed another half million kune to the "Mohammed" organization of Bosnia. He was never short of funds, because apart from the monies the Germans were paying him, he had treated the Waqf of Jerusalem, the Moslem widows and orphans fund, as his own. It was said in Arab circles that since the day in 1922 when the British had handed him the key to that figurative strongbox, not a single hospital, orphanage, or other charitable institution had been built in Palestine. All the funds had been used for political or personal use, a practice he was effectively continuing to this day. The Mufti was quoted as saying on Radio Bari that the killing of Jews was pleasant in the eyes of God and that the Moslems of Bosnia were the cream of Islam. The splendid German forces were eagerly waiting to welcome these stalwarts into their ranks.

Sufficiently enlightened for the day, I moved to the wrought-iron lift cage. My attention was attracted to the bulletin board on which hotels post golf tournaments, the hours for swimming, and religious services. There was a hand-lettered card in both German and Serbo-Croatian, announcing that this evening a folkloric soiree, dinner included, was being presented in the dining room. Reservations accepted by the concierge. I reserved a table, napped, changed for dinner, and descended into the dining room with its marble columns and heavy chandeliers.

Most of the guests were German officers, some of them in the company of ladies who did not appear to me to belong to the upper strata of Sarajevan society. The dinner was not bad under wartime circumstances, consisting of the ubiquitous oriental chopped salad, cevapcece—minced meat—on skewers, and a mound of rice. I noticed the Germans among my fellow diners turning their noses up at the somewhat gamey mutton, but after the addition of a fiery pepper sauce I enjoyed it thoroughly.

The folkloric program was exactly the sort that Dr. Steinbruch was expecting me to engage for the Kaukasus. It was, of course, abominable. The production had been mounted by a knowledgeable impresario, not for the benefit of the locals, who were raised on and appreciative of their own traditions, but for the benefit of the German officers and traveling men: simplistic dances by young men dressed in black shirts and sheepskin jackets, with black Turkish pantaloons and leather boots. They linked arms, hopped, skipped, did a sort of Balkan kazatska, and were joined by an equal number of girls, buxom and pretty enough in embroidered outfits, who joined the men in their gyrations. Between the dance numbers there were singers, at which time the conversational volume rose alarmingly in the dining room.

Except for the costumes and the melodies, it was the sort of program that seasoned and cynical Greek taverna owners put on for traveling groups of Swedish or German tourists. The hotel owners of Baalbek in Lebanon do the same for the parties of desiccated English spinsters who come on their mandatory Mediterranean journey. It was completely sanitized—melodies or numbers that might appear too strange to the hotel guests had been weeded out—and yet it gave the audience a chance to return home and tell envious family and friends that they had seen the real thing. The finale consisted of a quite beautiful Bosnian girl singing *Lili Marleen*, first in Serbo-Croatian and then in German. The applause, in which I joined, was tumultuous. German company-grade officers, their faces flushed with beer and rakija, shouted "Bravo!"

I called the maître d'hôtel, tipped him handsomely, and, giving him my room number, requested that the gentleman who had produced this extravaganza call me in the morning. I went to my room to retire. At least that was my intention.

February 14, 1944

I HAD JUST PUT ON MY SILK PAJAMAS—a present from Samira, it came to me in a flash of pain—when there was a knock on the door. While I was hesitating to open, the voice identified itself. "The waiter, with your tea, sir."

I had not ordered tea, and although I had been awaiting Steinbruch's waiter emissary, I had idiotically expected him under other circumstances. I unlocked the door and the waiter entered, tray in hand. He was a handsome man in his late thirties, more Mediterranean than Slavic in appearance, with the sort of good looks often seen among the Yugoslav men of the Dalmatian coast. He placed the tray on the table and started to pour the tea into the cup with his back to me. I was sure he had softly said "Baruch ha ba"—Blessed is he who comes—in Hebrew, but when he turned around he asked me in German if I wanted lemon or milk. I don't believe I answered, as we now frankly studied each other, each one ready to back out in case of a miscalculation. He was the more courageous.

"Daniel, I'm glad you've come. I am David Papo. My family is from Split, on the coast. I am known here as Milan Draskovic."

Papo was a family name I recognized as being traditionally Sephardic, but I decided to put him to the test, as we were still speaking German. "Had gadya," I said in the Aramaic which signifies "a little goat," being the refrain to an old Passover melody.

Papo smiled, closed his eyes in an effort to reach back into his childhood, and without stopping for breath told me what I wanted to hear: "Un kavritiku ki lu mirku mi padri por doz levanim"—A little goat which my father bought for me for two levanim.

He said it in the Judeo-Spanish fashion which no one, not even a student of Cervantes or a philologist, could have dissembled. In the old tradition we shook hands and kissed each other's cheeks.

"Listen to me, Daniel, every minute is precious. The others have arrived, but only two of them made it."

"What others? What are you talking about?"

"The parachute team. From Egypt. The drop was detected by the Ustashas. One broke his neck while in harness, and the other one shot at the fascists, so they killed him. No prisoners, thank God. The other two are here. A Scotsman and one of ours, both from Palestine."

I cursed Steinbruch as Samira must have cursed me. "What parachute team? I'm here to hire dancers and to find out if Moslems are joining the Waffen SS. I know nothing about partisans and parachutists. You're telling me too much, David. I know myself. If, God forbid, the Germans should arrest me, I would put all of you in jeopardy. So please stop. Don't tell me any names, and don't speak to me of your plans. I'm the worst coward you'll ever meet."

David Papo, far from being angry, drew me into an embrace. "Daniel, only stupid people are not afraid. When I killed my first Ustasha I was shaking so badly I could hardly get my knife into his belly. And he was asleep."

Far from reassuring me, this gory tale served to heighten my fear. I rationalized that they had not brought me all the way from Berlin to slaughter Bosnians in their beds, but I was certain I was not equal to the task that would be demanded of me.

David continued, my terror having gone unnoticed. "We must find out when the first draft of Bosnians leave. We're going to blow their train sky high. It will decrease their fervor to fight a jihad."

Insensitive as he was, he did not know that the blood had drained from my face, that my hands were ice-cold.

"The date of their departure, that's what we want from you. That's the really crucial information—the entire operation hinges on it. One more thing: the explosives were lost in the air drop. That will make it even rougher." He bared his even white teeth in a cruel smile and took my moist, limp hand into his own. "Shalom. I'll be back tomorrow night."

I was trapped. Steinbruch had played me like a trout on a line for years and had finally decided to land me. He had withheld the real goal of this theatrical casting journey from me, and as for Papo and his partisan friends, I was laboring under no misapprehensions about them either. If I proved recalcitrant, I was sure they would do away with me without the slightest hesitation. They would not permit a dilettante such as I to endanger their work. What was I to do? The answer came from my grandfather's lips. "Con el pie derecho y el nombre del Dio"—With the right foot forward, and with the name of God.

February 15, 1944

AT TEN O'CLOCK Thursday morning my telephone rang. A pleasant voice, age indeterminate, speaking good German, identified itself.

"Good morning, and many welcomes. This is Dr. Dusan Ivic, artistic impresario of Sarajevo. I am at your disposal."

I reciprocated the courtesies and in turn identified myself as the owner of the Kaukasus, which I modestly described as a cabaret of some note in Berlin. Again I was in luck. He knew it well. After having completed his studies he had visited Berlin and made the rounds at night. Thus he knew my worthy and highly regarded establishment. How could he serve me?

I complimented him on last night's spectacle, adding that it was something in that nature I was looking for, perhaps a bit more authentic, something less tailored for the tourist trade. Would he be my guest for dinner this evening so that we could discuss it further? My pleasure was his pleasure, he replied. He would collect me at seven o'clock.

I spent the rest of the day seeing the sights, actually visiting the mosques and the cathedral suggested to me by the helpful stranger. The walls of the Ali Pasha mosque were plastered with posters of the Grand Mufti, and it was not necessary for me to read Bosnian to understand their message.

I returned to the hotel late in the afternoon. Perhaps I had wanted subconsciously to avoid a meeting with Papo, but I need not to have bothered. We passed each other in the lobby where he was serving beer to German lieutenants, and he did not even dignify me with a glance.

Promptly at seven o'clock Dr. Dusan Ivic picked me up in his 1938 Opel. He appeared to be a Croat gentleman in his early forties, well dressed and barbered, smelling strongly of Trois Fleurs, a hair pomade with which I once had a passing flirtation. One good look told me that here was a man who enjoyed wine, women, and song. He had about him the telltale signs of corruption, like the tiny brown cracks rotting the creamy smoothness of a gardenia petal. Just the right sort of fellow with whom to spend an evening.

He drove carefully along rock-filled roadbeds until we reached the heights above the city, stopping at what he called a "svratishte," an old country inn. The night air was icy cold. The common room of the inn consisted of wooden benches and cubicles, their seats and backs covered with uncured sheepskins, surrounding a charcoal spit on which whole sheep were roasting. The few other guests were locals and several Ustashas in uniform, with whom my new friend exchanged greetings. I noticed, prominent in the buttonhole of his lapel, the Ustashas' party emblem. We avoided speaking of business until we had shared many gulps of fiery rakija, accompanied by slabs of travnicki sir, a pungent ewe cheese. I entertained him with stories of the delectable and exotic girls I had imported into Berlin from the Levant, speaking of minor scandals that had involved my girls and substantial and righteous Berliners. I spoke of angry wives invading my office, of telephone calls by lawyers representing their abused clients. It was the sort of chitchat designed to make Dr. Ivic feel at ease with a kindred soul, and it did.

The innkeeper asked us to come to the spit and choose our cuts of meat. With it he served rounds of home-baked bread, duvec, the local rice cooked with tomatoes, peppers, and meat, and flagons of country wine.

This compulsive writing about food is in direct ratio to how hungry I happen to be. Since Lohmann's Silesian idyll with his widow came to an end, I have been on short rations. I suspect that Lohmann is sharing his own food with me, but he would deny it of course. Before drifting off to sleep at night, my father's balcony is likely to appear before me. I am not sure if it is an expression of longing for my family or a growling stomach lusting for the pigeons and the fresh Arab bread. I hope it is the former.

February 17, 1944

I RETURN TO DR. IVIC and our dinner at the country inn. He had touched on the highlights of his career: the study of law in Zagreb, the courses he had read in a German university, and the opening of his practice. There had been some conflict of interest and he decided to go into the theatrical business, in which he was well served by his knowledge of contracts and the writing of agreements. He added that I as a foreigner could not appreciate how difficult it had been for a Croat such as himself to prevail in the legal profession against the Serbs and especially the Jews until the country had been liberated by the Germans.

This was the moment to discuss my needs for the Kaukasus. I explained that the time had come to stop indulging the German public with Levantine spectacles now held in ill repute by the ruling circles. Friends in high places, I said, had suggested that I draw on the enormous talents available in axis countries such as Italy, Romania, and Hungary. I told Dr. Ivic that I considered those suggestions laughable. Did anyone believe that the German public was in a mood to be entertained by Romanian or Hungarian Gypsies, members of yet another despised cosmopolitan race? Or that Italians with their opera buffo manners were fare for Germans who were beginning to see their ally with a jaundiced eye?

Dr. Ivic smiled his nodding approval of my analysis; he knew in which direction I was heading.

No, I said, all those suggestions were balderdash. Only our allies the Croatians, who had incorporated Bosnia into their territory, had the resources to furnish such a spectacle. The Bosnians with their spirited and masculine dancers, their handsome girls, had a primitive cleanliness about them that would be a relief from the bordello atmosphere of the belly dance.

I do not think Dr. Ivic believed a word of this drivel. But there was a business relation in the offing, and he would have helped me enlist the devil.

He agreed that the hotel spectacle was far too timid and unimaginative for a club like the Kaukasus, and he suggested that we visit some mountain villages where authentic dancers still existed, men who danced with swords to the beat of the tambour and the lyre. In passing, he mentioned how prohibitive the price of petrol had become. I put him at ease, saying that it was my intention to underwrite the expenses of the talent search.

I paid the innkeeper and we started the perilous return trip. Because of blackout regulations the headlights of the Opel had been reduced to thin blue slits. Dr. Ivic drove silently, slowly, and carefully. When we regained the streets of Sarajevo he said he needed a drink; would I let him treat me to a nightcap? I was agreeable and before long we pulled up in front of an elegant villa on a side street. A couple of German Kübelwägen, the personnel carriers of the German army, were parked discreetly under the trees. I followed Dr. Ivic under the portico, and shortly after he rang the door was opened by a handsome woman in a black evening dress.

"Madame Jovanka, I should like to introduce Herr Salazar; he owns Berlin's most successful nightclub, the Kaukasus," said Ivic.

I took her hand and kissed it. "Madame, my pleasure." She led us to a table in what must have been Sarajevo's most elegant whorehouse. It had a bar, a small dance floor, and round tables, their lamps topped with cone-shaped red lampshades. A couple of German officers sat with two girls, a bottle of local wine between them. The lack of animation indicated to me that the drinking was post-coital. Two girls approached our table wearing evening dresses that left their breasts largely exposed. Madame Jovanka shooed them away. "Go, darlings, the gentlemen will call you when they're ready."

A waiter brought a bottle of grasevina, a Slovenian Riesling, and after drinking deeply Ivic addressed himself to me.

"Herr Salazar, I think I like you, and I don't want to waste your time. I've been to Berlin and Vienna and Budapest; I've even been to Paris, and I think I know what a nightclub should offer. What you saw at the Bosphor last night was the best this region has to offer. That show, or one like it, would close after two days at your club. And that's the sad truth. Am I right, Jovanka?" he asked seeking her professional confirmation.

"Dr. Ivic," I started to say in all sincerity, "I am flattered and honored by your honesty and—'' but he stopped me with a wave of his hand.

"I know of a village in the mountains. It is known for its ancient mosque and for the fanaticism of its Moslems. These people are dancers; you have never seen anything like it. I am not an expert in these matters, but I think at one time they were disciples of the Turkish Dervishes."

"You mean the mosque at Ustikolina? Near the old fortress?" Jovanka asked.

"Exactly, but that's a restricted zone." He lowered his voice. "I think the Waffen SS is up there."

"Then there's no way of getting up there?" Jovanka asked.

"Not unless the Germans allow it," I suggested. I had just seen Sturmbannführer Ewald Rabe, his arm around a girl, make his entrance from behind a red velvet drape leading off the bar. It occurred to me that he had come directly from his seminar. I wondered if there was a connection. I immediately rose and went over to greet him, hoping against hope that he knew no more of Samira's disposition than I did. Obviously he didn't, as he appeared surprised but pleased to see me. I brought him to our table and introduced him to Jovanka and Dr. Ivic.

Rabe told us he had just arrived from Berlin, and that his fellow officers had recommended Madame Jovanka's as the one decent place in town. What in heaven's name was Salazar doing here? he wanted to know. I started to explain that it was my intention to produce a patriotic German-Croatian production in connection with a "Croatia Week" I was intending to advertise. Dancers, music, food of the country, that sort of thing. A production that would feature the Bosnian Moslems who, I had been told, were flocking to the colors by the thousands. I thought such a program would not only be educational in Germany but would spur local pride and increase recruitment.

Rabe concurred wholeheartedly, adding that he would do whatever he could to help his friend Herr Salazar. Dr. Ivic and I looked at each other, not sure how best to proceed.

Unexpectedly, Madame Jovanka took the reins away from us. She had slipped her arm through Rabe's and was whispering some intimacies into his ear that caused him to laugh. She turned to us and said that in honor of our presence, her establishment would present a little divertissement for our entertainment. Afterward the ladies would be there for our pleasure, but she was staking a claim. She was so smitten with the Sturmbannführer's charm and looks that she claimed him for herself. Rabe, flattered by her offer, gallantly kissed her hand.

A small orchestra consisting of violin, concertina, drums, and piano had materialized and was slipping into one of the Slavic tangos, which, to my taste at least, are easily as good as the pseudo-Argentine tangos we hear in the West. As a Spaniard I knew what was expected of me, and I asked Madame Jovanka to dance. Among my social graces I do not count tennis, golf, swimming, the equestrian arts, or skiing—all patently ridiculous pastimes for a Jew from Damascus. But I could dance, and I took Madame Jovanka out on the floor and proved it to her and to the club that was gradually filling up. I put on the cold mask of the professional tango dancer while I put Madame Jovanka through her paces. She responded to me, and we acted out the battle of the sexes which is the story of that dance.

When we were firmly entwined and I was bending her backwards, she suddenly whispered into my ear, "Let me handle the German; I'll get your authorization for you."

The number was coming to an end, and I threw caution to the wind. "He likes to be flogged. Put a chain around his neck and drag him around the room. That's the way to his heart."

Madame Jovanka preceded me back to our table to generous applause from the customers and their ladies.

"Muchas gracias, Señor Salazar," she said. I wasn't sure if she thanked me for the dance or the information.

"I am here to serve you," I replied in my best Castilian.

The orchestra started a slow bolero and the house lights dimmed momentarily. When they came up again there was a round mattress covered with a Spanish shawl on the dance floor. Madame Jovanka stood in front of the orchestra. She raised her white if slightly plump arms in a bid for silence. In her strapless black gown, with her thick dark hair, she was a damned fine-looking woman.

"Dear friends of the Salon Jovanka, and especially Kameraden of the German forces. To welcome our special guests tonight, we would like to present a little hors d'oeuvres which should heighten your appetite for a pleasant evening. With much pleasure, I present Natasha and Zuleika.''

There was appreciative applause, and a junoesque blonde with the tall body of an athlete and a petite brunette stepped out of the wings. They were both dressed in provocative underwear, which included brassieres, waist cinchers, cache-sexe, stockings, and garter belts. They danced to the strains of the bolero, rather artlessly, while the waiters rushed bottles of wine, beer, and rakija to the tables. I observed Madame Jovanka in action. As a nightclub owner I could appreciate her total command, sending waiters to this table, girls to another, making sure her customers were building up sizable bills. She joined us by the time the dancers had undressed one another and had commenced a lesbian spectacle on the mattress. To the applause of the crowd, the mattress now started to rotate slowly—in fact Madame Jovanka had installed a primitive revolving stage; I could envision a sweating employee under the floorboards, manually pushing the stage around, like the proverbial donkey grinding corn.

The slowly rotating turntable gave everyone at the club an unimpeded view of the activities. They were no better or worse than what most of us had seen in Port Said, in Marseilles, or in Berlin. In spite of the moans and thrashings there was the same nonerotic quality we all had seen in countless films produced in Cuba dating back to the twenties. The special quality of these proceedings lay in the disparity in the size of the girls. The brunette's head barely reached the breasts of the blonde. They completed their gyrations and, in the manner of stage actors, held hands as they took bows. Some soldiers tossed the flowers from their table vases onto the stage.

The lights dimmed momentarily again, and I could sense the rush of waiters bringing more drinks before the lights came back on. This time the audience gasped. The tall girl had strapped an oversize phallus, seemingly made of rubber, to her loins, and she now proceeded to fornicate her small partner with an expertise and staying power that would have been the envy of many men. The club became deadly silent at this display. As the brunette began to emit orgasmic shrieks, a commotion started at one of the tables. A German captain, drunk and heavily agitated, was making his way toward the stage. He brutally pushed those who impeded his progress out of the way. His face was red, drenched in sweat. He had loosened his tunic and was attempting to unbutton the fly of his breeches. He was shouting at the top of his lungs.

"Stop the Schweinerei! Let a real man do the job! I'll show you how to fuck these pigs!" He shoved aside a young aviator who tried to restrain him and stepped up on the stage. The girls fled in terror, the waving phallus comically preceding the blonde.

Rabe leaped onto the stage to face the lurching captain, and for a second they stood silently facing each other under the house lights. Dr. Ivic and I looked at each other with the same thought: the show was continuing, only the next act had started. Rabe, his right arm extended, his hand open, slapped the captain across the face with such force that blood gushed from his nose. Rabe then assumed a parade-ground stance and bellowed, "Shut your snout! Stand at attention! Hands along the seams of your trousers!" The parade-ground voice and the sight of the SS insignia did its job; the big man started to blubber. Rabe turned away from him, to the audience. "I want the most junior officer present to come forward and escort this man to the Military Police." A hapless young lieutenant presented himself and led the unprotesting man away.

On cue from Madame Jovanka, the music started and the whores led their customers onto the dance floor. Rabe returned to our table. He had done what was expected of a German officer and all eyes were on him. He was elated. One could sense the adrenaline pumping through his system. Madame Jovanka offered him her arm. "The Sturmbannführer deserves the best the house has to offer." They disappeared behind the velvet drapes behind the bar.

Dr. Ivic ordered another bottle. We toasted each other. It had been one hell of an evening so far. Ivic leaned toward me confidentially.

"This may turn out to be a lucky night for us. If anyone can get a pass for the forbidden zone, Jovanka can."

I was inclined to agree with him.

"I am only sorry you missed one thing," Ivic added.

"What's that?" I wanted to know.

"To see the little brunette fuck the big blonde. That's really something!"

"Shall we go?" I asked him.

"You're not interested in the girls?"

"Not in the slops left behind by the army."

"My sentiments exactly," said Dr. Ivic. "If you want a little company, let me know—I'll send you my secretary and her cousin. I call them Heaven and Hell. They are fantastic."

He dropped me off at the Bosphor. It was four o'clock in the morning.

February 18, 1944

IT WAS THE OLD LOHMANN *who has just left me. He had appeared, smiling, avuncular, carrying a large string bag, the sort used by local housewives on their forays to the greengrocer's. He emptied the bag silently, beaming ever more as he placed the contents on the table before me. There was jam, tinned sardines, condensed milk, sausage, bread, and even the cake which Berliners call Sandkuchen. He urged me to eat, and when he saw the cautious manner in which I approached bread and sausage, he told me to dig in, as there was plenty more where this windfall had come from. He lowered himself onto my groaning couch and only then chose to tell me of his new enterprise.*

In order to justify his repeated appearances in the building, he was still calling on Inge and Jutta, the two part-time prostitutes. He had run into them in a neighborhood bar, and they had told him that the ladies' wear shop in which they were employed had been bombed out of existence. They were loath to report to the Labor Exchange for fear of being sent to a defense factory. Lohmann had reevaluated the girls: they were still in their twenties, rather pretty in an unexceptional way, and he thought that with their lack of intelligence they would wind up as common streetwalkers. They were too lazy to hold down a more demanding job, Lohmann said, and he decided to come to their rescue. Drawing on his experience as a one-time procurer in the aftermath of the First World War, he had enlisted them without too much trouble. Lohmann would better their lot, and his own in the process. He took them to a beauty parlor and had their hair styled, their fingers manicured, their eyebrows plucked, and makeup applied in moderation. Next they went to the premises of the defunct eating club in the Kantstrasse. There were still a number of elegant dresses and some felt and straw hats left in the bedroom closets. Those remnants were certainly an improvement over what the girls had been wearing, and that evening, when Lohmann entered the confines of an elegant blacked-out bar in the company of Inge and Jutta, potential customers sat up and took notice.

Within days a selected clientele had been built up, and Lohmann assumed the time-honored function of the procurer: father confessor, treasurer, and paymaster.

"I hope it is not from the proceeds of white slavery that I am gorging myself," I said righteously.

"Indeed you are," said Lohmann with a chuckle, "And in the process we are keeping a couple of young girls out of the railroad stations, where they would pick up a dose of the clap within twenty-four hours."

Lohmann's logic won me over, and I cut myself a piece of the Sandkuchen.

February 19, 1944

I awoke at ten o'clock. There was an envelope under the door, German army issue. I opened it with some trepidation, but I need not have. It was a very mannerly invitation:

> The Officers of the Handjar Division
> request the pleasure of Herr Salazar's
> company at a lunch to be given in the
> Officers' Mess
>
> On *Saturday, 22 November 1941*
>
> Transport will be at Bosphor Hotel at 1000 hours.
> Please carry appropriate identification.
>
> Schlüter, Adjutant

The lunch was set for Saturday, so I had the day to myself. I would try to find a hamam, a Turkish bath, and laze the afternoon away. A knock on the door brought me Papo and breakfast: Turkish coffee, yogurt, and some nice local rolls. He set down the tray, and I handed him the invitation. He was impressed.

"I come off work at noon today. I'll be in front of the railroad station by twelve-thirty. When we spot each other I'll start walking. Follow me at a distance; you need not stay on the same side of the street. It's time you met the chaverim."

Friends indeed, I thought with misgivings.

At the station, I spotted Papo. He was wearing a cloth cap, his overcoat negligently thrown over his shoulder. When he saw me he turned his back and sauntered off the square onto one of the main streets. I followed at a leisurely pace, looking into an occasional shop window but always keeping him in sight. Soon we were cutting through side streets, streets that gave way to cobblestoned alleys, until we emerged in a gray, soot-covered industrial district. The streets here were mud, and I saw Papo disappearing between two wooden fences. Making sure I was unobserved, I followed. Papo waved me toward him. He was crouched beside a ground-level window, covered with wire mesh. Suddenly the window opened, the wire was pulled back, and Papo disappeared into it; I followed, helped by unseen hands. The window was replaced and I took my bearings. We were in a grain warehouse where countless sacks, neatly stacked, had created an impenetrable maze.

I followed Papo and two shadowy figures until we came to a crude office—really nothing more than a tally keeper's stall. There was a rude desk, a chair, and a bench. One of the men seated himself behind the desk; the three of us sat on the bench. We waited for a moment to adjust to the half-light.

"There ye are then, laddie," the man behind the desk said. He was a hirsute, balding Scotsman, with a fiery red mustache and huge forearms. He held out his hand. "Call me Ian."

"Shalom," said the man next to me. "I am Uzi." He gave me his hand. He was a carbon copy of the Scotsman, but dark and Semitic, with a heavy black mustache and dark hairy forearms.

Papo spoke of my invitation to the German bastion, and Ian produced a large map printed on what appeared to be parachute silk. Uzi lowered his voice, and we briefly conversed in Judeo-Spanish. His was distinct from mine, as over the centuries we had developed linguistic idiosyncrasies in the countries of our dispersion. Not only are there Turkish, Bulgarian, Greek, Yugoslav, Levantine, and North African variants, but those with a trained ear can tell if a man is a native of Rhodes, Melas, Corfu, Skopje, or Salonika.

Uzi was a native of Sarajevo, descendant of the Kajons, a family of printers. He had left as a boy of fourteen when his family had emigrated to Palestine. He still spoke Bosnian and Serbo-Croatian and had perfect recall of the place of his birth. He had joined the British army and, after service against the Germans in the desert, had volunteered for parachute missions in support of Serbian partisans who had taken to the mountains. He told me that since the Germans had occupied Yugoslavia, their Croatian puppets had murdered hundreds of thousands of Serbs, Jews, and Gypsies. Among the Jews, mostly Sephardim like ourselves, only those who had managed to escape to the benevolent Italian occupation of Dalmatia, along the Adriatic coast, had survived. I found this hard to believe, having seen the general tranquillity of the town. Uzi told me of deportation to Croat extermination camps. He told me of camps at Jasenovac, Stara Gradiska, Loborgrad, and Jadovno. There were many others whose names I cannot recall. It was a boast of the Germans that the Jewish problem in Yugoslavia no longer existed. It had been largely solved for them by the Croats.

But the most numerous victims of the German-Croatian coalition had been the Serbs. The Croatians, with their Ustasha regulars and the blessing of the Pavelic-Artukovic regime, had literally murdered hundreds of thousands of Serbs without the benefit of extermination camps. In a bloodletting of unparalleled cruelty they had shot, garroted, knifed, and hanged their former fellow citizens, occasionally sparing a few who agreed to convert from Greek Orthodoxy to Roman Catholicism. The butchery had been indescribable: pregnant mothers had the unborn rippled out of their bellies; wanton rape and general savagery was the order of the day. Uzi added that under the guidance of the Mufti of Jerusalem, the Bosnian Moslems had willingly joined the Croats in the extermination of the Serbs and Jews. He was here to settle old scores.

I felt ignorant when he spoke of generations of rabbis, writers, and sages; the Muchachos, Shabtais, Pardos, and Pereiras, the Finzis and the Maestros, who had settled here half a millennium ago under the benevolent rule of the Turks. Uzi said that all this murder and destruction would be paid for. He told me of others from Palestine who would parachute into their countries of origin, either to help save the remnant of our people or to support the local partisans. Uzi had come from a kibbutz. I wondered if they had managed to transform my mild-mannered brother, Victor, into a farmer-soldier.

We gathered around Ian. He was a born leader: captain from a parachute brigade, humorous, witty, modest, and with that inborn courage of Celtic warriors, parents to his bloodline. I was also impressed by Papo, who lived from day to day, cheek by jowl with the enemy, always aware of his fate in case of discovery: torture and death. I was similarly taken by Uzi, who had been a soldier all his life, fought the war, and finally parachuted into the country of his birth. I sensed his familiarity with arms and explosives, his capacity to kill, but I was still a product of the Diaspora, still the offspring of generations of merchants and peddlers, and I felt safer under the leadership of Ian than under that of my own people. I realized how illogical it was, but the dispersion had done it to us, and it would take men like Uzi to bring about a change.

I paid attention to Ian. "Listen to me, lads. I don't like to repeat myself. The concept of the mission is simple and logical. The execution may prove more difficult. It usually is. We've lost two of our men, and the explosives with them. Fortunately I carried the maps and the command is mine, so the locals cannot have discovered much from the bodies. Parachuting agents are nothing new in this war. We have Papo's partisan group to support us, some thirty in number. That's on the plus side of the ledger. Now let's run through it once. Save your questions for later. First the concept. The Jerries have started to recruit the local Moslems. The buggers think they've embarked on a holy war. Ideally, we want to blow up the first troop transport that leaves this region. From the Moslems' point of view it will cast the Evil Eye on this recruitment of their people. For the Germans it will make it a lot tougher to enlist the locals. The operation has various benefits. It might induce the Germans to bring more garrison troops into this area, or it might result in the replacement of the local command, who will be judged to have been incompetent. The peripheral benefits are many."

He lit his evil-smelling pipe and continued.

"The execution is something else. The plan was to blow up the train carrying the first draft out of here. We've no explosives, and Papo says there's no way of getting enough, which means we're going to have to derail the train by sheer manpower: by tearing the tracks apart with our bare hands, if need be."

He blew blue smoke into our faces.

"Two minor irritants are that we don't know when the draft is leaving or in which direction they're heading. Now, Daniel, you're going to be lunching with the brass of the Handjar Division tomorrow." He turned to Uzi. "What's it mean, chaver?"

"Handjar means sword in Bosnian," said Uzi.

"It's 'seif' in Arabic. Seif ed din: the sword of faith. The sort of imagery that appeals to the Moslems," I added.

"Let's stick it up their arse, then! Much of the burden is on you, Daniel. You're going to be eating and drinking with the Jerries; somehow you must find out when they're leaving." Ian grinned at me. "I know it's a tall order, but you're the only one who can get that close. Papo has people in the railway yards who will tell us if a transport is being assembled, but its destination is usually secret until the last minute. So bear that in mind. If you're not lucky tomorrow, try and get another pass to visit the villages in search of your dancers. Use your brains, lad, and good luck to you." He gave me a bone-bruising clap on the shoulder.

I was not to be dismissed that easily. "You men have been in the army all your lives; you grew up with guns. I've never even been a boy scout—and you're going to send me to a German fortification alone? What if I slip? What if I give myself away? Those Bosnians will make kebab out of me." The three men looked at one another as if I were mad. "You're safely hidden, while I can't sleep nights for fear that Samira, or Lohmann, or Steinbruch has been pulled in by the Gestapo—"

I had no chance to continue because the bearlike Uzi had grabbed me by the throat and was shaking me like a dishcloth. "Curse the day we laid eyes on you. What is so precious about your life? Good men are dying every day, and few were given the chance that you have to bloody the Germans."

He was still shaking me when Ian intervened. Uzi loosened his grasp. The Scotsman led me to the bench and sat down next to me. "Daniel, these are going to be the best moments of your life. You will think of them all your days. It will make you proud, and you will taste the sweetness of vengeance. I believe in you. You will sit with the Germans and you will listen to them and you will keep your eyes open and you will bring us the information we need. And when this is over, you and Uzi and Papo and I will meet and drink and talk about the grandest time we ever had." He took my hand into his powerful grasp and held it until I am sure some of his strength flowed into me.

Papo decided that I must return to the hotel. I should not be placed in a position in which I would have difficulty in accounting for my time. He would look me up after my return from my outing.

I got back to the hotel without incident. I felt so much better that I toyed with the idea of calling Dr. Ivic to arrange an evening with Heaven and Hell for me. I gave up the idea, however tempting. Superstitious as I am, I did not want to prejudice the events of the following day by unseemly conduct on the night before.

February 20, 1944

AT TEN O'CLOCK SHARP the Kübelwagen drew up in front of the hotel. The SS Rottenführer opened the door for me, and I was not surprised to see Dr. Ivic already installed in the rear. He was sporting a fur-lined coat and Bosnian sheepskin cap and cut a rather dashing figure. He was greatly pleased, not only at the prospect of being my agent in the hiring of entertainers but also at having been invited to the Waffen SS mess. According to Papo, Ivic was not only a member of the Ustasha Party but a major collaborator with the Germans. It appeared that his information was correct.

As soon as we had left Sarajevo behind us, we commenced our ascent into the rapidly thinning mountain air. Dr. Ivic pointed out mountain peaks and Bosnian churches of great antiquity as we continued our climb. Finally Sarajevo lay like a toy village on the floor of the valley. We had already driven sixty kilometers before we came to the first checkpoint at Dobro Polje. A mixed patrol of German regulars and Croatians examined our papers meticulously, and I noted that after the inspection of Dr. Ivic's credentials he was rewarded with an especially snappy salute by the Croatian sergeant. The climb continued for another twenty kilometers. We left the main road at Miljevina, where we hit another checkpoint, but this time it was manned by Waffen SS and soldiers of the Moslem division. It was the first time I had seen these young men exactly the way Amina and Samira had described them: in German field gray, but wearing a red tarboosh, the crown a little lower than the ones I had worn as a young man. They also inspected our papers and waved us on.

We followed a narrow road, playing hide-and-seek with the Bistric River. After half an hour, Dr. Ivic pointed off to the right of the vehicle. A large mosque lay close by, but we continued on. Dr. Ivic explained that we had passed Foca and were now in the heartland of unreconstructed Islam. After another fifteen minutes a great Turkish fortification loomed ahead of us. We could see a swastika banner and one with an Islamic crescent and star fluttering from its ramparts. We had arrived at Ustikolina.

We drove into the vast courtyard of this bastion and were received by the Officer of the Day. He asked us to sign the register in the guardroom and then escorted us into the officers' mess. There we were received with great cordiality by Sturmbannführer Rabe, who introduced us to his fellow officers, including the Colonel Commanding, Standartenführer Heinz Jürgen Novak, who had been identified for us by Samira. There were also a number of Bosnian Moslems present, mostly in the lower Waffen SS officer ranks. Out of deference to them, and to create a feeling of respect for their allies, the Germans served no liquor or wine in the mess. Turkish coffee was served in exquisite old copper finjans.

At lunch, Rabe asked me to sit next to him. He wondered if I had spoken with my office in Berlin and if I had any news of Samira. I was terrified that this question, so jovially asked, might in reality be a trap and I heard myself answering lamely that I had made no attempt to call my manager, Lohmann. Rabe said he had tried for forty-eight hours to get through to Berlin but had been unable to get a connection. The meal was brought to an end with coffee and a baklava that would not have passed muster in my mother's kitchen. The Germans ate it gingerly, and I could tell they were lusting for their smelly cheeses and sweet pastries piled high with whipped cream.

After lunch I excused myself, asking for the latrine. I was directed to the very end of a long drafty corridor. Ian had told me to be on the lookout for the bulletin boards to be found on all army posts; they usually contained a host of information. He had also asked me to enter offices under some pretext, in the hope that I would pick up some hint regarding troop movement. Indeed, there were a number of bulletin boards in the corridor, but they were all covered with canvas. As I lifted the cover of the first, I became aware of echoing footsteps, and I dropped the canvas just as a young Bosnian sentry came into view. As he passed me I mumbled "Toilet" and he motioned down the hall.

I had slowly shuffled down the corridor when the sign ADJUTANT stopped me. I surmised that an adjutant was a sort of assistant to the commanding officer, and I knocked softly on the door. There was no reply. I tried the door handle and the door opened. I closed it behind me. The office was in incredible order. There were hundreds of files and ledgers on rough shelves, and the adjutant's desk itself was neat as a pin. With pounding heart I tried the drawer. It was locked. I took a scissors off the desk and, like the amateur I was, started to poke at the lock with it. I quickly realized that if I broke it and opened the drawer forcibly, it would produce a hue and cry upon its discovery. I desisted, replaced the scissors, and made for the door. I opened it and found myself face-to-face with a young German soldier, a tray of file folders in his arms and steel-rimmed spectacles on his nose. He was as surprised as I but I reacted more quickly. In a flash the adjutant's name came to me—he had signed the invitation. I also knew from living in Germany that subordinates, especially in the military, were used to being shouted at. I took my chances.

"I am a guest of the SS. Where is Herr Schlüter, the adjutant?" I bellowed, emphasizing "SS" and "Schlüter." The poor clerk came to attention and, looking straight ahead, barked, "The Adjutant, at Officers' Mess, sir!" and then stepped aside to let me pass. I hoped he thought I was with the SS or the Ustasha; anyway, I had been credible enough for him not to sound the alarm. That he would report the encounter routinely, I did not doubt. But it added an element of urgency to my mission.

Frustrated, I returned to the mess. The officers had filed out to the crenellated rooftop overlooking the courtyard. With Dr. Ivic at my side, the adjoining mountain ranges were pointed out to me and, to our right, the ancient mosque of Ustikolina below us. The domed roof and minaret were of remarkable size and preservation. An authentic Turkish village was clustered around its base. The latticed second-story balconies hanging over the narrow streets were identical to those built by the Turks in Damascus in the Ottoman days. I could see old women wearing the yashmak, which concealed their faces. They wore dresses over their pantaloons and pantuklas, turned-up slippers, on their feet. It was a tableau out of the past.

My daydreams were shattered by the shrill blast of a bugle. A young officer came to ask that Dr. Ivic and I join the officers. Chairs had been set up, and little tables held cigars and cigarettes. The officers directed their gaze at the courtyard below. I heard the strain of a military band, but to my delight it was not the Dessauer or the Radetzky March but a plaintive Turkish melody, played on nasal horns, accompanied by threatening drumbeats. Even in my youth I had never heard anything like this, because the French had early on set the martial tone in Syria. Now a Bosnian military band marched into the courtyard through the main gate, followed by a thunderous pounding of boots on the pavement. Company after company of Bosnian recruits paraded in front of us. Their battalion and company commanders were obviously Germans, while junior officers and NCOs were all Bosnians. All were in field gray with red tarboosh. Instead of the German jackboots, the men wore short leggings over their boots; their rifles, leather gear, and bayonets were standard German issue.

Hateful as they were to me, it was one hell of a parade. It was, after all, what the Germans do best. I counted nearly five hundred men, and then desisted, not wanting to attract attention by being overly interested in the proceedings. Rabe joined us. He was immensely proud of his troops. He also was wearing a tarboosh now. For the first time I noticed the cap badge: an amalgam of swastika and crescent, symbol of the unholy alliance of Hitler and the Grand Mufti.

The parade came to an end, but instead of trooping off the young men stacked their rifles in pyramids and sat down in orderly ranks, lining the walls of the courtyard. It seemed as if we were to be treated to a football match.

Dr. Ivic and a Bosnian officer joined me. Ivic was immensely pleased.

"Captain Cengic tells me that the imam of the mosque has organized an exhibition of the local dancers, members of an old religious brotherhood. These are the descendants of the Whirling Dervishes of which Madame Jovanka spoke. He tells me that they practice self-flagellation on the birthday of the Prophet. They dance all day while the blood streams from their wounds." He grew confidential. "I think Sturmbannführer Rabe's hand is in this. It's his way of repaying you for your friendship."

In the meantime a straggle of villagers entered the courtyard. Judging by their appearance, they were the more important citizens, limited to men, of course. Young soldiers were setting up chairs for them while a group of Moslem clerics entered the courtyard. They were four or five in number, dressed in their high-collared, knee-length caftans. A white-bearded man, the white cloth of the Hajj wrapped around his tarboosh, walked under a black umbrella. I was sure he was the imam of the mosque. An older man followed, also in the white-wrapped tarboosh, but he wore dark glasses and walked stiffly with the aid of a cane. I believed him to be the muezzin, the cleric who calls the devout to prayer from the top of the minaret. These men are often blind. Tradition has it that thus they are unable to feast their eyes on the women in the harems that lie below, but I do not know if this story is true. I think it is cut from the same cloth as the tale that the sultans forbade cucumbers to be brought into the harem unless they had been sliced: the jealous sultans did not want their wives and concubines to abate their ardor without the sultan's personal participation. Or the old saw that castration led to the impotence the sultans demanded of the guardians of the harem. Even the tales of the *Thousand and One Nights* disprove this theory: its eunuchs are forever pleasuring the ladies, while the sultans decide weighty matters of state.

The program was about to start. The soldiers were seated quietly and patiently, the village notables and clergy sat on their chairs, the German officers lined the parapet above, much like the sultans or emirs of the East, ready to enjoy a "Fantasia" staged by their worshipful and grateful subjects. Now a small orchestra marched in, traditionally dressed in turbans, black pantaloons, and upturned slippers. They carried drums, shepherd flutes, and primitive lyres with short, highly arched bows. They seated themselves and started to play without the benefit of a chef d'orchestre.

This was truly primitive music out of the Ottoman past, whining phrases that continued unabated. Admittedly this cacophony is painful to western ears; I could see it on the faces of the Germans. But I had no difficulty assimilating the beat. I must have felt it at the same time as the Bosnian recruits, who now started to clap their hands in a deafening rhythm in time with the drumbeats.

A roar went up from the recruits. The Dervishes were cartwheeling into the courtyard. They came through the gate one by one, at least thirty of them. With ever-increasing speed they were wheeling into the center of the yard; finally an inner order emerged as they continued their gyrations in two concentric circles.

As the rhythm changed they linked arms, formed a large circle, and as it slowly moved the men began to rotate their heads ever more rapidly, making it look as if their heads were attached to their torsos by a swivel rather than a skeletal apparatus.

Their appearance was also startling. Their hair was knotted in long braids and the strands fell to their shoulders, covering their eyes. They wore pantaloons and sashes about their waists, nothing else.

As they danced there were subtle changes in rhythm and their feet began to stamp; they broke up into smaller groups and increased the tempo of their cranial gyrations. I sensed the beginnings of a state of hypnosis seizing the dancers. Without it their physical exertions would have been impossible.

Dr. Ivic spoke to me, but I could not keep my eyes off the dancers. "This is the show for you, Herr Salazar. I'll negotiate with the imam for ten of the best, and you'll fill the Kaukasus for months. No one has ever seen this, and it's only the beginning." Spellbound, I nodded my assent.

As I watched the Moslem clerics in the courtyard, an idea began to take shape. Since these imams, mullahs, and muezzins read and interpret the Koran to the faithful, it stood to reason that they could read Arabic. This did not mean that they could speak it or understand it; much as the Roman Catholic faithful recite the mass and prayers in Latin in complete ignorance of what is being said. But something told me that the two men with the white-covered tarboosh might speak Arabic. The white cloth indicated they had made the Hajj, the pilgrimage to Mecca, and there was an outside chance that at least one would be conversant in Arabic.

The mosque's proximity to the fort suggested to me that the clerics were spiritual advisers to the troops. Certainly the Allah-intoxicated soldiers went to pray at the mosque on Saturdays. It stood to reason that the mullahs would have full knowledge of any impending troop movements. It had been thus in garrison towns since the days of the Romans, the priest and the prostitutes always the first to know when the soldiers were moving out. Whatever the risk involved, I decided to stand among them and approach one or the other when the opportunity presented itself. What I would say, or how I would go about it, I did not know. I would follow the Moslem philosophy: everything is preordained; man can change nothing. I would let the fates guide my actions.

I turned to Dr. Ivic and said I was going into the courtyard so I could study the dancers at close hand. I left the parapet quickly, thus ensuring that he did not follow me. I worked my way around the soldiers and finally stood behind the clergy.

The dancing had become yet more orgiastic. Some of the men had begun to whirl, arms outstretched, heads bobbing, turning in ever more frenzied circles, urged on by the beats of the drum. Gradually the others joined them until they truly lived up to their name: Whirling Dervishes. It was interminable and I could see the Germans getting restless, but the Bosnian soldiers were getting caught up in it. Some of the dancers, glassy eyed and with spittle on their chins, were rotating like tops. I noticed with amazement that many had erections, which were bulging their pantaloons outward. There were occasional shouts of "Allahu akbar"—God is great—from the soldiery.

Two young soldiers carrying mameluke swords joined the circle of dancers, waving the swords over their heads. The music broke off and the Dervishes slowly spun to a halt. They stood swaying for a while, then followed the sword carriers in a procession around the yard. The soldiers picked up the Moslem clergymen, placed them on their shoulders, and, following the waving swords, started an unrestrained, jubilant, unbroken circle. A Bosnian song, religious or secular—it was incomprehensible to me—broke out as the men continued their shuffling around. Forgotten was the blind muezzin. He had remained seated, unattended.

I gained his side and gently led him to the relative safety of the wall. At least he would not be trampled there. " 'Id moubarak, yah hajj," I said. A blessed feast to you, O pilgrim.

He turned his dark glasses toward me. " 'Alaina wa 'alaik," he replied. May yours and ours be blessed.

I decided to throw caution to the wind. "You speak Arabic, yah hajj, and beautifully."

His bony hand sought out my own. He held it firmly. "The less I see, the more I remember. I have hardly spoken it since I studied in Cairo."

"I can tell by your speech and the elegance of the tongue that you are a learned man. You studied at Al Azhar?"

"Indeed, but that was forty years ago. No one bothers to learn Arabic anymore; they repeat the Koran like parrots."

The old man was still holding my hand. I was hoping that I was not being observed from the ramparts. I had given the muezzin an opportunity to speak Arabic, and he was making the most of it. He pointed to his dark glasses.

"I don't mind not seeing. There is too much ugliness nowadays, too much disrespect. But I miss the dance of the Dervishes; they were my joy at every feast. Now I am content to feel their wind on my face, to hear the cry of the flute, content to quote Rumi the Afghani, who gathered the Dervishes about him."

He turned his clouded eyes heavenward and declaimed,

"Listen to the reed, how as a flute it makes lament,
Telling how once from the reed-bed it was bent.

The poet Rumi was a soul in love with Allah!"

Again the muezzin quoted.

"I am the mote in the sunbeam, I am the ball of the sun,
I am the glow of the morning, I am the evening breath.

You see, when Rumi spoke to the Dervishes they whirled until they became one with God." He released my hand.

"Mashkour, yah hajj," I said, to thank him for the beauty of his words. May you be thanked, O pilgrim.

"Allah yehfazak, yah, ibni," he replied. May God reward you, my son. "And you, O gentleman, you are from where?"

I decided to answer obliquely and then to plunge into the matter at hand. "I studied at the university, but I am here as a guest of the Germans." I continued without missing a beat. "You must be very proud of all the fine young men who have joined their army?"

"May they be blessed. They will fight the jihad against the Jews, Inch'allah! I wish you had understood their song."

"Indeed," I said.

"The words are the Mufti's, Hajj Amin's: 'Oh, you Moslems! Kill the Jews wherever you find them! You will please God, history, and the Faith! This saves your honor! God is with you!'"

"Exactly my sentiments," I said to the old man. "This feast is in honor of the soldiers, then? Of their leave-taking?"

"Indeed," he said. "They are leaving et-tnain."

"Et-tnain" means the second day of the week. In Arabic Sunday is called the first day; thus the troops were leaving Monday: that is, in forty-eight hours. Now came the big question. I weighed my words carefully. "They are strong-looking boys. If I were a Russian, I would make water in my trousers."

The old man laughed. "The Russians have been spared. The boys are going to Split. From there they hope to sail for Libya. They want to march at the head of Rommel's army and liberate Jerusalem from the Jews."

It had been as simple as that. I took my leave.

"Bekhartikom, yah hajj," I said. By your leave, O pilgrim.

"Ma es salame, yah khawaja," he replied. Go in peace, O gentleman.

I pushed my way through the snake-dancing soldiery and joined the others on the rampart. It seemed I had not been missed.

This must be one of the longest entries in these boastful memoirs. The excitement of those days came back to me, and the hours flew. But now the sun is setting and my hand hurts. I keep myself warm with a blanket thrown over the heavy sweater Lohmann brought me, and the layers of newspapers between my undershirt and shirt help. It smudges newsprint onto my linen, but it keeps me relatively warm. February is an icy time of the year in Berlin, and my attempt to keep clean and warm is a losing battle.

February 21, 1944

WE DROVE BACK TO SARAJEVO; Sturmbannführer Rabe rode with us. I suspected he would be heading for Madame Jovanka's to be put through his paces. Suddenly he turned to me.

"I saw you talking to the blind muezzin. How did you manage? Surely he doesn't speak German?"

"I wanted to get closer to the dancers; he was left standing alone. I tried some of the Arabic phrases I've learned from the girls: Assalamu alaikum, Marhaba, that sort of thing. He was very appreciative. And the dancers were absolutely spectacular. I'm going to prevail on Dr. Ivic to represent me in my negotiations with them. I am deeply grateful, especially to you, Sturmbannführer." It did not seem very convincing, but it was the best I could do.

Rabe acknowledged my thanks with a curt nod. He stared into space while Dr. Ivic and I maintained an uncomfortable silence. Again Rabe turned to me. 'I've studied Arabic for months. All I can spout is simplistic tripe: 'God is great,' 'You are welcome,' 'Peace unto you,' 'Do you wish a cigarette?' total shit, and you a cabaret impresario—I believe that's the right word—were chatting up a storm with this old fraud."

In spite of the altitude I felt the sweat breaking out. "Herr Sturmbannführer. I am sure you are making too much of this. Over the years I've learned some polite forms; it made the old man very happy to hear them from a stranger."

Rabe did not reply. I could not tell if he was mollified or would go on the attack once more. He sat in silence the rest of the way. Once we arrived at the hotel, I asked them to join me at the bar. Rabe declined, pleading army business.

I gave Dr. Ivic carte blanche to negotiate for me; I needed ten of the dancers, no more, and they had to be in Berlin by the end of December. We would speak again. He took his leave.

At approximately ten o'clock Papo came into my room. He

wheeled in a large serving table set with a full dinner. It would give us an opportunity to speak for five minutes now, and again in an hour when he would come to remove the table. I filled him in quickly. The troops were leaving on Monday, headed for Split. Possibly to join the Afrika Korps. I also mentioned the unpleasantness with Rabe in the motorcar, but he praised me, saying he would report to Ian and Uzi after getting off work.

Approximately an hour later Papo came back to say that he would be bringing my breakfast around eight. By that time he would have orders from Ian and he would have seen the partisans who worked in the railroad yards. Probably orders for the assembly of a troop train were already known. We were sharing a smoke when agitated pounding struck my door. Papo withdrew into my bathroom, motioning for me to open. I did, and Rabe burst in. He was out of control.

"You son of a bitch!" he yelled. "I just got through to Berlin and spoke to your whoremaster, Lohmann. He said you fired Samira! By whose orders, you greasy dago? You knew she was employed by me, that she's working for the SS!"

"Sturmbannführer Rabe, please, she is a drug addict; no good to my club and a danger to your security—"

"The only danger to my security is you. You lied to me about Samira, and I don't believe the cock-and-bull story you gave me this afternoon. You're coming down to headquarters with me, and the security people are going to have a chat with you."

"I'll make a deal with you, Sturmbannführer," I said. "You leave me alone, or I'll tell them that you have a Syrian Jewess as a mistress who has to whip your arse so Captain Shawa can fuck you dog fashion. That should enhance your career with the SS."

Rabe turned white and his face started to twitch. I decided to follow up my advantage.

"I don't know why you're carrying on about Samira. You've got Jovanka flogging you here, and she probably has one of her waiters fucking you in the arse. I'll tell that to the Gestapo also." I continued. "I know Standartenführer Novak will be delighted to hear all this. Now let me be so I can hire my dancers. I'm doing more for German-Croatian friendship than you are." I had overdone it. Rabe had opened his holster and was pulling his Luger out. He pointed it at me, pulling the slide back with a shaking hand.

"No one will believe a word of what you say, you piece of shit. Look at you. You're some sort of half-breed anyway. I'm going to watch while the boys interrogate you. When they shoot the first charge of juice up your balls, when they stick a pressure hose up your arse, you won't be so smart. And now, hands up and march. March!"

He was so busy with his Luger he never heard Papo come up behind him.

Papo had taken off his shoes, and in one quick gesture he brought my razor strop about Rabe's throat, pulling the leather with such force that Rabe dropped to his knees, letting the Luger slip from his hands with a soft thud. While I watched in fascination, Rabe dropped to his hands and knees; Papo sat on his back, twisting the leather ends of the strop in desperate fury. Rabe looked up and gave me one last sad, knowing look. Then he collapsed.

Papo kept the pressure up for a moment longer and released the strop. He turned Rabe over with his foot. Rabe's face was purple, the eyes filled with blood. Papo pointed to a spreading stain on the crotch of Rabe's pearl-gray breeches. "Look," he said. "The son of a bitch came in his pants."

I was beside myself at the realization at what had happened within minutes in my hotel room. The thought of having to dispose of the body, the impending search, and the inevitable investigation had me on the verge of nausea. Not Papo. He disarmed the Luger and slipped it into his pocket, along with the extra clip of ammunition. His only comment was that it was a pity about the uniform; the partisans would have put it to good use, but there was neither the time nor the place to salvage it.

Papo instructed me to sit Rabe upright and to push his torso forward with all my might, so that Papo, with the use of Rabe's belt and braces, could tie him firmly into a U-shaped bundle, thus effectively reducing his bulk by half. Impatient with my efforts, Papo sat down so hard on Rabe's shoulders that I could hear the vertebras crack. When Rabe was fully trussed, Papo proceeded to remove serving dishes from the lower level of the serving table, piling everything on the tabletop. With my help we placed Rabe's body on the level just above the wheels. He hardly protruded. Papo rearranged the tablecloth, covering Rabe effectively, placed the uniform cap under Rabe's body, and declared himself satisfied.

"What are you going to do with the body? What do I say when the SS gets here? When will I see you?" The questions came tumbling out.

"Get hold of yourself. This is a big hotel; we've got ninety rooms, over half with their own bathrooms. We make lots of hot water. There are big furnaces in the basement, and that's where he is going to wind up. All I need is a little mazal. Before they sift for his fillings and buttons, I'll have disappeared into the mountains and you'll be back in your club in Berlin. If anyone asks about Rabe, say he came and left. It's the truth. Think you can find your way to the warehouse by yourself?" I nodded. "Then be there by ten."

He pushed the table out of the door and, once in the corridor, said audibly, "Good night, sir, and thank you very much."

I closed the door and looked around. There wasn't even a spot of blood. The whole episode had taken under fifteen minutes. I went to bed, but of course sleep would not come. I kept reliving the terrifying events that had occurred here just minutes before.

If Papo had not been in the bathroom, I would either be dead, executed by Rabe on the spot, or, worse, being interrogated by the SS in some basement in Sarajevo. Once they had extracted my confession, not a difficult task in my case, they would certainly have shipped me off to Gestapo headquarters in Berlin. There they would have made short shrift of me—using their rubber truncheons, their water hoses, their electrodes. They would quickly have unraveled my life in Berlin, my recruitment by Dr. Steinbruch, my change of name. I would have implicated Lohmann, Hilde, Frau Novikov, Samira, anyone still remaining from the Landau circle of friends. It was too ghastly to contemplate.

I also realized that another element of danger had entered my life: not the Germans or the Ustasha this time but my very co-conspirators Uzi and Ian, and foremost my compatriot David Papo. From the professional and cold-blooded way David had killed Rabe I deduced that they would not hesitate to do away with me if they felt even for a moment that my lack of enthusiasm threatened the success of their mission. I was flagellating myself with these thoughts when the shrilling of the telephone jolted me upright. I took a deep breath and prepared for the worst. It was the concierge.

"I apologize for the intrusion, Herr Salazar, but Sturmbannführer

Rabe's chauffeur is in the lobby asking for him. He thought he might be visiting with you."

"My God, it's one o'clock. The Sturmbannführer was here around eleven, but he only stayed about five minutes. He didn't tell me where he was going." And I hung up.

By ten o'clock Sunday morning I was at the entry of the grain warehouse. Ian and Uzi helped me in. I had brought them cigarettes and bread. Ian told me to sit and listen.

"Here's how it's working out. Papo was in the yards this morning; a train is being assembled today. It's not exactly the Flying Scotsman. They've got an Austrian locomotive, 1936 vintage, one Reichsbahn second-class carriage for the officers, a kitchen car, and a dog's breakfast of German, Yugo, and Austrian third-class carriages, nine in number.

"They estimate that, with their packs, bedrolls, and mobile company equipment, the train could carry between eight hundred and eleven hundred men. Depends on how they pack them in. Because of you we know the routing; toward the coast there's not a lot of choice. About ninety kilometers from here the train crosses a wooden trestle over a finger of Lake Jablanicko. The trestle is about eighty meters high. They say it's a marvel of engineering built by the Austrian army in the days of the Danube monarchy. It's all built of wood; with the exception of the tracks there's no steel up there."

Ian paused, while Uzi handed him a piece of bread. Ian took a bite and continued.

"Papo will learn the time of departure sometime during the day; then his lads will come out of the woods and together we'll derail the ruddy train. Unfortunately we don't have what it takes to blow it sky high."

"What about me?" I wanted to know. "What do I do now?"

"Your job is over, and a hell of a job you did. You finish your business with your local impresario and take the train back to Berlin. You've got to get back to your post. You've become important to us."

My God. Dr. Steinbruch was not through with me. Then something even worse occurred to me. "You mean I'm going to be left in Sarajevo after you sabotage the train? I'm going to be left behind when the real search for Rabe starts? My friend Dr. Ivic is one of the top collaborators in town. He'll deliver me to the Gestapo personally, even if he loses his commission."

Uzi spoke up. "Chaver. If they find you missing now, they'll start putting everything together. You've got to act as normally as possible. That's part of your job."

I realized immediately that this thick-headed kibbutz farmer could not understand my inner turmoil. He understood tractors and Sten guns, nothing else. I turned to Ian.

"For God's sake, Ian, I'm no hero. You know what Rabe said before we killed him? That the Gestapo was going to shoot electric charges up my zoub and jam a pressure hose up my tiz!" Both laughed at the Arabic vulgarisms. "If they pull me in I would last two minutes. Just the time it takes to get my pants off. I would tell them everything. I know myself. The only fight I was ever in was when I beat up a girl."

The two warriors looked at each other.

"I'll meet with Ivic today, but when you pull out, take me with you. Just like Papo."

Ian and Uzi got up and disappeared somewhere behind the stacks of bagged wheat. I was left to the terrors conjured up by my active imagination. They would be relatively safe in the mountains with a strongly armed partisan unit, while I was to be left behind to deal with the SS, the Ustashas, and the Gestapo!

Ian and Uzi concluded their council of war and emerged from behind the sacked grain. I could see I had finally gotten through to them. Ian spelled it out for me. I would have to take my leave of Dr. Ivic, settle my bill at the Bosphor, and take a taxi to the station. As far as Ivic was concerned my actions would arouse no suspicion, because with railroad travel in its disorganized condition it was quite logical that I would try to route myself out of Sarajevo by whatever avenue was open to me.

I was to leave my luggage with the baggagemaster's office, taking only documents and tickets with me. After the operation at the trestle, Papo's partisans would attempt to get me to a railroad junction from where I could work my way back to Germany via Zagreb, Ljubljana, and Klagenfurt. I was to join them tonight.

On the way to Dr. Ivic's office I stopped at a café, where I sat quietly and attempted to sort out the predicament in which I found myself. The importance Ian attached to my return to Berlin and the impending appearance of the Bosnians at the Kaukasus indicated to me that Dr. Steinbruch had other assignments awaiting me—assignments for which I had no appetite, especially since Samira was now out of Germany. I toyed with the idea of returning to Syria via Turkey, but Bulgaria had been occupied by the Germans since March of 1941, and travel authority of the sort I had obtained for Croatia could only be acquired in Berlin. I would be better served to return to Berlin, liquidate my assets, and—using my Spanish passport—head for neutral Portugal.

I finished my coffee and went to Dr. Ivic's office, where we worked out the details concerning my employment of the dance troupe. I decided to be generous with salaries, per diems, and travel allowances. I was resolved to recoup all this from Dr. Steinbruch's secret fund. Our leave-taking was more than cordial, and I think Dr. Ivic genuinely liked me. I also had a chance to meet his secretary, a truly striking-looking woman. I wondered if she was the Heaven or the Hell of his infamous duet.

At the hotel I had a bad moment. As I returned from Dr. Ivic's and asked the concierge for my key, I interrupted a whispered conversation between him and two German civilians in shiny leather jackets. As I headed for the lift I could feel their eyes boring into my back, but it may just have been my imagination.

Around three o'clock I paid my bill and took a taxi to the station. I left my luggage with the baggagemaster, bemoaning the fact that I was giving up several tailor-made suits, silk shirts, and pajamas. After a week my suitcase would be moved into the storage area in the rear of the baggagemaster's shed, to gather dust in the company of wicker baskets, carpet rolls, cartons, and leather cases abandoned by those fleeing war, revolution, wives with too many children, or jealous lovers. I drank coffee, took a leisurely stroll in the downtown area, and bought some sausage and bread. By six o'clock I was in the warehouse with Ian and Uzi.

I slept relatively well during the night, reassured by the rock-bound serenity of the two parachutists. We had spent the evening entertaining one another with stories out of our past. Ian spoke of a world of which Uzi and I were not a part, of growing up in a fine home in the highlands of Scotland, of hunting and fishing with his father and brothers, of a private boy's school where the emphasis was on classics and rugby, and of his service in a Scottish regiment before transferring to parachute training and the commandos.

Uzi's life had always been tinged with danger. He had been on patrol against Arab marauders commanded by the Mufti's military chieftain, Fawzi el Kauwakji, when he was only fifteen. From the very beginning of his enlistment in the British forces he had been motivated by revenge against the Germans, the Croatians, and their Bosnian allies who had butchered the remnant of his family and community.

My stories of dancers and the corruption of night life seemed trite in comparison. Before we retired Uzi handed me Rabe's Luger, which Papo had given them. By the time he was through with me, I knew its mechanical functions and the nomenclature of its parts; all that was left for me to do was to pull the trigger in earnest.

Early Monday morning before sun-up, a lorry pulled into the yard. Papo and a man with him, a taciturn Serb who shook our hands, came to get us out. They silently lowered the tailgate to the lorry, its interior empty except for a three-sided wooden box near the tailgate. The five of us filled the lorry with the heavy grain sacks in record time. All of us were drenched with sweat; I was dizzy with exertion.

Now the purpose of the box became clear to me. It was designed for Ian, Uzi, and me to slide under, covered as it was by the sacks. We slid in feet first, and Papo and his companion added several more rows of sacks until we were totally concealed. The tailgate was closed and the lorry started up.

It was only ninety kilometers to the trestle, but because of the weight of the lorry and the conditions of the road it took us over three hours to get there. We were bounced all the way in a kidney-rupturing jog on the steel bed of the vehicle, hitting our noses and foreheads on the rough boards of the box that enclosed us. We were only stopped once. We dimly heard Papo's voice, and possibly that of a soldier or gendarme, and then we rattled on.

When the lorry lurched off the roadway, we could not only hear but also feel the enormous weight of the sacks shifting and sliding above us. I think we were all in terror of being crushed. With a great bounce we finally came to a dead stop. Quickly the tailgate was lowered, sacks removed, and helpful arms pulled us out. We were surrounded by some fifteen men, all heavily armed, who shook our hands, some holding us to their breasts, some kissing us unashamedly. We had finally joined Papo's Serbian partisans.

We were in a ditch deep below the level of the road, and the partisans wasted no time in camouflaging the vehicle with branches and bullrushes.

We could hear the roar of water and followed a partisan deep into the underbrush single file, across a barrier of rocks. Suddenly we were under the trestle. Its struts resembled telephone poles, hundreds of them combined in a geometric pattern of great artistry. It reminded me of a structure built with infinite patience by enthusiasts who make bridges and towers out of thousands of toothpicks. Only these poles were anchored in the rushing waters of a gorge that emptied into a broader body of water downstream. The roar of the icy water was deafening. This would prove to be an advantage to us later on.

We gathered around one of the partisans, who drew patterns in the sand and spoke lengthily in Serbo-Croatian. Ian and I waited to be enlightened. Uzi translated. The troop train was due to leave Sarajevo at five-fifteen, which would bring it through here sometime around seven o'clock, or shortly before sundown. The problem was that a freight train, Sarajevo bound, was due shortly before six. This meant we could start the preparatory work almost any time, but we could not render the tracks impassable until after the freight train had passed.

We had no explosives. Our efforts would be reduced to removing the spikes that held the wooden ties in place and pulling the tracks sufficiently apart that the weight of the engine would dislocate them. The weight and impetus of the locomotive would cause it to careen off the trestle, pulling the train along with it. To ensure that the train slipped off toward the deepest part of the gorge, only one rail would actually be tilted outward. Uzi explained that the partisan in charge was a civil engineer by profession, who had already calculated at what point the train should be derailed to ensure that all eleven carriages took the plunge.

It had been decided that the engineer and a few selected men would mount the trestle and commence the preliminary work. Only after the passage of the freight train would everyone else be needed to pull the spikes and loosen the heavy rails. As the trestle represented a high point, observation from above was not going to be a problem; the Luftwaffe had concerns other than flying security patrols over the Yugoslav railway system. But it was up to us on the ground to be on the alert for traffic and above all for military patrols. Drivers of fast-moving cars or vans would not be able to observe the men on the trestle since the upper track level was out of the drivers' range of vision. Railroad workers' tools were taken from the underside of our lorry, and pickaxes and sledgehammers were passed upward.

Ian joined the Serbs on their ascent of the trestle, while I remained with Uzi and two other partisans. We sought shelter under the trees and kept our weapons at hand. From time to time Uzi translated the partisans' stories of massacres and atrocities committed on the Serbs for me; they repeated the figure of 500,000 martyrs and he told me that the carnage was still going on. They were living for the day when they would hang Pavelic and his premier, Artukovic. Their special hatred was reserved for the Bosnian Moslems, whom they perceived as the jackals who had outdone their Croatian masters in cruelty. Their own state, Serbia, was actually occupied by the Germans, whereas Croatia, as an ally of the Germans, enjoyed relative autonomy. This group of partisans had lived off the land for over a year, wreaking vengeance on German, Croat, and Bosnian alike.

Around four-thirty in the afternoon I became aware of a pain in the region of my kidneys and the overpowering urge to urinate. Never having been a soldier, I lacked the nonchalance with which the partisans, for reasons of security, defecated and urinated in one another's presence. Thus driven by some idiotic need for privacy, I wandered off a little way to relieve myself. I came into a leafy clearing, one side of it sloping down into a growth of young saplings.

I saw with some alarm that I was urinating blood, which I attributed to the fearful pounding my kidneys had taken on the metal bed of the lorry. Something caused me to look up from my fascination with my stream of urine, to see just a little below me two men in uniform, carbines slung over their shoulders. One had field glasses in his hand. I saw the dull gleam of an army-green motorcycle with sidecar next to them. They were pointing, looking off into the distance, and I could not tell by their demeanor if they had spotted a deer or if it was one of the partisans they had seen.

To my horror I realized that there was no chance of my backing out; they would see my slightest movement. I would have to shoot them! I hoped I would remember how to fire the Luger. I reached for the holster and our glances met, the surprise being theirs. Without adjusting my trousers I brought up the Luger, pushed up the safety, and fired. The man in field gray sat down slowly, heavily. The one in black was trying to unlimber his carbine when I shot him high in the chest.

The reports had reverberated, and Uzi and the Serbs were immediately at my side. There was blood on my trousers, and their first concern was that I had been injured. Words would not come and I pointed at the motorcycle. The German was dead. The Ustasha sat stupidly looking at the ground in front of him. One of the Serbs whipped out a hunting knife and finished him off. They threw the cycle into the water and disposed of the bodies. Gradually I could articulate, and it seemed I had withstood the baptism of fire.

There was only desultory traffic on the road. Shortly before six the men came off the trestle. They had loosened most of the spikes, but they were fairly sure the fright train would pass in relative safety. We did not have long to wait. While the rails sang and the trestle groaned, the train rumbled across the trestle. The rolling stock was old, the locomotive even older. We hoped that the troop train would show more impetus.

Now all of us scrambled up the rocks until we reached the tracks on the trestle. I tried not to look down. It was terrifying to see the water below. Under the guidance of the engineer we ripped the loosened spikes out. Some had been rustily embedded for half a century, and the effort was superhuman. The men wielded their picks and sledgehammers like maniacs. They pounded the spikes, they splintered the ties, we all fought the clock with desperation. Shortly before seven the rail was free. All of us strained to the point of rupture to move it off dead center. Like slaves of yore we chanted in unison to give more power to the common effort. Finally it came free. The engineer inspected the work and only then ordered us off the trestle.

Mercifully the sun was slipping down, casting heavy shadows of gray and brown that obscured our handiwork. Then we heard a hum on the rails, followed by the driving of the pistons and the asthmatic escape of steam. Finally the engine appeared, a narrow, high old model, followed by its coal tender and then the carriages. It was starting to cross the trestle, the beams groaning in protest.

In spite of orders to the contrary we all stood up, every eye riveted on the locomotive. It was probably only doing thirty-five kilometers when it came to the appointed spot. It seemed to sag, change its mind, continue a few meters, and then decided to peel off the trestle. Obediently, most of the carriages followed in its wake. On the way down the locomotive struck the struts at mid-level. A fearful sound of hissing and boiling steam gurgled up from the waters as the locomotive sank. Three carriages had become uncoupled and remained standing on the trestle, where we could see the fear-crazed soldiers climbing out of windows and doors. By now the trestle, mortally weakened by the impact of the locomotive, had started to sway like a rope ladder in a windstorm. When it finally gave way, the struts shot out like arrows from a bow and the remaining carriages plunged madly into the river. The partisans set up a roar, a primordial scream of blood revenge.

For a moment we watched the waters. Clouds of steam were still rising, and air bubbles like those released by a drowning beast were rupturing on the surface. The carriages were giving up the air within them, and bodies slowly floated upward. A surprising number of survivors now emerged amid the bobbing detritus of the explosion. Adrift on the roiling waters were packs and bedrolls, splintered beams, and wooden sections of the carriages. Here and there some poor devil clung to the debris for dear life. Others, mortally wounded, left a red wake behind them as they thrashed about in useless circles.

Suddenly a strut, perhaps released by the shifting of a carriage, shot out of the water like a projectile. This gruesome tableau drew the partisans like flies to rotten meat. They brought up their Sten guns, their Schmeissers, and with grim determination started to pick off the Bosnian survivors. Few were left when Ian appeared, greatly agitated, motioning for the firing to stop. The partisans lowered their weapons, awaiting an explanation. It came, translated by Uzi. A few survivors from a disaster such as this were beneficial, Ian said. They would return to their villages, greatly magnify the horror of the event, and assure everyone that this jihad for the Germans was cursed with the Evil Eye. The Serbs smiled and desisted.

February 25, 1944

LOHMANN CAME UNEXPECTEDLY *last night, just before dark. He had been drinking and was in a jolly mood. He brought a little bundle out of his overcoat and placed it on my table. It turned out to be his white linen handkerchief, its ends knotted together, containing a rather bruised mixture of pastel-colored petit-fours and assorted sugary biscuits. I scooped them up with my fingers and waited, like a child at bedtime, for the story to start. "Love works in mysterious ways" was Lohmann's introduction to his narrative. He had lost half his inventory, 50 percent of his stock-in-trade was gone, but he was nevertheless a happy man.*

"Please explain yourself, Lohmann, I am not following you," I remember saying. "I come from Jutta's engagement party" was his explanation.

It developed that Jutta, in the performance of her profession, had serviced a middle-aged businessman on a daily basis for almost a week. This Herr Sedlmeyer, an accountant from the Bavarian brewing community of Aying, had after two of Jutta's ministrations become suitor rather than client. He came to his assignations with flowers, candy, or even silk stockings. Finally he had proposed. Admittedly he was fifty-five, Jutta was half his age, but he had a substantial practice as a chartered accountant, and, more importantly in these dangerous days, he lived in the peaceful Bavarian countryside, too far away from Munich to be of much interest to the bomber squadrons of the RAF.

Herr Seldlmeyer had given his engagement party at the pension where he stayed. Lohmann was perceived to be a favorite uncle, who had come to give his niece away before her departure for the provinces. Lohmann was genuinely happy for Jutta; he shared her joy and was pleased that her life of shame had been so short-lived. In the approaching darkness I could see the smile on his face. Inge, although joyful at her friend's good fortune, had whispered tearfully to Lohmann that she hoped she would do as well. Lohmann had promised to be on the lookout for a suitable candidate.

There had been other guests at the party: some of the girls from the dress shop that had formerly employed them, an aunt of Inge's, and her daughter Ursula, Inge's cousin. Lohmann said he recognized a free spirit when he saw one and had drawn Ursula into a conversation. She worked as a typist for an insurance company, a job she hated for its poor pay and for the constant pounding of the keys, which ruined the scarlet polish of her fingernails. Lohmann had commiserated with her, later suggesting to Inge that her cousin move in with her after Jutta's departure and be apprenticed to the trade. Inge had laughed, saying that her cousin didn't need much of an apprenticeship; only the idea of doing it for money had to be brought home to her.

Lohmann anticipated my disapproval. "Keep eating, Herr Saporta. I am not a white slaver shipping virgins to Rio Bamba. I'm only helping a couple of girls turn their only asset into a nest egg for an otherwise bleak future. And if I can do as well for Inge and her cousin as I did for Jutta, I'll be the happiest man in the world." I believed him and finished off the engagement pastries.

I return to the massacre beneath the railroad trestle of which I spoke earlier. After Ian had stopped the killing of the last few survivors there was no time to waste. We broke into preselected groups. The Serb commandant kissed me, Ian smashed me on the shoulder, and Uzi held me by the nape of the neck. Fiercely he said. "If you live through this, come to Palestine. We'll be needing you." I had no chance to speak to Papo. My group had me in tow, and within minutes all of us had disappeared into the surrounding forest.

I am not sure how many days I was with them. They were all Serbs; two spoke a little German. I don't know how much they knew of my mission to the Waffen SS fortress but obviously something had filtered down to them; also, I had shot the German and the Ustasha before they could give us away. In short, they treated me with much respect and open affection. On several occasions we met with Serbs in the partisan network. They gave us food and accompanied us through the terrain with which they were familiar, before delivering us to someone in the next sector. Each time I was hugged by the partisans. Only this adulation kept me from protesting the killing pace of our forced march. Also I must confess that I was not displeased by the admiration shown me, and I made every attempt to react modestly to their praise.

In retrospect it was absurd that I was so honored. The history of my valorous conduct is that Dr. Steinbruch tricked me into joining his anti-Nazi efforts: that Ian and Papo, brutes that they were, frightened me into going to the Nazi stronghold; that my acquiring the information of the troop departure was elicited from an old blind muezzin. My shooting of the German and Bosnian had been an act of fear, nothing more. If heroics are compounded of such banality, perhaps there are other heroes even less deserving of the title than I.

In any event, the partisans saw their hero safely into the hands of a farmer, one of their own, who drove me into Banja Luka, a provincial town and rail junction, in a truck full of sheep. He put me on a train that brought me to Zagreb. Near the railroad station I went to a public bath house and bought a presentable if secondhand suit in an open-air stall.

My tickets and travel documents were in order, and to substantiate my presence I had my contracts for the Bosnian dancers on Dr. Ivic's stationery. I made my way back to Berlin via Graz, Prague, and Dresden. There was chaos along the way and endless rerouting because of the many troop trains. The people too were uneasy, warned about impending disaster on the Russian front. I was unable to get into first-class compartments; they were all taken by officers.

Between Prague and Dresden I found myself jammed onto the rear platform of a second-class carriage. The compartments were filled and even the passageway was congested, mostly with soldiers squatting on their packs. As the train slowly pulled into the extensive rail yard on the outskirts of Dresden we became aware of a drone, even over the noise of the train, followed by the thud of bombs going off nearby. The train lurched to a halt, sending people careening into one another in the corridor, while others came pouring out of their compartments. The result was a solid mass of terrified people crammed into the narrow passageway. The rain of bombs continued, and we could see a train several tracks away burning fiercely.

I had heard that during air attacks passengers normally sought shelter under the train, but this was clearly an impossibility. The bombs continued to fall, and explosions could be felt up and down the line. We were pressed together, a living, breathing, terrified mass.

I became aware that I was pressed against a young woman in the uniform of a ticket comptroller of the German railways. I recognized the little wings on the collar of her jacket. I looked into her face. She had the clean, unblemished beauty of the type of which the Germans were rightfully proud. Her eyes were light blue; her bobbed dark-blond hair spilled out from under her jaunty fore-and-aft cap. Her eyelashes were wet from the tears that were coursing down her face. They were not tears of fear, she was much too composed for that. Perhaps they were tears of sorrow that her young life should be over before she could live it to the fullest. Slowly she looked up at me, into my eyes.

As if in a dream she asked, "What are you called?" She had used the familiar German form, as if speaking to a child or to an intimate.

"Daniel," I answered.

"Where are you from?" she asked, and then shook her head. "It makes no difference, you needn't tell me." She had locked her hands around my forearms. "Do you want to die like this? Like an animal in the stockyards?" I shook my head. "Then come," she said.

She pushed an elderly sergeant out of the way and opened the door to the toilet behind her. She pulled me in after her and locked the door. Here we were, in the squalid, littered little compartment with its opaque gray window. The bombs were coming down again, and now an antiaircraft battery went off. She put her arms around my neck and kissed me on the mouth with the affection and longing usually reserved for a husband or lover. There was nothing carnal or brutal about her. I responded and she breathed her thanks at me, "Danke, danke." When she undid her tunic I could see the simple gold wedding band on her finger. She offered me her breasts, so white I could see the fine network of blue veins delicately tracing their fullness. She undid my trousers and with a quick movement stripped off her own. I was momentarily aware of dark gray woolen stockings encasing her sturdy legs; then she had seated herself on the washbowl and had locked her legs around my waist. While bombs went off and some nearby target erupted with a roar, we made love.

Suddenly the air was deathly still. The bombers had moved on,

February 26, 1944

I WAS BACK IN BERLIN on December 4, 1941, and I breathed a sigh of relief as the train steamed into the station. I had been gone three weeks. I joined the exodus of soldiers and airmen, the small number of civilians, in leaving the dirty, malodorous train. Once we were on the platform we were stopped by military police. The reason was obvious. An ambulance train had pulled into the other side of the platform minutes before our arrival, and the wounded were given priority to leave the station. We stood with our backs against the sides of our filthy train, observing the spectacle of stretcher-bearers carrying the wounded and mutilated off the ambulance train. Many hobbled on crutches, helped by medical orderlies; some blinded, heads bandaged, were being escorted by nurses. It was a grim spectacle.

Suddenly I was jostled by a stretcher being carried by two orderlies. The young soldiers were held up by a contingent of wheelchairs ahead of them, and I could not help looking down at the man on the stretcher. I recognized the face with the dueling scars at once. It was Herr Stemmler! His legs had been amputated above the knee, and I could see the bloodied, gauze-covered stumps.

Stemmler saw me at the same time. With superhuman strength he pushed himself into a sitting position. His right hand shot out and, clawlike, fastened itself on my jacket. His emaciated, stubbly face was contorted with hatred, purpling with rage.

"Saporta," he started to keen. "Saporta, give me my cheese sandwich!" Only the absurdity of the remark saved me from the now morbidly interested crowd. The orderlies, convinced that their charge was hallucinating, tried to break Stemmler's hold on me, but Stemmler continued to shrill, "Saporta, my cheese sandwich!" and would not relinquish his iron grip on my jacket. I already suspected what was to follow and, with violence triggered by mounting fear, tore myself free. I could hear the ripping of cloth and, finally released, pushed unheedingly through the congested crowd.

When I reached the top of the exit ramp, I could hear Stemmler shrieking at the top of his lungs, "That was Saporta! A Jew! Saporta, he got away!" I plunged down the stairs, aware that a piece of my jacket was gone. The patch of white lining on my breast seemed to proclaim my vulnerability as effectively as if it had been the yellow Star of David, emblazoned "Jude."

An hour later I was in my office at the Kaukasus.

February 27, 1944

LOHMANN CAME TODAY *just after noon, an unusual time for him. He watched me eat, then sighed heavily and brought a carefully folded newspaper out of his overcoat pocket. He handed it to me without comment. I have translated it in its entirety.*

RÖHM PUTSCH: NEW REVELATIONS
Munich, February 21

Almost ten years after the suppression of the attempted Putsch by the SA under the leadership of the traitor General Ernst Röhm, the Bavarian State Procurator has released additional details concerning the case. On June 30, 1934, the Reichsführer, at the head of his personal SS guard battalion, arrested Röhm and his clique in various inns on the shore of the Wiessee Lake. In the process a homosexual orgy was uncovered in the quarters of SA Führer Edmund Heines, which adjoined those of Röhm. Those arrested at Lake Wiessee were brought to Stadelheim Penitentiary in Munich, where they were executed on July 2nd.

An Italian national among them has been identified. He was Mario Gambalonga, approximately 25 years of age according to the Munich coroner's office. Of interest is the fact that Gambalonga, a hermaphrodite possessing both male and female sexual characteristics, was the one-time star of Klub Kaukasus, known as a Berlin meeting place for the decadent Jewish intellectual circles that once dictated public tastes in the Reichscapital. That this repulsive accident of nature, this spawn of obscenity, the sight of which would cause instant revulsion on the part of normal people, should have been the companion, or worse, of elements aspiring to the leadership of the nation, is living proof, if such were needed, of the degeneracy and moral decay of the Röhm clique.

I read the article in silence; what could I have said? That at least Maria-Mario had enjoyed some years of comfort, of excitement, even of adulation while in Berlin; that these few years were worth a lifetime in the goat shed that had been her home? That she had been saved from an early death as a consumptive hermit, who after the death of her mother would have been delivered into the hands of primitive and hateful villagers? That it was better for her to be shot to death by the SS after suffering God knows what indignities? Am I playing God? I know I am rationalizing to put my guilty conscience to rest.

Lohmann had predicted this sad outcome from the outset. Lohmann, who had been both pimp and thief, knew where to draw the line. In my exploitation of Maria-Mario, I had not been willing to exercise the same moral judgment.

February 28, 1944

I RETURN TO THE MORNING of December 16, 1941. It had been twelve days since my return from Sarajevo. Lohmann and I were busy with preparations for Christmas and the ensuing New Year's festivities. The three weeks in Bosnia now seemed like a fever dream, which I could not believe I had actually experienced. I had not yet reported the details of the operations to Dr. Steinbruch. I had merely indicated to him on the telephone that "things had gone as expected." I knew he was speaking from a public telephone box, but I thought I detected more than ordinary caution in his voice. We agreed to meet on the evening of December twentieth on Unter del Linden, where we would disappear in the anonymity of masses of Christmas shoppers.

While we were drinking coffee in the Kaukasus kitchen, Lohmann again described to me how he had managed to put Samira on the train to Istanbul. I was like a child who could not tire of hearing his favorite fairy tale.

"Herr Salazar, when I handed her the letter of dismissal, she really went to pieces. I think she understood it was your way of getting her out of Germany, your way of terminating her affair with Rabe. Perhaps because of my years and my appearance, she saw in me a father confessor. She ranted. She said that both Rabe and you had used her, used her like a beast. She said she didn't know which of you she hated more. Herr Salazar, I told her what I think she wanted to hear. I took the liberty of telling her that you loved her, that although I knew nothing of the cause of your breakup, I, as a man, was convinced that you loved her still."

Then Lohmann told me something that he had so far withheld.

"I did not want to leave the decision of her departure in her hands. I wanted to see her on the train because I had determined that she was leaving—not because she had suddenly decided to leave or, for that matter, to stay. It was too risky. I'm afraid I did not endear myself to Fräulein Samira."

He paused. I asked him to continue.

"I knew how dependent she had become on her Hungarian drug supplier. I used to see her pacing up and down in the foyer, waiting for him. I grabbed him in the courtyard and told him I would break every bone in his body if he sold cocaine or anything else to Fräulein Samira, that I would buy it from him myself. He didn't care, as long as he made his sale. I bought a week's supply. I saw her the following evening, pacing like a tiger in a cage. The Hungarian did not show. I asked her into the office, showed her the packets, and said she could have them all once she was on the train. I gave her a pittance and next day put her into her compartment on the sleeper. She asked me for the drugs. I said the sleeping car attendant had a 'box of chocolates' for her once they crossed the border into Hungary. I had given the man twenty-five marks, no questions asked. She cursed me, but I stayed on the platform until the train pulled out."

It was with mixed feelings that I had listened to Lohmann's recitation of Samira's departure. I was deeply grateful to him for having spirited Samira out of Germany. He was proud of "having gotten Fräulein Samira out of the Sturmbannführer's clutches." Lohmann of course did not know that Rabe had ended up in the furnaces of the Bosphor Hotel. But the cost had been too great. I had single-handedly forced her into an unspeakable relationship with Rabe—God only knows what transpired when Captain Shawa Nawa joined them in their "lovemaking." It was I who was responsible for her narcotic addiction, and, more reprehensible yet, it was I who must have destroyed whatever innocence she had maintained after years as a belly dancer in the nightclubs of the Arab world. Whatever faith she had in her fellowman, I had also sacrificed. Was it worth it? Probably not. Did the death of a few hundred recruits really change the course of the war? As a sop to my conscience I tell myself that victory in war is made up of thousands of seemingly unimportant skirmishes and acts of momentary bravery.

On that fateful morning we had discussed the direction the war was taking. Less than two weeks before, the Americans had declared war on the Axis powers, the result of the Japanese attack on the American naval installations in Pearl Harbor. The Japanese had also delivered lightning strikes against the British in Hong Kong and

Singapore and against the Dutch in Indonesia. Their initial success was remarkable. According to Lohmann this gave rise to two schools of thought. The school of optimists believed that the entry into the war of so formidable an ally as the Japanese would hasten the day of an Axis victory, with victorious German and Japanese armies linking up somewhere in Asiatic Russia. The school of pessimists, to which he belonged, included those whose historical memory extended as far back as 1917. They remembered the early trickle of inexperienced doughboys arriving from America, a trickle that rapidly turned into a torrent of fresh, well-fed, and enthusiastic troops. These American divisions had beefed up the exhausted French and British, thus snatching victory from the grasp of the hitherto triumphant Germans. Lohmann thought that history would repeat itself. He hoped that when the day of reckoning came, it would be the Yankees who occupied Germany and not the Russians. It was one of the few times in our relationship that I chose not to air my views in the matter. Although I owed him my life, he was a German with deep roots in his country, and it would have been a gratuitous hurt to reveal to him my hope that the Russians would exact bloody vengeance here.

Lohmann was pouring a second cup of coffee for us when a fearful pounding sounded on our front door. Lohmann recognized the source of its vehemence. He immediately took charge. First he took my cup and saucer and threw them into the dishwater in the sink. Then he emptied the ashtray containing my Simon Artz cigarette stubs.

He pushed me into a refuse bin and upended the other bins on top of me so that I was covered by a thick layer of garbage. Only then did he open the door. I could hear the Gestapo slamming doors and breaking furniture, and, I imagined, ransacking my office. They came into the kitchen, Lohmann on their heels.

"Where is that Jewish swine?" the man in charge bellowed.

"What Jewish swine?" Lohmann wanted to know.

"Saporta, the owner of this whorehouse."

Lohmann became indignant. "I know of no Saporta, and I don't work for Jews. I'm a veteran Party member; I was fighting Communists in the streets when you had mother's milk on your chin. My Herr Salazar is a Spaniard. He has a picture of General Franco in his office. Go and see for yourself."

The man became conciliatory. "He's fooled a lot of people, your Spaniard. When did you see him last?"

"Today is Tuesday the sixteenth; we're closed on Mondays, so it was around three o'clock in the morning on Sunday the fourteenth. He has not been here since. Have you been to his flat?"

It was a question Lohmann could safely ask, with me under the refuse.

"That pimp's nest, you mean? Only silk shirts, and more perfume in the bathroom than in a French whorehouse."

"Well, you know the type," Lohmann said. "He sleeps around a lot, mostly actresses. He has a lot of low friends in high places." Lohmann laughed, and the Gestapo laughed with him.

"If there is anything else I can tell you, ask," Lohmann volunteered.

The Gestapo was mollified. "Come down to headquarters, Prinz Albrechtstrasse, Number Eight, Room Two-twelve, tomorrow at nine. We'll take your statement. Heil Hitler!"

"Heil Hitler!" Lohmann barked, and I could hear him bring his heels together.

Lohmann followed them out through the courtyard and, satisfied that they had driven off, had me out of the trash bin, out the back door, and into a taxi within minutes. He knew enough about police procedures to realize that it would be relatively safe to follow the police out the door but that they would be back later to padlock the Kaukasus; of that he was certain. Lohmann directed the taxi to take us to an underground station in Zehlendorf, where we got out. We walked several blocks to his aunt's apartment, where I spent the day. Lohmann picked me up that night and brought me to my attic, where I have been ever since.

Lohmann then reported to Gestapo headquarters as he had been instructed. He had dressed carefully for the occasion: dark overcoat, oversize veteran Nazi Party emblem on his lapel, bowler hat, and a copy of the *Völkischer Beobachter* negligently stuck in his coat pocket. He had his Party membership card dating back to the twenties in his wallet and probably would have walked out of this point of no return unharmed, even had luck not favored him once more.

While looking for the room to which he had been summoned, Lohmann was addressed by a man in his mid-fifties in civilian clothes with a short Hindenburg haircut. Lohmann recognized him as an attorney of no great note but, like himself, a veteran Party member. He had made a name for himself in the days of the Weimar Republic by defending Brown Shirt hoodlums arrested for drunkenness, brawling, smashing shop windows, and grievous assault. He told Lohmann he was now a Public Prosecutor—a function that conferred on the office holder the right to demand that defendants be decapitated; usually they were. This man was delighted to see Lohmann, and when informed by him what the nature of the visit was, he offered to accompany him to Room 212, the officials therein being well known to him.

The presence of the Public Prosecutor had a magical effect, and after pleasantries Lohmann was dismissed. Lohmann said he was not surprised. His credentials were too good, and no blame or complicity relating to his employer could be attached to him.

February 29, 1944

THIS HAS BEEN THE STORY *of my life, which ground to a halt on December 16, 1941. I have skimmed through it. It is compounded of bombast and disgrace, but also of my not immodest pride at my perseverance, and my sense of accomplishment that I, spice merchant turned cabaret owner, should have struck an important blow against the Nazi war machine.*

Above all I hope that my love and devotion to my family, whose hopes had been so high for me, have been dutifully recorded.

To the Lord God I say "hatanu"—we have sinned—and "patanu"— we have transgressed—when I think of Mario, of Chayim Spiegel, and of Samira.

To the reader, should these pages ever be found, I say, temper your judgment with mercy.

Through my little window I see the fine tracings of a new moon against the darkening sky. It seems fitting at this time to repeat the blessing I said at my father's side upon the sighting of each new moon:

> *May it be a good sign and a good fortune*
> *for us and for all of Israel, Amen.*

And now I shall put these pages away. I will bring them out only at the hour of deliverance, if with God's help (and Lohmann's) there should be one.

April 22, 1945

MY LAST ENTRY *was dated February 29, 1944. It has been over a year. I have survived, but at some cost. But this is not the time for a recital of aches and pains. Lohmann came this morning, greatly agitated. The Russians are at the outskirts of the city. To the citizens of Berlin it is now becoming evident that it will be the Russians, hell-bent for revenge, and not the more benign Anglo-Americans who are going to be marching into the capital. To aggravate matters, the Führer bunker, where Hitler, Goebbels, and his entire staff are ensconced, is still operative. The Berliners know it, and the Russians know it also. They will certainly make every attempt to capture this prize. Lohmann is clearly worried—he has memories of the First World War.*

"If we can survive the first week after Ivan enters the city we shall be all right. The Russians will install a military government and there will be order. But during that first week, the troops will be turned loose, to do as they please—that's what the French did in 1918. They unleashed their colonial infantry in the Rhineland. The Senegalese raped everything between eight and eighty."

I don't know if this story was true, but I have heard the Germans tell it many times.

Lohmann left me a meager ration and cautioned me to use it sparingly.

April 25, 1945

LOHMANN FINALLY CAME *after an absence of two days. He came after dark, and we discussed the meaning of a new development. Since early this morning I had become aware of a new sound: a sound like huge bedsheets being ripped in the sky, or the roar of freight trains rumbling overhead. It is of course the sound of Russian artillery. Occasionally I hear a crump when the shells strike home.*

Lohmann reports that the city is now completely surrounded. What we hear is a Russian artillery symphony, orchestrated to reduce Berlin to rubble.

"Lohmann," I said. "Do you think it might be safer if I left the attic and took my chances in the streets? I cannot imagine that under these conditions the Gestapo is still looking for me."

"Herr Saporta. You still don't know your Germans. Half of Berlin is destroyed, but the mail is still being delivered. The police are still writing citations for littering. The judges of the People's Courts are still in session, sentencing to death defeatists and traitors. 'Ordnung muss sein'—There must be order—even in the midst of chaos."

"I rely on you to get me out as soon as you think it's safe. I must admit to you that I am more frightened now that the end is so near."

"Don't concern yourself, Herr Saporta. Lohmann will get you out. We'll soon be opening the Kaukasus for the Russian brass, just wait and see."

And he was gone.

April 28, 1945

THE ARTILLERY BARRAGES *are not only gaining in intensity but the sound of the trajectory has changed, indicating that the fieldpieces have moved into the heart of the city. When I look out of my dormer window, I see great palls of gray dust. At night I can see fires everywhere.*

Lohmann did not come on the twenty-sixth. He did not come on the twenty-seventh. There have been longer absences in the past, but the situation is more dangerous now, and I am not very stable myself; my nerves are frazzled to a dangerous degree.

I am also out of food, save for an impossibly hard roll, but I will soften it with my saliva.

I slept away the afternoon. I had my recurring dream of Damascus: safe in the bosom of my family, in the never-never-land of my father's balcony. But with awakening, reality descended on me. My father, alav ha shalom, was dead. My mother, sisters, and brother dispersed. There was no balcony to which to return. Not anywhere.

My concern for Lohmann grows by the hour. Has he been arrested? Has he been killed by a Russian shell? Is he lying wounded under a mound of rubble?

I strain my ears for the comforting sound of his footsteps, but all I hear is the whoosh *of incoming artillery shells.*

April 29, 1945

NO LOHMANN *since the twenty-fifth. Also without food since then. It is clear to me that something must have happened to him. Even if I ran into the streets, where would I find him? At his aunt's in Zehlendorf? Absurd. I know he would be here if it were physically possible. The conclusions are obvious. He's dead, badly wounded, or has been arrested. Arrest these days usually means execution.*

I now realize, more than ever, how much Lohmann's friendship means to me in this alien land. The food with which he sustains me is not part of it. It is the strength and common sense he exudes that give me peace and an anchor to my existence.

Here is my plan, then. I will stay in my attic until the shooting stops. The firing now is so intense and the explosions so close by, that the end can only be days off. Provided I am not killed by shell fire first, I will take my chances in the streets. Should crazed rearguard Nazis shoot me or vengeful Russians kill me, ma'alesh, it cannot be helped.

I am not afraid to join my father Ezra. I long to kiss his hand, to sit next to him, with the smell of mimosa and jasmine enveloping us. I would lay the ledger of my accomplishments and failures before him.

Would he see my cruelty toward Chayim Spiegel as a sacrifice in the name of a greater task? Or would he see it through his gentle eyes as the betrayal of one Jew by another? How would he judge my dealings with Samira? Samira with whom I could have stood under the wedding chupah; Samira who would have given him the grandchildren for which he yearned. What verdict, O Father?

And the Bosnian country boys, plunging to their deaths off the railroad trestle, drowning in the icy waters of a lake. Would my father see me as a soldier, fighting for a noble cause, or as an unseen assassin playing a shadowy part in a dirty game? An agent of the night, causing the deaths of a thousand apple-cheeked boys? What verdict, O Father?

These are all ramblings of a disordered mind. I am faint with hunger, empty-headed. When I lie on my couch I drift from sleep to daydreams, outlandish fantasies of my childhood and the later years. I visit my Aunt Regine with my mother; there are other guests, we drink tea, eat pastries; older boys tease me, I am nervous, I wet my pants, I can feel the dark hot stain spreading across my lap. Then I am with Cousin Eli; we are visiting the sharmutas, but I am not sure with whom I am coupling, Frau Landau, Hilde, Latifa, Samira?

Samira. There are recurring dreams of Samira. They are always the same. We appear side by side in a brown monotone. She is standing, she wears a summer dress with white stockings, there is a garland of flowers in her hair. Her look is demure, her right hand rests on my shoulder. I am seated on a straightback chair; I wear a striped suit; I can see the high-topped shoes. The tarboosh is on my head, in my right hand is a ring of amber worry beads. I ask myself, why does that which never happened seem so normal, so completely a part of my life? Suddenly it comes to me. It is the wedding picture of my parents, hanging in its gold frame in our living room, only it is Samira and I who are united for all eternity.

I stop for today. I am intensely agitated; I can feel that a chapter in my life, perhaps the last, is coming to an end.

April 30, 1945

EARLY THIS MORNING *I heard small hesitant steps on the wooden attic floor. Then a soft knocking and the voice.*

"Herr Saporta. Herr Salazar! Help me get in. It is Hilde."

I pushed against the heavy cupboard, and Hilde stepped through the crevice between the cupboard and the wooden slats of the attic partitions. Even in her head scarf and stained mackintosh I would have recognized her at once. She chose to ignore my bearded, pallid, malodorous condition. Before giving me an explanation of her presence she insisted that I eat the two slices of bread with ersatz jam and drink the liter bottle of thin coffee and milk that she brought out of her coat pocket.

She told me how she had come to me. The janitor of the former eating club in the Kantstrasse had come to her employer's house to fetch her. They had immediately gone to the Kantstrasse. Lohmann had sought refuge there. He had been shot, once in the arm, once in the side; he was bleeding profusely. She had attempted to staunch the flow of blood, but she feared that his arm had been shattered, that he would go into shock. It is clear that Lohmann needs medical care desperately.

According to Hilde, Lohmann had been stopped by a patrol of the Volkssturm. These were patrols consisting either of elderly men or of heavily armed teenagers, some as young as fourteen, brought to the colors to stop the Russian invader. The boys were usurping their authority by shooting suspected "defeatists" out of hand. One of them had stopped Lohmann and ordered him to open his briefcase. The briefcase was full of contraband food—most of it intended for me. Lohmann had fled into the hallway of a bombed-out building, but not before the boy had unslung his rifle and fired a volley of shots at him. Lohmann had taken refuge behind the charred doors of the entry, and when the boy entered the hallway in pursuit, Lohmann had smashed him in the face with a brick. Lohmann still had sufficient strength to drag the boy into the hallway with his good arm and pitch him down into the cellar.

He had applied a rough tourniquet and after nightfall had made it over to the Kantstrasse. This is where Hilde had joined him, thanks to the janitor. Once Lohmann and Hilde were alone, he had told her of me and voiced the fear that I was starving to death in the attic. She was to try and keep me alive until the hour of capitulation. Those were his instructions.

Hilde now added her concerns for Lohmann's safety to mine. She did this by describing the situation in the streets of Berlin for me. Units of the Russian army were now less than a kilometer away from us. Refugees from other districts, already occupied by the Russians, brought fearful stories. Russian artillery pieces were firing point-blank, demolishing buildings one by one, reducing them to hillocks of rubble. Occasionally they spared a building where white sheets were draped over the balconies in sign of surrender. But once the tanks and the artillery were displaced forward, platoons of infantry combed the surviving apartments, dredged those cellars that had not caved in, and brought terrified groups of humanity into the open. Women and girls, regardless of even age, were repeatedly raped by the men, who queued up to take their pleasure. Men of military age or those wearing remnants of military uniforms were shot out of hand.

Hilde was terrified that if the Russians found Lohmann they would execute him in spite of his years, in the belief that his wounds stemmed from some Nazi rearguard action against them.

"You must take me to him, Hilde," I said. "I speak Russian with enough authority to protect him."

"That is impossible, the streets are crawling with Volkssturm patrols, and if you'll excuse me, Herr Saporta, with your appearance, without proper identification, they'd hang you from the nearest lamppost." She finally agreed that she would come for me at nightfall, the darkness increasing our chances of reaching Lohmann.

Hilde left me several hours ago. I have finally managed to lace my shoes on my swollen feet. I have put on the coat with which I came here over three years ago.

I see things very clearly now, and I am no longer afraid. This I must do:

Gain Lohmann's side and see that he gets medical care and comes to no harm. Then I must go to Istanbul, seek out Minassian, and learn if he has word of Samira. Should he fail me I will go to Aleppo, to the Bahsita quarter, and go from door to door until I find Moshe Zechariah, the ritual butcher, and ask for the whereabouts of his daughter.

I pray to Him on high that He should hear my plea. Not for my gratification, nor to expunge my guilt. Only to restore Samira to the lifelong love and protection I have pledged to her.

These memoirs I will place into the drawer of this crude wooden table. May the reader read them with compassion or disdain; pass them on or throw them away. It has been written. It is out of my hands.

I hear Hilde's footsteps. And now, "Con el pie derecho y el nombre del dio," I go forth.

Daniel Saporta, son of Ezra
Berlin, April 30, 1945

From *The Los Angeles Times* of May 19, 1990:

DIARY RESTORED TO LA DEVELOPER
Document Bridges Eras, Cultures

At a ceremony held in Beverly Hills, a diary was returned to Daniel Saporta, 79, prominent local developer, by Reinhard Dinkelmayer, director of the Goethe Institute. Saporta had left the diary in the Berlin attic where he had been in hiding from the notorious Gestapo from 1941 until the capture of the city by the Allies in 1945.

After the razing of the Berlin Wall and the reunification of the city, a number of abandoned buildings in the eastern sector were condemned. A wrecking crew discovered the diaries and turned them over to police. As the contents were deemed to be of cultural value they were given to the Goethe Institute, a German foundation with branches throughout the world.

Saporta, who is a native of Damascus, Syria, attended with his wife, Samira, a former artist, and sons Alan and Barry, both developers.

In accepting the diary Saporta said he wanted to use the occasion to honor a former employee, Otto Lohmann, manager of the "Kaukasus," a Berlin nightclub, which Saporta once operated. Lohmann not only kept him alive but probably gave his own life in attempting to protect him, Saporta said.

Saporta, until his retirement in 1982, was CEO of the Shop-Rite Discount Marts and a pioneer in the shopping mall concept. He is president of Congregation B'nai Sefarad and active in community and cultural affairs.